Derek Fee was born in Dublin in 1947. He was educated at Trinity College and University College Dublin, where he received a PhD in economics. He worked as an oilfield engineer in the North Sea and Iran, and as an oil consultant to the Irish government, before joining the European Commission in 1978. He is currently a principal administrator in the Energy Directorate General. He has written six books and numerous articles on the oil industry, and has travelled widely both inside and outside the European Community. He lives in Brussels with his wife and two children.

DEREK FEE

CARTEL

Town House, Dublin

Published in 1994 by
Town House and Country House
42 Morehampton Road
Donnybrook
Dublin 4

A CIP catalogue record for this book is available
from the British Library

ISBN: 0-948524-96-0

Cover design: Jack Hayden Design and Art
Typeset by Typeform Repro
Printed in Ireland by Colour Books Ltd.

For John, Eileen and Mamo

CHAPTER ONE

PAMPLONA, JULY 8TH

Bruno Cavelli moved carefully through the crowd. It was 6.00am, but already the narrow cobbled streets of Pamplona were crammed with both locals and tourists, all making their way towards the Plaza del Castillo. There, lured by the prospect of danger and bloodshed and by the legend created by Ernest Hemingway, they would watch the running of the bulls, the spectacle that forms part of the city's annual celebrations in honour of its patron, Saint Fermin.

The majority of the crowd, both male and female, wore, like Cavelli, the traditional dress of those taking part in the running of the bulls — red neckerchief, white shirt and white trousers tied with a red sash. Despite their brave costumes, almost all the tourists would keep well clear of the bulls, leaving the foolhardy Navarrese youths to enjoy the risks they would take.

Cavelli was not a tourist, and he had no knowledge of Hemingway. Nor did he intend to pit his courage against the bulls, although his costume and his olive skin allowed him to fit perfectly into the guise of a local bull-runner. Bruno Cavelli was in Pamplona to do what he did best — he was there to kill.

Michael Joyce didn't know a single word of the song being sung by the huge crowd dancing in front of the Café Irun in the Plaza del Castillo, but that didn't stop him from joining in. His lack of understanding of Spanish had been more than compensated for by the quantities of wine and cheap champagne that he had consumed during the night in the notorious 'Street of a Thousand Bars'. The uniformed brass band systematically beat out the ancient Navarrese melodies, stirring the blood of the revellers. Joyce bounced up and down in the centre of the crowd and not for the first time asked himself what was he doing prancing about in an old cobbled square at six o'clock in the morning, and about to entrust his precious skin to the whims of several tons of Spanish beef. The answer was always the same — he was simply making a living. The editor of *International Traveller* was paying Michael to write the definitive piece on the Fiesta de Saint Fermin, and that meant becoming a part of the week-long madness. At this point in time, Michael Joyce was pondering the wisdom of his decision to accept the assignment. He had already concluded that completing the whole week of Saint Fermin would require the constitution of a horse, and a liver to match. The question was not whether he could develop prose suitable to describe the experience, but whether his recollections would be sufficiently lucid to permit him to write anything at all. However, as long as his potential Pulitzer Prize winning series of articles on his role as a liaison officer with the French Legionnaires in the Western Desert of Iraq lay gathering dust on some bureaucrat's desk in the Pentagon, assignments from *International Traveller* and magazines like it would help keep body and soul together.

Bruno Cavelli reached the Plaza del Castillo just as the singing, dancing throng in front of the Café Irun began a slow shuffle around the edge of the square, moving steadily towards the start of the bull-run. The majority of the dancers were drunk — full of Dutch courage before they risked facing the bulls. The Corsican had no such problems. During his time as a 'para', he had often faced death in the sweltering wastelands of Chad. The bulls of Pamplona were nothing to the black devils of N'jamena or the 'flics' of Marseilles. Cavelli fingered the knife hidden in the folds of his red sash. The idea of murdering his 'mark' in Pamplona had been inspirational. Death and Pamplona were synonymous, so who would look closely at the unfortunate demise of another otherwise healthy man under the horns of the on-rushing bulls?

Cavelli was borne along with the general movement towards the bottom of the square. He noticed a head of lank blond hair, but when the crowd parted momentarily to reveal the face, Cavelli saw that it was not his man. The Corsican started to push his way through the throng, spurning a hand that tried to drag him into an impromptu dance. It was important to locate the 'mark' before the crowd reached the top of the square and began to congregate for the prayers that traditionally precede the run. The *mozos*, experienced runners who oversee the event, were located near the centre of the crowd, recognisable by the rolled-up newspapers that they brandished proudly in the air directly over their heads, badges of honour indicating the location of the 'bravest of the brave'.

Cavelli pushed towards this central group. The crowd swayed and the Corsican caught sight of the man for whom he had been searching. He was struck by the ordinariness of his intended victim. If the Corsican had been another kind of person, he might have wondered why somebody was willing to pay a large sum of money to see what appeared to be a very ordinary individual dead. But Bruno Cavelli didn't burden himself with such questions. With over twenty contract 'kills' to his credit and a growing reputation in the Unione Corse, Cavelli had learned that there was no percentage in knowing why somebody had to die. The only thing that paid was being the hand behind the death. The fact that Finn Jorgensen had offended somebody powerful enough to order his killing was of no consequence to the Corsican. Cavelli moved closer to the central group and saw that they were not like the drunken youths who formed the perimeter of the moving throng. These were hard-faced older men without the flushed features of the young wine drinkers.

The object of Cavelli's attention was a slightly built, fair-haired man who stood with the group of *mozos*. The Corsican moved closer and noticed that the thin face beneath the lank fair hair was slightly flushed, though whether by alcohol or excitement Cavelli could not tell. He looked into the Dane's blue eyes and held them for a second before breaking contact. For Cavelli there was something almost sensual about the moment when his and his victim's eyes first met. There was no closer relationship than that of murderer and victim. In the moment when the victim left the world, the relationship with the killer far transcended the closeness enjoyed during the momentary coupling of bodies. Cavelli moved slowly to the edge of the central group, keeping the Dane in sight, and maintained his position close to Jorgensen as the crowd reached the edge of the square and began to filter to the top of the street known as the Estefeta.

Michael Joyce heard the band end their playing abruptly, and as if somebody had given an unseen signal, the previously boisterous crowd fell suddenly quiet. Without the music to stir the blood, the runners were faced in the silence with the true extent of their involvement in the event that was about to take place.

Away to his left, Michael could see the strengthened wooden pens that held the bulls and steers. Directly in front of him and along the full length of the right-hand side of the Estefeta, a double row of wooden posts stood embedded in the open side of the cobbled streets. In the distance, he could see a crew of grey-clad workers proceeding in the direction of the bull-ring, sweeping the glass and plastic from the littered streets as they went, before laying down a covering of sawdust. Across from the wooden barricades, the bars and shops which had been the scene of last night's revels had disgorged their customers and now stood barred and empty. Above on the balconies, privileged spectators, glasses of wine in hand, had gathered to watch the event in complete safety.

The runners, gathered at Santo Domingo near the top of the Estefeta, turned to face the large building at the corner of the Plaza del Castillo. The disorganisation of the singing, dancing crowd from the Plaza had been replaced by a quiet discipline. Michael watched as a priest on a balcony led the congregation in prayer, his sing-song Spanish washing over the heads of those who were about to risk their lives.

The prayer ended and the crowd roared as one man. A single rocket blazed into the sky, indicating that in ten minutes' time the bulls would be set free.

This was the point of no return, Michael thought. Once into the cobbled streets behind the Plaza del Castillo, the only exit was the bull-ring where the run ended. This was what the editor of *International Traveller* was paying for — a real life experience of running with the bulls. Michael shook his head in an attempt to banish some of the cobwebs caused by the booze and the lack of sleep. If he was going to do this thing, it was important that he be in one piece afterwards so that he could write about it.

He was already well versed in the etiquette of survival. There were certain cardinal rules that had to be followed if one wanted to emerge unscathed. Firstly, not even the most foolhardy first-time runner attempted to run the entire course with the bulls. Therefore, Michael's initial object was to get himself far enough forward so that his running time would be limited. The second rule was to locate oneself close enough to the huge wooden barriers so that in the event of a mishap, one could throw oneself over or under the stout wooden planks. Michael examined the impressive barriers as he marched along with the other runners. Those watching the run were contained behind an inside barrier of wooden beams. Outside this barrier was a *cordon sanitaire*, which was patrolled by local police. Beyond the *cordon sanitaire* was a second line of wooden barriers. Some of the youths in front of him practised jumping onto the wooden beams. A group of *mozos* passed along, advising on suitable starting locations. A second rocket sounded behind Michael and many of the youths surrounding him instinctively began to run forward.

He found a spot midway down the run and established his line of escape over a low section of the barricade some hundred metres along the Estefeta. It was one thing to satisfy the requirements of the magazine. It was quite another to die in the process. Runners streamed past Michael's position and he could feel his heart pounding in his chest as he awaited the first sight of the bulls.

Bruno Cavelli braced himself. Every muscle in his sinewy body was prepared for action. It would be simply a question of timing. Jorgensen had become separated from the other *mozos* and was busy shepherding some youths to the side of the street. The sound of hooves striking cobble-stones turned the level of apprehension up by several notches. The first of the bulls powered past Cavelli, veering as the white-clad runners scrambled out of its way. Cavelli let his right hand close on the hilt of the knife in his sash. He looked over his shoulder at the line of on-rushing runners and beasts. The pandemonium of the scene behind was more than he could have hoped for — white-clad bodies were rushing in every direction to avoid the bulls, and some had already abandoned the run and were scrambling over and under the stout wooden beams that led to the safety of the *cordon sanitaire*. Despite the confusion, the Corsican had managed to maintain a two-metre distance from Jorgensen, who was totally absorbed in his role of shepherding the bulls away from the less well co-ordinated runners.

Cavelli purposely stepped into the path of an on-rushing bull. Jorgensen reacted almost immediately to the potential danger, moving quickly to Cavelli's side and preparing to deflect the bull with his rolled-up newspaper. He grabbed the Corsican's arm and pulled sharply. Previous experience had taught him to use maximum force, since a first-time runner confronted by several tons of Spanish beef tends to exhibit the panic of a drowning man. He was therefore surprised to find that the runner offered no resistance, and he pitched forward uncontrollably.

Michael looked back along the Estefeta. The bulls were clearly visible in the midst of the white-clad runners, and the confusion was total. Bodies ran in zigzag patterns along the cobbled streets, colliding with each other, the boarded up shop fronts and the wooden barriers. Michael was preparing to set off when he saw one of the runners collide with a fair-haired *mozo*. The two men careened across the cobbled street straight into the path of an oncoming bull. The impact spun them to the side in a grotesque parody of a ballet step.

Cavelli had maintained a superb balance as he and Jorgensen lurched across the Estefeta. Brushed aside by the bull, the two men continued spinning until they crashed into the base of the wooden barricade. In an instant the knife was in Cavelli's hand and he swiftly plunged the blade into the point just below the ribs on Jorgensen's left side and pushed it upwards towards the man's heart.

Jorgensen's breath escaped from his body in a giant whoosh as the two men hit the barrier. The Dane was trying to rise when he felt the sharp pain of the knife under his ribs. He pushed up against the weight of the Corsican but found himself in a vice-like grip. The pain in his side was intense and he looked down to see a patch of dark red blood staining his white shirt. The hand of the young man he had rescued seemed to be stuck to the patch of blood.

Cavelli's facial muscles contorted as he tried to push the blade to the very centre of the Dane's being. An expression of pain and surprise covered his victim's face. Jorgensen's eyes were already beginning to cloud over and the Corsican increased the pressure on the blade, and began to twist it so that the wound would look as though it had been inflicted by a bull's horn.

Michael's attention was withdrawn from the two men by the proximity of an on-rushing bull. He leaped for the safety of a window sill and as soon as he had established his position glanced back at the fallen *mozo* and the man he had rescued. A shaft of early morning sunlight was momentarily reflected from the latter's right hand. Although he would have had difficulty standing up in court and swearing to it, Michael was sure that the man had been holding a knife. He looked again, but it was now nowhere in sight. Surely he had been mistaken.

Cavelli's sixth sense smelled danger. He looked quickly around the sea of faces that squinted from every gap in the stout timbers of the barricades, but none showed any indication that they had seen what happened. But then the Corsican tossed his dark head back towards the cobbled street and looked through the scrambling bodies directly into the eyes of Michael Joyce, who was perched some distance off the ground with his hands fixed tightly to one of the wooden shutters that covered the window of a bar. The look on the man's face was enough to convince Cavelli that he had been observed.

'*Merde!*' The expletive exploded from Cavelli's lips. He gave the knife a final twist before extracting it from Jorgensen's side and slipping it back into his red sash. He looked into the Dane's grey face and knew that his work had been successful. He jumped onto the nearest barricade and scrambled into the *cordon sanitaire*.

Michael Joyce leaped from his perch when he saw Cavelli making his escape and pushed his way across the street. The *mozo* he had seen fall to the ground was lying on his back just beneath the nearest barricade. The left side of his white shirt was already covered by a vivid red stain, and a patch of sticky red liquid soiled the yellow sawdust that covered the street. The pallor of the man's face indicated the seriousness of his condition.

'Ekeller.' The sound emanating from the stricken man's parched lips was hardly audible.

Michael bent over and put his ear to the man's lips.

'Ekeller.' The word was repeated in a whisper and then Jorgensen shuddered before going still.

Michael jumped onto the top of the barricade and dropped into the *cordon sanitaire*. He looked quickly along the length of the gap between the two barricades but saw only the uniformed police. The young man with the knife must have already scrambled over the inner barricade. Michael climbed to the top of the inner barrier, but there was no sign of the man. Now that the bull-run was over, the crowd was already beginning to move towards the Plaza del Castillo and it would have been easy for him to slip into the human stream. Michael jumped into the crowd and tried to push his way towards the open streets. A siren sounded behind him and he assumed medical help was on its way to the *mozo* he had left lying at the foot of the barrier. He tried to look above the head of the crowd in a vain attempt to catch a glimpse of the fleeing assailant. The narrow streets leading away from the Estefeta were crammed solid and progress was slow. By the time he had covered the fifteen metres to the open spaces of the Plaza, a large section of the thousands of people who had been watching the running of the bulls had already preceded him. Whichever way Michael looked he was confronted by scores of dark-haired youths who resembled the man he had seen with the knife in his hand. The bull-run had only lasted a few minutes and already the staff of the bars were beginning to re-open their doors and remove the shutters from the windows. Michael walked slowly around the square, staring at the groups already breakfasting on bags of chorros and hot chocolate. Where in hell had the young man disappeared to? Perhaps the whole thing had been a figment of his tired wine-addled brain. The American turned and made his way back in the direction from which he had come.

Cavelli sat with a group of young Spaniards at a table just outside the entrance to the Café Irun. He watched the tall dark-haired man who had seen him murder the Dane exit from a narrow street at the side of the café and begin to look around the square. Cavelli moved behind his neighbour and watched as the man moved slowly around the perimeter of the square, examining the faces of those he passed. He wondered how much of his own face had been seen and whether the bastard would be able to recognise him again. No one had ever witnessed the Corsican at work before. He had succeeded in fulfilling his contract to kill the Dane, but had he succeeded in making it look like an accident? The conditions of the contract had been quite explicit. The death was to appear accidental and no official investigation was to ensue. The man stalking the square could prove to be an embarrassing problem. Cavelli contemplated staying in Pamplona to make sure that his employer's wishes were conformed to. But that would add to his exposure and could lead to the very consequence he was trying to avoid.

Michael Joyce walked back down the narrow street beside the Café Irun. He made his way back to the point in the Estefeta where he had seen the two men fall. The injured man had been removed and the only evidence that Michael had not imagined the whole incident was a patch of red-soaked sawdust. Perhaps he had been mistaken after all. Maybe the two men had brushed one of the bulls and the *mozo* had been injured. Michael tried to go over his recollections of the run for his article. He remembered very little except the look on the injured man's face. The man had said something to him, but he was damned if he could remember what it was. Tomorrow he would have to go through the whole nerve-shattering run again in order to satisfy the demands of his editor. Right now he was tired and hungry. It was time to get back to the Café Irun for the traditional post-run breakfast. Then some sleep.

Cavelli eased his rented Seat into a slot in the underground garage of the Hotel Gran Ercilla in Bilbao. He was dressed casually in a red Lacoste shirt and blue Levi jeans. The bloodied white shirt and trousers as well as the red sash and neckerchief had been burned along the deserted road between Pamplona and Vitoria, while the murder weapon had been cleaned and tossed into a deep *baranca*. He cleaned the interior of the car and then removed the gloves he had worn while driving the vehicle. The precautions he had taken would probably prove to be superfluous. Nobody among the thousands who had earlier thronged the streets of Pamplona would remember one youth from among so many.

Cavelli entered the hotel through the side door and went directly to his room on the fifth floor. It was four o'clock in the afternoon. He crossed to the phone and dialled a number.

'*Oui.*'

'I was at the running of the bulls in Pamplona this morning,' Cavelli said.

'Ah, yes,' the voice replied.

'I'm afraid I have some bad news concerning a mutual friend.'

The voice did not reply.

'It appears that our friend was gored to death by a bull.'

'How unfortunate,' the voice said.

'I'm staying here tonight and returning to Marseilles tomorrow. You can reach me there if you need me.'

'Everything should be under control now,' the voice said quietly. 'But do not take any commissions for at least a week. There may be some further business to transact. The funds we agreed on will be transferred to your bank tomorrow morning.'

The line went dead.

Cavelli replaced the receiver and started to peel off his clothes. His bank account was now larger by one hundred thousand French francs. He needed a shower and then some sleep. The hotel porter had promised him an exciting companion for the evening. Cavelli hoped that the lady was renowned for her stamina.

Jean Claude Blu replaced the handset on his personal telephone in his office on the thirtieth floor of the Tour Chemie on the outskirts of Lyons and walked to the window. The early summer evening was perfectly clear and the city shimmered under a fading sun shining from a near perfect azure sky. Blu looked towards the southern part of the city and saw the steel vessels of the Chemie de France plant reflected in the orange sunlight. He had begun his career in that very plant as a young engineer thirty-two years earlier. His life had been dedicated to his company and to the giant steel tubes that climbed skyward at the edge of the city. Nothing would be allowed to endanger his company's health.

Blu moved away from the window and back towards his desk. He removed a bottle of champagne from the fridge in the bar behind his desk and opened it. The chairman of Chemie de France had known that the Corsican would succeed in his mission. He poured a glass of the bubbling liquid into a fluted crystal glass. Only part of the danger had been removed by the death of Jorgensen. Jean Claude Blu would prove his worth by removing the rest.

The three white-aproned waiters standing near the entrance of the Maison des Cygnes busied themselves as Jean Claude Blu strode into the single first-floor room that constituted one of the most exclusive restaurants in Brussels. The chairman of France's largest chemical company was a regular visitor to the restaurant and was well known among the waiters for his generosity. The *maître d'* appeared and shepherded Blu towards a table that had been set in the window directly overlooking the Grand Place, the very heart of Brussels. Blu was pleased to see that his instructions regarding the discreet distance to be observed between his table and the neighbouring tables had been followed to the letter.

His dinner guest had already arrived.

'Monsieur Blu.' Lucien Dubois rose, as one of the most recognisable men in French business circles approached. The official of the European Commission had been in a sweat all day wondering why such a powerful man had invited him to dinner.

'Monsieur Dubois.' Blu extended his hand, which was taken eagerly by the younger man. 'What a pleasure to finally meet you.'

'It is an honour to meet you, monsieur.' Dubois exuded admiration. The career of a rising civil servant could be made or broken by powerful individuals such as Blu.

'Two Kirs Royales,' Blu told the waiter as he took his seat across from Dubois. He looked at the fawning face opposite him and concluded that it was going to be a long and tiresome evening. However, Dubois had a very important role to play in his plans. His file gave his age as thirty-five, but already too close an acquaintance with the rich cuisine of Belgium had caused his stomach to spread. He was dressed impeccably in a charcoal grey suit tailored perfectly to conceal the expanding girth.

'I understand that we have many friends in common,' Blu said, fingering the menu. 'Jacques Biron speaks most highly of you.'

'The minister was undoubtedly being too kind.' Dubois was now doubly intrigued. The mention of one of France's most senior ministers in Blu's opening gambit was quite unexpected.

The waiter brought the Kirs. 'Is Monsieur ready to order?' he asked, withdrawing a notepad from his apron pocket.

Blu did not bother to consult the menu. 'Bring foie gras to begin with, selle d'agneau to follow.' He raised his eyebrows in Dubois's direction.

'An excellent choice,' the younger man said.

'And a bottle of Chateau Batailley 1976,' Blu added, handing the unopened menu to the waiter. Dubois would certainly go far in his chosen career. It was necessary for those who served egotistical politicians to display the characteristics that the English writer Dickens had ascribed to his character Uriah Heep. A short acquaintance with Lucien Dubois was enough to confirm that he had these qualities in abundance.

'I'm grateful that you were free to join me this evening,' Blu said. 'I understand that you and I have many things in common. We are both 'X' and 'enarques'.'

'Nothing would please me more than to be of service to you.' With just one statement Blu had established a bond between himself and Dubois that was infinitely stronger than any other in France. The former pupils of the Ecole Polytechniques, or the 'X' as they are known, form a business and civil service élite which has effectively ruled France since the time of Napoleon. Being a member of such an exclusive club entitled one to the privilege of entry into the inner sanctum of French business. Virtually every business leader in France who counted had been trained at the Ecole Polytechnique. As 'enarques', both Blu and Dubois had completed their education at the prestigious Ecole Nationale d'Administration. The membership of such high status societies was much more prized in France than membership of a masonic lodge.

The waiter deposited delicate portions of paté de foie gras before the two men while the wine waiter served Blu with the Chateau Batailley. Blu nodded without tasting the wine, and the two waiters withdrew discreetly.

'You must tell me something of your work for the Commission,' Blu said, spreading a little paté on a slice of toast. He already knew exactly what Dubois did for the European Commission but it was necessary to allow the younger man to assist him in setting the scene.

'I have the honour of being the *chef-de-cabinet* for Monsieur le Commissaire Combes.' Dubois forked a large piece of foie gras directly into his mouth. 'As I'm sure you are aware, our Commissioner has the important responsibility of dealing with competition policy. The number of mergers and acquisitions has been growing rapidly over the past few years.'

'An altogether weighty and important dossier.' Blu spread a morsel of foie gras on toast and pushed the plate away. 'You are fortunate to have a superior of the quality of Combes to oversee such a matter.'

Dubois gulped a glass of the excellent Batailley and wondered exactly what Blu was up to. Everybody in France knew that his boss was a total incompetent who had been dispatched to Brussels as a damage limitation measure by the French Socialist Party. 'Yes,' Dubois said as he put his glass back on the table.

'However, I understand that no matter how competent Monsieur Combes is, he still depends on the senior members of his staff to direct the day-to-day operations of his office. In that respect he is indeed fortunate to have somebody of your experience to assist him.' Blu was well aware that Dubois was running Combes's office. The Commissioner knew as much about international law as Blu's five-year-old nephew knew about atomic energy. This situation was not uncommon among the seventeen Commissioners who constituted the college of the European Commission, and who mostly depended on a coterie of advisers who were responsible for formulating their Commissioners' view on various topics. The top adviser, or *chef-de-cabinet*, had an exceedingly powerful influence on the Commissioner, and if a Commissioner was particularly weak, was the *de facto* top official.

Dubois bathed in the warmth of Blu's obvious praise and the glow of the Chateau Batailley.

A waiter removed Blu's scarcely touched plate and Dubois's empty one.

'Minister Biron and I are convinced that there is a great future ahead of a man who can direct the policy of the European Community in so vital an area as competition policy,' Blu said, as the waiter laid two plates of lightly cooked saddle of lamb before them. On either side of the lamb, small circles of puréed potato and spinach lent more to the aesthetics of the dish than to the satisfaction of hunger.

'It is very gratifying to know that one's work is appreciated.' Dubois began to slice his knife through the pink slices of lamb.

'I understand, of course, that during your period of office with the Commission you are bound to be *communautaire*. However, our common heritage of service to France must not be forgotten.'

'I assure you, Monsieur Blu, that I am first and foremost a servant of France.' Dubois washed down a mouthful of lamb with a slug of wine. Whatever happened during his four-year stint with the European Commission, his ultimate career would be decided by the mandarins of the Quai d'Orsay.

'Good,' Blu said, cutting a tiny sliver of the pink meat and depositing it delicately in his mouth. 'Then I presume that I may speak openly and in complete confidence.'

'Of course,' Dubois said cheerfully, pleased at being taken into the confidence of the good and the great of France.

'The industry I represent is of vital importance to both France and the European Community. Therefore it is crucial that we remain profitable if we are to serve our clientele.'

Dubois nodded in agreement.

'Ever since the 1950s the petrochemical industry has experienced what could only be called spectacular growth. However, by 1980 the industry was faced with its first fall in demand, and while we could have accommodated a small drop, the actual fall was of truly dramatic proportions. By the time the industry realised what was happening, it was too late to halt the huge investment programmes that we had put into operation in the late 1970s. Moreover, new entrants began producing into an already declining market. The result was a crash and the virtual disappearance of profit for the established companies. In order to survive, each participant in the market was forced to enter into commercial arrangements with certain of our competitors.'

Dubois straightened himself in his seat. Being taken into a confidence was one thing, but he was getting the feeling that he was about to be compromised. 'Forgive me, Monsieur Blu,' he said carefully, hoping that without offending the industrialist he could stop the conversation developing in an embarrassing way, 'I don't really see the point of discussing your commercial arrangements with a Commission official. Especially one like me with the responsibility of overseeing the competition portfolio.'

'I thought that we had already established that your first allegiance was to France.' There was a threatening tone in Blu's voice.

'That is true. However, I would not like to find myself compromised.'

The waiter came and removed the plates. 'A dessert?' he asked.

'Fresh strawberries,' Blu said, and looked across at his companion. 'For two.' Blu's eyes seemed to bore into Dubois. 'I will tell you nothing that is not already known to Minister Biron.'

Dubois nodded, his apprehension rising by the second and dispelling the mellow feeling that the wine had created.

'Let me return to my narrative,' Blu said. 'The almost catastrophic events of the 1980s convinced us that in order to avoid a repetition in the future, a certain degree of co-operation between competitors in the petrochemical industry would be necessary. These commercial arrangements have continued and now form the basis of a loose association.'

The waiter placed a plate of fresh strawberries before each man.

Dubois watched Blu pop a piece of the ripe red fruit into his mouth. He looked at his own plate, and although his hunger had scarcely been sated, his appetite had disappeared. 'What you're talking about is a cartel,' he said, looking directly at his host.

'Come now, Lucien. Such commercial agreements are commonplace. I prefer to call it a pricing arrangement based on the maintenance of market share. Such a compromise has been proven to be in everybody's interest and, in fact, I would go so far as to say that it has allowed the European chemical industry to survive during very difficult times.'

Dubois looked through the Tudor style window across the cobbles of the Grand Place. The square was full of tourists lining up camera shots or drinking beers in the sidewalk cafés. Blu had compromised him totally. He was now privy to the fact that the European chemical industry had in effect been operating a cartel. As a civil servant he was obliged to report the fact to his superiors, but that would undoubtedly finish his career. And he was in no doubt that if he betrayed Blu's confidence, the chairman of Chemie de France would make sure that he never again held a responsible position.

'You've told me all this for a reason,' he said, returning his glance to his host. But he wasn't sure that he wanted to hear the reason, which would inevitably draw him further into a web of dishonesty.

'Just recently some papers have fallen into the hands of a Commission official.' Blu noticed Dubois's eyebrows raising. 'Don't worry, he was a very low level official. Those papers could be very damaging to my own company and to other European companies. Therefore it is vitally important that we recover the documents in question.'

A smile passed over Dubois's thin lips. So that was the point of the dinner invitation. 'There's another fact about the European Commission that you should know,' he said. 'The members of staff tend to be very single-minded and stubborn individuals. If I, as *chef-de-cabinet*, were to insist that an official surrender specific documents to me, that person could cause a lot of trouble.'

'What if the official in question was no longer living?'

Dubois sat erect in his chair. The hairs on his neck began to rise. 'What exactly do you mean by that?'

'The official in question, one Finn Jorgensen, was in Pamplona for the running of the bulls,' Blu said softly. 'Unfortunately, he was severely gored by one of the bulls. He is now no longer with us.' The chairman of Chemie de France popped another plump strawberry into his mouth and crushed it.

Something in his intonation put the wild idea into Dubois's mind that the death might not have been an accident. He gazed at the industrialist, wondering if the man could possibly be capable of murder. 'What do you want me to do?' he asked, a tone of resignation in his voice.

'Quite simply, I want you to recover those papers for me.'

'And if I can't?'

'Can't is a word that does not exist in the world I inhabit. You will carry out a very careful search of Jorgensen's papers and as soon as you locate those pertaining to our operation you will report instantly back to me.'

'What if I were to decline?'

'Then Commissioner Combes will receive a telephone call from Minister Biron tomorrow morning and by this time tomorrow evening your office will be cleared out and you will be on your way back to Paris to a job where your undoubted talents will be allowed to wither.'

'You don't offer much of a choice,' Dubois said, avoiding Blu's stare by looking out the window. He had no doubt that the chairman of Chemie de France was deadly serious.

'Some day, Lucien, you will wish to leave the service of your country and enter the private sector. Perhaps at that time you will be in a position to consider joining Chemie de France or one of our associated companies.' Blu was watching the young man carefully. He had already used the stick and now it was time to offer the carrot. 'While a man of integrity is very much appreciated in some types of employment, a man of unquestionable loyalty is a much rarer and therefore more appreciated bird. In this case you can be of assistance to us. In the future we will try to return the favour.'

Dubois hesitated only momentarily before lifting his cognac and tilting it towards his host. *'Pour la Patrie, les Sciences et la Gloire.'*

The two men touched glasses as Blu repeated the motto of the Ecole Polytechnique. They drank their cognac without further discussion.

It was almost eleven o'clock when Lucien Dubois left the Maison des Cygnes. At the main door he nearly bumped into a group of tourists surrounding the brass effigy of Evard t'Severd, a noble Belgian who had served his country loyally. The leg and forearm of the brass statue were shiny where thousands of tourists had rubbed the effigy of the dying knight in the hope that it would bring them luck. Although Dubois had passed the statue dozens of times, he had never succumbed to the temptation to try to improve whatever Dame Fortune had in store for him. Tonight he felt different. He had just passed a very important initiation ceremony and he was aware of having done so. Lucien Dubois stroked the thigh of the brass effigy, knowing that he had sacrificed his principles for the promise of a future, and in doing so had joined a line of human kind that stretched back to the First Man.

CHAPTER TWO

The table and six chairs that stood in the centre of the 'Horizon' room at the Brussels Sheraton Hotel looked cheerless in the otherwise empty suite. As was usual for the meetings of the cartel, the room had been cleared and carefully screened for listening devices.

Jean Claude Blu sat at the head of the table awaiting the arrival of the other members of the committee. He was pleased that the recruitment of Dubois had been accomplished so easily. The poor fool had little choice but to comply with their wishes. It would be a considerable feather in Blu's cap if he could report to his colleagues that the whole sorry mess of the documents being leaked to the European Commission had been successfully resolved. As the chairman of the cartel, it was his responsibility to retrieve the papers before any damage could be done. He was already eighty percent of the way to getting the documents back.

'Good morning, Jean Claude.'

Blu looked up from his papers and saw Henk Van Veen, the chief executive of the Dutch chemical giant, Elver, striding through the door. As usual the big Dutchman had a black cigar hanging from his lips.

'Good morning, Henk,' Blu said, turning up his nose as the pungent aroma of the cigar reached his nostrils. The Dutchman never ceased to amaze him. Van Veen was dressed as usual in dark blazer and grey slacks, attire that in Blu's mind was more associated with yachting than a business meeting. Also, Van Veen appeared to the Frenchman to look younger as the years progressed, whereas Blu was constantly aware of the deepening lines on his own gaunt face. But the Dutchman's most distinguishing features were his voice, which had the timbre of a rusty chain being pulled through a bed of gravel, and the fact that his grasp on thrift was such that not even the expenditure of a single centime escaped him.

Van Veen dropped his briefcase onto the floor beside one of the chairs and proceeded to pour himself a cup of coffee from one of the thermos flasks that had been set on the table.

'I'm surprised that I'm the first to arrive.' The deep gravelly voice filled the room as its owner allowed his long body to slump into one of the chairs. 'The traffic between Rotterdam and here was almost impenetrable.'

'The others should be here shortly.' Blu returned to the examination of the papers before him on the table, while reflecting with amazement that Van Veen, who was the top man in a company with sales in the billions and profits in the millions of dollars, would still travel by car.

The door to the suite opened and three other members of the cartel entered together. Blu stiffened as he saw leading them the grey-haired figure of Sir Roger Morley, the chief executive of Commonwealth Chemicals. Morley had the distinction of being a member of the cartel almost as long as Blu. Directly behind him came the American Dan Newton, who represented the US chemical interests in Europe. Bringing up the rear was Professore Enzo Di Marco, the chief executive of Italchemichi.

'Welcome, gentlemen.' Blu stood up from his chair and went to greet the three men. He avoided Morley and grasped Newton's outstretched hand. 'Good to see you, Dan.' Although Blu had attended Oxford University and could speak English perfectly, he affected a heavy French accent.

'Good to see you too, Jean Claude.' Newton squeezed the Frenchman's hand. The American stood 190 centimetres in his socks and weighed in at something over 127 kilos. He was one of those citizens of the US who give credence to the theory that everything is bigger in America. Or perhaps like some of his countrymen he was simply the product of years of indirect hormone treatment.

Blu extracted his hand and offered it to the Italian. *'Professore, come stai?'*

'Bene, grazie, et lei?' the slim and urbane Milanese replied.

'Bene, grazie.' Blu enjoyed using Italian. He was aware that Morley spoke only English. He also liked Di Marco, whom he considered to be a cultured individual.

'Roger, how are you?' Blu had pasted a smile to his face and extended his hand towards the chief executive of Commonwealth Chemicals. The Briton's taste in clothing appalled the Frenchman. Morley was wearing a red striped shirt which was already causing Blu to avert his gaze. Why was it, Blu wondered, that Morley could never rise above his lowly beginnings. Despite his exalted industrial position, Morley had never succeeded in throwing off either the demeanour or the appearance of the delivery boy he had once been. His off-the-peg suit hung awkwardly on his paunchy body and his thinning grey hair shot out in twin spikes behind each ear.

'Good, thanks,' said the Englishman, who hailed from the north-east and had never lost his Geordie accent. He gave the Frenchman's hand a perfunctory shake and then let it go. 'Have you any idea how long this meeting is going to last?'

Huff and puff, Blu thought, watching the Englishman's red face. With all Morley's rushing, Commonwealth Chemicals was sliding down the drain. Blu simply prayed that he would be around when the last vestiges of the British company were about to disappear, so that he could stick in the plug. 'It will be as long or as short as necessary,' he replied imperiously. 'Why don't we take our seats and we can begin immediately?'

'Where's Werner?' Van Veen asked, pouring himself a second cup of coffee.

Blu sat down and the others followed suit. 'Werner will be arriving shortly. We received his confirmation by fax.'

'There's no agenda for today's meeting?' Newton asked.

'Not today,' Blu replied. 'There are only two items to be discussed.' He passed around a number of blue folders. 'The secretariat have as usual prepared a report on the current state of the industry and on our pricing policy for the coming half year. You will also find included the quotas you have each been allocated.'

The five men opened their folders and began to read the columns of figures that were presented in the report.

'We may have some problems with these quotas.' Newton's mid-western accent broke the silence. 'I have to tell you that the US members are more than a little worried by the continual scaling down of the amount you guys allow us to sell in the European market.'

'We could make the same complaint about our allotment on the American market,' Blu said coldly. 'I shouldn't have to remind you, Dan, that these are recessionary times. Most of us sitting around this table are having to accept constriction of our sales, but we have made an effort to keep everyone's profits as healthy as possible.'

Sir Roger Morley ran his eyes over the figures a second time. The changes from the last half year were negligible, but there was a discernible downward trend in his company's allocation. Ever since the Frenchman had become chairman of the cartel, he had been chipping away at the British quota. Morley could feel the anger welling up inside him. He was between a rock and a hard place. Ideally he would have liked to tell the Frog to stuff his quotas up his arse and go it alone. But that course of action would leave Commonwealth Chemicals exposed to the combined pressure of the cartel, which had the muscle to drive him out of business. His only hope of improving his company's situation was to get Blu out of the chairman's seat. However, the cartel's rules were that the eldest member was automatically the chairman, and Blu was senior to him by several months.

'I notice that Commonwealth's share has been reduced yet again.' There was an edge in Morley's tone.

'Roger, we've all had our quotas cut.' Blu was delighted at Morley's discomfort. Difficulties for Commonwealth were market opportunities for Chemie de France.

Some more than others, Morley said to himself.

'I think the secretariat has done a good job. *Excellente*.' Di Marco slipped the papers back into the folder, displaying a set of perfectly manicured nails in the process. The Italian was growing weary of the feud between the Briton and the Frenchman. The cartel was simply a commercial arrangement and not an opportunity to fight the Hundred Years War over and over again.

The door to the suite opened and the five men turned in its direction. Werner Von Schick, the chief executive of Mannheim Chemicals, closed the door behind him and strode to the table at the centre of the room.

'*Guten Tag, die Herrschaften,*' the young German said, dropping his briefcase on the floor beside the empty chair. 'Jean Claude, Roger, Henk, Enzo, Dan.' The members of the cartel nodded a greeting. Dr Werner Von Schick was the youngest man in the suite by at least twenty years. At thirty-five years of age, he was already the chief executive of Germany's largest chemical company and a major influence on German industrial policy.

'We've just begun,' Blu said, talking directly to the pale-faced German. His eyes were constantly drawn to the duelling scar that ran from the young man's left ear to the corner of his thin-lipped mouth. The chairman had developed a deep respect for the young Prussian's business skills and was acting as the German's mentor on the cartel committee. The Frenchman was sure that some day Werner Von Schick would take over as chairman.

Von Schick was already examining the contents of the plastic folder. 'It looks about right to me.' The young German spoke English with a pronounced Boston accent, a legacy of three years spent at the Harvard Business School earning a doctorate in Business Administration. 'I think, Jean Claude, that both you and the secretariat are to be complimented on an excellent job.'

Blu smiled at his protégé. He could always depend on Werner for support. 'If everybody is agreed, we can move on to the next item on the agenda,' he said.

The six men around the table straightened themselves involuntarily.

'As agreed at our last meeting,' Blu continued, 'I took the first steps necessary to recover the documents that fell into the hands of Finn Jorgensen.' The chairman of the cartel looked accusingly across at his British colleague. Although there was no evidence to prove that Morley was the culprit, Blu was certain that when they located the source of the leak, the chief executive of Commonwealth would be put firmly in the dock. 'The unfortunate Dane was gored to death during the first day of the running of the bulls in Pamplona.'

'Was that entirely necessary?' Morley's voice cut sharply across the Frenchman. 'Couldn't the poor bastard have been bought off just like everybody else who's ever threatened our operation? Now we have a dead body to explain.' Morley didn't give a horse's ass whether Jorgensen lived or died. He smelled an opportunity of embarrassing Blu and he wasn't going to neglect it.

'As I remember it,' Di Marco's English was heavily accented — almost a music hall parody of an Italian speaking the language with an 'a' being added to every word, 'this group gave Jean Claude *carte blanche* to resolve the situation. The death of this young man, however regrettable, must be placed against the damage that public disclosure would do to our industry.'

'Not to mention the pockets of our companies,' Newton added. 'If Jean Claude hadn't succeeded in stopping Jorgensen, we could be looking at fines in the region of ten percent of our turnover. Jesus Christ! That type of money allied to the recession would bring the companies I represent to their knees. I'm sorry the guy's dead, but that's the way the cookie crumbles.'

'Perhaps I haven't made myself clear,' Morley articulated slowly, as if doing so might make the stupid foreigners understand better. 'By arranging the death of this man Jorgensen, we have committed a crime. I just wonder whether we all realise that.'

'Don't be naïve, Roger,' Von Schick said in his smooth Boston accent. 'Up to now the very existence of the cartel has never been threatened. Only those of us sitting at this table are privy to the arrangements that we've made over the years. The risk of having those arrangements exposed is worth much more than the life of just one man. I think Jean Claude reacted properly and with admirable haste. While I deplore the death of Jorgensen, I fully support the actions taken by our chairman.'

'Which brings us to an even more delicate point.' Blu let his gaze run around the faces of his colleagues before stopping at Morley. 'How did Mr Jorgensen come by papers that, if properly deciphered, could lead to the destruction of all our companies?'

The chief executive of Commonwealth stood up. Red streaks of anger radiated from the skin at his collar and extended up his neck to his face. 'I don't like the fact that you just happen to be looking at me every time you talk about finding the source of the leaked documents. If you've got any proof that the documents originated from my company, then you had better put it on the table. If not, then I'd advise you to keep your insinuations to yourself.'

'Sit down, Roger.' Blu was enjoying himself hugely. 'Your paranoia is beginning to show.'

Di Marco's sing-song English cut through the tense air in the room. 'How do you intend to expose whoever passed the documents to Jorgensen?'

'I have a problem in answering that question, Enzo,' Blu replied. 'The person who passed those documents to our hapless Dane is in all probability sitting at this table right now. Therefore any discussion on the steps I hope to take will inevitably alert him, or indeed them, since there might be more than one person involved in the conspiracy.'

'What guarantee do we have that you're not the person in question?' Morley asked, looking directly at Blu.

'You have no guarantee,' Blu replied, looking around the faces peering in his direction.

'Does anybody mind if I make a comment?' Newton said. 'What in hell would anybody in this room have to gain in having the cartel exposed? We're all agreed that if the European Commission was to get the goods on our operation, then all of our companies would be fined and our business arrangements ruined. That would impact on every man jack sitting here. I want those documents back and I want the skin of the rat who leaked them, whether he's currently in this room or not. For my money we should leave no stone unturned in exposing the bastard. What I'm saying is that I want all the bases covered, including those in all our individual companies.'

'Dan's got a point,' Morley interjected. 'Unless of course the whole document business is simply a scam dreamed up by our esteemed chairman. The cartel is in danger and only Jean Claude Blu can pull our collective chestnuts out of the proverbial fire. How very convenient.'

'*Conard!*' Blu said, beginning to rise from his chair.

Von Schick looked at the two elder statesmen of the cartel and sighed. 'There is no point in personalising this affair,' he said.

Van Veen nodded in agreement. 'The rest of us haven't come to Brussels to see you two putting on your own personal piece of theatre. Jean Claude, why don't you tell us what exactly you intend to do?'

Blu allowed himself to drop slowly back into his chair. 'I have taken the steps necessary to recover the documents that were leaked to Jorgensen. When those documents are in my hands, I will have the evidence that will put whoever leaked them into the dock.' The Frenchman resisted the temptation to stare at his British counterpart.

'*Va bene,*' Di Marco said. 'But no more killing without consultation. Considering the state of relations between Jean Claude and Roger, I suggest that they, along with Werner, constitute a mini-committee. If all three are agreed that further action is required to protect our cartel, then such an accord should constitute a green light from the rest of us.'

Blu looked around the other four members of the cartel and saw them nodding in agreement. 'That motion appears to be carried.' It was a clear dilution of the Frenchman's power as chairman of the cartel, but he had no problem in agreeing. Dubois was his ace in the hole. Combes' *chef-de-cabinet* would retrieve the documents and Blu would again be the hero of the cartel, with his own position as chairman consolidated as never before. He held out his hands magnanimously towards his two colleagues. 'If there is any need of further action that might lead to bodily harm, I shall seek the approval of both Roger and Werner before acting. However, I suggest that instead of unanimity it should be on the basis of a simple majority vote.'

'Agreed,' four voices echoed in unison.

The single dissenter was Sir Roger Morley. The chief executive of Commonwealth knew that he should be happy at the slight erosion of the Frenchman's power, but he had been skirmishing with Blu for long enough to be troubled by the fact that the chairman of the cartel had surrendered so easily. The crafty Gaul had something up his sleeve and Morley would have dearly liked to know what it was.

'*Bon,*' Jean Claude Blu said, gathering up the papers from the table before him. 'Our strategy is now clear. I will endeavour to recover the documents without further incident and the question of who was responsible for the leak may be solved at that time. May I wish you a safe return to your respective countries.' He deposited the documents in his leather briefcase and began to stride towards the door.

Sir Roger Morley watched as the Frenchman left. Some day he was going to bury that arrogant bastard. Blu was what they described on Tyneside as 'all shit and wind', nothing but a pompous little bugger in a six hundred pound suit. For ten long years he'd suffered the smarmy bastard without ever having the opportunity to nail his garlic-eating hide to the wall. The current difficulties of the cartel had seemed to present the perfect opportunity to make the Frenchman squirm, but Blu had responded in typical fashion by putting him on the defensive. However, there was still time for a battle or two on the question of the documents. Morley felt that the Frenchman had exposed himself by ordering the death of the Dane, but how in heaven's name could that be turned against him after the approbation of his colleagues in the cartel?

The expansive office of Nicholas J Elliot, the director general of the Competition Directorate General, was on the eighth floor of the European Commission building in Brussels. The furniture could have been called Scandinavian chic — stained wood and stainless steel. A genuine Mercator map of the British Isles hung directly behind Elliot's desk and tasteful prints were displayed on the rest of the wall space. The only concession to Elliot's exalted position in the hierarchy of the European Community was a rather tattered wall map of the twelve Member States which was secured to the wall by four thumb-tacks.

The phone rang.

'Yes?' Elliot's English accent was of the clipped military variety.

'Schuman on the line,' Elliot's secretary said.

'I'll take it,' Elliot punched the black button on his handset. 'Mr Schuman.' Elliot wondered why these businessmen insisted on these stupid pseudonyms when they were informing on their colleagues or their competitors. In general, the pseudonyms were quite ridiculous: Nightingale, Bigfoot, or some childish quirk or remembrance. 'Schuman' had taken it one step further by opting for the name of one of the founders of the European Community.

'I just happened to be in Brussels and I was wondering how your inquiry was proceeding,' Schuman's smooth voice came over the line.

'Everything is proceeding according to the time-scale we originally discussed. As I'm sure you are well aware, the preparation of such a complex and wide-ranging case with repercussions not only inside but also outside the Community can take some considerable time.'

'I understand the difficulties, but there may be some hiccups on the horizon.'

Elliot sat bolt upright in his seat. He didn't like the sound of that. 'What exactly are we talking about?'

'My colleagues are feeling a little restive,' Schuman said. 'It would be a pity to see the whole case go down the tubes just because you didn't act soon enough.'

'Soon or late isn't in question. Secrecy is. Progress is restricted by the fact that I can only put a very limited number of trustworthy staff on the case. If one word of the inquiry were to get out, we would probably have to abandon the case. You may be sure that we are processing the material as quickly as humanly possible under these constraints. In the meantime, you must do your best to quieten the rumblings of your colleagues.'

'I'll do my best. What about Combes?'

Elliot winced at the mention of the name of the French peasant. The world was ill-divided when a Wykehamist was set to work for an idiot like Combes. 'Neither the Commissioner nor any member of his staff knows anything about the inquiry.' And there's no reason why they should, Elliot added in his own mind.

'That's comforting to know. I'll be in touch.'

The phone went dead in Elliot's hand and he returned the handset to the cradle. He wondered why Schuman had decided to rat on his colleagues. Cases of conscience were not unknown in the business community, but they were rare birds indeed. The case against the chemical giants of Europe and the United States, when it was completed, would be one of the biggest ever handled by the European Commission. And the man prosecuting that case would be guaranteed his photograph in the pink pages of the *Financial Times* on more than one occasion.

Such things do not go unnoticed in higher places. Schuman had been a godsend. Elliot had kept control of the dossier himself and he was the sole European Commission link to the cartel member. Not a soul in Elliot's Directorate General had any idea about the source of the documents they were processing. Schuman and the chemical cartel were the keys that would open the box containing Elliot's knighthood.

Schuman handed the phone to the stewardess on the executive jet and sat back in his seat. The plan was going exactly as he had conceived it. Jorgensen had proved to be a better red herring than even he had expected. The documents leaked to Jorgensen had simply been sufficient to whet the Dane's appetite for pursuing a solitary quest. At the same time Schuman had delivered a veritable mountain of documents directly to Elliot. Now while the cartel was turning itself inside out trying to recover the documents that had been in Jorgensen's possession, Elliot and his team were examining a full set of incriminating documents that would eventually lead to the destruction of the petrochemical cartel. The sound of the powerful jet increased and they began to roll across the tarmac to the take-off runway.

The cartel had served its purpose, and now it was time for one man to structure the future of the European industry. Schuman smiled as he thought of the look on the faces of the cartel when the final curtain was rung down on them. Their comfortable arrangements had made them fat and feeble — perfect targets for a hungry predator. Schuman felt no remorse for Jorgensen. He would have consigned a battalion of European Commission officials to their fate if it would help him accomplish his plan. The jet engine screamed as the Lear accelerated along the runway. Schuman removed the latest cartel document from his briefcase and looked at the figures that divided the market between the members. Soon there would be only one name on that list, and he was not going to share the market with anyone.

'Merde!' Lucien Dubois kicked the small cardboard box across the floor of his office. The box landed close to the door, spilling out its contents of pens, staplers, punches, Scotch tape and all the paraphernalia associated with office work. Three other empty plain brown cardboard boxes sat on the floor beyond Dubois's modern semi-circular desk, their contents in piles around the sofa and easy chair that stood across from Dubois's working area.

Dubois's secretary entered the office and surveyed the scene of disorder. *'Est-ce-que je peux vous aider?'* she asked, contemplating her boss's sudden and uncharacteristic flirtation with office anarchy. She had never known Lucien to behave as he had that day.

'Non, foutez-moi la paix.'

The secretary beat a hasty retreat from the chaotic office.

Dubois looked around the mess. Was this really all that constituted the working life of a senior Commission official? Following his conversation with Blu, he had arranged for the *hussiers,* Commission porters, to load the contents of Jorgensen's office into a series of boxes and to deliver them to his office. The *chef-de-cabinet* had cancelled his complete programme in order to examine them. And all to no avail. The boxes contained nothing but a series of routine files which any fool in the organisation could have dealt with. With his reputation as a plodder, Jorgensen was hardly the type of individual who was going to be trusted with major cases. The problem remained as to where the documents relating to Chemie de France and the chemical industry were located. Routine files, office equipment and some personal items, which included a photograph of a very attractive dark-haired girl, possibly the cretin's girlfriend, were the sum total of Finn Jorgensen's office possessions.

'Oui.' Blu answered his personal phone on the first ring. He listened intently as Dubois made his report on the search for the incriminating documents among the rubbish in Jorgensen's office. 'You're absolutely positive that you have had access to all Jorgensen's papers.'

'Every scrap of junk that was in the man's office is lying strewn around me at the moment. I can assure you, Monsieur Blu, that I have personally examined every piece of paper and there is nothing concerning your operations.'

Blu sat silently pondering the news from Brussels. 'There is no possibility that he had already passed the papers to his hierarchy?' he asked at length.

'It's possible, but very unlikely. A case such as the one you outlined to me would be a considerable plum for a Commission official. It is highly improbable that Jorgensen would willingly hand over such a plum to one of his colleagues.'

'If there's even the slightest chance, I want it checked out.'

'I'll make some enquiries and get back to you.'

Blu put down the phone and walked to the picture window that made up one side of his office. The same pale yellow sunlight that was illuminating Brussels reflected off the glass-panelled buildings surrounding the Tour Chemie de France in central Lyons. Blu looked out over the medieval city, but on this occasion saw none of its beauty. Plan A had failed, as Dan Newton would say, and it was time to move ahead to plan B. Except that for the moment there was no plan B. And on the horizon was the tubby and somewhat dishevelled figure of Roger Morley. If the papers were not recovered quickly, Morley would be at his throat like a cornered rat. Nothing would please the Englishman more than to wrest the chairmanship of the cartel from him before it was time for him to go. He thought back over the many battles he had fought with the Briton. The recollections only served to convince him that, despite protestations to the contrary, the source of his present predicament was lying directly across the Channel. However, he would need the documents to put the final nail in Morley's coffin. And thus far he had been singularly unsuccessful in retrieving them. If they weren't in Jorgensen's office, then he would simply have to find out where they were.

Blu retraced his steps to the desk and typed in the code that released the lock on his secret drawer. The smooth teak panel slid open, exposing a small notebook and a buff-coloured file. Blu extracted the file and placed it on the desk before him. He flipped the buff cover and looked into the face of Finn Jorgensen staring back at him from a glossy black and white photograph. As he examined the photo, he reflected on the exquisite technical skills of Cavelli. The young Corsican had raised the dispensing of death to an art form. Men such as Cavelli were a precious commodity and were every bit as important to the smooth operation of the cartel as the executives who sat on the committee.

Blu turned the photograph, banishing the accusing stare of the stark black and white image, and leafed absentmindedly through the pages of the report he had commissioned on the Dane's life. Somehow he had to try to ascertain where the documents might have been stored. Jorgensen had not been stupid, and would have been quick to recognise the value of the papers. His impetuous call to Mannheim Chemicals had, however, exposed his possession of the documents. Blu read on through the pages describing Jorgensen's training as a lawyer, entry into the Danish Ministry of Foreign Affairs, and eventual recruitment by the European Commission. Would a lawyer, raised on caution, leave such valuable documents in his office? Even under lock and key, such a treasure trove would not be entirely safe. Perhaps Jorgensen had deposited the documents in a bank vault. Possible, thought Blu, but unlikely. Such documents were to be worked on and studied. The logistics of depositing them in a bank vault and retrieving them almost daily would be too cumbersome. Blu came to a second black and white photograph — a strikingly beautiful woman with thick, dark curly hair forming a perfect crescent around an oval face from which a pair of dark piercing eyes looked directly at him. The girl's face had been caught in a sensuous smile. Blu felt a slight stirring of lust. He read the section of the notes concerning the woman. They were sketchy. She was Welsh and also worked at the European Commission. Would not the Dane tell his lover about the treasure he had discovered? A man would confide the very depths of his soul to a woman such as the one in the photograph. Blu skipped back to the photograph and looked once more into the dark Celtic eyes.

Plan B was quickly formulating in his mind. The woman in the photograph would be the key to its success. Blu picked up the telephone and began to dial the number of a telephone in the small village of Cassis on the Mediterranean coast. He had reached the final digit when he remembered the stupid undertaking he had given his colleagues in Brussels. The handset of the phone almost shattered as Blu slammed it into its cradle.

Calling Morley to ask his approbation for an action that he wished to take was unthinkable. Blu picked up the phone again and began to dial the private number of the chief executive of Mannheim Chemicals.

'Ja,' Von Schick's tone was businesslike.

'Werner, it's Jean Claude.'

'So soon.' There was a tone of self-satisfaction in Von Schick's voice.

'Something has come up which I need to discuss with you. I had made certain arrangements,' Blu continued smoothly, 'to have Jorgensen's papers examined. I was sure that the leaked cartel memoranda would be located among these papers. Unfortunately I was wrong. In the circumstances we will have to throw our net a little wider. Such a casting has consequences that are at best unpredictable if we are to be sure of success. Following the decision of the committee at Brussels, I'm consulting with you on our future course of action.'

'Have you spoken to Roger yet?' Von Schick asked provocatively. He knew that the Frenchman would prefer to swallow a bottle of arsenic than humble himself before the chief of Commonwealth Chemicals.

'I decided to call you first,' Blu said, putting the best face on his reluctance to consult Sir Roger.

'What exactly do you propose doing and what are the risks involved?' the Prussian asked.

'The papers weren't in Jorgensen's office. It's unlikely that he would share such important knowledge with his colleagues. Only a fool would want to share the kudos of exposing an operation the size of ours. Such papers are precious and would need to be kept away from prying colleagues, yet close enough for constant examination. They must be somewhere in his apartment.'

'What do you intend to do? Burgle the place?'

'Initially, yes. I'd like to send the same man who helped us out with Jorgensen.'

'Is somebody of that type really necessary?' Von Schick queried, knowing that it wasn't the Frenchman's usual policy to crack a walnut by using a sledgehammer.

'There may be complications,' Blu replied. 'Firstly our man is excellent at what he does, but he may not be in a position to recognise the papers when he sees them.'

'Have him destroy the apartment,' Von Schick said coldly.

A typical German solution to a problem, Blu thought to himself. 'That may or may not have the desired result. In order to find the source of the leak we must actually recover the documents. Jorgensen had a live-in girlfriend. My guess is that although she doesn't know much of the detail, she probably knows where to put her hands on the papers. My man will endeavour to obtain them from her without excessive force, but we must be prepared for the worst. Although it's unlikely, the woman may actually know something of our business.'

'I'm afraid that I'm beginning to see where your line of thought is leading. The feeling I got from our colleagues was that they were not happy with the new departure you've established.'

'What about you, Werner?'

'We need a cartel if we are all to survive. But protection of the cartel at whatever cost is a completely different matter. This is a tough one to call.' Von Schick could imagine the proud Frenchman squirming on the other end of the line.

'What about the effects of disclosure on your own company? Mannheim would have a very difficult job surviving in a purely competitive situation. Especially after paying a fine of seventy or eighty million dollars.'

'You present me with quite a dilemma.'

Von Schick was tiring of his little game. The chairman of the cartel was so predictable that there was no pleasure in manipulating him.

'OK,' Von Schick said at length. 'You have my agreement to go ahead with the recovery of the documents. I presume you'll call Roger.'

'Of course,' Blu replied affably. 'Don't worry, Werner, your confidence in me will be totally justified. I have never failed in my duty to the cartel. You may rest assured of that.'

'I hope you're right, Jean Claude. *A bientôt.*'

Immediately Blu redialled the number in Cassis and waited.

'*Oui.*' Cavelli's Corsican accent came over the line.

'It's your employer in Lyons.' Blu got a certain degree of satisfaction from playing the stupid 'no-names' subterfuge.

'I'm listening.' Bruno Cavelli had no time for small talk.

'I have another job for you. It's a follow-up of the work you did for me in Pamplona. The individual you had dealings with on that occasion had in his possession some official papers which must be recovered. We have reason to believe that they can be found in his apartment.'

'Not my line of work,' the Corsican said sharply.

'There may, however, be some of your line of work involved in retrieving the documents.'

'How would I know which papers?'

'Easy. I'll fax you some examples of what we're looking for. You remove everything that looks like them and you deliver them to me.'

'How does my line of work come into it?' Cavelli gazed through the patio doors at the blue Mediterranean.

'Do you still have the file we sent you?'

'Yes.'

'Good. There's a photograph of a woman in it — she's Jorgensen's girlfriend. If you can't locate the papers in the apartment, then she must be made to assist you.'

Cavelli could smell the man's fear even across the telephone line. So the Dane had been killed because the wrong information had come into his possession. The Corsican's awareness of the reason behind the killing was academic. The fat-cat bastard sitting in Lyons must want those papers pretty badly if he was willing to contemplate a second murder. Once you've ordered one killing, the second is always easier. There is an erosion of conscience which comes with the power of life and death, Cavelli knew.

'And the money?' Cavelli asked.

'As usual. One hundred thousand francs for the job, fifty thousand of which will be deposited tomorrow morning in your Geneva account.'

'One hundred and fifty thousand,' Cavelli said, sipping white wine from the glass in his hand. Blu's need for results was palpable and he should be made to pay for the satisfaction of such a need.

'Agreed,' Blu said.

Cavelli cursed himself. Blu had agreed so quickly that he could have undoubtedly squeezed another fifty thousand francs from the industrialist. 'I'll leave for Brussels in the morning.'

'And you'll inform me as soon as you have completed your mission.'

'Of course.' Bruno Cavelli replaced the phone and sauntered through the open door that separated the livingroom from the terrace. He walked to the edge of the pool where the young Swedish hitch-hiker he had picked up the previous day lay tanning herself. He glanced across the rocky Calanques that separated his villa from the blue Mediterranean Sea. Cavelli drained his glass and then refilled it from the bottle of Chablis that stood in the ice-bucket at the girl's feet. *La vie est belle*, the swarthy Corsican thought to himself. How does a baby born in a hovel in the hills behind Bonifacio on the southern coast of Corsica gravitate to a villa overlooking the Mediterranean on the most exclusive stretch of real estate in Europe? To make such a jump it is necessary to employ the skills of the gutter to the full and be prepared to leave conscience in the hovel along with poverty. Cavelli had never seen any dignity in poverty. The Corsican's mother had succumbed to a life of hard work and deprivation before Bruno had completed his eighth year. He had watched as his eldest sister had begun to sell herself almost before she had begun to menstruate, her initiation into her career having been provided by Cavelli senior. Bruno had slit the old bastard's throat after the pig had offered his youngest daughter to a group of his drunken friends. There was no future for Cavelli in his birthplace, so he was forced to disappear into the filthy streets of Ajaccio. He sipped the cold white liquid and watched the sun heading towards the western horizon. Tomorrow he would have to head north to the capital of Belgium. Tonight he would dine in the village and then prepare himself to carry out his new commission.

Michael Joyce strolled along the rue du Spa feeling the early morning humidity causing sweat to trickle down the back of his neck. He had arrived back in Brussels two days earlier after his five-day sojourn in Pamplona, and had spent the interval setting down his impressions of that boozy, dangerous, pagan festival. It had taken two days to expel the alcohol he had consumed in the Navarrese capital. As he reviewed the notes of the first day of the fiesta, Michael had once again relived the moment when he was sure he had seen the young man stab the blond-haired *mozo*. On the second day of the fiesta, he had made enquiries at the hospital, and had been assured that like many visitors to Saint Fermin, the unfortunate man had been gored by one of the bad ones. The rest of the week had produced several more badly gored runners. A nagging doubt still ate away at Michael's mind.

'The wanderer returns.' Richard Fryer looked up from his word processor as Michael pushed through the door of the small office the two men shared. Their relationship was not that of landlord and tenant but rather that of occupier and squatter. Fryer, as the Brussels correspondent of the *Scotsman*, rated an office, and his magnanimity towards the minnows of his profession had led him to invite Michael Joyce to share his humble station. 'The most complimentary thing I could say, me old son, is that the red colour that currently adorns your cheeks is simply the result of the Spanish sun. However, that assumption may not be correct given the reputation of the Fiesta de Saint Fermin for alcohol consumption and the fact that the silly bugger at *International Traveller* was rash enough to extend you an advance.'

'It's a bit of both, actually.' Michael flopped into the battered office chair that faced Fryer's desk. The small fifteen-square-metre room was just large enough to accommodate the journalist's desk and an assortment of dented metal filing cabinets. Since both men spent most of their time outside the office, the cramped conditions were never seen as a problem.

As he looked at his benefactor, Michael thought that it was a bit ripe of Fryer to comment on his russet complexion. The Brussels correspondent of the *Scotsman* was renowned for his partiality to liquor, which was testified by his own ruby-red blotched face. Michael leafed through a wad of press releases that had arrived during his absence in Spain. 'There doesn't appear to be much happening on the European Commission front,' he said, tossing the papers into the wastepaper basket on Fryer's side of the desk.

'You are about to witness a great European phenomenon, my old fruit,' Fryer said, looking at the eager face of his young friend. 'Listen to your uncle Richard while I teach you the facts of Brussels life. The months of July and August represent for us journalists a silly season. The European commission and all its attendant functions virtually closes down for two full months. The well-heeled officials head off to their summer residences, leaving behind a skeleton staff to keep the show just barely on the road. There's no news, because nothing happens.'

'That wasn't exactly what I wanted to hear.' As a freelance journalist, Michael lived by the rule of 'no story, no pay'.

'Hie thee back to thy native city in the New World for the summer, and sponge off your parents,' Richard Fryer advised.

He had inadvertently hit on the single alternative that had a zero probability of occurrence. Michael could just imagine the self-satisfied look on his father's face as he deposited his bags in the hallway of the family's home on Cape Cod. Patrick Joyce still spoke in the sing-song accent of his Aran Islands birthplace. The scions of the Joyces of Boston had often been regaled with stories of the hard life their father had endured on the barren island off the coast of Galway. But Patrick Joyce had escaped all that and had become part of the Irish-American dream. Arriving in New York in the mid-fifties as a penniless immigrant, he had, through hard work and an inherent cleverness, ended up as the majority shareholder in one of Massachusetts' biggest construction firms. Michael's pragmatic father looked upon him as a throw-back to an older age when Ireland was the island of saints and scholars. There was no place in the elder Joyce's world for people who were content to squander their talents and the money that had been lavished on their education by living in squalor in Brussels and eking out a living by penning occasional articles for journals that nobody had ever heard of. 'All that good money spent on educating him,' Michael's father had pontificated on his son's last visit to his home. 'The fancy schools and the WASP college, and for what, I ask you? So he can live like a penniless tramp. I need somebody to help me run the company. And I'm not gettin' any younger.' Patrick Joyce was fifty-six years old and had the constitution of a horse.

'And so,' Fryer said, letting his eyelids close. 'How was Pamplona?'

'A real endurance test.'

'So I've heard. Only for the young and fit.' Fryer patted his expansive girth.

'There was one peculiar happening.' Michael launched into his story of the death of Jorgensen on the first day of the fiesta. 'I rang up the hospital later in the day and learned that Jorgensen lived here in Brussels and worked for the European Commission in the Competition Directorate General. I also found out that the body was collected by a Sandra Bishop who works in the Commission as a translator.'

'So,' Fryer said without opening his eyes when Michael had finished his narrative. 'First off, me young feller-me-lad, don't believe what you think you saw. Bulls and people running hither and thither. Bumping and boring, bashing and goring. Anything could have happened to the poor bugger who was killed. The knife might have been a shiny belt buckle — any metal object.'

'But maybe there's a story in it.' Somewhere deep in his gut Michael knew that something extraordinary had happened in Pamplona. The more his mind replayed the scene in the Estefeta, the clearer he saw the flashing blade that had ended Finn Jorgensen's life.

'Only for the poor fools who live in the arse-end of Aarhus or whatever Danish burg the dead man came from. During the silly season the only thing the rags will buy from you are stories about the officials of the European Community and drugs and sex and rock and roll. You know the kind of headline they're looking for — "Boozed-up and doped Commissioner ate my knickers". Dead EC officials are a dime a dozen, old boy.'

'But what if he was murdered?'

'So bloody what? Several months ago a lady official murdered her step-daughter and buried the body in the back garden. The story made page twenty in the local Belgian papers. None of the international press even bothered to carry it.'

'What if the reason he was killed had something to do with his work at the Commission?'

'My dear old chap, there's about as much chance of that as there is of a snowball lasting in hell. The major competition cases are staffed by tens of lawyers, none of whom rank highly enough to be the target of a hit-man. If your friend Jorgensen was indeed murdered, then I suppose there's a minuscule probability that it involves sexual or work jealousy. However, it's far more likely that the poor bugger was simply the victim of a freak accident on the first day of the running of the bulls.'

'But let's look at the journalistic possibilities,' Michael said. 'If it was a lover's quarrel, then there won't be a morsel of interest from the dailies or the wire services.'

'The boy's learning,' Fryer said.

'But if he was murdered and it has something to do with the Commission,' Michael continued, 'then there might possibly be a story waiting to be uncovered?'

'Woodward and Bernstein have a lot to answer for,' Fryer said. 'Yes, the only possibility that you could make a few pounds from this poor man's death is that there is some untapped scandal within the Commission which led to it. Michael, me old pal, me old beauty, there is no story, and you'll be wasting your time trying to find one. But if you've really got nothing better to do, then the Commission is as good a place as any to begin nosing around.'

'I don't suppose you have any connections in the Competition DG?'

Fryer opened his eyes and observed his squatter. A fresh young face not yet ruined by either booze or cynicism stared back at him. The correspondent from the *Scotsman* couldn't help liking the American. Behind the Boston accent and the Harvard degree, Michael Joyce was what Fryer's Irish relations would call 'a sound man'.

'So, despite advice to the contrary, the intrepid investigative reporter decides to proceed with his enquiries.' Fryer opened the top drawer of his desk and withdrew a thick filofax. 'Let the search for "deep throat" begin.' He flicked through the pages and then came to a stop. 'I don't know whether even you are intrepid enough for this particular fellow.'

'Tell me.'

'Dirk Van Waarde,' Fryer looked up for a second from the filofax. 'A diminutive Belgian popinjay whose career has gone wallop and who now puts his energy into amateur British theatre groups and the collection of office gossip. If your Danish friend was involved in anything shady, whether of a sexual or work nature, Dirk will be completely up to date on it.'

'He sounds ideal. How do I contact him?'

'First I have a question, my excited young friend. Have you managed to spend all of the advance that the editor of *International Traveller* lavished on you?'

Michael furrowed his brow and looked at Fryer. If Richard was looking for him to pay for the information, he'd knocked at the wrong door. 'I still have a few thousand francs languishing around in my pockets somewhere.'

'Good. The picture I gave you of Van Waarde was the up-side. Although the little bastard earns a fortune as an international civil servant, there's nothing he likes better than sticking some poor unsuspecting journalist for an expensive lunch. Forewarned is forearmed, old boy. Talking to Dirk is going to cost you money. Everybody thinks that because Van Waarde is a little fellow, then by definition he doesn't eat very much. They couldn't be more wrong. Dirk Van Waarde can out-eat and out-drink most men with three times his bulk. The man must have the metabolism of an Andean mountain goat.' Fryer watched Michael for signs of hesitancy and second thoughts.

All he saw was unrestrained keenness. Fryer tried to repress a smile. His young charge reminded him of one of those big shaggy dogs who always conspire to lose sight of the stick they were chasing but who charge around enthusiastically nonetheless. Michael Joyce had seen a murder in Pamplona and he wasn't going to let go of that idea until he was convinced that his chase was going to be either fruitless or too costly.

Fryer slid the filofax across the desk so that Dirk Van Waarde's number was facing Michael. 'Call him.' There was the element of a dare in Fryer's voice.

Michael picked up the phone and dialled Van Waarde's office.

'Van Waarde a l'appareil.'

'Mr Van Waarde,' Michael began hesitantly. He wondered exactly how and when he should broach the subject of Jorgensen. 'My name is Michael Joyce. I'm a friend of Richard Fryer.'

'Ah! A fellow hack, no doubt.'

Van Waarde spoke with a perfect English accent which would have done Larry Olivier proud. Michael could well imagine him as a star turn of the expatriate theatre community. Even with the restricted frequencies of the telephone, the voice was pure magic.

'After a fashion. Richard suggested that you would be the person to talk to about the operations of the Competition DG.'

'He's probably right.' There was a hint of amusement in the voice. 'What I don't know about the goings-on of my colleagues isn't worth knowing.'

'I was wondering whether I could drop by your office for a chat.' Michael said a silent prayer.

'Love to, Michael, but you know the saying "the walls have ears". Well, it goes double for this place. I'm afraid candid discussions would be out of the question. You hacks always seem to be swanning around on expense accounts. Why don't you invite me for lunch?'

Michael wondered whether he should explain to Van Waarde that he wasn't the expense account type of hack, but thought better of it. 'Have you anywhere in mind?'

'What about the Villa de Brussellas in the rue Archimède at twelve thirty? I'll leave you to make the arrangements. We wouldn't want to create any confusion in the staff's mind as to who's picking up the tab. Looking forward to seeing you at twelve thirty then.' The sonorous voice disappeared and the line went dead with Michael still holding the handpiece of Fryer's ancient black plastic phone to his ear.

'What did I tell you?' Fryer said gleefully, as Michael replaced the handset. 'Where?'

'The Villa de Brussellas,' Michael answered still in shock.

'Ouch,' Fryer said, screwing up his face in pain. 'You better not be hungry, old fruit. The only damage limitation you can hope for is that on this occasion he only eats for one.'

'I hope this is going to be worth it.'

'It probably won't be. Take my advice and let the whole thing drop.'

'How do I recognise Van Waarde?' Michael asked.

'He'll be the fellow wearing a silk scarf over a bow tie. Just look for somebody who'd be just as much at home in a campy theatrical pub as in the Villa de Brussellas, and you've got your man.'

'Assuming I strike out with him, is there anybody else I could talk to?'

'Why not go to the top? Why not try to talk to the director general himself.' Fryer flicked on the word processor. This conversation with Michael was beginning to become trying.

'Who's that?'

'I don't have to look in my filofax for that one, chummie. Once you've met him there's no possibility that you'd ever forget Nicholas J Elliot.'

'Why's that?'

'Elliot is one of those quintessential English civil servants who look down their noses at all but the high and the mighty of their own little island. The man has spent the last thirty years climbing up politician's bums in the hope of landing that great British accolade, a knighthood. He is the most pompous ass I've ever encountered and since I've spent most of my journalist career in the company of politicians, that is quite an accomplishment.

'It doesn't sound too encouraging.'

'Elliot does have one redeeming feature — he's basically honest. So if there was something not quite right about Jorgensen's death and Elliot was aware of it, he'd probably do something about it.'

'Can you get me in to see him?'

'I suppose so.' Fryer lifted the handset of the old black telephone.

Michael sat back and watched in admiration as the correspondent for the *Scotsman* used all his charm to organise a meeting with the great man. He'd learned a lot from Richard Fryer over the past six months.

'He's too busy today but he can see you for a quarter of an hour tomorrow morning at eleven.'

'Thanks, Richard, I really appreciate that.'

'If it helps you solve the mystery of the dead Dane, old boy, I suppose it won't have been in vain. However, if the sponging Van Waarde and the obnoxious Elliot are insufficient to divert your search for dirty deeds, please enlist somebody else as your next willing helper. Sancho Panza is not one of my favourite characters from literature.'

Fryer started to tap on the keys of the word processor. 'Now go away and leave me alone to earn what's left of this dreadful living.'

The offices of the European Commission were already disgorging their complement of well-heeled government officials into the streets surrounding the Rond Point Schuman as Michael braved the traffic on the roundabout and began to make his way along rue Archimède. He knew that the Villa de Brussellas was located at the end of the short cobbled street near the corner with Square Ambiorix. He walked past the kerb-side tables, fingering the five thousand francs that nestled comfortably in his right-hand pocket. Such a sum would, under normal circumstances, have been sufficient to feed him for a week, but might scarcely be enough to settle a business lunch in the Villa de Brussellas.

The restaurant was located in a four-storey brick building on the right side of the street. Michael stood outside the open doorway examining the menu which was exposed in a glass-fronted box attached to the wall. He gave up after looking at the entrées. The five thousand francs was definitely gone. Michael was borne through the open door and into the restaurant by a tide of customers and found himself standing at the top of the marble steps at the entrance to the restaurant proper.

'Vous avez une réservation, Monsieur?' the head waiter asked as Michael looked about for his luncheon companion.

'Oui, au nom de Joyce, comme le fameux écrivant,' Michael replied in fluent French. The money that Patrick Joyce had lavished on private schooling had given Michael language skills not normally present in the average American.

'Votre invité est déjà à table.' The waiter led Michael towards a small table at the rear of the restaurant on the ground floor.

The man seated at the table fitted Fryer's description to a tee.

'Mr Joyce, I presume.' Dirk Van Waarde stood and shook hands with his host in continental fashion. 'No relation, I suppose?' When the Belgian stood, his head stopped at Michael's shoulder. He was dressed in a smart grey suit, blue cotton shirt and red paisley bow-tie. A red cashmere scarf hung loosely around his neck.

'Pleased to meet you, Mr Van Waarde.' Michael took the Belgian's hand in a firm handshake. 'And no, the great man was no relation.'

'Call me Dirk.' Michael's guest resumed his seat. 'I took the precaution of ordering myself an aperitif.' He lifted a glass which to Michael's experienced gaze contained cassis and champagne. 'You look too young and fresh to be a hack.'

Michael took the seat facing the Belgian. 'I've just started trying to make my way in journalism. Richard Fryer has more or less taken me under his wing for the moment.'

'And which of the American papers do you represent?' Van Waarde sipped at his Kir Royale. The deep voice seemed to come from the very depths of his well-padded stomach.

'None, I'm a stringer.' Michael noticed the look of disappointment on his guest's face, displaying the recognition that there was no fat expense account to dig into.

'I had assumed that you represented the *Herald Tribune* or the *Wall Street Journal*.'

'Only in my dreams, I'm afraid.'

'Vous désirez commander?' The waiter stood at their shoulder.

Michael picked up the menu and glanced through it. Everything appeared expensive to a man who lived on hamburgers and the ubiquitous Belgian frites. The only good value appeared to be the lunch menu, which was priced at about $20.

'Je prends le menu,' Van Waarde said, somewhat reluctantly.

So the Belgian was not totally without scruples. A certain amount of pity was being shown to the unattached journalist. This would be news for Fryer.

'*Je prends aussi le menu, s'il vous plaît,*' Michael said, relief flooding through him. It would seem that only half his five thousand francs was going to disappear.

'*Et apportez une bouteille de Muscadet.*' Van Waarde had requested a relatively cheap but good French white wine. The Belgian emitted a theatrical sigh as the waiter departed. 'I hope this won't put too deep a hole in your pocket?'

'I can just about manage it,' Michael answered.

'So what can I do for you?' Van Waarde asked, conscious of the fact that he was going to have to work for his lunch.

'Richard recommended you as someone I could talk to about the inner working of your Directorate General and perhaps a particular problem that I have.'

'Which do you want to tackle first?'

The waiter laid an ice-bucket containing a chilled bottle of Muscadet on the table and proceeded to offer a glass for tasting. Van Waarde did the honours and declared the bottle drinkable, although the look on his face said it was only barely so.

'Why don't you tell me exactly what you do?'

'Right.' Van Waarde drained his aperitif and filled his wine glass. 'The Directorate General for Competition has several functions. Firstly, it looks at mergers and acquisitions to make sure that consumers are not being boxed into a corner. The 1970s and 80s were the era of the conglomerates. Company A buys up company B, giving economies of scale as the reason. But maybe the real reason for the acquisition is that the new AB company would have a dominant role in the market and they can begin to jack up the prices to the hapless customers.'

The waiter had placed their first course on the table and Van Waarde broke off his narrative to attack his *crudité* with gusto.

'The second thrust of the DG is the question of deregulation. We're there to cut the bonds that tie various companies together.' Van Waarde waved his knife in the air as though cutting the imaginary bonds. 'You people in the States have already managed to deregulate your airline industry while we're only scratching at the surface.'

'That's why my fare to Bilbao recently cost me more than a flight from New York to Los Angeles.'

'Right,' Van Waarde said, polishing off the remnants of his starter. 'The airline boys have got the total market organised. They parcel out the routes and they keep the fares at rates that would give the average American air traveller a heart attack. Our DG has been trying for years to force the airlines to deregulate but, unlike the States, Europe is dominated by state-owned carriers. So the people in government don't want to bankrupt their inefficient state-run enterprises. Third, and maybe most importantly, we're in the cartel-busting business. Every now and then we get wind of a juicy cartel operation whereby the principal market operators stay independent but share out the market between them in order to keep the prices up.'

Two plates of steaming monkfish arrived on the table. Van Waarde filled himself another glass of wine and downed half of it in one swallow.

'So the third is basically an amalgam of the first and the second?'

'More or less. Let me give you an example.' Van Waarde sliced a piece of monkfish and put it in his mouth. 'Everybody talks about the IBM case because it was the biggest case we ever handled. Ever heard of it?'

'No.'

'IBM were holding on to some proprietary technology that was effectively keeping competitors out of a very lucrative market. They had an interface without which nobody could gain entry to either the hardware or software side of the market. IBM wouldn't licence other firms in Europe to use their interfaces, so they had a virtual monopoly.'

'Seems like a straightforward business situation to me,' Michael said.

'Your Yankee free market spirit is beginning to show.' The man from the Competition Directorate General laughed, and poured himself another glass of wine. 'Anybody with a position as dominant as IBM in the marketplace could have set their own prices and fleeced the customers. Competition is essential for customer protection, whether it's in the United States or Europe.

It took us three years and a team of thirty lawyers before we managed to compel IBM to let the other poor buggers into the market. But we won, and that started us looking into a lot of other areas.'

'So the effort you have to put into each case is pretty considerable?' Michael asked.

'It sometimes takes years before we can even assemble enough evidence to pounce.' Van Waarde demolished the remainder of his main course and washed it down with a glass of Muscadet. 'We usually set up a team of lawyers to collect and examine whatever evidence we can assemble. The kind of people we deal with tend to be pretty secretive about their dirty business, so the evidence-collecting phase can be long and dreary.'

'Don't you have the right to subpoena evidence?' Michael asked.

'You may have read in the newspapers about the lightning dawn raids carried out by Commission officials at the premises of the miscreant. Stern-faced officials carrying out cardboard box after cardboard box of incriminating documents. That only happens when we're very sure that there's something to investigate.'

Michael waved away the dessert that the waiter offered, and asked for a coffee.

Dirk Van Waarde poured the last of the wine into his glass. The diminutive Belgian had already drunk most of the bottle and his face was becoming flushed. Michael still had to finish the single glass he had taken at the start of the meal.

'The dawn raids are the only exciting parts of our jobs,' Van Waarde continued. 'In the main, we pore over hundreds of documents trying to ferret out how these companies are screwing the poor unsuspecting public.' He motioned to the waiter and ordered himself a cognac. When he returned to Michael he said, 'Now, how about satisfying my curiosity by telling me what exactly you're working on.'

Michael wondered whether he should open up to Van Waarde. It was pretty obvious from the way the Belgian made the wine disappear that he was very partial to liquor. But he was

Michael's only lead into the working life of the man who had died in Pamplona.

'I don't suppose you knew Finn Jorgensen?' Michael said, looking into Van Waarde's now glassy eyes.

Van Waarde sipped his cognac and looked sad. 'I worked very closely with the boy. It's a scandal when somebody has to die so young. But what exactly is your interest in Finn?'

'I was in Pamplona doing a piece for an international travel magazine and I happened to be in the Estefeta when he was killed.'

'And now, in typical American fashion, you're doing a bit of ambulance-chasing. Sometimes I'm actually happy that I'm a civil servant and don't have to stoop so low to earn my living.'

Michael contemplated interjecting a remark on the ethics of well-paid officials of the European Commission sponging lunches off impecunious would-be journalists, but spurned the opportunity.

'I'm interested because I don't agree with the official version of your colleague's death. From where I was standing I have no doubt that he wasn't gored by a bull. I'm pretty certain that I saw someone stab him.' Michael saw again in his mind's eye the sallow olive face looking up at him from Jorgensen's prone body.

'You're certainly mistaken,' Van Waarde said, but there was a stunned look on his face which belied his disbelief. He picked up his cognac and took a liberal swallow. 'Who in their right mind would want to kill Finn? He was one of the most innocuous chaps I've ever worked with — one of those intense Scandinavians, all bound up with honour and dark thoughts about life and death.'

'I guess I could be mistaken, but every time I replay the incident in my mind I see it as murder. Do you know of any reason associated with his work for the Commission why someone would want him dead?'

Van Waarde thought for a few moments. 'No.' He paused again for a few seconds as though thinking something over. 'Nothing from a work point of view, anyway. Finn was living with this rather attractive young lady. I only had the pleasure of meeting her once. I thought that they formed a rather odd couple — she was all Celtic fire and he all Scandinavian frigidity. I suppose she might be the kind of woman someone would kill for.'

Michael got the idea that there was a piece of information Van Waarde was not divulging.

'These cases that you follow up,' Michael said, changing the point of his enquiry. 'How do they come to light? How do you get wind of the evil doing, as it were?'

'In every conceivable way.' Van Waarde's accent was now thick with liquor. 'Disgruntled ex-employees, articles in journals or trade papers pointing out curious practices that should be followed up. Any one of a thousand and one ways.'

'Could Finn Jorgensen have unearthed something fishy all on his own?' Michael asked.

Again Van Waarde paused before answering. 'It's highly unlikely. Being noticed in an organisation as large as the Commission is quite difficult. Headline-making cases can also be career-making cases, so any possibility of landing a big case is eagerly snapped up by the potential high fliers. Most of the normal casework is passed down through the hierarchy, while the top cases tend to get passed to lodge brothers. If you know what I mean.' The Belgian tapped the side of his nose and smiled. 'Not being a lodge brother, very little has come my way.'

'Are you sure that Jorgensen wasn't working on something that could have had major repercussions?' Michael asked.

'Not that I know of. But then again, he probably wouldn't have confided in me. In fact, until he was sufficiently sure of the facts he wouldn't have confided in anyone.' Again there was a perceptible hesitation in Van Waarde's train of thought.

'Why do I get the feeling that you're holding back on me?' Michael said, staring into the Belgian's florid face.

'There's something I probably shouldn't tell you.' Van Waarde wondered if his own face had ever displayed such eagerness and enthusiasm. There was no point in such idle thoughts. He kept telling himself that cynicism was a function of age and experience. It would not be long before Joyce's innocence had turned to hard-bitten scepticism. Finn Jorgensen was dead. A death that had merited scarcely a comment from his colleagues and would be marked by a two-line obituary in next month's staff magazine. Nobody, from the top to the bottom of the building that housed the European executive, cared. Whether Jorgensen died by fair or foul means was totally academic to all of his colleagues. And that included Dirk Van Waarde. He stared again at the young journalist. Maybe it was as well to have at least one person who cared. Even if he was an ambulance-chaser.

Michael watched as Van Waarde mulled over his disclosure.

Van Waarde swirled the remainder of his cognac in the bulb of his glass. 'A couple of months ago I loaned Finn one of my law books. I went in to his office this morning to retrieve it before everything disappeared.' Van Waarde started to laugh. 'That's a joke. Everything was already gone, including my precious book. The office had been completely cleaned out. There wasn't even a scrap of paper left in the desk drawers. I asked around but nobody seems to have any idea how or why.'

'That's unusual?' Michael asked.

Van Waarde's face went suddenly serious. 'You're not kidding. I've seen the powers that be shuffle the working remains into cardboard boxes and leave them on the office floor for months. If you want my opinion, somebody systematically cleaned out every scrap of paper from Finn Jorgensen's office.'

Michael felt like shouting 'Eureka'. It was the first indication he'd received that there was something not quite right about the whole affair. Perhaps pursuing the question of Finn Jorgensen's death was not a wild goose chase after all. 'What's your own conclusion?' he asked.

'I have none,' Van Waarde said, bundling the napkin from his lap and tossing it on the table in front of him. 'Now I have to thank you for a very pleasant lunch.'

'May I contact you again?' Michael asked.

'I'd prefer if you didn't. Whatever killed Finn might be catching, and I don't care enough about my non-career to lose my life for it. One of our ex-colleagues is currently a professor at a business school in Paris.' Van Waarde fished around in the inside pocket of his jacket and removed a small electronic organiser. He flipped open the case and typed on the keys before passing the machine to Michael. 'If you've got any more questions, I suggest that you direct them to him. He knows as much about competition policy as I do, but he managed to get out of the system.'

Michael put the small plastic machine on the table in front of him, and copied down the business and home addresses of Alain Jeaune, a professor at the Institut Européen d'Administration des Affaires in Paris.

'Good luck, Mr Joyce.' Van Waarde closed the organiser and popped it into his pocket. He pushed his chair back from the table and stood up. 'Even if you aren't a relation of the great man, I shall tell people that you are and that I dined with you.'

Michael took the Belgian's outstretched hand. 'You don't speak Danish by any chance?' he asked.

'I have a smattering,' Van Waarde said. 'Like many Commission officials I've dabbled in languages a bit.'

Michael thought back to the prone figure on the cobbled streets of Pamplona. The word had been whispered and faint, but Michael had heard it. 'What does "Ekeller" mean?' he asked.

The Belgian stood pondering for a moment. 'I'm not quite sure but it sounds like something to do with a cellar. "In the cellar" or "at the cellar". You'll have to check it out with a Dane.'

CHAPTER THREE

It was already dark when Bruno Cavelli deposited his bag on the bed in the small room of the decrepit hotel in the backstreets behind the Gare du Nord in Brussels. He looked through the grime on the window at the garish red strip lights surrounding the windows of the bars lining the street in which his hotel was located. The Corsican used part of the tattered curtain to wipe off some of the dirt in order to focus on the denizens of the windows across from the hotel. A lady of indeterminate age, dressed only in a set of black underwear, sat bathed in red neon light in the centre of one window. The white flesh of her thighs and torso contrasted vividly with the black of her garments, and the expression on her painted face was tired and bored. In the window of the bar to her left a black girl dressed in a tight red miniskirt gyrated to blaring music. Two men walked slowly along the neon-lit street, their passage marked by signs of animation in the red-lit windows, which subsided into bored lethargy as soon as the potential customers had passed.

Cavelli had chosen to spend his short stay in Brussels at the flea pit in the centre of the Brussels red-light district. The Moroccans who ran the dump would have been embarrassed to ask any of their guests for a passport and the local police probably only visited the hotel to collect their monthly pay-off. Cavelli could see the tower of the Sheraton Hotel just two streets away. In that monument to the world-wide spread of Americana, jaded businessmen would be settling down for the night between crisp white sheets after receiving their nightly dose of CNN to convince them that there was a real world on the other side of the Atlantic Ocean. The Corsican looked at the bed which dominated the tiny room. A faded brown cover was draped over grey used sheets which Cavelli knew would have the texture of sandpaper. The chair and table combination that stood in one corner of the room looked as if they had been rescued from the rubbish tip, while the wardrobe in the other corner slumped to the right in a sad imitation of the Leaning Tower of Pisa. A cracked and filthy handbasin was located beside the window, the pitted faucet dripping droplets of water directly onto a brown stain at the base of the ceramic bowl. The toilet was ten metres down the hall, yet the room stank of stale urine. He wondered what stories that sagging wooden bed would tell if it could speak. It was the same room as could be found in a thousand dumps in every big city in Europe. Rooms like this were the price of anonymity.

Cavelli would have preferred to travel to Brussels by air. However, he had eschewed that pleasure and crossed the border into Belgium by train from Paris. The practice of the Belgian bureaucracy of registering every incoming air passenger on the police computer at Zaventem Airport had made that port of entry taboo to the European criminal fraternity. With any luck he would be out of Brussels the next day and nobody would be the wiser. The day after that at the very latest. He flopped back on the bed and the springs creaked as they extended towards the floor. The ceiling above his head was marked by a large water stain from which cracks emanated to every corner of the room. Cavelli wondered when he would be able to stop living in shit-holes like this. He hadn't always been so discerning. The hovels on the outskirts of Ajaccio were infinitely shittier than the room in which he now lay. But they had acted as a spur to the young Cavelli to aspire to something better.

Bruno Cavelli hadn't needed much of a spur to push himself into the arms of the Unione Corse. Every street urchin who hustled a bag in Ajaccio or who rolled a drunken tourist, aspired to be taken on by the gang bosses who ran the Mediterranean island and were also firmly implanted on the southern coast of France. Cavelli had been among the most talented. The death of his father cast him onto the streets. Without any means of making a living other than crime, he graduated from petty thievery to mugging by the time he was sixteen. At seventeen he had been admitted to the Unione as a 'soldat'. The French Army had completed Cavelli's martial education by sending his unit to prop up the ailing regime in Chad. The twenty-two-year-old who left the barracks in Marseilles was

60

already a consummate killing machine with a ready market for his skills and a bright future in the Unione before him.

Cavelli closed his eyes. Tomorrow he would retrieve Blu's precious papers. A picture of the girl floated into his mind. The photograph of the woman in Jorgensen's file had excited him and he hadn't yet made up his mind whether he would take her or not. That would have to wait until he saw her in person. If he found the papers during the search of her apartment, then there would be no need to bother with her. Cavelli half wished that his search would prove fruitless.

It was ten minutes to eleven when Michael Joyce walked through the glass doors of the Commission building on the Avenue Cortenberg. He had been mulling over the information that Van Waarde had already given him. Obviously there had been something of importance in Jorgensen's office. The big question was what had it been? And how did that something relate to the bizarre events on the cobbled streets of Pamplona? Maybe Nicholas Elliot would know the answers. And if he did, would he be willing to share his knowledge with a lowly reporter?

Michael stepped out of the lift at the eighth floor, still holding in his hand the piece of paper that had gained him entry. He looked around the vestibule and started walking towards the exit with the legend 'Office Nos. 34-57' above it. Elliot's office was distinguished from the others by the stretch of green carpet leading to it. Pecking order is very important in the bureaucracy, and no doubt could be left in visitors' minds that the person whom they were about to meet had senior status and that mystical but attainable quality, gravitas.

The legend outside Elliot's door read 'Nicholas J Elliot - Prière de s'addresser au secrétariat'. An arrow pointed in the direction of Elliot's 'secrétariat'. Nobody could gain access to the holy of holies without passing through Elliot's secretary.

'Good morning,' Michael said, as he entered the room.

The two ladies sitting in the office ignored his greeting.

Elliot apparently liked his secretaries on the older side. Neither woman would ever see fifty again, and Michael estimated one to be nearing sixty. The office was wall-to-wall greenery. Plants of every type and description stood on the floor and in the nooks and crannies. If the two ladies had decided to save the Amazon rain forest by moving it to their office, then they had made a pretty good start on the project.

Michael cleared his throat in the hope of attracting attention. 'My name is Joyce,' he continued somewhat hesitantly. 'I've got an appointment with Mr Elliot for eleven.'

The two grey-haired ladies turned their pallid heads to gaze at him from the green background like a couple of exotic birds in their cages at the zoo. The one sitting by Elliot's door stared at the intruder. Her face was thin, with two hollows where the skin was pulled taut across her prominent cheekbones. The skin itself was the colour and texture of parchment. 'Mr Elliot will be with you in a moment.' The accent was Germanic, although the English was perfect. She bent over her work without further comment.

Michael ignored the omission of the offer to take a seat and plonked himself in the nearest empty chair. The two secretaries continued to ignore his presence. Michael had been struck during his contacts with those constructing the new Europe by the fact that this Herculean task had managed to drive all humour and humanity from them. The two secretaries in whose office he now sat were typical of the grim-faced warriors who laboured at the coal-face of European unity.

A buzz on the secretarial set on the desk in front of the grey-haired lady broke the deafening silence in the room. She picked up the handset and listened for a moment.

'Mr Elliot will see you now,' she said.

Michael entered Elliot's office and saw the great man sitting behind his desk at the other side of the room. The top of Elliot's bald head stared back at the young American. Michael quietly crossed the carpeted gap between the entrance and the desk. Elliot continued to pore over the papers laid out before him.

'Mr Joyce.' Elliot raised his great bald head and stared at the young man seated across the desk from him. He shuffled the papers before him, and moved them to one side. 'Richard Fryer of the *Scotsman* called me concerning you. Which paper do you represent?'

Michael stared into the stern lined face of the Englishman. 'I'm doing a series of articles on the European Community for the *Boston Globe*,' he lied, guessing that Elliot would give him little consideration if he had revealed some less formidable affiliation. Pander to the pompous was a rule of the journalistic profession.

'The *Boston Globe*,' Elliot said thoughtfully. Joyce looked remarkably young to be associated with such a quality paper. Still Fryer was a serious enough individual. 'You're an American?'

'Yes, sir. Born and bred in Boston, Mass.'

'What can I do for you?' Elliot asked.

'First off, I'd like to thank you for agreeing to see me, Mr Elliot. Richard Fryer told me how busy you are.'

'My time is rather limited.' Elliot shuffled the papers on his desk to emphasise the point. 'How exactly can I help you?' The clipped diction turned the 'help' into 'hilp'.

'Although the people in the States don't know much about the European Community, the business community knows enough to be afraid of your competition policy.'

'We have a very informative series of handouts which describes in detail our work here. I can arrange for a set to be delivered to you,' Elliot said.

'I've read all the background material,' Michael lied. 'I'm trying to get a personal view on the running of your operation. For example, do you have any big cases pending at the moment?'

'I'm afraid our current workload is confidential.' Elliot sat up straight behind his desk. 'I can discuss cases that have already been completed, but we are very careful not to alert those we are presently investigating.'

'But you do have some significant cases under consideration?' Michael asked.

'We always have cases under consideration, Mr Joyce.' Elliot sometimes found Americans quite tiresome. 'But our investigations are confidential until we actually have proof of some breach of competition law. Then we generally announce ourselves through a dawn raid. The "smoking gun" evidence we find during these raids augments the evidence we have already collected.'

'What sort of sanctions do you have against the firms who are found guilty?' Michael asked.

'Firstly, any cartels are broken up, and secondly, and perhaps most importantly for the firms in question, we fine them ten percent of their annual turnover. Let me give you an example — we fined Tetrapak, a Swiss-Swedish drinks carton maker, seventy-five million ECUs. That's about ninety million American dollars. That level of fine really hurts.'

'Does anybody ever get injured in these dawn raids?'

'Never,' Elliot said smugly. 'The officials are accompanied by police officers. The offenders may not like being caught, but after all they are businessmen.'

Michael was tempted to say that Robert Maxwell and those involved in the Guinness and US insider-trading scandals had also been businessmen, but their morals had been closer to those of a gutter-rat.

'Are you aware that one of your officials was killed last week in Pamplona?'

The smug look faded from Elliot's face and was replaced by a scowl. 'I am aware that one of my officials died in an accident during the running of the bulls. What has that to do with the matter we're currently discussing?'

'I happened to be present in Pamplona at the time of Finn Jorgensen's death.' Michael weighed up his next comment carefully. 'For my money his death wasn't an accident. I was wondering whether there was any reason why someone might want Jorgensen dead and I thought that perhaps it might have had something to do with his work for you. I understand that his office has been cleaned out.'

A smile played across Elliot's thin lips. 'You Americans are so melodramatic. The work of the European Commission is not consistent with its officials being assassinated. As to his office being cleaned out, that's normal procedure. Office space is at a premium here.' The professional smile faded from Elliot's featureless face. 'I think you may have been less than honest with me as to the purpose of this interview.' The director general looked down his long nose at the journalist. There was something not quite pukka about the young man. Elliot would have words with Joyce's mentor concerning this particular interview. 'Perhaps you would be so kind as to get to the point of this charade,' he said sharply.

'I don't buy the official version of Finn Jorgensen's death,' Michael said, bridling under the back-handed insult. 'For my money he was murdered.'

'Then I suggest that you should have gone to the police with your information. After all, they are the professionals.'

'You can imagine what the police would have thought. Pamplona isn't known for the sobriety of the participants.'

'I was thinking the same thing myself.' Elliot picked up the telephone and pressed a buzzer. 'Georges? Perhaps you'd join me in my office. And bring the task file.' He turned back. 'As you might understand, Mr Joyce, I am the head of a rather large Directorate General, and unfortunately I am not aware of exactly what each and every individual is doing at any point in time. However, I think we had better scotch this absurd idea of yours about Jorgensen's work straight away.'

The door opened and a swarthy man dressed in a dark checked sports-coat and grey slacks entered. The clothes hung on his thin frame. He looked immediately at Elliot and then at Michael from under a pair of the bushiest eyebrows that the American had ever seen.

'This is my assistant, Georges Lafonde,' Elliot said. He nodded in Michael's direction. 'Mr Joyce is a journalist who has a theory that our ex-colleague Finn Jorgensen was murdered.'

Lafonde expressed no emotion but continued to stare through a set of hooded dark brown eyes in Michael's direction. Michael had seen many men like Elliot's assistant before. He had been around his father enough to recognise Lafonde as a professional crawler, an acolyte ready to do his master's bidding at a moment's notice.

'Was Jorgensen working on anything special for us?'

Lafonde looked away from Michael and consulted his file. 'No. Routine cases, that's all.' The voice was laconic and although Elliot's assistant was certainly European, the accent was American.

'You're sure?' Elliot asked.

Lafonde nodded and closed the file.

'It appears that we can't help you.' Elliot moved the shuffled papers back to the centre of the table.

Michael knew enough about body language to know when his presence was no longer required. He had learned nothing from Elliot and there was no way he was going to be entertained further.

'Thank you for your time,' he said, rising from the chair.

Elliot made no move to speak or to acknowledge Michael's remark.

After the American had left, Lafonde walked slowly across the room and closed the door.

'Who cleaned out Jorgensen's office?' Elliot asked sharply.

'I wasn't even aware that it had been cleaned out.' Lafonde slouched in the chair so recently vacated by Michael.

'Could Jorgensen have been working on something that we didn't know about?' Elliot asked.

Lafonde thought for a second before replying. 'There's no way of knowing whether he was working in a private capacity. If he was working on something, he's managed to keep it pretty quiet. There isn't a whisper in the corridors.'

'It couldn't have anything to do with the Schuman investigation?' Elliot said. Breaking up the chemical cartel would be the biggest single case ever brought by the European Commission. Every time that Elliot contemplated the possibility that the investigation might screw-up, his bowels eased slightly.

'No way,' Lafonde said without hesitation. 'The team handling the investigation knows that if anyone breaks a confidence they leave this place by rocket with their career in flames behind them. Don't worry. They're all such ambitious bastards that they'll kill anyone who screws it up.'

'A rather unfortunate choice of words. Is there any possibility that this Joyce fellow's theory about Jorgensen is correct?'

'Not a chance in hell,' Lafonde said wearily. He came out of the slouch and pushed himself off the chair. 'Jorgensen was killed because he stood in front of a bull at the wrong moment. That's all there was to it.'

'I want you to ask around and see if he was working on something in private. Also find out who cleared his office.' Elliot returned to the papers on his desk and ignored the retreating back of his assistant. He was so close to attaining his life's ambition, and a tiny dark cloud had suddenly appeared in his clear blue sky. The Schuman investigation would be complete in a few weeks and he would be on the front page of the *Times* and the *Financial Times* for long enough for him to bag a 'K' in the next honours list. A faint thrill of anticipation ran through the civil servant.

'Sir Nicholas Elliot,' he said softly under his breath. He liked the sound of it.

Sandra Bishop was having a bad day. Every day since her return from Pamplona and Denmark had been a bad day. The hassle with the Spanish authorities over Finn's dead body had been unpleasant enough, but that had been compounded by the necessity of putting her lover in the ground in his home town, to the disapproving glances of the Jorgensen clan. Finn's father, the Reverend Kurt Jorgensen, had made quite clear the family's position with regard to Sandra. She was a fallen woman and as such should be on her way back to the den of iniquity from whence she came as soon as was humanly and decently possible. The whole episode had been a nightmare from start to finish. She looked around her office and wondered whether she had been right to resume her work so soon. Maybe those who had counselled a trip to the Seychelles had been right. She looked out across the trees of the Parc du Cinquantenaire. The Triumphal Arch of the Belgians stood out in the bright sunshine above the verdant foliage of the park. However, the view brought her no joy. She longed for the hills around the north Wales coast and the rushing waters of the Irish Sea as they rippled across the beach at Llandudno. Finn's death had only served to remind her of the loneliness she felt in Brussels. Hundreds of miles separated her from the people who could comfort her and help her through the pain. But amid the pain there was also recrimination. The night before Finn's death they had sat in a small restaurant and she had told him that their affair was over. She wondered whether her decision had led her lover to a recklessness that certainly was not part of his nature.

The ringing of the telephone on her desk brought her out of her reverie.

'Good morning. May I speak to Sandra Bishop?' The accent was American, and she recognised the Boston twang which the Kennedys had made famous.

'Speaking,' Sandra replied tentatively. Since Finn's death, strangers made her nervous. They generally brought problems about insurance or some other bureaucratic nonsense.

'My name is Michael Joyce and we've never met.' Michael was annoyed at himself for the trite opening, but he had been unable to come up with anything more novel. 'I'm a journalist working here in Brussels.'

Sandra fought down the urge to slam the receiver onto its cradle. What stopped her was the voice on the other end of the line. There was something kindly and sensitive in the American's inflection.

'I don't really want to bother you,' Michael continued, 'but I was wondering if I could meet you some time to discuss the death of Finn Jorgensen.'

Sandra let out a silent scream. How many times would she be called upon to repeat the nauseating facts? Was there no limit to the people who 'needed to know' how a Danish Commission official died on the streets of a nondescript Spanish town. She composed herself before speaking, fighting hard to control her Celtic temper. 'Is there any particular reason?' she asked.

Michael recognised the Welsh lilt in her voice. It wasn't the pronounced bass of Richard Burton, but a high treble sound like a thousand bells tinkling in an evening breeze. 'I was in Pamplona when Mr Jorgensen died. In fact I was in the street right beside him. There are a few things that I'd like to talk to you about.' Despite himself, Michael couldn't help wondering what the woman looked like. The voice intrigued him.

'How did you get my name and my phone number?' she asked, a note of apprehension in her voice.

'The AP, that's the Associated Press, carried a report on the first day of the running of the bulls which included details of Mr Jorgensen's death and gave your name. As to your phone number, I simply rang up the switchboard at the Commission and they put me through to you.'

'What kind of things do you want to discuss?' she asked.

'Like I said, I happened to be standing nearby when Mr Jorgensen was killed. From where I was standing, your friend wasn't gored by a bull. I may have been mistaken but I believe I saw a young Spaniard stab him.' Michael heard the sharp intake of breath on the other end of the line.

'That the most ridiculous thing I've ever heard. I'm sure that you're mistaken. There's no earthly reason why anyone would want to murder Finn. It's absurd.'

'I wonder if you would mind answering a few questions?' Michael asked. 'Perhaps we could have a drink together this evening.'

'I don't think so. I don't really see the point of it.'

'I promise not to take up too much of your time, but there may be some little fact that you've overlooked that would help me.'

If it wasn't for the obvious pleading tone in Michael Joyce's voice, Sandra would have considered his call some sort of ghoulish hoax. 'OK,' she said after a short pause. 'But let's have the drink at my place. I'm not sure that I want to be seen on the circuit just yet. Why don't we say six-thirty.' She gave him an address in Square Marguérite, which Michael knew was close to the main European Commission building. 'My name is on one of the buttons in the hall.' She regretted the invitation as soon as she had delivered it.

'Great. I'll be there at six,' Michael said.

Sandra put down the phone and stared out at the sun-lit park. Concentrating on the translation of the papers that sat on her desk was impossible. What a fool she'd been to agree to meet that young American. He might be intending to rob her — not that there was much in her flat to steal — or he could even be a rapist. But he had sounded genuine, and, in spite of herself, she was intrigued by what he had said about Finn. Murder was something that occurred only on television or in the movies, and Finn as a murder victim just didn't fit. And yet there had been something strange about him during the few weeks before their trip to Pamplona. Normally so phlegmatic that at times she could have screamed, he had been excited about something. At first she had made the obvious deduction that he had found another woman, but when she challenged him on that score he was so genuinely astonished that she had abandoned the idea, and in fact he had firmly denied that anything had changed in his attitude or his interests. She suspected that he was lying, but it didn't seem worth worrying about, especially since she had already half decided to end their liaison. But could Michael Joyce's bizarre theory have anything to do with Finn's excitement? Surely he couldn't have been involved in anything illegal — his idea of crime was travelling on the Metro without punching his ticket.

The thoughts swirled round her brain. The more she thought about it, the more absurd the idea of murder seemed. If Finn had been stabbed, surely the doctors would have seen that the wound had not been inflicted by a bull's horn. Oh, it was all a lot of rubbish! I'm a twenty-five-year-old woman,' Sandra said to herself. 'Not unattractive and with one of the most sought-after jobs in Europe. My whole life is in front of me. The man I lived with for over a year has just died in tragic circumstances, but there's no need to over-dramatise the situation. His death was an accident, and the sooner I can forget about it and get on with my life, the better. And when the American reporter comes, I shall open the door with the safety chain on, and tell him to go away.'

She picked up the paper she had been working on before Michael Joyce had interrupted her. She could make a start on this new life of hers by getting back to work.

Cavelli had easily gained entry through the electronically operated front door of the apartment house where the Bishop woman lived in Square Marguérite. Near the single lock, the steel frame of the door was slightly bent where an amateur had tried to jemmy it. The Corsican needed no such brutality to gain entry. One of the advantages of membership of the Unione Corse was access to the skills and the tools of many trades. Cavelli pocketed the set of skeleton keys as soon as he entered the ground floor hallway which contained the door to the concierge's flat and the lifts which led to the apartments. Screwed to the wall beside the lifts was a metal plaque indicating the layout of the apartments on the ten floors above.

A small black plastic sticker bearing the legend 'Bishop/Jorgensen' in white lettering was set against one of the two apartments located on the fifth floor. Cavelli pushed the lift button and heard the apparatus begin to trundle its way towards him.

There were two doors on either side of the corridor on the fifth floor. A similar sticker to that in the lobby told Cavelli that the Bishop/Jorgensen apartment was on the right. Neither the Yale lock nor the mortice were more than minor obstacles, and within moments he stepped inside the entrance hall of Sandra Bishop's flat. A simple phone call had been enough to establish that the woman was already at work, and he would be free to carry out his search unimpeded. He moved confidently across the hall and into the large dining/living area, which was lined with book-shelves. The taste of the Bishop/Jorgensens ran from classical Italian leather couches to a Scandinavian ultra-modern dining suite. Cavelli moved swiftly around the other rooms. The kitchen was small and narrow in the Belgian fashion, with presses which would require searching. He passed quickly along the narrow corridor at the rear of the apartment and opened the door to a small bedroom which had been converted into an office. A computer sat on a white Formica table and cardboard boxes littered the shelving which had been set into the wall. This is where the search would begin. First, however, Cavelli continued along the corridor and entered the master bedroom. A photograph of Jorgensen sat on a bedside table on the left side of the bed. The Corsican picked up the silver frame and looked into the smiling pale face of the man he had recently murdered in Pamplona. A rush of pleasure filled Cavelli as he re-lived those moments when he felt the life ebb out of the fallen body. The Apaches had been right, he thought, a killer subsumes the spirit of the person he kills, growing in the process into something superhuman. Cavelli felt the power surge through his body. He replaced the photograph, deciding to concentrate the search on the study and the living-cum-diningroom.

'*Merde!*' Bruno Cavelli slammed his hand into the back of the leather club chair in the livingroom. He had been over every inch of the apartment during the afternoon and had turned up precisely nothing. Jorgensen's office had been neatly organised and therefore easily searched. Rows of files consisting of every bill Jorgensen had ever paid, car insurance certificates dating back ten years, and every bureaucratic contact the man had ever had, littered the shelves in the tiny room. The living-cum-diningroom had been equally unproductive. Cavelli had donned a pair of plastic surgical gloves as soon as he had started, and had searched assiduously, carefully replacing each item he removed for examination. He had gone over everything in the kitchen, bathroom and bedroom twice, but to no avail. If Jorgensen had papers belonging to Chemie de France, they certainly weren't in his apartment.

He crossed to the drinks cabinet in the livingroom and poured himself a scotch. In was not his practice to drink while on a job, but the lack of success with the search had left him frustrated. He sat on the couch and examined the picture of the happy couple that sat staring at him from its perch on the coffee table. There was now no way of avoiding involving the woman. Cavelli looked at his watch. It was almost five fifteen. Sandra Bishop would soon return from her work. The two smiling faces looked back at him from the photograph. The woman would know where Jorgensen had hidden the documents and she would be only too happy to impart this information to Cavelli before he was finished with her.

Sandra Bishop was still regretting her hasty invitation to Michael Joyce when she turned the key in her apartment door and entered her entrance hall. She removed her light cotton jacket and hung it in the cupboard. The apartment was something else she was going to have to decide about. It was much too big, and costly, for one person. She looked around the empty apartment and a chill ran down her spine. The conversation with Michael Joyce had spooked her. She was more aware than ever of living alone, despite the fact that she was completely surrounded by people. That was a major joke, she thought, walking into the livingroom and dropping into a leather club chair. In the year she and Finn had been living in the apartment in Square Marguérite, they had not met any of their twenty or so neighbours. They had, of course, nodded to the other denizens of the building as they had entered or left and they had seen the names on the plaque at the lifts, but putting names to faces or vice versa just didn't happen. It was all so different in Llandudno. There people not only knew who you were but could make a pretty good guess at what you might be thinking. The sense of loneliness which was becoming a constant companion welled over Sandra. Finn had been her one human contact. Although he could be withdrawn, the Dane was always there when she needed somebody to talk to. Perhaps that had been the basis of their relationship, she thought. Maybe that was why she had decided to finish it. There should be something more to love than simply companionship. There should be some passion.

As soon as Cavelli heard the key entering the lock he slipped into the small office. Through the gap between the door and the wooden frame he had a perfect view of the hall. The woman who entered was the one whose photograph he had been examining and whom he knew to be Sandra Bishop, Jorgensen's lover. He waited while she closed the door behind her. She was alone. Cavelli watched her remove her coat and hang it in the wardrobe. The photographs had not done her justice. Her dark hair hung in curly tresses to her shoulders, the strands of hair spreading across the white silk blouse which set off her creamy skin. A short black skirt showed off a pair of perfectly formed legs. She turned her head in his direction and he saw two dark brown eyes staring out from a high-cheeked oval face. Cavelli resolved to screw her before he killed her. The Corsican watched through the gap in the frame as she left the hall and made her way into the livingroom. Normally he felt no remorse over the people he dispatched in the course of his work, but this time it was different. To rid the world of such a beautiful creature would indeed be a shame. But not to enjoy the fruits of her body before killing her would be a sin of equal magnitude. He slipped quietly out of the office and moved along the corridor towards the double doors that led to the livingroom. She was sitting with her back to the door. Cavelli moved back to his previous position in the office and slipped a knife from the scabbard fitted to his calf. He picked a file off the desk and dropped it on the ground.

Sandra jumped when she heard the sound from the corridor. My God, I'm becoming paranoid, she thought. A small noise in one of the rooms at the rear and my heart immediately leaps into my mouth. Why the hell had that stupid journalist called her? He had well and truly spooked her with his crazy theories, and now she was beginning to jump at her own shadow. She stood up slowly and started to move towards the corridor. All Finn's clothes had been packed and sent to charity. Soon she would have to get stuck into cleaning out his office. All those bloody files containing useless never-looked-at documents. The detritus of an ordered life. When that lot was bundled together, there would be the biggest bonfire that Square Marguérite had ever seen. She pushed open the door and looked at the mess of paper spread out over the parquet floor. The sooner all this crap is out of here the better, she thought, preparing to bend down and pick up the litter.

Sandra gasped as the hand came from nowhere and clamped itself on her mouth. Fear like nothing she had ever experienced gripped every fibre of her being. She tried to scream, but the force of the palm over her mouth turned what she had intended as a full-blooded scream into a strangled whimper.

All thoughts of struggle evaporated when she felt the steel edge of the knife pressed against her throat. Bile rushed out of her stomach and entered her mouth. She wanted to throw up, but the hand was clamped firmly over her lips. Her legs began to tremble and almost gave way, only the grip of her assailant keeping her upright. The hand that was clamped around her mouth was also restricting her nose and she struggled for breath.

'Quiet little one.' The heavily accented voice spoke into her right ear. 'There is no need for you to be afraid.'

The voice increased Sandra's fear and she began to struggle, but stopped immediately when she felt the knife press closer to her skin. What the hell had her instructor in the self-defence classes said? She had to start deep breathing and get herself under control. Some bloody advice when there was a hand like a vice clamped over your mouth and nose. She knew that she had to calm herself, but there was a demon in her head which was telling her to panic. Although the words that had been spoken into her ear were English, the man who was holding her was undoubtedly French or Belgian or perhaps, God forbid, Moroccan. Chances were that she had disturbed the bastard while he had been burgling her apartment and landed herself into a rape scene. Had she been able she would have kicked herself for not heeding the stories in the newspapers and fitting an alarm. The hand tightened on her mouth and nose and she felt herself losing consciousness.

Cavelli released his grip slightly when he felt the girl go limp. 'Don't struggle, or it won't be very nice. Promise not to scream, and I'll let you go.'

Sandra nodded.

'Break that promise,' the voice said, 'and I'll hurt you very badly.'

Sandra spluttered as the air slipped through the gaps in Cavelli's fingers and flooded her starved lungs. She took a deep breath, preparing to scream as loudly as she could, when the hand tightened on her mouth again. The bastard must have been psychic.

'Stupid bitch!' the voice said, almost gently. 'You scream, and you'll get it!'

Sandra quickly ran over her options. Stuck like this there was no chance. Her assailant was male and was armed, but seemed very calm. She reasoned that he was probably a professional burglar rather than an amateur, and perhaps her luck was in. Professional thieves didn't go around stabbing and maiming people. She nodded again.

She felt the pressure immediately release on her mouth and nose.

The evening sun was still warm as Michael walked west on the rue de la Loi heading in the direction of Square Marguérite. The traffic streaming along the main arterial road leading into Brussels was beginning to thin as the end of the Brussels rush-hour approached. He had been replaying his interview with Elliot all afternoon. As with Van Waarde, Michael was sure there was something that Elliot hadn't told him. Sandra Bishop would be his last avenue of enquiry. If she could think of no good reason why her lover had been stabbed to death, then Michael would be obliged to let the whole thing go and assume that the young man with the knife had been a Rioja-induced apparition. However, something inside him said that this was not about to happen.

Michael walked along the rue Archimède. The couples sitting at the tables outside the cafés that lined the street made him think of his current lack of female companionship. This was another bone of contention between Michael and his father. The older Joyce children had behaved like good Catholics and married as soon as they had left college. Patrick Joyce was already a grandfather six times over, but the unmarried status of his youngest son was a constant source of irritation. Michael looked at the gaily dressed women who decorated the cafés along the rue Archimède. Perhaps the elder Joyce was right. Journalism and writing had given Michael very little encouragement and no money. Maybe it was time to implement plan B — a return to Boston and a conventional existence.

'Quite a looker, aren't you?' Cavelli said as the woman turned to face him. 'Better than your photo. Be a pity to spoil that pretty face, so not a sound. *Compris?*'

'Who the hell are you and what are you doing in my apartment?' Sandra put as much righteous indignation into her voice as she could muster, but she was aware of Cavelli's eyes dropping to her breasts. The intruder was only slightly taller than herself, but his body was hard and muscular. Her mouth still stung from his iron grip. This was not a man to trifle with.

'Don't worry about me. Worry about what you've got that I want.' Cavelli let his knife slide under the top button of Sandra's silk blouse and then jerked it up, severing the thread holding the button. The blouse slipped open.

Oh God, no, she thought as she watched Cavelli's eyes stare at her exposed cleavage. It was going to be a rape scene after all. She pulled in a deep breath, trying to calm her befuddled nerves. Things like this didn't happen in her ordered world. The man before her was strong and armed. And ruthless. She felt instinctively that he wasn't going to be taken in by any of the moves she'd learned in the self-defence classes. She would have to try and humour the bastard and wait for her opportunity to escape.

'What exactly do I have that you're looking for?'

A slow smile spread over Cavelli's lips. He already had an erection, and he wondered whether he should take her now or wait until the papers had been located. He decided that he could wait. Tomorrow he would leave for the south of France, so there was a whole night to enjoy the woman. He lifted his free hand and let it slide inside the blouse and cup her breast. The flesh was warm and firm. His fingers found her nipple and he brushed it until it erected. He was going to enjoy this.

Sandra watched the smile spread over the intruder's face, and prepared to bring her knee up into the bastard's groin. Perhaps that would put a stop to his ardour.

The ringing of the bell caused Cavelli to step back sharply.

'Who is it?'

'I have no idea,' she replied.

He pointed the knife at her throat. 'Don't fuck with me!'

'I honestly don't know.' But it was almost six o'clock, so it had to be the American journalist. Perhaps she would be able to use him to her advantage.

The bell rang again.

Cavelli eased the knife against Sandra's neck. 'Get rid of 'em!' The Corsican motioned towards the parlaphone which stood just inside the door.

Sandra moved slowly towards the hallway. The door was only a few metres away, but even beyond it there would be little chance of escape. The outer hallway contained only the lifts and the door to the stairwell which ran through the centre of the building. She turned and found that the intruder had replaced the knife he had been holding with a gun. The open door and a mad rush down the stairwell was no longer an option. She could feel her legs shaking as she lifted the phone from the cradle.

'Remember I understand English.' Cavelli stood beside her, pistol in hand, and leaned his ear towards the phone.

'Yes?' Sandra said.

'Hi there! It's Michael Joyce.' The American accent crackled through the speaker. It sounded young and strong.

'I'm not feeling well, Mr Joyce.' Sandra's voice was breaking under the strain. 'Perhaps you could come back another time.'

Michael could hear the tension in the voice which percolated through the tiny speaker in the wall panel in the hallway, but the end of the road on the Jorgensen investigation was approaching and he preferred to get it over now if possible. 'I'd really prefer to see you now,' he persisted. 'It won't take that long.'

Sandra turned to face Cavelli.

'Let him come up, then get rid of him.'

Sandra expelled breath with relief. 'I'm buzzing you up.' She pushed the button on the side of the parlaphone. 'But it's only for a moment. I'm on the fifth floor.'

Cavelli grabbed her by the throat and put the pistol to the side of her head. 'Listen, sweetheart!' His spittle sprayed her face. 'You speak any word or do anything I don't like, and I'll kill both of you. Get rid of him quickly, and you'll be all right.' The Corsican released his grip on her throat and moved towards the corridor at the rear of the apartment. 'I'll be able to hear and see everything. Don't screw up.'

Sandra began to breathe more easily when Cavelli removed the gun. While he had been speaking she had been looking into his coal black eyes. There was no emotion present in those eyes and Sandra was sure that their owner was not a man who made empty threats.

The sound of her doorbell made her jump. Neither of the alternatives presented to her was particularly palatable. If she tried to escape, both she and the man at the door would be murdered, while if she managed to get rid of Joyce, she would be totally defenceless. She walked to the door and opened it.

'Sorry for disturbing you, Miss Bishop.' Michael looked into the drawn face of the woman standing in front of him. 'I realise that you're probably still in mourning.'

My God, I must really look dreadful, Sandra thought, staring into the hallway beyond Joyce as the lift doors closed and the mechanism took her only possible lifeline away. 'Come in Mr Joyce,' she said.

'Call me Michael, please.'

Terrified though she was, some part of Sandra's brain registered that Michael Joyce was behaving with the smooth casualness normally associated with educated Americans. He was tall and well built without being bulky. His dress was casual — a rugby shirt under a loose cream cotton jacket, and Levi jeans. He passed her and walked into the entrance hall of her apartment. She glanced over her shoulder and saw the half-open office door.

'Exactly how can I help you, Michael?' Sandra's voice shook nervously as she ushered the journalist into the livingroom.

'Like I told you on the phone,' Michael began, 'I was in Pamplona when Finn Jorgensen died. In fact I was standing not five metres away from him when the bulls came through. Although by now I'm beginning to doubt it, I thought I saw a young Spaniard plunge a knife into your friend. Right now I'm trying to find out whether there was any reason why somebody would have wanted him dead.'

Sandra fought to control her emotions. She wanted to scream but forced herself to be calm. 'Would you please sit down, Michael? A drink?' She realised that the intruder would not be too happy with the invitation to Joyce, but she badly needed a drink herself.

'I don't suppose you stock Bushmills,' Michael said, slumping into the armchair.

She lifted the distinctive square bottle from the back of the cabinet and held it aloft. He watched appreciatively as she poured two liberal measures of whiskey into highball glasses. Her hands shook, sending more water than Michael would have wanted to see cascading into the glass on top of the amber liquid.

'I'm afraid you were mistaken in Pamplona.' A picture of the man hiding in the study flashed into her mind at the moment she proffered the glass to Michael, and she almost released her grip on the tumbler.

Michael reached forward quickly and removed the glass from her hand, aware that his whiskey had almost bitten the dust.

My God, Sandra thought, trying to control the spasm of panic that was spreading through her. The intruder, who now was listening to every word they said and who was in possession of a pistol, could very easily be taken for a young Spaniard. It was only the accented English that had made her think he was French or Belgian. She looked into the American's tanned face. His features were craggy and manly, with the dark tint of his skin betraying more than a hint of his Celtic heritage.

'Finn was a rather unremarkable individual,' Sandra said. The quake in her voice was more pronounced. 'I can think of no reason why anyone would want to kill him, unless of course it was simply a random act.'

Michael lifted his glass. 'Cheers,' he said. 'I don't think it was random. I got a pretty good look at the guy who was wielding the knife, and if anything, I'd say that he was the kind of person who knew what he was doing.'

Sandra's hand shook perceptibly as she raised the glass to her lips and drank. Could the man hiding in the study have murdered Finn, and if so why? The whole idea was ridiculous. But Finn was dead and there was a thoroughly unsavoury character not twenty metres away.

'I'm... I'm afraid I can't help you,' Sandra said.

Michael could see that his hostess was under considerable strain. Van Waarde had called him an 'ambulance-chaser', and now Michael was beginning to feel that the cap actually did fit. What sort of a ghoul was he turning into? This bloody quest for some semblance of understanding of what he had seen was beginning to strip him of his basic humanity. He would have to accept that he had drawn a blank. It was time to let the whole affair drop.

'Just one last question,' Michael said, draining his glass. 'Do you have a cellar?'

One last question, Sandra thought. What happens when Michael Joyce walks out of the door?

'What a strange question.'

'I was with Mr Jorgensen just before he died and he whispered something to me. I didn't realise it was in Danish, but when I tried it on one of his colleagues he said it was something about a cellar.'

'We don't have a cellar but we do have a *cave*.' Her hands were beginning to shake again.

'What's a *cave*?' Michael asked.

This was a scene straight out of a nineteen-forties B-movie, Sandra thought. My life is being threatened and I'm sitting here talking to this man as though nothing was happening. The fear she had felt earlier crept over her like a dark blanket. She quickly raised her glass to her lips and drained the contents in a single gulp. The fiery liquid helped her to compose herself. 'It's a type of storeroom in the basement of the building. Finn was a sports freak and he kept most of his stuff down there along with our collection of wines.'

'Can I see it?'

'What for?' She was sure that a trip to the cave with Joyce wasn't on the intruder's agenda.

'Over the past few days I've been trying to find some reason why somebody wanted Finn Jorgensen dead. Everything I've touched so far has been a dead-end. The only thing I've got to go on now is the last words of a dying man. Perhaps Finn had some reason for turning his dying breath into the Danish word for cellar. If there's nothing down there, I'll make my way out and leave you in peace.'

Sandra felt her mouth go dry. How on earth could she extricate herself from this situation?

Cavelli felt the time was right to put in an appearance. He stepped into her livingroom. 'Don't move,' he said, pointing his pistol directly at Michael.

Michael knew enough about firearms to recognise the gun as a Bodyguard version of the Smith and Wesson 38. That meant that the man holding the gun was no amateur. There is no external hammer on the Bodyguard, so that it can be brought into action quickly from a pocket or a holster without snagging.

The mutual recognition between the two men was instantaneous. Michael leaned forward in his seat.

'Don't stand up yet,' Cavelli said, a smile spreading over his olive face. 'Seen you before, haven't I?'

'Yes,' Michael said. The man holding the gun was dressed differently, but he was indisputably the young man Michael had seen killing Jorgensen. 'The last time was on a street in Pamplona.'

'You know this man?' Sandra said incredulously.

'Not personally,' Michael said. 'This is the man I saw stabbing Finn Jorgensen in Pamplona last week.'

The certainty that Finn had been murdered by the man standing before her hit Sandra like a sledge-hammer. She started to retch, but all that came from her mouth was a thin string of yellow bile. She slumped back in the chair, her mind recoiling, unable to take any more punishment.

'I wouldn't have thought about the cellar,' Cavelli said, holding the gun pointed steadily at his captives. What a stroke of luck! Fate had been kind enough to give him the vital piece of information while at the same time dropping into his lap the only witness to the events in Pamplona. 'Pity I wasn't there when Jorgensen croaked his last words — it might have saved me a lot of time.'

'What do you want?' Sandra asked.

'Nothing much.' Cavelli was genuinely sorry that he would not have the opportunity to fuck the woman. 'Just some papers your fancy man had.'

Michael looked into Cavelli's dark eyes and knew for sure that he and Sandra Bishop were as good as dead. The accent marked the man as being French, and it was ironic that the last time Michael had seen that same look was on the faces of the French Legionnaires in the Iraqi Desert. The man holding the gun was the same breed.

'We'll go to this *cave* together,' Cavelli said, and smiled. 'She'll lead the way and you'll follow.' Cavelli motioned at Michael with his gun. 'Try any funny business and the first bullet goes in her head. And I'm not kidding.' He moved into the room and away from the door. 'Let's go.'

Sandra Bishop tried to rise but felt that she was glued to the chair. Michael stood and helped her to her feet. She slumped against him and tears began to roll down her cheeks.

Things like this don't happen to ordinary people, Sandra was thinking as she fought off the fog that was trying to envelop her brain. She could feel Michael's arms supporting her and she was dimly aware of the strength that flowed from him. She wiped the tears from her face and felt her legs strengthen under her as a wave of indignation swept through her. Who the hell were these people who felt that they could go around killing and invading people's homes with impunity? She lifted her head and stared across at the man holding the gun. A wave of revulsion and hate swept over her. She had never wanted to see anyone dead in her life but she was willing to make an exception for the man who had killed Finn and had been about to rape her.

She removed Michael's hand and stood facing Cavelli. If she was going to die, then she wasn't going to go whining and whimpering.

'You pig!' she said with as much venom as she could muster. 'You filthy murdering piece of shit!' She started to move towards Cavelli, but Michael restrained her before she had gone more than one step.

'Let me go.' She tried to pull her arm away from the American, but he held her fast.

'I don't advise it,' he said, holding firmly to Sandra's arm. 'This man would kill both you and me without blinking an eyelid. Why don't we help him find whatever he's looking for and then perhaps he'll be on his way.'

'He's got the right idea,' Cavelli said, enjoying the woman's display of anger. He motioned with the gun towards the open door of the livingroom. 'Don't forget the key to the *cave*. I'm only making one trip.' The *cave* would be an ideal resting place for the two bodies. Whether the documents were located or not, neither of Cavelli's captives were going to leave the cellar alive.

Sandra moved reluctantly towards the door of the livingroom, with Michael directly behind her. She slipped a bunch of keys from a hook on the wall beside the apartment door and opened the front door. The fifth-floor hallway was dark. Sandra punched the plastic button set on the wall, and the six-square-metre space was flooded with light. She moved to press the lift button.

'Not the lift,' Cavelli said from behind Michael. 'Don't want to meet anyone, do we? Open the door to the stairs and start down.' As soon as the Corsican had gained entry to the apartment, he had immediately scouted the escape routes, one of which had been the stairwell, which ran through the centre of the building.

Sandra pushed open the door to the stairwell and pressed the timer-switch behind the door. The narrow square cavity containing the stairs was lit by a dim series of lights which ran the complete height of the building. Sandra started to move down the stairs with Michael close behind her, Cavelli brought up the rear, noiselessly closing the door behind him.

The trio made their way down the centre of the building, moving slowly around the tightly pitched stairs. Michael's brain was racing. There was no doubt that the murderer of Finn Jorgensen planned the same fate for Sandra Bishop and himself. The question was how could such an outcome be avoided. This man was a professional killer who would leave nothing to chance. Trying to overpower him in the restricted area of the stairwell would be well nigh impossible. A gun in such a confined space was an overwhelming weapon.

Sandra continued to lead the way down past the second floor and towards the first. Soon they would be in the basement and they would find out whether the damn documents Finn's killer wanted were there. Then what? Her mind refused to consider what the intruder with the gun would do once they had completed their examination of the *cave*. She passed the door leading to the ground floor and began the descent into the basement area.

Cavelli watched the two in front of him descend towards their fate. By tomorrow he would be back in his villa on the hill overlooking Les Calanques, playing boule with his lovely Swedish companion.

The coolness of the basement made Sandra shiver momentarily.

'The individual cupboards are in here.' Sandra pushed against the heavy door at the foot of the stairwell.

'Not yet,' Cavelli said, from the edge of the stairs. He nudged Michael in the back with the Smith and Wesson. 'Change places with her. Try anything, and she'll be the first to get it.'

Sandra held the door while Michael brushed past her and entered the cool basement. He pushed the switch just inside the heavy door and as the light flickered into life found himself looking into a large subterranean room with a corridor running down the centre away from the entrance door. In the dim light cast by the naked bulb over his head he saw that several small passages ran off the main corridor at intervals, each containing a series of small storerooms where the occupants of the apartments could keep whatever they wished. Each passage was lit by a single dim naked bulb such as the one that hung over Michael's head.

'Move,' Cavelli said, motioning with the Smith and Wesson.

Sandra walked along the main corridor and turned into the second passageway on the right. The others followed. There was hardly any light in the passage, away from the dim bulb that lit the main corridor. There were three storerooms — simple concrete-block structures with a wooden door in the centre — on each side of the passageway. Stout locks hung from all the doors. The Bishop/Jorgensen *cave* was the middle one on the right-hand side.

'Open it,' Cavelli said. 'You,' he pushed Michael forward. 'Help her look.'

Michael walked forward several steps and pushed the plastic timer-switch which was fixed to the wall of the passageway. If the timer was the same as those on the floors above, they would have light for something approaching two minutes. Sandra had already opened the *cave* door and had stood aside. Michael looked into the storeroom, surveying the array of junk that was accumulated there. A metre-high rack of wine bottles lined the back wall of the small room. The floor was littered with assorted cardboard boxes and sundry sporting equipment. Two sets of skis were propped in one corner along with ski boots and ski poles. Two sets of ice skates were on the floor beneath the skis. The dim light from the corridor barely lit the room. Michael adjusted his eyes to the darkness of the interior and tried to locate something that could be used as a weapon. A graphite bow hung on the wall on the *cave*, its string hanging loose from one side of the arched frame. His eyes darted around the remainder of the small room but there were no arrows in sight. It was probably just as well, since the killer would have them dead and buried before Michael would have time to assemble the bow. The rest of the contents of the storeroom consisted of ancient football boots and assorted wine bottles. A cardboard box stood on the floor just inside the door. Michael bent to examine the contents.

'Any papers there?' Cavelli asked. He stood clear of the door of the storeroom, giving himself a clear field of fire.

Michael rooted through the cardboard boxes on the floor. All except two contained paperbacks. 'There are two boxes,' Michael said, dragging a box of bound papers towards him. He pulled out a volume of about four hundred pages. The leaves were annotated in a tiny but precise hand. Something told him that he had just located the papers their captor was seeking, and if that was the case then the moment of his and Sandra Bishop's death was not very far away. The lights would be going out in less than one minute and that would be his last chance to avoid the fate that the man holding the gun had in store for them. He glanced over his shoulder and saw that Sandra had retreated to the far end of the passage, as far away as possible from Cavelli. Above his head the graphite bow hung on the wall.

'Bring them out here.' Cavelli kept the gun trained on the doorway.

Michael pushed the boxes of documents out through the entrance to the storeroom with his foot.

Cavelli moved forward carefully. 'Open 'em!'

As Michael leaned forward to open the first of the boxes, the light in the passageway went out. Although the dim bulb by the basement door was still alight, the darkness in the passage and the storeroom was almost absolute. Michael arched backwards and ripped the bow from the wall.

Cavelli had been about to move forward when the corridor was plunged into darkness. He turned and saw the dim glow from the plastic knob of the timer-switch two metres behind him. He moved for the switch, and then stumbled as a cord gripped at his throat.

Michael had gripped the graphite bow in his right hand and wound the string around his left hand. He propelled himself through the doorway, prepared to receive a bullet from the killer's gun, but instead saw the murderer's back. His eyes were accustomed to the dark from rooting around in the storeroom. He looped the string around the killer's head and down onto his throat, and then pulled back on it with all his strength. He could feel the strain on his hands as the killer's body was almost lifted from the ground. During his service with the US Army, Michael had practised garrotting many times, but he had never actually used the technique. The string bit into his hand as he drove his knee into the killer's back and pulled the man's body towards him.

Bruno Cavelli would have cursed himself for his inattention if he had had the time. The cord bit deep into his throat, cutting off the supply of air to his lungs. He lashed back with his feet, and felt his heels slamming into the American's shins, but the pressure of the string on his throat was maintained. His only chance was to get the gun over his shoulder and shoot his assailant. He raised the gun and pointed it over his shoulder. The explosion of the first shot reverberated around the basement, and the bullet ricocheted off the concrete walls of the storerooms. Cavelli fired four more shots in rapid succession, and still the pressure on his throat increased. The girl screamed and Cavelli hoped that he had hit her.

Sandra had pressed herself into the wall at the end of the passageway as soon as the lights had gone out and the fight had begun. Her first impulse was to go to Michael's aid, but she realised that in the narrow corridor she would almost certainly be more hindrance than help. In any case, terror seemed to have paralysed her. If the intruder overcame Joyce, that would certainly be the end for both of them. Then a series of flashes from the muzzle of the killer's gun lit up the passageway, and she could see sparks flying from the concrete as the bullets sang off the walls. The pungent smell of cordite filled the air. Sandra screamed, and screamed again.

Bullets whipped past the side of Michael's head. The sound of Sandra's screams made him redouble his efforts to neutralise the killer. Ignoring the growing pain in his hand, he sawed the cord back and forward across the throat, opening up a gash into which he pulled the cord ever tighter. The Corsican was wriggling and flaying his feet and hands around in every direction as the cord bit deeper into his throat, severing blood vessels and cutting into his windpipe. Michael pushed with all his might on the killer's back, forcing him in the opposite direction to the penetrating cord.

Cavelli felt blood running down his chest. His feet and lower limbs were already numb and his arms were rapidly losing feeling. He knew that one last effort was required, but he could not lift his hand. The empty Smith and Wesson slipped from his grasp and clattered on the stone floor of the storeroom. The Corsican's mind was suddenly full of the people he had already murdered. Their faces floated before his eyes before disappearing into a sea of blackness.

Michael felt the man's body go limp. Adrenalin pumped around his body and he held onto the killer for several seconds before he let the string go slack. The body immediately slumped to the floor. Michael dropped the graphite bow and was aware for the first time that the cord had embedded itself in his left hand. He carefully unwound the string, feeling the sting as the last turn unravelled. He moved forward and punched the plastic light switch. The killer's body lay slumped in a pool of dark red blood. His head hung grotesquely to the side like a propped up Pierrot doll. It would not be necessary to check for signs of life. The cord had almost severed the head from the body. Cavelli's shirt front and trousers were stained a vivid red.

Sandra put her fingers to her lips. The scream that she felt emanating from her stomach would not force itself through her mouth and she stood silently biting on her fingers. The corpse at her feet could not possibly be real. It looked like a crumpled image of the man who had invaded her life earlier in the evening and whose death she had so fervently desired.

'Is he dead?' she asked quietly, turning to look at Michael.

'Yes.' He bent and picked up the Smith and Wesson from where it had fallen, and slipped it into his pocket.

Sandra couldn't bring herself to look down again at the intruder's corpse. 'This can't be happening. I know that I'm going to wake up and find that this is some kind of crazy nightmare.'

'It's all too real. He murdered Finn at Pamplona and he would just as easily have slit our throats or whatever else he might have had in mind for us. All he wanted was the papers in the boxes and to leave no witnesses behind.' Michael bent down and started to go through the man's pockets. A wave of euphoria washed over him. Not only had he survived a potentially deadly situation, but he had been right about the importance of what he had seen in Pamplona. The story of Finn Jorgensen's death was one notch nearer the surface. He now had part of the answer and the rest of the story undoubtedly lay in the two boxes they had discovered in the *cave*. He had no intention of handing the boxes over to the police or any other authority until he had discovered what secrets they held.

'Who the hell *are* you?' Sandra asked, as though seeing Michael for the first time.

'Michael Joyce,' he answered mechanically, withdrawing a bundle of bank notes from the corpse's pocket.

'That's your name, but who the hell are you? How come an ordinary man like you is able to overpower and kill a professional?' Sandra shivered as she remembered the animal noises in the dark. 'You killed so easily.'

Michael thought about that for a second. 'I killed him only because if I hadn't, he would certainly have killed both of us.' He bent down and examined the corpse. The man's pockets contained only the bundles of French and Belgian francs and a box of shells for the Smith and Wesson. There was no identification, no letters, not even a paper handkerchief. The labels of the cotton shirt and jacket he wore had been removed. The corpse was and would probably remain a mystery man. Michael made a quick count of the money. There was almost twenty thousand Belgian francs and ten thousand French francs in notes. That made a total of almost two thousand five hundred dollars. He slipped the money and the box of shells into his pocket.

'We have to call the police,' Sandra said, moving into the main corridor. She carefully skirted both the intruder's body and Michael. They would probably be in court for years over this business, she thought to herself.

'We have to think this thing through first.' Michael pulled the body towards the opening to the *cave*. He was wondering how he could avoid the next logical step, the call to the Brussels police. 'The police are going to have a lot of questions about the hows and the whys. And right now we don't have a lot of the answers. Why don't we leave our friend here for a few minutes while we run through some of the possibilities.'

'I've had just about enough,' Sandra said, watching Michael deposit the intruder's body in her storeroom. There was an edge of fear in her voice. 'I've been absolutely scared out of my wits by both of you. One hour ago I was sure that I was going to be raped and then I was convinced that I was going to be killed. Right now all I want is to hand the whole damn thing over to the police and go back to living the boring drab life I lived before all these things started to happen.'

'Maybe you won't be allowed to go back to your drab boring existence that easily,' Michael said, closing and locking the *cave* door.

'What do you mean by that?' Sandra asked.

'Think about it.' Michael had been trying to rationalise the events in his own mind. 'The mystery man was quite willing to kill both of us. Yet he was a professional who was sent here simply to do a job. So there are people behind him who want to suppress whatever is in those boxes. Let's suppose that the contents of the boxes are the reason that Finn was murdered. That means it's likely that your boyfriend was killed because he discovered some secret he wasn't supposed to. We haven't an idea of what he found, but maybe somebody thinks we do know. Our lives would then have the same value as Finn's. The presence of the killer here tonight is evidence enough of that. Think of what might have happened if I hadn't made the arrangement to meet you this evening. As for the police, can you imagine what they'd think about such a theory?' Michael thought again about his interview with Elliot. What the hell had the director general been holding back? Perhaps Elliot was behind Finn's murder and the visit of the mystery man. At this point in time anything was possible.

Sandra tried to make sense of what Michael Joyce was saying. There was little or no doubt that her life had been threatened. Maybe he was right and whoever was after the documents would kill her whether they went to the police or not. 'I need a drink,' she said. 'In fact I think I need a drink more than I've ever needed one in my life before.'

The apartment, which had been the most familiar surrounding for Sandra, now seemed strange and threatening. She quickly checked all the rooms before going into the livingroom. Michael Joyce was already demolishing the remains of the whiskey she had poured for him earlier. She walked to the drinks cabinet and poured herself a large brandy.

She looked across at the man who had undoubtedly saved her life. 'OK, so what next?' she asked, taking a deep draught from the glass. She noticed that her hand was shaking.

'I don't know,' Michael said, casting a glance at the boxes which he had deposited on the coffee table in front of him. 'I'm sure the answer to this whole goddamn riddle is in there somewhere.' Michael opened one of the boxes and removed a bundle of papers. The white sheets were covered with rows of figures, company names and what looked like chemical symbols. As far as Michael was concerned he might have been looking at a document printed in Japanese. The pages were written in a language only decipherable to lawyers and accountants. For the first time in his life Michael wished he had taken his father's advice and followed his brother into the Harvard Law School. The only way they would ever discover the reason why Finn Jorgensen had been murdered would be to find someone who could translate the sheaf of paper in the boxes into layperson's English. Using words of one syllable if possible. When he understood as much as Finn Jorgensen had, he would have the full story.

Sandra refilled her glass and sat down across from Michael. 'If we're going to call the police we should do it now.' Oh my God, she thought, remembering the seemingly endless sessions with the Spanish police in Pamplona. The prospect of repeating the experience, this time with the Belgian police, was horrifying. 'Good Lord, your hand!' She stood up and walked across to where Michael was sitting. An ugly red welt had risen on both the palm and the back of his hand. 'I'll get some antiseptic for it.' She started to move towards the door.

'My hand's OK.' He was touched by her concern. 'I think we should try to find out what's in those papers before we start explaining ourselves to the police.' Strange things were apt to happen when a person wandered into a police station and said that they'd just killed somebody. Evidence had a habit of getting lost or being made to disappear. Without knowledge of the contents of the boxes, Michael Joyce was simply a man who had murdered another human being. And murderers were inclined to spend long periods in jail. Whoever had sent the mystery man wanted the contents of the boxes badly enough to kill for them. That kind of person wasn't above juicing the local police officers. And if the Brussels constabulary were as badly paid as Boston's finest, the boxes and their contents would have disappeared long before Michael's trial. No, Michael certainly didn't want to explain himself to the agents of law and order right now. What he wanted was to find out what piece of information was so important that Finn Jorgensen had to die because he knew about it.

Sandra had retaken her seat and was sipping her brandy. Her face was pale and drawn. The trauma of the evening's events was beginning to set in.

Michael could see that deciding the next step was up to him. Firstly, they needed somebody urgently to decipher the documents. Dirk Van Waarde was out of the question. As was anybody in the European Commission. Michael fished around in his jacket pocket and came up with the piece of paper on which he had transcribed the details about Alain Jeaune.

'I've got the name of this professor in Paris who's supposed to be a doozie on this sort of stuff,' Michael said. 'If he agrees to help us, would you come there with me? When we find out what's behind Finn's murder, we'll present the police with the whole case.'

'You're crazy,' Sandra said. She wanted to get out of this bloody nightmare, not to become more embroiled in it. Drop everything and go to Paris? Have you forgotten the little matter of the man lying in our *cave* downstairs?'

'Let me call this guy. If he agrees to see us tomorrow, then what difference will one day make? We can go to the police with the whole affair wrapped up. Just think what might have happened if I hadn't shown up this evening when I did.'

He was right, Sandra thought. Michael Joyce had been her saviour. Why the hell should she worry that the bastard lying in the *cave* had died before he could kill them? A sudden coldness came over her when she realised how easily she could dismiss the fact that he had been murdered. But Finn had been murdered too. The whole situation was both horrific and wildly absurd. But it was not a nightmare — it was real, and there was no way that she could escape from it. Perhaps it would make sense to do as Michael wanted. Perhaps she owed him that. 'All right,' she said.

The number Michael called in Paris was answered on the second ring.

'Professor Jeaune?' Michael asked.

'Yes.'

'My name is Michael Joyce. I'm a journalist working in Brussels. One of your ex-colleagues at the Commission, Dirk Van Waarde, suggested I call you.'

'And how is the old reprobate?' Jeaune asked.

'Pretty good, I guess.' A picture of the small tubby figure of Van Waarde waddling out of the Villa de Brussellas came into Michael's mind. 'Some documents have come into my possession which could have something to do with the kind of legal work you did at the Commission. I was wondering whether you'd take a look at them.'

'Why not have Dirk examine them?' Jeaune asked.

'I'd prefer to have someone independent run an eye over them.'

'We are just about to break up for our vacation and I'm really quite busy. Do you have any idea what's involved in terms of time?'

'No, but I can bring you the documents tomorrow morning, and then you could see for yourself.'

There was a short silence on the line from Paris. 'OK,' Jeaune said eventually. 'I can't promise to help, but you can come to my office at the institute at ten o'clock. However, I should warn you that any time I spend on this project will be billed and my time does not come cheap.'

'That's fine.' Michael was thinking of the two and a half thousand dollars he had purloined from the dead man's pockets.

'How do I find the institute?'

'When you get to Fontainbleau it's signposted. Until tomorrow then.'

'He's agreed to look at the papers,' Michael said, putting down the phone.

Please God, Sandra thought and sipped her brandy, can I please go back to my safe boring existence?

Michael could see the apprehension on her face, but there was no way he could leave her behind. Whoever had sent the man lying dead in the *cave* knew where to find her. Tomorrow or the next day someone else would be around to continue where Finn's murderer had left off.

'We'll be back the day after tomorrow at the latest,' Michael said in his firmest voice. Sandra Bishop looked frail and vulnerable. He wanted to hold her but restrained himself.

'Then will it all be over?'

'Yes,' Michael answered with a certainty he didn't feel. 'Do you have a car?'

'Yes.'

'Great!' Michael looked at his watch. 'It's seven thirty now. If we leave straight away we could be in Paris by ten thirty.'

Sandra looked at him and wondered again whether she was right to trust him and to fall in with his plan. Her instinct was still to go immediately to the police. Michael Joyce had killed the man in the basement, she hadn't. By going to Paris with him she would be making herself an accessory after the fact, or whatever they called it, and would be as guilty as he was in the eyes of the law. Or was he guilty of anything? He had killed in self-defence, and to save her too. She felt utterly confused. A crazy, mixed-up kid, that's what she was. Then she remembered the moments just before Michael rang the bell and a shiver ran down her spine. She looked around the apartment and suddenly felt very vulnerable. Perhaps Paris was not such a bad idea after all.

'I'll pack a bag and be with you in a few minutes,' she said, heading for the rear of the apartment.

CHAPTER FOUR

A shaft of golden light was streaming in through the gap in the curtains of the small hotel room when Michael awoke from a troubled sleep. As the surroundings emerged from the fog that covered his eyes, he realised that they were totally alien to him. It took several moments before he remembered where he was and how he had come to be there. The throbbing in his left hand assured him that it had not been a nightmare but stark reality.

Sandra and he had stumbled into the crumbling hotel on the rue Gavarni close by the Eiffel Tower just before eleven o'clock. Thankfully the hotel had several vacancies. Michael was asleep almost as soon as his head had hit the pillow — the events of the day had exhausted him both physically and mentally. His eyes focused on the tiny room. Pushing aside the duvet, he fished around with his hand beneath the bed. The cardboard boxes containing the documents that had already claimed the lives of two men were exactly where he had left them.

The shower was down the hall, and Michael suddenly felt that he needed one badly. He had joined an exclusive club — he had killed another human being with his bare hands, and the smell of blood seemed to emanate from every pore in his body. Besides, he had been in his clothes for almost twenty-four hours. He stood under the shower for fifteen minutes, letting the hot water sting and redden his skin. When he emerged, the smell of blood was still in his nostrils.

'You look surprised to see me,' Sandra said, as she joined him at the breakfast table on the ground floor.

'I suppose I am,' Michael replied, pouring some thick black coffee from the porcelain jug into her cup. 'I had to pinch myself this morning to really believe that I was in Paris.'

'Me too.' She looked across the table at the man with whom she had travelled from Brussels. Nobody in their right mind would call Michael Joyce handsome, but he had what might have been described as a rugged attractiveness. She guessed him to be in his mid-twenties, but he looked older. There was determination in his blue eyes. 'Have you ever heard of Hunter S Thompson?' she asked.

'I majored in gonzo journalism at Harvard,' Michael replied.

'I would have been much more confident last night if I'd known that you were a Harvard man.' Sandra buttered a chunk of baguette. There was a lot more to Michael Joyce than met the eye. 'Harvard man' living in the same body as a man who could kill when he needed to — a combination of the intellectual and the elemental. 'As the good Dr Thompson would say, "I've been wondering whether this trip was really necessary". I'm afraid I wasn't thinking too clearly yesterday evening.'

'You couldn't be blamed for that.' Michael noticed that sleep had banished some of the dark lines that had etched her face in Brussels.

'I was scared out of my wits,' Sandra said, biting on the baguette. 'But you were the essence of coolness. I know I've already asked you this question, but who the hell are you?'

'An unemployed journalist who happened onto a murder and then had the stupidity to follow it up.' Michael drained his coffee cup. 'We'd better be on our way. I understand from the hotel manager that if the traffic is kind, Fontainebleau is about an hour away, and there's something I want to do before we leave.'

'Before we go anywhere,' Sandra said refilling their coffee cups, 'I want to know how come an unemployed journalist has the presence of mind to pull a bow from the wall of my *cave* and strangle that horrid bloody man. Don't get me wrong — I'm glad that you stopped him, but maybe you're as dangerous as he was.'

'At college I was in the ROTC.' Michael noticed the puzzled look on her face. 'Reserve Officer Training Corps. You put in some time on military training and they give you some money towards your tuition. Normally it's a pro forma kind of thing. Basic training and not much more. I got unlucky. Sadaam Hussein invaded Kuwait and as part of my service requirement I was called up to play my insignificant part in Desert Storm.'

'That still doesn't explain what happened in the basement.'

'Maybe I should add that because I speak French pretty well the powers that be made me a liaison officer with the French Legionnaires. Six months of training in the desert with those guys is apt to give one skills that one probably shouldn't have.'

'It all sounds plausible enough,' Sandra said, finishing the last of her coffee. 'But I suppose it's just as plausible as Finn being murdered during the running of the bulls or finding that man in my apartment. I've got to trust somebody, and I suppose it might as well be you.' She stood up. 'I have to call Brussels and tell them I'm taking a few days' leave. Then I'll get my things and meet you at the reception, and we can decide who pays the bill.'

'That's already been decided.' Michael produced the wad of French francs from the pocket of his jeans. 'I doubt very much if the police are going to find the next of kin of the man who tried to murder us. He might as well pay for our accommodation since he's the one who inconvenienced us.'

Sandra looked at her travelling companion. A grin lit up his face, and she smiled back at him. It was easy to forget that there was a body in the basement in Square Marguérite and that he had put it there.

Michael had already paid the bill by the time Sandra appeared at the reception.

'There's a copy shop around the corner,' he said, as they opened the battered doors of the hotel. 'I think before we hand over the documents to Jeaune we should make a copy. And I guess I should invest in a new shirt. This one is beginning to grow mushrooms.'

The owner of the copy shop gratefully accepted the five crisp five hundred franc notes before loading both sets of papers into individual plastic bags. Each of the plastic bags weighed approximately five kilos and contained more than a thousand sheets. The car was parked on a traffic island at one end of the rue Gavarni. In most American cities it would have already been towed away, but this was Paris. Cars were parked everywhere, and the Peugeot sitting on the traffic island certainly was not the worst impediment the early morning drivers would encounter.

Cars stood bumper to bumper on the Périphérique as Michael and Sandra made their way painstakingly towards the south-western edge of Paris and onto the motorway leading to Fontainebleau. Not for the first time Michael wondered what secrets, if any, the papers would reveal. If there were no secrets, he could look forward to a protracted stay in Belgium, some of it at least as a guest of the Belgian government. He had killed a man, and although the self-defence argument, backed up by Sandra's evidence, would undoubtedly lead to an acquittal, the trial would inevitably be costly, and as he sat in the tiny car crawling along the Paris motorway system, he could see only one way that he could pay for such proceedings — through the good offices of Patrick Joyce. His father would only be too pleased to fund Michael's defence as long as certain conditions would be met. And one of those conditions was sure to be a nine-to-five occupation in one of the Joyce group of companies.

'How long have you been in Brussels?' he asked, trying to dispel the visions of himself in prison grey.

'Only three years,' Sandra answered. 'I joined the Commission one year after leaving university.'

'What exactly do you do there?'

'I'm a translator,' she replied. 'And if I do say so myself I'm very good at what I do. I was brought up speaking both English and Welsh so I've always had a feeling for language. I studied Spanish and French at university and I was damn lucky to get a job in Brussels.'

'It must be exciting working in such a multi-cultural environment,' Michael said.

They left the feeder road and the motorway south stretched away in front of them. Sandra relaxed at the wheel of the Peugeot. 'I suppose it should be exciting, but quite honestly the nationalities don't really mix.'

'What about you and Finn?'

'That didn't work out.' She had been trying to put the feelings of guilt about her relationship with Finn out of her mind. 'We hadn't really been together for months.'

'Why?' The word was out before Michael realised that he might be prying.

'I like watching Ingmar Bergman films but that doesn't necessarily mean that I like living in one. I used to think that the Danes were a bit like the Welsh. They can be quite jolly when they have a few drinks under their belt. But hidden somewhere inside them is a manic depressive waiting to get out. Finn didn't just drink. He drank until he couldn't get another drop in. Then he would collapse. The problem was that once he'd passed a certain point of drunkenness, the angst would set in and the tears would begin to flow. I've never met someone who could be so intense on every subject under the sun. It got so I couldn't take it. The violent ups followed by the equally violent downs. After meeting his family in Jutland I could understand it better. A childhood of Lutheran strictness doesn't exactly prepare one for a life of a certain amount of money and privilege as an international civil servant. Anyway, I decided that our relationship was going nowhere.' It was strange, she thought, Finn seemed long ago and far away. Now he was gone forever, and she wondered whether in a few months their year together would seem like a dream. 'In a way you've done me a favour. Other than saving my life of course.'

'How's that?' Michael asked.

'Over the past week I've been thinking that I might have been responsible for Finn's death. Perhaps I've read too many romances, but I was half convinced that the poor fool had thrown himself under a bull because I'd rejected him. Now I know that however stupid it sounded, your version of how he died is closer to the truth. I'm glad that it had nothing to do with me.'

The journalist in Michael wanted to probe deeper, but he sensed that his companion had opened up as much as she was going to for the present.

They had left the suburbs of Paris behind and were now travelling through green countryside. Clumps of trees stood in the middle of grasslands. Michael noticed that there were no crops in the fields and no farm animals nibbling on the green grass. It was a countryside laid waste, awaiting the ominous approach of the housing constructor.

They reached the town of Fontainebleau almost one hour after they had left Paris and twenty minutes before the appointed time of their meeting with Jeaune. Michael picked up the first sign for the Institute Européen d'Administration des Affaires near the centre of the town.

'What exactly are you going to tell this professor?' Sandra asked as she manoeuvred the car through the traffic which virtually blocked the narrow street leading to the centre of the town.

'We must keep him in the dark as much as possible on how the papers got into our hands. After all, we're only looking for a reason why somebody should want to murder Finn and then be willing to go to such lengths to retrieve the papers. If Jeaune can present us with just such a reason, then there's no point in telling him things he doesn't need to know.'

They followed the signposts until they arrived at a series of glass and concrete buildings set in green grasslands and forests on the outskirts of the town. Michael could see why it had been easy for Jeaune to desert the concrete monstrosities of Brussels for this scene of peace and tranquillity. This was a campus on the American model. The institute's buildings, which consisted of a series of glass cubes straight out of a space invaders game, were deposited around well-manicured lawns which were dotted with stands of trees. Sandra eased the Peugeot along the gravel driveway until they arrived at the car-park beside the Administration Building.

'Good morning.' Alain Jeaune rose and extended a skeletal hand towards his visitors. The INSEAD professor was thin to the point of being emaciated and the collar of his shirt hung loosely around his neck.

'I'm Michael Joyce and this is Sandra Bishop. Thanks for seeing us on such short notice.'

'You're quite lucky to get me,' Jeaune said. His English accent was flawless. 'We just finished our second semester, so there's a lull before the storm of thesis preparation. You mentioned on the phone that Dirk Van Waarde had recommended me and that you wanted me to look at some papers. Perhaps you'd like to expand a little on what exactly you want me to do.'

'That might be a little difficult.' Michael deposited the plastic bag containing one copy of the documents on the table before Jeaune. 'I'm a journalist and so is Miss Bishop. These documents were passed to me by one of my contacts without any explanation. The contact simply said that there was something of great interest in the papers which would make a good story. I'm afraid I have no idea what it's about.'

Jeaune tipped the contents of the bag onto the desk. A thousand or so loose leaves of close typing and tables tumbled across the light grey surface in front of him.

'This is quite a job you ask me to do,' Jeaune said, looking at the mass of paper. 'Starting from scratch, it could take either hours or weeks to analyse this material.'

Michael and Sandra glanced at each other. Both were aware that they had little time before the body in the basement would be discovered.

Jeaune sorted through the papers and then removed fifty or so pages from the centre of the pile. 'It appears that someone else has already begun the analysis.' He held the pages out to Michael.

The American looked at the leaves in Jeaune's hand. Notes had been scribbled in the margins. 'It means nothing to me, I'm afraid,' he said, examining the mixture of tables and indecipherable text. 'But we're not really looking for a detailed analysis. A short explanation of what it all means would do us just perfectly.'

Jeaune was still shuffling through the papers. 'How exactly did you say that you came by these documents?'

'I didn't say exactly how I came by them,' Michael said, feeling a trickle of sweat running down the centre of his back despite the air-conditioning in the office. 'I'm a journalist. People tell me things in confidence. People send me documents. It's against the journalistic code to reveal our sources.'

'These documents come from the archives of some of the biggest companies in Europe,' Jeaune said, replacing the papers in the plastic sack. 'I am amazed that such companies managed to *displace* them.' The INSEAD professor looked up and stared into Michael's eyes.

Michael willed himself to hold the brown-eyed stare. 'Will you be able to give us a quick analysis or not?'

'What I'm really asking Mr Joyce is whether you came by these documents legally?' Jeaune said.

'Let us say that they were leaked to me in the public interest,' Michael lied.

Jeaune shifted his stare to the girl. Sandra returned the gaze without flinching.

'I should be able to give you an opinion by tomorrow. My fee will be five thousand francs.'

That was almost one thousand dollars, Michael thought. Not bad for a day's work. He still had eight thousand French francs and twenty thousand Belgian francs. Michael silently thanked the man he had killed in Brussels for providing the finance for their quest.

'That's agreeable,' Michael said. 'When do we contact you?'

'Call me here tomorrow at noon. I'll have a preliminary analysis of the material which may give you what you want.' Jeaune stood and extended the bony hand again.

Michael shook the professor's hand without comment.

'Until tomorrow then,' Sandra said, taking Jeaune's hand.

Jeaune walked from behind his desk as the couple left his office. He crossed to the window and looked across the perfectly manicured lawns bathed in bright July sunlight. It looked like a scene from Manet at this time of year — green, hazy and perfectly still. All that was missing were the figures for a reproduction of *Le Déjeuner sur l'Herbe*. Jeaune watched as Michael and Sandra left the building and made their way towards the car-park. He wondered if they were lovers. The woman was beautiful.

The summer sun baked the city of Lyons, turning the brick buildings into giant storage heaters which would continue to radiate a ferocious heat long after the sun had set. The specially tinted windows of the Tour de Chemie reflected the sun's rays, but enough heat penetrated the building to warrant the air-conditioner's constant hum.

The knock on the door of Jean Claude Blu's office was almost imperceptible. He looked up from the papers on his desk as his executive assistant, Dominique Leriche, entered the office discreetly. Blu watched her close the door and approach his desk. She was both intelligent and beautiful, and Jean Claude Blu wanted to make love with her very badly. He had managed to get all her predecessors into his bed, but Dominique Leriche was proving a formidable opponent.

'You haven't finished the reports!' The look of astonishment was clear on Leriche's beautiful face. The chairman's ability to plough through the paper that swamped his desk was legendary in Chemie de France.

'No.' There was an edge in Blu's voice which was never normally there when he spoke to his assistant. He looked up from the desk and was filled with lust for her.

'You are preoccupied?' she asked, gathering up the small amount of documents Blu had already dealt with.

'I have several things on my mind.' Their conversations these days often had a sexual element to them and Blu wondered whether she was preparing herself to succumb to his charms.

'Is there anything I can help with?' Leriche asked.

Again Blu felt there was a sexual opening. 'Will you have dinner with me this evening?' he asked.

'I'm afraid I have another engagement.'

Blu saw the smile she tried to suppress. She was playing with him. 'That's all,' he said sharply. 'I'll call when I need you again.'

'Your wife called,' Leriche said smugly. 'I told her you were busy.' She turned and started towards the door.

Blu watched her as she crossed the office. She would succumb just like the rest. He would enjoy having her and he would make her pay for teasing him and making him wait so long. Several years pushing a pen in personnel should help her to develop the right level of humility. He made a note to return Charlotte's call later.

Blu looked at the mass of paper that still littered his desk and then at his watch. It was midday and he wasn't near clearing the dross. The powers of concentration that were his trademark had deserted him, and that worried him. During his sixty years, Blu had recognised within his being the existence of a sixth sense. That extra dimension to his character had saved his life at Dien Bien Phu and in Algeria, and had led him successfully through the political minefield of climbing the executive ladder at Chemie de France. Although he tried to suppress the feeling, his sixth sense was warning him of some impending disaster. All he had to do was identify the danger and take the necessary steps to eliminate it. Earlier in the morning, Blu had run through the possible portfolio of potential threats. On the personal front there were none. His wife and son were two strangers whom he rarely met — two blood suckers who fed voraciously on his ample bank account. Chemie de France, which had initially been his mistress, had long ago become his true wife, while a procession of young mistresses catered to his sexual needs.

The source of the feeling of dread that had overtaken him was certainly located somewhere within Chemie de France. The greatest threat to the company was undoubtedly the exposure of the cartel. He thought about the promise he had made to the other cartel members. Whatever threat lay in the leaking of the documents would soon be eliminated. One did not employ the likes of Cavelli and contemplate failure. Even if the ground ended up littered with bodies, Cavelli would certainly arrive with the documents, presenting Blu with the coup that would be the climax to his career. He would expose Morley for the traitor that he was and then put the squeeze on Commonwealth Chemicals. Maybe there would be an upside to the document fiasco. With Morley out of the way, he could try to grab a part of Commonwealth's business and thereby increase Chemie de France's quotas.

Blu got up from his desk and walked into the small washroom that annexed his office. He ran the cold tap and splashed his face. The cold water felt refreshing against his skin. The face staring back at him from the mirror over the handbasin looked more haggard than usual. In five short years Blu would normally have to give up the post of chairman and tread the path into retirement. However, he had already set in motion events that would overturn company policy and permit him to continue in the post, which was not so much a job as his whole life. He smiled at his reflection in the mirror. He felt certain that for once his sixth sense was off-beam. As soon as he had recovered the documents, he would take a short break in the Caribbean, preferably with Dominique Leriche in tow.

The town of Fontainebleau was crammed with tourists as Sandra piloted the Peugeot back towards Paris. She turned into the square southwest of the town by the Château and ground to a stop. A huge tour bus attempting to negotiate a tight corner was blocking the entrance to one of the narrow streets that led towards the north of the town and the motorway to Paris.

Sandra sat quietly at the end of the queue. 'Where to now?' she said, nodding at the traffic jam ahead.

'I guess we could go back to Brussels this evening,' Michael said, 'and return here tomorrow for the meeting with Jeaune.'

Sandra thought about the recent events in her apartment. A return to her former home was not the most appealing alternative at that point in time.

'Perhaps we should stay here,' she said. 'We could play tourist for a day, if you like.'

'That's the best offer I've had all day. You seem to know the place pretty well.'

'Well enough.' Sandra eased the Peugeot out of the traffic and slipped it into an empty parking space outside the Château. 'I spent a year at the Sorbonne as part of my degree course. I think it would be a good idea to begin our tour at the Château.'

'I'm in your hands.'

'What did you make of Jeaune?' Sandra asked, as they passed through the ornate gates and made their way towards the scattered buildings that make up the Château of Fontainebleau.

'I suppose he knows what he's doing, and if he doesn't, at least he knows how to charge.' Jeaune's fee for a one-day consultation was exactly equal to what Michael had earned for the previous month. And that had been a particularly good month.

They walked along the gravel path that led to the main building of the Château, skirting a group of Japanese who formed a neat circle around their guide and photographed everything in sight.

'So what is Michael Joyce doing in Brussels?' Sandra asked as they emerged on the Château side of the Japanese.

'Trying to earn a living, or perhaps running away from earning one.' Michael was beginning to like this girl.

'Perhaps you'd explain some of these cryptic remarks to me as we go along,' Sandra said, smiling.

'My father has always had his children's lives mapped out for them. My two brothers and my sister fell perfectly into step, but I turned out to be the black sheep in the family.' Michael hesitated. He wasn't really into bar-room confessions.

'Keep going,' Sandra said. 'It's much more interesting than looking at one of the very minor châteaux of France.'

Michael glanced at the string of buildings that stretched in front of them. 'It looks quite imposing to me.'

'It would, you being an American.' The warm sun was beginning to have its effect and Sandra felt herself relax. 'Anything over two hundred years old seems imposing to you lot. This place isn't a patch on Versailles or even some of the smaller Loire châteaux. It's exactly what it looks like — a glorified hunting lodge.'

They had reached the left corner of the Château and Sandra led the way through an ornate gateway into a park that skirted the edge of the building. A small fountain in the centre of a lake sent a thin stream of water into the warm air. A trio of tame peacocks strutted around the fringe of the lake, expanding their exquisite feathered fans for the cameras of the tourists.

'You were telling me about you being the black sheep,' Sandra said.

'My father is a self-made man,' Michael said. 'I'm sure you've heard the story before — penniless emigrant arrives in the States and builds up huge fortune. My dad hasn't exactly built up a huge fortune, but let's say that he's worth substantially more than a million dollars. One of his big priorities was to set up the Joyce dynasty before he passes on. My eldest brother, Liam, is the family flagship, so to speak. He finished law at Harvard and immediately found a place on the staff of the Mayor of Boston. His path is already mapped out — State Legislature, Congress and then the Senate. My sister Kathleen is a CPA and my other brother Joe is an engineer. Both of them work for Dad's company. I was supposed to form part of the triumvirate — the engineer, the CPA and the legal eagle — a new generation that was going to lead the Joyce group of companies to bigger and better profits.' Michael suddenly felt sad standing there in the grassy garden of an ancient French château. Whenever he thought about his family he was overcome with a profound melancholy. Ever since his mind had begun to function properly he had realised that he was a member of a two-tier family. On one side there was Liam, Joe and Kathleen. who always seemed to have so much in common. At least they all shared a burning interest in the future of Patrick Joyce's enterprises. On the other side there was Michael, the family dreamer, or ne'er-do-well, as his father would say. While his two brothers and his sister played at the Three Musketeers, vowing all for one and one for all, Michael walked over the sand-dunes of the Cape trying to be something different from that which Patrick Joyce tried to make him. It would have been a lonely existence if it hadn't been for Maureen Joyce. His mother, with her finely sculptured face and raven hair could have been a model for Cathleen Ní Houlihan, the embodiment of Ireland. In the summers when the Three Musketeers invaded the offices of Joyce Construction to wreak havoc on the employees, Maureen had insisted on sending Michael to care for his grandfather on Inishmore, the largest of the Aran Islands. While his brothers and his sisters had been exploring the mysteries of cash flow and the balance sheet, Michael had been sitting at the feet of old Seán Joyce, listening to stories about men who were seven feet tall and in whom all the power and wisdom of the world was concentrated. He had once confided to his father the pleasure he took in his grandfather's stories. Patrick Joyce's riposte had been that those Irishmen who possessed any modicum of power or wisdom had had the good sense to leave the accursed island and emigrate to the US. God bless America. There had been many times when Michael wondered whether he belonged in the Joyce family. As a small child he had harboured the idea that he was an orphan taken in by the Joyces and raised by them.

Sandra noticed his melancholy mood. 'We can all do with a little bit of silver spoon from time to time. It's really nothing to feel guilty about.'

'Who said anything about feeling guilty?' Michael said turning to look at his companion. 'I loved every goddamned minute of it. The fact that I had to be my own man before I was my dad's is the only thing that saddens me. I just wasn't cut out to travel the well-worn route to the top of the corporate ladder.' Michael wondered who he was trying to convince.

'So instead you became a horrendously successful journalist in Brussels.' She smiled at him.

They were standing at the rear of the first set of buildings of the Château. Later additions extended away ahead of them, but neither of them was really interested.

'Brussels I can do without, but at least I'm doing what I want to do, not what my father wants me to do. What about you? Are you doing what you wanted to do?'

'I always wanted to get away from Wales,' she said, continuing to stroll along the gravel pathway that skirted the rear of the Château. 'My father and mother run a small guesthouse in a resort on the north coast of Wales called Llandudno. It's one of the bleakest and most beautiful places in the world. A wind rips in off the Irish Sea that cuts straight through you. Don't look so worried — you'll probably never go there. These days hardly anybody does. But in the days before everybody could afford to go to Spain, Llandudno was one of the places where the Welsh workingman spent his holidays. My earliest memories are of cleaning that tumbling old wreck of a guesthouse. Being an only child, I was constantly being told that some day the dump was going to be mine and I could then spend the rest of my days cooking bacon and sausage and chips in between scrubbing my hands off. The thought of serving up a million cups of tea didn't exactly excite me. I wanted to see a bit of the world before I became a glorified charlady.'

Michael pointed at the peeling rear of the Château. 'Is this the height of the cultural tour?' he asked.

'If you really feel interested we can go inside and see where Napoleon slept.'

'Fascinating as it sounds, I think I'd prefer to seek out some local diner and put away some lunch.'

They turned together and began to retrace their steps. 'There's a little town quite close to here called Barbizon,' she said, slipping her arm into his. 'It's an artists' hangout and really very pretentious. But there are a few places that serve a fairly decent lunch.'

'Sounds just about right.' Michael enjoyed the feel of her arm on his. Life was strange. His being in the wrong place at the wrong time had already led him to take the life of another human being and to stroll through the gardens of a French château with a woman he found both beautiful and charming. Just a few miles away a French professor was examining a set of papers that might ultimately lead to the opening of a lot of journalistic doors for Michael Joyce. *La vie est belle,* Michael thought. Life really was beautiful.

It was early evening in Lyons and Jean Claude Blu paced nervously across the breadth of his office. It was now almost two days since he had instructed Cavelli to search out the documents and there was still no word from the young Corsican. That was completely out of character. The telephone rang and Blu walked quickly to his desk and snatched up the handset.

'*Oui.*' The sharpness in Blu's voice indicated his irritation.

'*C'est* Sir Roger Morley,' the secretary said, recognising her boss's bad humour.

Blu stabbed at the black button on his phone without speaking.

'Jean Claude.' Morley's north-east accent made Blu's first name sound Arabic.

'How nice to hear from you, Roger.' Blu composed himself so as not to betray his anxiety.

It was there, Morley thought. Well disguised, but there nonetheless. The chief executive of Commonwealth Chemicals had heard enough fear in men's voices to recognise it. 'I expected to hear from you before now.' He would have to play Blu like a wily trout. 'My understanding of our last meeting was that you would contact both Werner and myself concerning the recovery of the documents. Am I to assume that you already have the papers to hand?'

'Not quite.'

Morley smiled as he detected the almost imperceptible tremor in the Frenchman's voice.

'The documents weren't in Jorgensen's office as I had anticipated,' Blu continued quickly. 'However, I've taken the necessary steps to recover them.'

'Without consulting Werner or myself as agreed at our meeting in Brussels,' Morley probed.

'I discussed my course of action with Werner.' Blu could feel the heat creeping into his face. 'My secretary tried to reach you but you were unavailable,' he lied.

You sneaky little bastard, Morley thought. 'What a pity,' the Englishman said. 'I would welcome the opportunity to show that I'm as anxious to retrieve the documents as you are. What exactly did you agree with Werner?'

Blu could feel sweat trickling from the edge of his hairline. 'I've sent one of my men to Brussels to search Jorgensen's apartment. Since the documents weren't in his office they must be at his home.'

'Or maybe in a bank vault or at the home of a friend or God knows where.' Morley was enjoying himself thoroughly. 'I suppose we can anticipate another dose of the rough stuff?'

'That shouldn't be necessary,' Blu said, remembering that he had authorised Cavelli to eliminate Jorgensen's woman if it was unavoidable. 'The papers will be in my hands within hours and then we'll know who is behind the attempt to destroy the cartel.' Blu hoped that what he was saying would actually come to pass, but the fact that Cavelli had not yet contacted him was most disquieting.

Increasingly Morley could feel the fear coming across the telephone line to him. The old fox was on the run over the documents. Now it was up to him to make sure that if Blu failed to produce the goods, the cartel would dump him as chairman. 'I hope for all our sakes that you're right, Jean Claude,' he said. 'I may have gauged the mood of the other members of the cartel wrongly, but I have a feeling that if you screw up on this one then you may have officiated over your last cartel meeting.'

'Really, Roger,' the Frenchman said, controlling his rising temper, 'if you have nothing further to discuss, then I suggest that we terminate our conversation. I'm sure you're as busy as I am.'

'*Au revoir.*' Morley pronounced it 'or vor'. 'I wouldn't want to keep you away from clearing up your little mess.'

Blu replaced the handset gently on its cradle. He wanted to slam it down but there was always the possibility that Morley was still listening on the other end of the line and the sound of the handset crashing into the cradle would only give his rival added pleasure. He had been a fool to ignore the warning bells that had been ringing in his head all day. Cavelli should have reported the retrieval of the documents by now. Unthinkable as it was to consider Cavelli's failure, it was safe to presume that something had gone wrong.

He stabbed at the button on the intercom that connected him to his secretary. 'Get me Tahir.'

Blu sat back in his chair and ran his fingers through his thick grey hair. Morley had smelt that something wasn't quite right. There had been a sound of triumph in the Briton's voice. Unless he could get his hands on the documents within the next few days, the initiative would pass to the Englishman, and the other members of the cartel might agree to ditch him as chairman. If that happened his position at Chemie de France would be undermined and it would be only a matter of time before he would be ousted there too. The rapid recovery of the documents was beginning to take on a new importance.

The phone buzzed. 'Monsieur Tahir,' the secretary announced as the door to Blu's office opened and a tall well-built man in his late fifties entered Blu's domain.

'Take a seat, Patrick,' Blu said looking up into the cold blue eyes of his chief of security. 'It's good to see you.'

Tahir dropped his long body into the chair directly in front of Blu's desk and looked at his boss. 'You look fucked, *mon capitaine*,' he said, pulling a packet of Marlboro cigarettes from his pocket. He knew that smoking was prohibited in the chairman's office but he also knew that the rule didn't apply to him. 'You need some time in the sun to rid yourself of the office pallor.' He lit a cigarette and let it dangle from his lips.

In Blu's eyes Tahir had hardly changed since the day the two men had met at the paratroop barracks in Hanoi in 1954. Even then Tahir's hair was steel grey and cut as close as possible to the scalp. 'It always astonishes me that you never seem to age,' Blu said.

'Hard bloody work and clean fucking living,' Tahir laughed, pulling on the Marlboro and sending a cloud of smoke skyward.

'Do you want a drink?'

'I'll get us both a pastis.' Tahir stood up and walked to the drinks cabinet which was concealed behind a bookcase on the office wall. He poured two glasses and added the water, which turned the liquid a cloudy white.

'*Salut.*' Tahir toasted his superior, drank deeply, put the empty glass on the desk and flopped back into the chair.

Blu sipped at his pastis. 'I have a very serious problem.' He wondered how many times he had used exactly the same opening phrase to Tahir in the thirty-nine years they had known each other. Whenever Jean Claude Blu had hit deep shit, whether it was in Vietnam or Algeria or at Chemie de France, Patrick Tahir had always been there to pull him out of it. Appointing Tahir as his chief of security at Chemie de France was the smartest move he had ever made.

Tahir's blue eyes never strayed from Blu.

'You remember some weeks ago we discussed the problem of the documents that had fallen into the wrong hands.'

Tahir nodded. 'I assumed that had been taken care of by Cavelli.'

'Cavelli removed the threat of the Commission official involved, but the documents were still at large.' Blu explained the role of Dubois in searching Jorgensen's office and his failure to locate the papers. 'Two days ago I sent Cavelli to Brussels to retrieve the documents from the dead man's apartment.'

'So what's the problem?' Tahir blew another cloud of smoke into the air.

'He hasn't reported back.' Blu saw the flicker of surprise in Tahir's eyes.

'It's not possible,' Tahir said, dropping his cigarette into the glass that stood on the desk in front of him. 'Something else must have come up.'

'That wouldn't be very professional, Sergent. Cavelli is, after all, your man. You recommended him.'

'I don't mean he took another job,' Tahir said calmly. 'People like Bruno Cavelli don't screw up, because if they do they know that they'll never get another commission. If Cavelli hasn't reported in, it's probably because he can't.' He eased himself forward and pulled the phone towards him. Without looking at Blu, he punched the button giving him an outside line. 'Do you have the file we made up on Jorgensen?' he asked as he tapped out a series of numbers on the phone.

Blu opened the side drawer of his desk and removed a sheaf of papers. He pushed them across the desk to Tahir.

'Michel, it's your old Sergent,' Tahir said as soon as the voice came on the other end of the phone. 'Shut the fuck up and listen. Go around to — ' Tahir riffled through the papers in the file and gave Sandra's Brussels address. 'We sent a man to do a job there and he hasn't reported back. Scout around and see if there's anything off-beam. And check with your police contacts whether anybody has been lifted there over the past few days.'

Tahir listened attentively while his correspondent replied. 'I want to know fucking yesterday, OK?' he shouted into the receiver. 'Call me back within the hour.' He replaced the handset and pushed the phone back across the desk. The file lay open before him and he flicked through the pages, stopping at the photograph of Jorgensen's woman. She wasn't to his taste but the thought flashed through his mind that she could be the reason for Cavelli delaying in Brussels. The little Corsican fancied himself as a cocksman.

'Well?' Blu said.

'We'll know shortly,' Tahir said, standing up and turning towards the door. 'One fucking way or the other.'

Michel Gnechte drove up the Chaussée de Louvain and turned into the rue Pave. The call from Tahir hadn't exactly been convenient. Even though Gnechte had a pressing engagement with some men who wanted to buy two kilos of the best Moroccan hash, it was more than his skin was worth to disobey an order from 'Le Sergent'. Gnechte had run across some of the greatest bastards that God had deposited on the blue and green planet but none of them held a candle to Tahir. So as soon as his former colleague in the paras had broken the connection, Gnechte had immediately telephoned one of his friends at the Etterbeek police station and made enquiries about miscreants who had been arrested in the region of Square Marguérite in the past forty-eight hours. For the villain, there was one major convenience about the Belgian police — they were the worst paid police force in Europe. For the modest expenditure of three thousand Belgian francs, Gnechte had found out that nobody had been lifted in that part of town. One part of Tahir's orders had already been complied with and in a few minutes he would run a quick eye over the apartment and then get back to 'Le Sergent' within the time he had been allotted.

There wasn't an inch of free space to be found around the square when Gnechte arrived. Almost fifty percent of the parked cars sported the special blue 'EUR' plates, which indicated that their owners were officials of the European Commission.

'Bastards,' Gnechte said, as he swept past the line of cars. Like most Belgians Gnechte hated the Euro officials who, in his humble opinion, had fucked up Brussels. The foreigners drove up the rents and flaunted their spending power in front of the locals. However, there were compensations. The well-heeled international civil servants and their spoiled brats were good customers for his mind-expanding products. Gnechte hated the European officials, but he would have been the first to resist the idea of them moving elsewhere. He looked at the numbers and located the address Tahir had given him. It was one of the older buildings on the square and stood ten storeys high, crowding over the two-storied house beside it. Gnechte slipped his car into the next street on the right. He parked directly in front of the gates of a school despite the tow-away sign.

The panel inside the doorway of the building in Square Marguérite showed that apartment 3a was occupied by a Bishop/Jorgensen combination. Gnechte pushed the black button in the metal panel opposite the name tag. If either Bishop or Jorgensen was at home, then Tahir would have the answer to his question. There was silence from the speaker at the top of the metal panel. Nobody at home. Gnechte was as dismissive as Cavelli of the lock on the outer door. He slipped a narrow iron pick into the mechanism and flicked the lock open. On the third floor he found two doors. Both had spy holes cut at eye level. He moved quickly to the door marked 'A' and slipped a pick into the mortise lock in the centre of the door. The lock turned easily and Gnechte pushed the door open quietly but quickly. The apartment had a musty smell as though the windows hadn't been opened for some time. The Belgian moved quickly through the empty rooms. In the bedroom he found clothes littered across the double bed. The place was empty, but somebody had left in a hurry.

Gnechte heard the police siren when he was standing in the entrance hall of apartment 3a. The wail started away in the distance and continued to grow in intensity until it stopped very close to the building in which he was standing. That was too much of a coincidence. His first instinct was to run. But many a clever thief had been nabbed because he had bolted when there was no need. Gnechte let himself out the door and pushed the button of the lift. He stood with his face turned away from the apartment on the other side of the hall just in case some busybody should hazard a look through the spy hole. He half expected to find two beefy uniformed Flemings waiting in the lift for him, but the small metal box was empty when it arrived. Still keeping his face averted from the door of 3b, he stepped into the lift and pushed the button to descend to the ground floor. This was going to be the hard bit. If the police had come to arrest a burglar, then they would be waiting for him in the vestibule. Gnechte stepped out of the lift into what could have been a station full of police. The men were piling through a door directly facing the lift. Gnechte could see stairs both ascending and descending through the door, which a young policeman held open for his colleagues. He let out a sigh. It had been a coincidence after all. There was no point in prolonging his visit. He moved into the vestibule and saw a number of police cars and an ambulance drawn up outside the front door. A door on the right of the vestibule opened and a small dark-haired lady of about fifty looked out.

'Excuse me, Madame,' Gnechte said, 'what's the reason for all the activity?'

'One of the tenants found a body in the *cave*. I haven't seen it myself — I just called the police.'

This was definitely Gnechte's cue to leave the scene. He had already gone way beyond the call of duty on this one.

'*Bon soir*, Madame.' Gnechte scuttled out past two policemen and through the open front door of the vestibule. Hopefully nobody would remember him. He was absolutely certain that Tahir was in some way connected with the dead body. But that was none of his business. He had to find a phone straight away and report on his visit to 'Le Sergent'. Then he would get back downtown and see whether those hash buyers had bothered to hang around.

As soon as Roger Morley had put down the receiver from his call with Blu his mind had begun to race. The old bastard was on the rack and Morley was adept enough to recognise it. Now all that was required was a little tightening of the screw.

There was only one course of action. Morley pushed the button on the intercom that connected him to his secretary and ordered the girl to set up a conference call with Van Veen in Rotterdam, Di Marco in Milan, Newton in New Jersey and Von Schick in Frankfurt. They were all to be on the line with him before the evening was out and he didn't care where they were to be found — at the office, at home, in a plane, at the opera or in their mistresses' bed. He wanted to speak to them immediately.

An hour later his secretary still hadn't been able to organise all four calls for one time. Morley walked to the window of his seventeenth-floor office. The evening sun cast a pale orange glow over Tyneside, lighting up South Shields and turning the shores of the North Sea a golden red. If this was the result of the greenhouse effect, Morley thought, then somebody should be working full-time at getting more carbon dioxide into the atmosphere. Whatever the weather, Roger Morley loved the north-east of England. His job had permitted him to travel all over the world, but he'd never seen another place that could compare to Newcastle. Nor had he met finer folk than Geordies. Morley's whole life had been dedicated to building up a company that would stand as the flagship of the area. Away in the distance the sun cast golden shadows over the derelict shipyards which had once been the pride of Tyneside. Commonwealth Chemicals had replaced the shipyards as the area's largest employer and financial engine. It hadn't taken a membership of Mensa for Morley to recognise the threat of the cartel documents as a crude attempt by Blu to launch an attack against him and Commonwealth. If and when the documents turned up he would have to ensure that either he or one of his men was in the vicinity to make sure that their origin was fully investigated. The Frenchman's theory that somebody was trying to bring down the cartel was just so much pie-in-the-sky. Nobody would benefit from such a manoeuvre. One thing was sure, Blu had provided him with a heaven-sent opportunity to rid the cartel of the Frenchman's influence. Morley was going to prise Blu out of the chairman's chair and lay claim to it himself.

The chairman of Commonwealth Chemicals turned sharply as the phone on his desk buzzed. He crossed quickly to the desk and pulled up the phone.

'Two minutes, sir.' Morley's secretary sounded more than a little exasperated.

Morley slipped back into his leather armchair and made a mental note to have a little extra put in the girl's pay cheque next month. It had been his experience that nothing motivates like money.

'This had better be good, Roger.' Dan Newton's American twang was the first to come over the line. 'Your secretary has just pulled me out of a very important budget meeting.'

'That's not as bad as being pulled away from dinner at La Scaletta,' Di Marco said sourly.

'Sorry about the abruptness of the need to speak,' Morley said confidently. 'Do we also have Werner and Henk on the line?'

'I'm here.' An echo bounced Von Schick's American accent back and forth across the line. The technology of the conference call was still prone to occasional gremlins. 'Unlike Marco I'm still at the office. What's the problem, Roger?'

'So am I.' Van Veen's husky voice was superimposed on Von Schick's last remark.

'Perhaps I'm being obvious, Roger,' Newton said, 'but is it a coincidence that all of the committee members except Jean Claude are on this conference call.'

'Jean Claude was specifically excluded,' Morley said, hearing his voice echo across the line. 'In fact, I organised this call in order to discuss Jean Claude's performance. We all agreed in Brussels that our commercial arrangements must be preserved at all costs.'

'For Christ's sake, Roger!' Newton's irritated voice boomed across the line. 'I wasn't dragged out of an important meeting to listen to the minutes of our last meeting. Get to the fucking point.'

'The point is,' Morley said calmly, 'that Jean Claude has screwed up retrieving the documents and that there's a very good chance that not only will we all be looking for new jobs in the near future but some of us may get to find out what the inside of a jail looks like. And that's without the Jorgensen affair ever coming to light.'

'I think we're all well aware of the consequences of failure,' Von Schick said. 'What exactly are you suggesting, Roger?'

'Jean Claude must be removed as chairman immediately,' Morley said. He waited for the protests but heard nothing. 'The recovery of the documents must be entrusted to someone else.'

'Who did you have in mind?' Van Veen's growl was laced with sarcasm.

'I think we are jumping the gun,' Di Marco said in his sing-song accent. 'Jean Claude has never failed us before. Perhaps we should give him a chance.'

'There's always a first time for failure,' Morley said. 'His past record stands for nothing if failure now succeeds in bringing the whole house of cards to the ground.'

'I'm with Roger,' Newton said. 'Let's get this fucking thing over with and get back to the business of making money. If Roger feels he can clear this mess up, then I'm four square behind him.'

Morley smiled to himself. He had managed to set Blu on top of the trap door — now all that was required was for the other members of the cartel to pull the switch.

'I tend to agree with Marco,' Von Schick said. 'Perhaps Jean Claude's performance to date has been a little less than we've come to expect. However, his position among us dictates that we at least give him an opportunity to recover lost ground. This view must of course be tempered by the overriding requirement that the cartel be preserved.'

'Get to the point, Werner,' Newton said. 'I've got a roomful of highly paid jokers waiting on me.'

There was irritation in Von Schick's voice when he spoke again. 'Why don't we give Jean Claude twenty-four hours to recover the documents? I suggest that Enzo call him and give him until this time tomorrow evening to recover the papers. If he fails, the torch passes to Roger.'

'Agreed,' Van Veen growled.

'*D'accordo,*' Di Marco said.

'OK,' Newton said. 'Keep me in touch.'

The Europeans heard a click on the line.

'Agreed.' Roger Morley had no choice but to be gracious. He had managed to push Blu nearer the brink but he hadn't yet managed to get him over the edge.

Enzo Di Marco broke the connection and then asked the operator for a number in Lyons. He looked back across the foyer of the restaurant at the table containing his guests. His wife was keeping the conversation going in his absence and probably hating every minute of it. Giovanna was increasing the pressure on him to accept a professorship at Northwestern University in the United States. Perhaps the demise of the cartel would make the decision for him. His position as chairman of Italchemichi was precarious at the best of times, but a major financial scandal would certainly see him off. Di Marco waited nervously while the operator put the call through. He saw his wife glance inquiringly in his direction. He waved at her and threw his eyes upwards. Something Morley had said was worrying him. Being removed as chairman of Italchemichi was the kind of threat that he could deal with, but what about the threat of prison over the Jorgensen affair which Morley had raised? Di Marco would happily spend his declining years in the groves of academe now that the other option might be a cell in the San Vitore Prison. They must have been crazy to agree to Jean Claude's course of action.

'*Oui.*' Blu was sitting in his semi-dark office. Patrick Tahir sat across the desk from him.

'Jean Claude,' Di Marco laughed nervously, 'it's Enzo calling from Milan.'

'Enzo,' Blu said, hearing the noise of the restaurant in the background. 'What makes you call me at this hour?'

Di Marco steeled himself to pass on the bad news. He decided that honesty was the best policy. 'Roger Morley set up a conference call between the members of the cartel.'

'And I couldn't be reached I suppose,' Blu said, laughing.

'He made no attempt to reach you,' Di Marco continued. 'Roger is not very happy with the way that you are handling the recovery of the documents. He thinks you should be removed from your post as chairman of the cartel committee.'

'He does, does he?' Blu said leaning back in the chair. 'And what do the rest of you think?'

There was a silence on Di Marco's side of the line. 'They've made me the spokesman to transmit a message to you. We are all agreed that in the interest of the safety of the cartel, the documents must be recovered as quickly as possible. Therefore, we are giving you twenty-four hours to find the documents or we will be forced to turn to someone else.'

Good old Enzo, Blu thought, the old Milanese would have made a wonderful diplomat. That was if he could spare the time from playing Judas Iscariot. Blu would not demean himself by asking who they had in mind as the 'someone else'. 'Was that the opinion of Werner and Henk as well?' He would expect Newton to side with his Anglo colleague. There had always been a 'special arrangement' between the American and the Englishman.

'Morley wanted you out immediately. The others and myself thought that you would come up with the papers within the twenty-four hours and the whole situation would be defused.'

Blu felt no warmth in the empty vote of confidence Di Marco was trying to relay. 'Thank you for passing the message, Enzo. You can go back to your dinner.' Blu abruptly placed the telephone handset on its cradle.

'Bad news?' Tahir asked.

'The sons of bitches have given me twenty-four hours to come up with the documents,' Blu said. 'My colleagues have just conferred, and if I don't produce then I'm out and that stupid *con* Morley will take over my position.' Blu's neck flushed.

'And that would anger you greatly?'

'More than anything in this world. Morley and I can hardly bear to be in the same room with each other. I despise him, and the feeling is mutual. Whatever happens, Patrick, we must get to those documents first.'

'That may not be so easy. With Cavelli out of the way and the girl missing, we have no way of finding out where they are.' Tahir had been incredulous when he'd heard the news from Brussels. Gnechte had reported that the flat was empty and then added that a dead body had been found in the *cave*. 'Le Sergent' had informed his agent not to rest until he found out whose corpse it had been. Tahir had fully expected the body to be that of some civilian that Cavelli had been forced to stiff. However, the description of the corpse that Gnechte had been able to obtain from his police contacts left Tahir in no doubt that it was Cavelli.

'Then we must find the woman,' Blu said, rising from the desk and beginning to pace the floor. Who do those turds think they are? he thought as he strode towards the office window. They give ultimatums to the chairman of Chemie de France the same way they would scold a naughty child. Somehow he would turn the tables on them, but he would never forgive the indignity they had forced on him.

'We've got plenty of friends in France, but our network in other countries is fucking weak,' Tahir said. 'I've already put out the message to our flics and government agency contacts, but I don't hold out much hope. Since his body was found in her apartment building, Cavelli must've made contact with her. If he's thrown a scare into her and she's run, then she could have gone fucking anywhere.'

Blu pulled the file on Jorgensen from his desk. He was sure that they had collected some information on the woman, although he hadn't bothered to read it. He flipped quickly through the pages until he came to the sheet headed 'Sandra Bishop', and read quickly down the page.

'She comes from the North of Wales, some place with an unpronounceable name.' Blu skipped over the rest of the details. 'She may have run there.'

'We'll get one of our British contacts to cover the address tomorrow,' Tahir said calmly.

'How the hell did Cavelli end up dead?' Blu asked, handing the single sheet to Tahir. 'She's not exactly a black belt in some mystic martial art. How did she manage to kill a trained assassin?'

'I've been trying to work that out myself,' Tahir said, taking the sheet. He read Sandra's profile. Cavelli's death had been bothering him more than a little. Men in Cavelli's line of work didn't just keel over and they didn't tend to be accident prone. The Corsican had been at the height of his powers. He finished reading the page. 'She can't have had anything to do with it. But what the hell did happen?'

'That's why you're on the pay-roll,' Blu said angrily, continuing to pace the office. 'I haven't paid you a fortune over the past twenty-five years for you to tell me that you don't know what's going on and that you can't help me.'

Tahir looked at his boss and mentor. He had served Blu loyally for almost forty years. For Blu he had been pimp and bodyguard and strong arm man, and still his former captain treated him like the garbage collector. All the women procured, the rivals eliminated and the petty scandals that had been swept under the carpet now counted for nothing. The present predicament was the imperative and if Tahir somehow managed to solve this one, then it too would be forgotten within the week. Perhaps it would be better that this one should not be solved, Tahir thought. During this last year he had begun to feel his age and he had already prepared his retirement. His white-washed cottage in Ceuta on the extreme tip of the North African coast had cost him a small fortune because of its location in one of the remaining European-controlled enclaves on the dark continent. But he would only go there when his Capitaine had no further use for him. 'Gnechte and his boys will be going over the woman's apartment with a fine-tooth comb,' he said, rising smoothly from his chair. The smooth feline movement was inconsistent with his sixty plus years. 'In a few hours we'll know every fucking thing there is to know about Sandra Bishop. We'll start the search for her early tomorrow morning. Sooner or later she'll use a credit card or a cash machine and then we'll have her.' The chief of security of Chemie de France would not have bet a *sou* on their chances of locating the woman within twenty-four hours. It was too bloody easy to disappear in a Europe without frontiers. The woman could only be found now by way of a miracle.

Michael picked up a cooked crab and began to poke the meat from the interior of the crusty shell. He looked across at Sandra. The day exploring Paris in her company had managed to dispel all thoughts of documents, dead bodies in *caves* and INSEAD professors from his mind. They were ensconced in a corner table of Sandra's favourite restaurant in Paris, on a corner of the Place de la Concorde. Before them on the table sat a *plateau des fruits de mer* — a steel plate containing a dazzling mixture of shellfish. A chilled bottle of Pouilly Fumé sat beside them in an ice-bucket.

'I want to propose a toast.' Michael raised his glass. 'To the woman who led a hapless American around Fontainebleau, showed him the culinary delights of Barbizon, conducted him on a tour of the Seine by Bateau Mouche, and ended by showing him Notre Dame by night.'

'It was my pleasure.' Sandra flushed slightly and touched her glass to Michael's. She loved the atmosphere of 'Le Congrès'; even when packed with the late evening clientele, it always managed to give her a mellow feeling. She adored the way excited arguments bounded from table to table, the constant chatter interspersed with brief silences in which the food gradually disappeared.

'Have you always liked fighting your food?' Michael motioned to Sandra's plate, which was covered in a mountain of shells.

'I suppose it comes from living beside the sea. Anyway, you're no mean hand at wielding the shell-cracker yourself.'

'Have you ever been to Boston?'

Sandra shook her head.

'You'd love it. My parents live on Cape Cod. Right on the edge of the ocean. In the summer we'd all pile into my dad's boat and head out fishing. We'd eat everything that came out of the sea.'

'Sounds wonderful.'

'Maybe you'll go there one day.'

'Perhaps I will.' Sandra drank some of her wine, feeling the cold bitterness refreshing her mouth. It had been a strange and wonderful day. Every time she had tried to immerse herself in the pleasure of seeing Paris again, the events of the past week would intrude to spoil the moment. It was only at 'Le Congrès' that she had succeeded in forgetting them. 'Whenever you talk about Boston or your family I get the feeling that that's where you'd really like to be.' She pushed away her plate. 'Is there a blond all-American girl waiting for you over there that you haven't told me about?'

'I'm all out of luck in the blond all-American girl stakes at the moment.' He looked across the table at Sandra. They had met scarcely twenty-four hours ago, but already he felt he had known her very much longer, and the thoughts he was beginning to have about her were quite disturbing. Perhaps tomorrow they would discover the mystery behind the papers and they would be back in Brussels explaining to the police about the dead body in the *cave* in Square Marguérite. At that point their relationship wouldn't even have the shallowness of the exchanged addresses at the end of a holiday.

'Would you like a coffee?' Michael asked.

'No, I'm exhausted.' Sandra stifled a yawn. 'Fresh air and walking, followed by copious amounts of good food and wine, tend to do that to me. Maybe I'll get a full night's sleep tonight.'

They left the restaurant and begin to walk along the Place de la Concorde.

Michael smiled as he saw the cars parked three deep on the edge of the roundabout. 'Not even in New York would you get away with something like that.'

'This isn't New York.' Sandra slipped her arm in his and led him in the direction of the nearest taxi rank. On their return to Paris they had abandoned the Peugeot in a parking lot close to the hotel.

In the taxi on the way to the rue du Passy, Sandra's head fell on his shoulder. Michael put his arm around her and held her close despite the clammy heat of the Paris night. He wished tomorrow didn't have to come.

It was almost one o'clock in the morning when Alain Jeaune turned the final page of the documents that Michael Joyce had handed him at Fontainebleau thirteen hours previously. Since he had started examining the documents in the early afternoon, he had plunged deeper and deeper into the intricate web of fraud that had been established by Europe's chemical giants. As a practitioner in the field, he was forced to admire the scale of the deceit. The top of the desk looked as if a bomb had hit it. In one corner, the supper that Jeaune had put in the microwave earlier in the evening was scarcely touched. Coffee-stained notepaper lay in front of him and opened books filled every other space. Jeaune took his coffee cup and made his way to the tiny kitchen of his studio flat in the Sixteenth Arrondissement. The seventy-five square metres he inhabited had been bequeathed to him by his aunt and would sell for something in the region of two million French francs — enough to buy a mansion anywhere in the provinces. He poured himself another cup of the thick black coffee he had been drinking all evening, and added a good measure of brandy. He did not normally drink during the week, but felt that he deserved this particular treat.

Although on the edge of exhaustion, he could not have slept without completing at least a preliminary examination of the papers. Like an addict of detective fiction, he had gradually unravelled the mystery locked within the documents, discovering that the companies had been operating a very successful cartel. The sums they were ripping off were mind-boggling. Whoever had selected the documents for leaking had done so with infinite care. There was enough in the pile of pages lying on the desk to expose the plot, but not nearly enough to form the basis of a successful prosecution by the European Commission. Jeaune flopped into an easy chair situated beside the grand piano that dominated the bottom floor of the duplex studio. The documents were the most explosive that he had ever examined in his career as a competition lawyer. He would have to consider carefully how he could fully benefit from his part in this affair. He sipped the mixture of coffee and brandy, enjoying the gentle glow that it gave him.

Michael came to slowly as he heard the knock on his door. He slipped from the bed and crossed the threadbare carpet to the door.

Sandra stood on the landing. She was wearing a thin cotton kimono over silk pyjamas. 'I don't seem able to sleep,' she said.

'Lying in there on my own isn't helping, I'm afraid, and I don't need to be alone right now.'

'Wait a second while I get decent.' Michael slipped back inside and stepped into his jeans. 'OK. Come on in.' As Sandra entered the tiny room he looked round it. There was just one rickety chair. 'Why don't you lie on the bed?' he said. 'I won't bite, you know. I'll just sit here in this chair.'

'Thanks.' Sandra lay on the bed. For a few moments she said nothing. She tried to smile at him, but her lips were trembling and she was near to tears. Suddenly the words came tumbling out in a frightened whisper. 'I've never been so confused or scared in my life. I'm so frightened, Michael — terrified.'

Michael knew instinctively that this was not the moment to speak, but that he should wait until she was ready.

After a while Sandra relaxed a little, letting her head fall back on the stiff pillow. She took a couple of deep breaths and then seemed able to continue more calmly. 'A few weeks ago,' she said, 'I was leading a pretty normal life. Work wasn't wonderful, but it wasn't unbearable either. My personal life was a bit of a mess, but at least I'd recognised that and was almost ready to do something about it. Then I watch while a man is killed, and I discover that the man I'd been living with was murdered. And then we come to Paris with a whole lot of papers which don't seem to make sense to anybody, and I don't know what I'm doing here. Honestly, I don't, Michael. I don't understand what's happening to me. And I'm frightened. When I woke up in the dark just now I was absolutely paralysed with fear.'

'Yes I know,' Michael said softly. 'I know just how you feel.' He could see that she was trembling.

'I don't think you do. You say it's your military training, but you were pretty calm and cold-blooded back there in Brussels. I find that scary too.'

Michael remembered the feel of the dying man twitching in his grip as he pulled the cord tighter and tighter on his windpipe. Calm and cold-blooded were the last words he would have used to describe himself in those frantic moments. But he could not argue with Sandra in her present state of tension, even if there had been any point. Somehow he had to try to soothe and reassure her, which wasn't easy when she was absolutely right to be frightened. A sudden inspiration made him think of his childhood.

'When we were kids,' he began, leaning back in the chair, 'whenever one of us was sick or we broke an arm or something, my mother would always try to comfort us with the fact that the pain was transitory. Soon enough we'd be back to normal when the bones had knit or the sickness had passed. This damn mess is just like one of those bouts of sickness. When you're in the middle of it, there's pain and you feel lousy and it seems like it's never going to be over. Then one day you wake up and there's no pain and you just continue on as if you'd never been sick at all.' He paused and looked at Sandra. The trembling had stopped, and the panic had faded from her eyes. 'Tomorrow or the day after we'll clear this mystery up and you'll be able to go back to your normal life. Next year it'll be a dim memory and the year after that you'll wonder whether it was just a dream.'

'Yes, I suppose so,' Sandra said. She sounded sleepy. 'Go on talking. That accent of yours is very soothing.'

Michael began to tell her another anecdote from his childhood, but before he had spoken more than a few words, her eyelids closed, her breathing became regular and deep, and he knew that she was asleep.

She looked so peaceful lying there. He was glad that he had not told her how much she had to be afraid of. The people who had murdered Finn Jorgensen were out there somewhere. They probably knew by now that the man they had sent to Brussels had failed. He wondered what their reaction to that piece of news would be. There was nothing that he and Sandra could do except pray that Jeaune would come up with some answer to the riddle of the documents. He stretched out his legs and lay back in his makeshift berth.

Professor Alain Jeaune arrived at the lush campus of INSEAD at nine o'clock. He parked the Opel Omega and removed the plastic bag containing the precious documents from the trunk before carefully locking the doors. He wondered whether a Mercedes 280 would look too ostentatious in the staff parking lot. Probably not. Most of the other professors drove prestige cars. There might not even be any need to park at the institute after today. He strode towards the concrete steps which led him into the building in which his office was located.

The tiny room looked different today. Somehow or other it appeared bigger and brighter. Jeaune put the plastic bag in his filing cabinet and locked it. Then he locked the door of the office, and went to pick up the phone.

In his bedroom on the top floor of the Tour Chemie, Jean Claude Blu awoke from a troubled sleep. There were enough demons in his past to keep a thousand men awake for ever, but those ancient misdeeds had never bothered the chairman of Chemie de France. He had dispatched his boardroom enemies with the same ruthlessness that he had employed to destroy the enemies of France on the field of battle. Blu left the small bedroom and went into the bathroom. The face that stared back at him from the mirror looked haggard and scared, the kind of face that the chairman loved to see across the boardroom table from him, the face of a man whom hope had deserted. He was facing possibly his last day at the helm of the petrochemical cartel. Somewhere deep in his being he begged the Fates to give him one last chance to rescue himself.

He showered, shaved and breakfasted, with the thought of somehow finding the documents uppermost in his mind. The daily travail of running one of the largest companies in France would have to be sacrificed to saving the skin of its chairman.

He watched as the light on the top of his phone buzzed like an angry bee. He had left strict instructions with his secretary that he was not to be disturbed. The girl would have to be fired. The light continued to buzz. Blu whipped up the handpiece angrily. 'I told you I wasn't to be disturbed!'

'But Monsieur Blu,' the secretary's voice quaked. 'The caller is most insistent.'

'You've just signed your own dismissal notice.' Blu's voice soared with fury.

'He told me to tell you it concerns the cartel,' the girl persisted.

'What!' Blu's voice exploded.

'It's a Professor Jeaune calling from Paris,' the secretary continued. 'He says that he wishes to talk to you about the cartel.'

'Get Tahir to my office straight away,' Blu said, the irritation disappearing from his voice. He pushed the black button which would put him in direct contact with the caller.

'Good morning, Monsieur le Président,' Alain Jeaune said on the other end of the line. 'My name is Alain Jeaune, I'm a professor at the Institute Européen d'Administration des Affaires in Fontainebleau. We met once but you probably don't remember. My institute organised a top management briefing for Chemie de France.'

Blu had no recollection of the man. 'What can I do for you, Professor?'

'It is not what you can do for me, Monsieur le Président, it is what I can do for you.' Jeaune paused for a moment. The phrasing had to be just right. 'Some documents have recently come into my possession which cast an interesting light on the business arrangements that Chemie de France has with some of its competitors.'

Blu sat bolt upright. He could feel the presence of an approaching miracle. 'And may I ask how these documents came into your possession?' he asked.

'We will come to that later,' Jeaune said. 'I notice that you do not deny that such arrangements exist.'

'There are always commercial arrangements.' If the game was going to be 'tripping around the bushes', Blu could play that one too. 'Even on occasion between rivals.'

'I'm speaking about long-term co-ordinated commercial arrangements between the main companies in a certain field, aimed at protecting market share and keeping commodity prices at specified levels.'

'Assuming that such arrangements do exist, how do the documents you spoke about relate to them?'

Patrick Tahir entered the chairman's office and Blu motioned him to pick up the extension telephone that sat on the meeting table.

Jeaune continued, confident that he had struck pay-dirt. 'I've only made a preliminary examination of the papers, but it is my view that a good competition lawyer would glean enough information from them to instigate an investigation of the operations of some very large European and American companies. I should add that until a year ago I myself was just such an individual. My previous employer was the Commission of the European Communities.'

Blu realised that this information was intended as a threat, but he felt no panic. A man who is about to inform on someone doesn't call up the intended victim first to gloat.

'How interesting,' Blu said. 'And what do you intend to do with these documents?'

'That's the point. Getting back to your first question, the documents are not mine to do anything with. They were brought to me by a Brussels-based journalist named Michael Joyce and a woman called Sandra Bishop. I was employed simply to give an opinion on the contents of the papers.'

Blu could see Tahir scribbling the journalist's name on a pad that sat on the table.

'I should advise you, Professor Jeaune,' Blu's voice hardened, 'that the papers currently in your possession are stolen property and that anybody assisting this theft will be prosecuted with the full vigour of the law.'

'That is the purpose of this call,' Jeaune said.

They were finally getting to what the Americans called 'the beef in the sandwich', Blu thought. He had heard enough pitches in his life to recognise one a mile off.

'If as you say, Monsieur le Président,' Jeaune continued, 'these documents are indeed stolen property, then my only concern is to see that they are returned to their rightful owners. However, the contents are of such an explosive nature that I am at a loss as to whom I should entrust the papers. It might be that the European Commission would be the proper body to decide on who the documents should be returned to. Or conversely, I could return the papers to Mr Joyce and wash my hands of the whole affair.'

Blu smiled to himself. The man on the other end of the line was an absolute amateur at blackmail. 'Then we would be left with the question of finding the mysterious Mr Joyce. Which might be a considerable inconvenience. Perhaps you've already thought of a solution to that particular problem?'

Jeaune was very satisfied with the progress of the conversation. He had managed to lead Blu to the position he wanted without too much difficulty. 'I have given that matter some thought, Monsieur le Président,' he said confidently. 'If perhaps there were a representative of Chemie de France present when I handed over the documents to Joyce, then that representative could discuss the source of the documents with the person who brought them to me in the first place.'

'What an admirable solution,' Blu said in his best ego-massaging tone of voice. 'What exactly did you have in mind?'

'It's quite simple. Joyce will be telephoning me tomorrow morning to arrange a meeting. I will suggest seven o'clock at my apartment.'

'Excellent,' Blu said. He could imagine the next part of the conversation.

'There is however the question of my fee,' Jeaune said hesitantly.

'Chemie de France would be most pleased to cover your expenses and add a considerable honorarium. Shall we say a total of half a million francs?'

'Considering that you will recover documents that are potentially very costly to you, I think one million francs might be closer to the real value.'

We have left the realm of blackmail and have entered the realm of extortion, Blu thought. However, the recovery of the documents was paramount. 'Agreed,' he said. 'Now give me the address of your apartment.'

Jeaune almost let the phone fall with excitement. The million francs would be simply the first instalment. The cartel papers were worth a fortune. The companies would pay billions of francs in fines if the documents fell into the hands of the Commission. A few million francs every now and again would keep Alain Jeaune in luxury in the Caribbean. Trying to keep the excitement out of his voice, he gave an address in the fashionable Sixteenth Arrondissement. Blu watched as Tahir noted it down.

'My representative will be my chief of security, Patrick Tahir,' Blu said.

'He *will* bring the money?' Jeaune said.

'He will indeed, Professor. I must thank you for the responsible way in which you've handled this affair. Please don't let there be any slip-ups.'

'There won't be.'

'Until this evening,' Blu said, and hung up the phone and turned to face Tahir. 'You said it would take a miracle to find the woman, and that stupid greedy bastard in Paris has handed her to us on a platter.'

'Somebody up there must certainly love you,' Tahir said, grinning at him.

'He does, Patrick. Remember how we almost bought it in Indo-China and in Algeria. Every time the deck was stacked against us something always came along that pulled us out of the fire. How many times have politicians tried to topple me from my post as chairman of Chemie de France? Every time they've failed. Now Jeaune has presented me not only with a reprieve, but with the perfect chance of dealing a mortal blow to Morley. The Englishman will rue the day he ever heard the name Jean Claude Blu.'

'How the fuck did this journalist' — Tahir looked at his notepad, — 'Joyce become involved? Maybe we should try to find out more about him.'

'I don't know and I don't particularly care.' Blu stood up from behind his desk and crossed to where his chief of security was standing.

'What do you want me to do?'

'You heard the whole conversation. Just take care of it.'

'You mean permanently?'

'I mean very definitely permanently.'

CHAPTER FIVE

Nicholas Elliot sat at his desk examining the pages of the *Financial Times*. He sighed perceptibly. The 'Observer' column of Britain's most respected daily paper was speculating on the candidates from the Civil Service for the Honours List and Elliot's name was not mentioned.

There was a knock on his door and Georges Lafonde entered the room.

'Have you seen the newspapers?' Lafonde asked.

'I'm just finishing the *Financial Times*,' Elliot replied, clicking his fingers and pointing to the chair directly before his desk. 'And damn depressing reading it makes too. Whatever fool is compiling the *Observer* column these days is speculating on the Honours List and he neglects to mention my name.'

Lafonde sat down in the chair indicated by his master. 'Probably just an oversight,' he said laconically, viewing Elliot through his bushy eyebrows and hooded lids.

'Don't be so bloody naïve.' Elliot folded the pink-coloured paper and tossed it to the far edge of his desk. 'A remark like that shows just how much you know about the British political establishment. Anybody who has spent more than a weekend in Brussels could well be considered to have gone native. And since I've spent ten years here, there are probably those at the Foreign Office who consider me to be as Belgian as Hercule Poirot.'

'I don't suppose that you've read today's copy of *Le Soir*?' Lafonde asked.

'In all my time living in this poor excuse for a capital city, I have neither felt the need to read a local newspaper nor to watch one of the local television channels.'

'There's a rather interesting report.' Lafonde opened a blue cardboard file cover and produced a newspaper cutting which he laid on the desk before Elliot.

The competition director general ignored the piece of newspaper. 'What does it say?'

'A man was found dead in the basement of the apartment building where Finn Jorgensen used to live,' Lafonde said, removing the cutting and replacing it in the folder. 'The mystery is that nobody seems to have any idea who the individual was or what he was doing there. I only remembered the address myself because I went through Jorgensen's file again after that journalist visited you.'

'Is this something that should worry us?' Elliot asked, beginning to open the first item in his stack of morning mail.

'It could be just a coincidence.'

'Continue,' Elliot said, reading the second letter in the pack.

'You told me to keep an eye out for anything that could jeopardise the investigation into the chemical cartel, and that's just what I'm doing.' Lafonde slouched back in the chair, trying to fight down his annoyance at Elliot's inattention.

'I'm depending on you, Georges,' Elliot said, to ensure that there are no screw-ups in preparing the case. A dead man being found in the basement of Jorgensen's apartment building is not my idea of a threat.' Elliot picked another letter off the pile and continued reading.

Lafonde stood and began to move towards the door. He had seen Elliot terminate enough interviews to know that his own was over.

Elliot's phone buzzed almost as soon as Lafonde left the room.

'Mr Schuman on the line for you,' the secretary said.

'Schuman.' Elliot had pressed the black button as soon as he had heard the name. 'Two calls in such a short period of time. My, but we *are* getting anxious.'

'You've got to speed up the progress of the case,' the voice on the line said calmly. 'Some of my colleagues on the cartel committee are beginning to take fright.'

'No can do, I'm afraid. These things must follow their course.'

'If the course is much longer then there won't be anything incriminating left in the offices when you raid them.' Schuman's voice was calm but firm. 'The cartel might split apart before you have the opportunity to bust them, and that would be a pity. For all concerned.'

'The papers you supplied to us are being processed as quickly as possible, but as I've already explained at length, some legal niceties have to be observed. You can't just start breaking down the main doors of established companies one morning without making sure that there will be no serious repercussions. Is there something else that I should know about?'

Elliot paused, listening to the sound of breathing on the other end of the line. Schuman would not have called again unless there was some pressing reason. Although there was no concrete evidence to support him, the competition director general was sure that his informant was holding something back. Schuman was so bloody cool. There hadn't been the slightest sound of panic in the man's voice. It was to be expected that informants should keep back some kernel of information which they could trade at the last minute, but Elliot had the feeling that this was something different. Something was beginning to smell.

'My colleagues are particularly jumpy at the moment,' Schuman said quietly. 'I can't put my finger on the reason for their apprehension but I think that what I considered as an urgency a few days ago has now become an imperative.'

'I'm getting your message loud and clear.' Elliot's accent was more clipped than usual. 'And I will take the necessary steps to speed up the investigation. But I just hope to God that you're being totally frank with me.'

'You can count on it,' Schuman said. 'You must arrange to raid the offices as soon as possible. I'll be in touch.'

The phone went dead in Elliot's hand. What the hell was Schuman up to? Elliot knew that there was no point pushing his lawyers any harder than they were being pushed at the moment. The case was only days away from completion, but the calls from Schuman were worrying. They were almost there. The final touches were being put to the organisation of the dawn raids. And Nicholas Elliot would tolerate no slip-ups.

Michael awoke with pains shooting along his legs. He turned awkwardly in the chair and felt the hard wooden arm biting into his side. Sandra lay on the bed, her dark hair streaming across the white pillow. Michael eased his feet off the bed and put them on the floor. He had spent more uncomfortable nights, but not very recently. The hands of his watch said nine-fifteen. Breakfast finished at nine, so they would have to forgo the pleasures of the hotel diningroom.

Sandra stirred and opened her eyes, squinting into the bright sunlight. A smile spread across her lips when she saw Michael in the chair at the foot of his bed.

'Sorry for evicting you last night,' she said, sitting up in the bed. 'If I'd stayed in my own room I never would have got back to sleep. And thank you for not trying... anything.'

There was an awkward pause.

'I'm sorry', she said. 'I shouldn't have said that.'

'That's OK,' Michael replied. 'If you want the real low-down on me I should tell you maybe that my class at college voted me the guy least likely to rape his date.' He laughed. 'But I wouldn't want you to get the wrong idea. They didn't give me that title because I'm gay, which I most certainly am not, but simply as a tribute to my exquisite manners. In fact, I'm almost as well-behaved as an English lord. Or maybe I should say a Welsh lord. Do they have lords in Wales?'

Sandra knew that he was fooling in the hope of removing any embarrassment she might feel. She smiled. 'What's on the agenda today?'

'We've missed the coffee and baguette provided by the hotel, so I guess we should immediately locate a kerbside café capable of providing a little sustenance. But before we eat I'd like to call Jeaune and find out what, if anything, he's been able to deduce from the documents.'

Sandra stood up and stretched. 'I'm absolutely famished. It's a pity that the cooked breakfast is not a French tradition. Right now I could murder a plate of bacon and eggs.'

'A good night's sleep tends to give one an appetite,' Michael smiled. 'See you in the lobby in twenty minutes.' He watched as Sandra left the room. Soon it would be impossible not to show the attraction he was feeling for her. After today it was likely that their paths would diverge as they rejoined their separate lives, but he wished there was some way that he could stay in contact with her.

They left the hotel and walked towards the small café on the corner of the rue Gavarni and the rue du Passy. Michael left Sandra at the table and reluctantly went inside to find a telephone and make the call that would lead ultimately to the break-up of their partnership.

'Professor Jeaune, it's Michael Joyce here. You asked me to call you today.'

'Good morning, Mr Joyce.' Jeaune did not subscribe to the Anglo-Saxon habit of using first names. 'I have been examining the papers you left with me. However, I shall need several hours more before I can form a definite opinion.'

'Can you give me any indication at all of what the documents relate to?'

'I shall have the work completed by the end of the day. May I suggest that you come to my apartment at seven this evening, and I will present you and your charming companion with my findings.'

'You'll have nothing before then?' Michael made no attempt to hide the note of disappointment in his voice. The longer they stayed away from Brussels, the deeper the hot water he would be in over the dead man in the basement in Square Marguérite. Another day might just be the straw that broke the camel's back.

'I'm afraid not,' Jeaune said. 'You may consider that I am doing you a favour. There are not many who would consider a summer day in Paris in the company of a beautiful woman as a penance, Mr Joyce.'

'Then I suppose that it will have to be seven at your apartment,' Michael said. 'What's the address?' He wrote the address on a sheet of paper that lay on the bar.

'*Au revoir,* Mr Joyce. Until this evening.' Jeaune replaced the telephone and sat back contentedly in his chair. He remembered a phrase that had been continually used by the leader of the television 'A Team'. 'I love it when a plan comes together,' he said.

'Jeaune won't be ready with the papers until seven this evening,' Michael said, dropping into the wicker chair directly across from Sandra. 'He's invited us to his apartment where he will disclose all.'

'I've ordered us some coffee and croissants,' Sandra said.

'You're obviously a lady who likes to concentrate on one thing at a time.'

'I think your little homily last night might have struck home. I've been thinking the whole business over and I've decided that I have no other option than to follow the trail to the end. We're both implicated in a killing and the only possible way I can ever rejoin the sane part of the human race is to try and help you clear yourself and by implication clear myself as well.'

A waiter arrived and laid two large cups of coffee and a pannier of croissants on the table.

Sandra picked up one of the fresh pastries and took a bite. 'If Jeaune can't be ready until seven this evening, all the talking in the world won't change it,' she said through a mouthful of croissant. 'Right now I'm hungry, so I'm going to concentrate on having a pleasant breakfast. Was he able to give you any hint of what the documents are about?'

'He was very unforthcoming,' Michael said. 'Or maybe he was telling the truth and he hadn't yet formulated an opinion. Anyway we'll find out the details this evening. In the meantime the ball is in your court.'

'I suppose for a first-timer in Paris a visit to the Louvre might be in order.' Sandra smiled and picked up a second croissant.

It was midday when the Lear jet bearing the logo of Chemie de France rolled to a halt in the private section of Charles de Gaulle Airport on the eastern outskirts of Paris. The howl of the twin engines gradually reduced and Patrick Tahir eased himself out of his seat. The ex-para made a final check of the on-board fax machine. He had instructed Gnechte to fax him as soon as he had compiled details on the journalist Michael Joyce.

'I hope you enjoyed the flight, sir.' The blond hostess exuded charm.

Tahir passed her without responding.

The hostess shivered involuntarily as Tahir ducked through the exit of the cabin. Something about that man made her skin crawl.

'*Bon jour, Chef,*' Philippe Lepape stood at the foot of the steps to the plane, holding open the passenger door of a decrepit Citroën CX.

'Hello, Philippe.' Tahir got into the scruffy car. He could have been met by a Chemie de France Mercedes, but he preferred to deal with his tried and trusted friends. He heard the rear suspension groan as the rotund figure of Lepape settled itself behind the wheel. 'Have you got what I asked for?'

'Everything's waiting for you back at my place.' Lepape smiled, revealing a row of rotten teeth.

'And how's business, Philippe?' Tahir asked as the Citroën moved away from the jet and towards the exit from the tarmac.

'Which business?' Lepape gave a booming laugh. 'The drugs business is wonderful. The flics bust some of my pushers from time to time but *grace à Dieu* they still accept my money and leave me alone.' Lepape steered the car through a set of wire gates and onto the road leading to the centre of Paris. 'The girl business works less well. The Algerians and Moroccans still form a queue, but the brave Français are worried by the disease.'

Tahir looked across at his ancient comrade. Lepape was worth many millions of francs, but he was dressed worse than the shabbiest *clochard* who slept under the bridges of the Seine. The only caprice the old miser had was his stomach. Some day a distant relative of Lepape was going to be very surprised to find himself a millionaire.

'I will pay twenty thousand francs for your help in the business this evening,' Tahir said, looking at the solid block of traffic inching towards the Périphérique.

'I don't normally attend to such matters personally.'

Tahir shot a sideways glance.

'Of course I would be happy to help you out, but you might prefer to have one of my younger men along.' Lepape waited anxiously for Tahir's response. 'Le Sergent' was one of the few men on earth that Lepape feared.

The security chief of Chemie eased back in his seat and ran his right hand through the sharp pines of his steel grey hair. 'You know bloody well that I don't work with people I don't know. Send your young men out to push their dope on the streets. What I have in mind requires somebody of your subtle talents. And there's absolutely no risk.'

Lepape piloted the Citroën into the right-hand lane and up the ramp onto the circular road that runs around the centre of Paris. He knew better than to argue with the man sitting beside him. They were members of a very élite club who had carried out atrocities in the name of France but who had managed to escape with their skins from Algeria. Lepape left the motorway and made his way to the Boulevard de Magenta, swinging right into the Boulevard de Strasbourg. At the corner of the Boulevard Saint-Denis and the rue de Boukia, Tahir saw the first streetwalkers. Their white faces stared from the darkened doorways as they waited to alight like a hoard of locusts on any car that was stupid enough to stop. The people walking the streets were mainly North African, with a sprinkling of darker skins from further south.

'Not the place to run as a National Front candidate,' Tahir said, nodding towards the street.

'Fuck Le Pen and the skinhead mob,' Lepape said, spitting on the floor of the Citroën. 'I can't stand people who never screw or who prefer beer and wine to the products of the Riff mountains. If those bastards had their way, people like me wouldn't be able to make even the meagre living we do.'

Lepape stopped the car in front of a decaying four-storey *maison à maître* which had seen much better days. Two youths who wore leather jackets despite the high temperature lounged against either side of the open doorway.

'Problems?' Tahir said, opening the door and stepping out onto the street.

'No.' Lepape put his left hand on the roof of the Citroën to lever himself out of the driver's seat. 'They belong to me. Although my drug operations are strictly small time, there's always some bastard who's trying to grab what little turf I have left.'

The two young men by the door of the building shuffled as their boss emerged from the Citroën.

Lepape gave the two guards a cursory nod as he passed them. 'I bring up a consignment from Corsica every now and then.' Lepape led Tahir past the youths and through the open door.

'They'd cut their own mothers for a one franc piece. It takes them varying times to become addicts, but when they do, I fuck them out. One thing I've learned in this business is never ever trust an addict.'

The ground floor of the building was dark after the bright sunlight of the street. A single naked bulb shone a dim light over a scene of creeping decay. Paint had peeled from the walls and the marble tiles were covered with an ancient scum. This Paris demi-monde of dirt and decay was in stark contrast to the plush offices of Chemie de France, but both were dedicated to the same end — the making of money.

'This is where I conduct my business.' Lepape strode on towards the staircase. 'But I live on the third floor. We've been here almost one year. Soon it will be time to move our base of operations.'

The sound of Arabic music came from overhead and the two men looked at each other.

'Our friends are waiting for us,' Lepape said, leering.

Walking beyond the wooden door that led to Lepape's living area was like entering another world after the squalor of the lower floors. The entire third floor had been turned into a single apartment. A person being shown a photo montage of the apartment could not have been blamed for thinking that it was located on the Avenue Foch and not in the emigrant quarter of Paris. The rooms were tastefully furnished with antiques, while expensive Shiraz carpets covered the polished marble floors.

Lepape strode on towards the source of the music. 'I think you're going to like this, mon Sergent,' he said over his shoulder. He threw open a door at the rear of the apartment and stood back.

Tahir stood in the doorway and smiled. The room had been set up in the manner of an Algiers brothel, with large cushions strewn around a floor several centimetres thick in gaily coloured Moroccan carpets. The only pieces of furniture were low coffee tables consisting of beaten copper plates atop carved sandalwood stools. Tahir let his eyes wander around the room, taking in the hunting scene tapestry that covered the window. Subtle lighting had been placed in the roof to create a shadowy ambience. The security chief felt a glow gradually spreading through his body. The two girls were standing beside a state-of-the-art stereo system in the corner of the room. Both were dressed in traditional Berber costumes, long flowing red and blue gowns threaded with gold. Both wore headgear with strands of small gold coins dangling over either ear.

'Wonderful,' Tahir said.

'After you, mon Sergent.' Lepape smiled happily. It was difficult to impress Tahir, but he felt he had succeeded. 'The beauty in red is Farhana and the girl in blue is called Selima.'

Farhana and Selima approached the two men, and each in turn took and kissed Lepape's hand.

'This is my friend and my guest.' Lepape motioned towards Tahir. 'We must ensure that his stay in my house is as pleasant as possible.'

The two girls turned towards Tahir.

'They are seventeen, and fresh from the Riff mountains,' Lepape said. 'Both virgins. I have been saving them for you.'

Tahir noticed a wicked look in Farhana's eye which gave the lie to Lepape's claim. The girl might be only seventeen, but she had been a *putain* for more than a couple of months. Farhana laid a hand on Tahir's arm. Her dark eyes smiled at him and he noticed the tribal facial marking she had applied to her brown skin and the ornate henna-coloured lattice patterns, which would have taken her hours to apply, on her palms and fingers. He was indeed an honoured guest. He allowed the girl to lead him into the room.

'Would you like to see me dance?' the girl called Farhana said in halting French.

'I would like that very much,' Tahir replied in fluent Arabic. He dropped onto the cushions next to Lepape while the two girls went to the stereo and changed the music.

Lepape opened an onyx cigarette box that lay on the coffee table between the two men. He removed two fat cigarettes and offered one to Tahir.

'My own private stuff,' Lepape said, rolling the joints between his fingers. 'Grown high in the Riff mountains especially for me.'

Tahir looked at the hash cigarettes.

142

'Of course if you prefer something more exotic,' Lepape said, looking into the grey eyes of 'Le Sergent', 'I have a stock of almost any drug that you can mention.'

'This'll do,' Tahir said, accepting the joint. 'But not too fucking much of this stuff. We've got business this evening.'

'There is plenty of time, mon Sergent.' Lepape leaned across and lit their joints. They turned together as the pounding beat of the tambour came through the speakers.

Tahir sucked in the sweet blue aromatic smoke and felt it swirl through his lungs. He blew the smoke out slowly and watched the two young Berbers moving rhythmically to the music. It was a scene fit to transport a man through time. Farhana started to sing the high whining music of the North African mountains, and Tahir was a young man again sitting beneath a clear desert sky looking down at the festivities in a Berber camp set in a stony plain. The hash swirled around in his brain as he watched Farhana. There had been so many like her when he had been in Algeria. Some of them had succumbed willingly, while Tahir and his colleagues had sometimes been forced to hold down the more reluctant. He wondered idly whether there were any of his progeny running around North Africa. Tahir smiled at the thought of a Berber with some of his genes. Lepape made a grab at Selima as she danced close to him and the young Berber moved agilely away from the fat man's grasping paws.

The drumming rose to a crescendo and the two girls gave themselves over completely to the music. It was strange, Tahir thought, that such a repressive society could have produced a music that fired the blood of both men and women, and a style of dancing that was incredibly sexual. Lepape had not lied about the quality of the hash. Tahir's concentration on the movements of the girls was total, and a desire was rising in him that would soon have to be satisfied. Farhana moved close to 'Le Sergent', and made no move to escape when he pulled her to the floor beside him. Her tongue darted across her lips and she pushed her firm young body against him. Tahir smiled. Only Lepape could find a seventeen-year-old virgin with the skills of a practised whore. He slipped his hand around the girl and leaned forward to kiss her. Her tongue flicked into his mouth as her hands made their way towards his crotch. Soon the girl had his penis out of his trousers and her head bent lower. Lepape had briefed her well. Tahir took a deep toke of his joint as the girl began to fellate him. He looked across at Lepape and saw that Selima had lifted her skirts and was preparing to sit on the fat drug peddler's exposed penis. And there were still six hours to go before their appointment with Joyce and Bishop.

Sir Roger Morley had been stalking his office at Commonwealth Chemicals all day. The senior executives had often seen him in this mood and most had made hasty arrangements to visit clients or play golf during the afternoon. Morley was on the brink of one of his finest triumphs since he had pulled himself up by his bootstraps from the mail office at Commonwealth to his current position as chief executive. There was no way that Blu could haul himself back from the brink. In a little over six hours the Frenchman would be history as far as the cartel was concerned. But getting rid of Blu would only be half the battle. The recession was cutting deeply into Commonwealth. Morley had spent the morning reviewing the figures for the current year, and they were little short of disastrous. There were already rumblings in the City, and the Commonwealth share price had come under sustained pressure. An investigation of the cartel operation by the European Commission and the consequent heavy fine might be just enough to drop the share price through the trap door. Therefore, once Blu was out of the way, Morley would immediately have to turn his attention to the matter that had led to Blu's downfall, the recovery of the documents.

Morley pressed the button on his intercom. 'Get me Von Schick in Frankfurt.'

The chief of Commonwealth didn't particularly like the German, but he was the only member of the cartel committee who was worth his salt. Morley subconsciously ran his finger along the side of his cheek, tracing the path of Von Schick's *schlager* scar. He wondered what sort of mentality was associated with someone who geared up and then stood there while some fool took a swing at him with a sword. Morley tended to agree with the British Conservative politicians who had a pathological fear of the Krauts taking over Europe or possibly the world, but he needed a bed-fellow right now, and while he would have preferred to see Newton filling the bill, Von Schick was the man who could be counted on.

The light buzzed on his phone.

'Hello Roger,' Von Schick said. 'Not another of your conference calls, I hope.'

'Not today, Werner,' Morley said, with a lightness he didn't feel. 'I wanted to talk to you about what happens after this evening.'

'Might you not be a little premature? After all, Jean Claude hasn't failed yet.'

'You and I are realists, Werner. After this evening Blu will no longer be the chairman of the cartel, and I'm going to need someone to help me pick up the pieces.'

'What exactly did you have in mind?'

'I want to reorganise the cartel committee. It's time we created the post of deputy chairman, with a stipulation that the deputy chairman automatically replace the retiring chairman.'

'And you'd like me to become the deputy chairman,' Von Schick interjected.

'Yes,' Morley said, slightly peeved at being denied actually offering Von Schick the post.

'That's very flattering, Roger. Jean Claude has already made somewhat the same offer.' Von Schick smiled, enjoying the silence from the other end of the line.

'Our industry is going to have to battle its way out of this recession and I personally don't think that Jean Claude Blu has the balls to keep the cartel in operation.' Morley paused.

'You may be right,' Von Schick said.

'I know I am. You and I together would be just the right team.' Bite, you Kraut bastard, Morley said to himself.

'There's a certain amount of logic in what you say. What exactly do you intend to do?'

Gotcha, Morley thought. 'Firstly, we've got to locate the documents that were leaked to Jorgensen. Blu has ballsed-up the operation from day one. Once we've safeguarded the future of the cartel, there'll have to be a redistribution of the quotas. Some companies are suffering worse than others, so perhaps some will have to make a sacrifice so that others can survive.'

'Your half-yearly results are due out shortly if I'm not mistaken,' Von Schick said.

'Next month.'

'The rumour in Frankfurt is that you're looking decidedly shaky.'

'Nothing we can't get over.'

'Glad to hear it, Roger. It would be most inconvenient if the incoming chairman of the cartel found himself fighting to keep his own business alive.'

'It won't come to that, Werner.'

'I hope not. Anyway if Blu fails, then you can count me in on your scheme.'

'Good.' Morley was well satisfied with the result.

'As long as you can guarantee me at least a five percent increase in my quota.'

'That's extortion and you know it, Werner. Two and a half percent would be absolute tops.'

'Let us agree on four percent,' Von Schick said.

'Three and a half.'

'Agreed. I'll be in touch after we hear from Jean Claude. I hope you have a very pleasant evening, Roger.'

'So do I, Werner. We'll talk again soon.' Morley put down the phone. The Tories were right about the Germans. Morley had the distinct impression that Von Schick had managed to get exactly what he wanted.

Werner Von Schick put down the telephone and smiled. It had all been so predictable. Morley had expected him to negotiate an increase in market share in exchange for his support. It was really all so pointless. The old men were busy chasing their tails while doom was staring them in the face. Within a few days the cartel would be in tatters and Mannheim Chemicals would be ideally placed to pick up whatever pieces the others would be forced to throw onto the market. Von Schick began to doodle on a sheet of white paper lying on the desk before him. The fact that the old men had not yet recovered the papers he had leaked to Jorgensen was a measure of their incompetence. Jean Claude had certainly lost his touch, and they were just about to find out whether Roger Morley still had what it took. Von Schick looked down at the complex doodle he had drawn on the paper. He had drawn a phoenix rising out of its ashes. He ripped the sheet of paper from the pad and dropped it into his desk drawer. It might prove to be a prophetic drawing.

Michael Joyce's feet felt like two lumps of raw meat. He and Sandra sat in a café on the Avenue des Nations Unies across from the Eiffel Tower. What they had accomplished in one day had at first seemed impossible. They had scurried around the Louvre, and had then spent the absolute minimum of time admiring the huge plexiglass sculpture known as 'Mittérrand's madness'. Then a visit to the Ile de la Cité and Notre Dame before a sustaining lunch in a Greek restaurant in the rue Saints Pères. After lunch they had checked out of their hotel before continuing their sightseeing with a visit to the Bourbon Palace, Les Invalides and the Ecole Militaire and finishing off with a trip up the Eiffel Tower.

'I'll never forget my first visit to Paris,' Michael said, taking a slug from his frosted beer glass. 'Every time I get sore feet I'll be reminded of this trip.'

'At least the two days went quickly,' Sandra said, looking at her companion. 'In just over an hour we will know what is in the documents and hopefully why Finn died.' She lay back in her director's chair, letting the fading rays of the sun warm the length of her body. 'Then it will all be over.'

Michael was tempted to say something about the hours they would spend in Etterbeek Police Station back in Brussels, but he didn't want to burst her bubble. His hand strayed, as it had so many times since they had left the hotel after lunch, to the pocket of his cotton jacket. The loaded Smith and Wesson Bodyguard weighed down the pocket. He had taken the gun from the car on the off-chance that something could go wrong. Sitting in the evening sun he was beginning to think that he was being more than a little paranoid. After all, Jeaune was their man. The professor had been recommended by Van Waarde, who was completely unaware of the existence of the documents. Despite this, Michael had somehow felt compelled to bring the damn thing along to the meeting. He involuntarily pushed the gun further into the recesses of the pocket, certain that every passer-by was staring at the bulge it made.

'Then it will be back to Brussels to pick up the pieces and go back to life as it was.' Michael watched Sandra turn her face to catch the rays of sunlight. He definitely didn't want this interlude to end.

'I don't think so,' Sandra said, her face still turned to the sun. 'What's happened in the last few weeks has been horrible, but I think it's been a kind of watershed for me. When I get back to Brussels, the first thing I'm going to do is clear the apartment. When I was in Denmark, the Jorgensens said they wanted to have Finn's belongings. In fact they made it quite clear that there was no way they were letting me get away with anything. I'm going to have the whole lot, including the furniture, packed up and ready for them to collect.'

'What about the apartment?'

'It's only rented. I'll just cancel the contract. I've been wanting to leave Brussels for some time, but it's very difficult to break out of a golden cage. Now I've got the perfect excuse. I'm going to take at least a year's leave of absence and I'm going to see a little bit of the world. Maybe I'll go to Australia.'

Michael wondered whether there were any jobs for impecunious Harvard graduates down-under. 'Sounds great to me,' he said, putting as much enthusiasm into his voice as he could muster.

Sandra smiled at him. Finn would have come up with a thousand reasons for staying put, with reason number one being money. She watched Michael sip his beer and wondered what might have happened if they had met under a totally different set of circumstances. It was useless to speculate. This evening or tomorrow morning they would go their separate ways.

'What about you?' Sandra asked.

'The first thing I'll do is make my peace with the Brussels police.' Michael smiled. 'The last thing I want to be famous for is a jail journal. Other than that I suppose I'll spend a few more years avoiding the inevitable.' Michael drained the cold beer. 'When I look back from my vantage point as a great industrial leader I'll be able to say that I at least gave my dream a try, even if it was a miserable failure.'

'My, but we are being negative today! What happens if you write a Pulitzer Prize winner and get a job on the major paper in Boston?'

'Result, happiness or maybe just imagined happiness. From the first day I picked up the *New York Times* and read Jimmy Breslin's column, I've always wanted to write for that paper. About the only way that dream is going to come true is if my dad makes it big enough to buy the paper.'

'Stop putting yourself down.' The image of Michael as the lost waif made her want to throw her arms around him and cuddle him. 'It's only a defence mechanism. If you keep saying that you can't do it, it's easier to accept failure when it arrives. It could also lead to what's known as a self-fulfilling prophecy.'

'Sorry to change the subject, but shouldn't we be thinking about moving? We've only got forty minutes to make it to Jeaune's apartment.' Michael lifted his jacket off the back of the chair and felt the weight of the Smith and Wesson in the pocket.

Sandra stared across the Seine at the Eiffel Tower, not wanting to move from her seat on this sunlit pavement. Perhaps she would forget about going back to Brussels and stay on here for a few days. She had plenty of leave coming and she had been indefinite about when she would return to her job at the Commission.

'At this very moment we are sitting in the Sixteenth,' Sandra said, finishing her beer. 'Jeaune's apartment is located just off the opposite end of the rue de Passy, so it shouldn't take us more than twenty minutes to walk it. Very swish it is, too.'

'What about taking the car?' Michael asked. He was feeling uneasy about carrying the gun on his person, and if they returned to the car he could always deposit it there.

'You've got to be joking. The car is quite okay where it is, but by the time we get to Jeaune's the only places that will be available will be on top of the lamp-posts, and even they might be taken.'

'You've got a point. Let's go. Maybe we can manage to turn a twenty-minute walk into a forty-minute stroll.'

Alain Jeaune had arrived home early from Fontainebleau and had spent what was left of the afternoon organising his notes on the cartel documents. In order to strengthen his future negotiating position, he had made a copy of the documents and had locked them away carefully in his office.

The INSEAD professor went to the fridge and removed one of the bottles of champagne that he had bought to celebrate the occasion. There should be a celebration when one comes into money, and he considered that he had just come into an inheritance. However, unlike other inheritances which consisted of one single payment, his was an inheritance that would produce enormous sums annually, or indeed whenever he wanted. He crossed the livingroom of the duplex and set the champagne bottle into the ice-bucket which had been placed on top of the grand piano. The clock above the bricked-in fireplace said six-forty. Jeaune had been glancing at it every few minutes since he had entered the apartment. He checked around the room. Everything was set for what would undoubtedly prove to be the most propitious evening of his life.

Patrick Tahir slipped out of the passenger seat of the battered Citroën and sucked in great breaths of polluted Paris air. He watched as Lepape levered himself onto the street on the driver's side of the car. The two ex-comrades in arms had left their two young Algerian prostitutes fast asleep amid the cushions on the floor of Lepape's make-believe brothel. The drug-baron motioned to the rear of the car and both men walked to the boot.

'An afternoon to remember,' Lepape said slapping 'Le Sergent' on the shoulder. 'One to bring back pleasant memories of our days in the kasbah.'

'Perhaps I will visit Paris more often, Philippe.' Tahir could still feel the delicious pain in his loins. Lepape's 'virgins' had been performers without parallel. He thought of the two naked girls lying asleep amid the cushions at Lepape's, their long black hair splayed out about their heads. So young, and yet neither had the stamina of their older partners. As soon as their business with Jeaune and the two from Brussels was finished, Lepape and he would return to continue their pleasure. On their way to

Jeaune's apartment they had stopped at the Paris office of Chemie de France and picked up the single sheet of paper that constituted Gnechte's report from Brussels. It appeared that Michael Joyce was exactly what he had represented himself to Jeaune as, an unattached journalist. Joyce was from Boston and Gnechte had faxed one of his contacts there for more information. It would arrive too late. Joyce was about to die. Gnechte had included the information that the Brussels police were looking for Sandra Bishop for questioning about the death of the still unidentified man found in the basement at Square Marguérite.

Lepape pushed the button that opened the Citroën's boot. Tahir looked around the deserted street.

'You must have been feeling nostalgic,' 'Le Sergent' said, as he looked into the boot. A 9mm MAT 49 sub-machine gun sat nestling on the black rubber matting which covered the floor of the boot. He lifted the steel machine gun and felt the weight. 'It's been one hell of a long time since I've handled one of these.' Tahir had lived with a gun similar to this as his constant companion for more than six years. The butt of the MAT was closed, making the gun at about forty-five centimetres total length ideal for concealment .

'I forgot to return it to the stores after we left Algeria,' Lepape said, smiling. 'It comes in useful now and then in my current line of work. The magazine is always full.'

Tahir handed Lepape the machine gun and the fat man slipped it under his jacket. 'Le Sergent' reached into the boot once more and lifted out a 9mm PA15MAB.

'You're not completely nostalgic,' Tahir said, slipping the pistol into his waistband.

'It's important to move with the times. I understand fifty of those pistols disappeared from an Army storeroom just two months ago.'

'How convenient.' Tahir looked at his watch. 'What about the drugs?'

Lepape put his hand in the right-hand pocket of his soiled suit coat and pulled out a fifteen by seven centimetre plastic box. 'Exactly as you requested. What way do we play this?' he asked.

'None of them makes it out of there. It's just another middle-class sob story. Three professional people who happened to get themselves some very bad dope to hold an orgy with.'

Lepape watched 'Le Sergent' stride erectly away from the Citroën and make for the rue Richpin where Jeaune's apartment was located. He wondered whether the old bastard was anxious to get on with the killing or in a hurry to get back to his *putain*. Just like the old days in Hanoi and Algiers, the fat man thought.

'*Plus ça change plus a reste la même,*' Lepape muttered under his breath.

Michael and Sandra stood before the imposing building on the rue Richpin. A series of bells had been imbedded into what was probably one of the original concrete columns that stood on either side of the door. The bells and the roughly gouged hole in which they stood represented the victory of technology over art. Sandra looked along the line of bells and pressed the one opposite Jeaune's name.

'When I see houses like this I wonder whether families actually lived in them,' Michael said, looking up at the rows of windows.

'Don't the Joyces have a mansion in Cape Cod?'

'We have what most people would consider a large house, but nothing on the scale of this one.'

'*Oui.*' The tinny sound of Jeaune's voice came from a loudspeaker embedded in the column.

'Michael Joyce, Professor,' Michael said, speaking into the column.

'Come right up. I'm on the third floor.'

Michael pushed open the door and he and Sandra entered the house. The hall in which they found themselves was the size of Michael's garret in Saint Josse. And considerably cleaner. The floor was white marble, and a marble staircase climbed upwards from the left-hand side of the hallway. The steel frame of a lift stood at the far end of the hall.

'Very grand,' Michael said, moving towards the lift.

They rode up the three flights of stairs in the rickety steel cage, the lifting mechanism groaning in agony with each centimetre they climbed.

'Welcome.' Jeaune stood on the landing directly across from the lift door.

Michael accepted the professor's outstretched hand, noticing the change in his host's demeanour from their meeting in Fontainebleau. This had to be Jeaune's 'home' persona. The professor's face looked even more pinched than it had at Fontainebleau, and dark bags graced the underside of his eyes.

'Please come in.' Jeaune took Sandra's hand and ushered her and Michael through the open door of his apartment. 'I hope I didn't put you out too much by asking you to come here.' He closed and locked the door behind them.

'It was really quite convenient,' Sandra said, descending a short flight of stairs and entering the living area. 'We were staying in a hotel in the rue Gavarni.' She looked up and saw that the ceiling was at least six metres above them. The part of the living area that looked out on the street was dominated by a grand piano, a stereo and two very old stuffed couches. The rear had been turned into a small office.

'Good,' Jeaune said, crossing quickly to the piano. 'I hope you enjoyed your visit to Paris.' He looked at Michael before wiping the sweat from his face with a handkerchief.

'Very much,' the young American said. 'Only I don't think that a two-day visit does a city like Paris justice. Have you finished examining the papers?'

'So like an American to want to get down to business quickly.' Jeaune picked the bottle of champagne from the ice-bucket and proceeded to tear off the foil wrapping. 'The pace of business is somewhat more sedate in Europe.' He eased out the cork with no more than a faint plop, and proceeded to fill three of the four fluted glasses which sat on a silver tray set beside the ice-bucket. His hand shook perceptibly as he poured the champagne.

'Miss Bishop.' Jeaune handed Sandra one of the glasses. 'And Mr Joyce.'

He lifted his glass in a toast. 'To Paris.'

Michael touched his glass to both Sandra's and Jeaune's and sipped the sparkling wine, thinking how over-rated it was.

'Miss Bishop and myself are anxious to get back to Brussels, and while we very much appreciate your hospitality, we really would like to get on with the business we came here to conduct.'

'I'm sure your father would be very proud of you,' Sandra whispered to Michael, smiling at him.

'Ah yes! The documents.' Jeaune placed his glass carefully on the silver tray. 'Perhaps you would like to sit down.'

It was hot in the apartment, and Michael removed his jacket and pushed it into the corner of the chair.

'I have carried out a preliminary examination.' The professor nodded in the direction of the papers, which were stacked on the piano. A buzzer sounded. 'Please excuse me,' Jeaune said, and climbed the short flight of stairs to the parlaphone which hung on the wall just inside the door.

'This guy has a lot of class, but I wish to hell he'd get on with it,' Michael said softly. 'The sooner we're back in Brussels the better.'

'Relax.' Sandra sipped her champagne. 'We're almost home.'

'Just wait one moment and I'll be right with you,' Jeaune said, before unlocking the door and slipping out through it.

'That man needs a course in relaxation techniques,' Sandra said.

Michael didn't reply. He could hear the sound of the old lift creaking in the hallway outside. The arrival of the unforeseen guest was one coincidence too many for Michael. He could ignore Jeaune's nervousness, but the new arrival was something that certainly wasn't in his script. He slipped the Smith and Wesson out of his pocket, took off the safety-catch and pushed the gun into the gap between the side and the seat cushion of the couch. One way or another the pistol would be his ace-in-the-hole in case Jeaune was up to no good. Michael smiled to himself. He was becoming paranoid. It was probably Madame Jeaune. The noise of the lift stopped and the sound of male voices speaking in French came from the landing outside the open door. If it was Madame Jeaune, then she had been blessed with a fine bass voice.

Michael looked up as the three men walked through the door in single file. Jeaune was in the lead and some of his jaunty 'mine host' air had disappeared. As soon as Michael got a good look at the two men behind Jeaune he could see why the professor's mood had changed. Neither man was young, and indeed Michael guessed them both to be close to sixty. The one directly behind Jeaune, despite the fact that he could have been considered an old man, looked lean and hard. He was dressed in a well-cut sports jacket and slacks, wore his grey hair cropped to the skull, and moved with the assurance of a man who was confident that he could handle any situation. His companion, who was fat, almost bald and wore a grubby light blue suit, turned and locked the door behind him just as Jeaune had done when Michael and Sandra entered.

'Mr Joyce, Miss Bishop.' The smile was pasted onto Jeaune's thin lips. 'May I introduce Mr Tahir and — Jeaune paused for a second.

'Monsieur Lepape,' Tahir prompted.

'Monsieur Tahir represents a very important French company who believe that they have some business with you.'

'Don't bother to stand,' Tahir said, and pushed Jeaune onto the second couch. He removed the pistol from his waistband and Lepape lifted out the MAT from underneath his jacket.

'Oh God, no!' Sandra exclaimed.

'Don't worry, it'll be all right,' Michael said, putting his arm around Sandra's shoulder.

'*Qu'est que vous faîtes?*' Jeaune began to stand up, but Tahir punched him hard in the stomach, and he collapsed on the floor, holding his abdomen.

Tahir looked at Joyce and Jorgensen's woman. He was impressed by the man's cool. No bluster like Jeaune, just calm acceptance. There was something about that coolness that troubled him. The sooner they had it over and they were out of there the better.

'So you're Michael Joyce,' Tahir said, looking at the young man. The American was almost dark enough to be of Latin extraction. Tahir estimated that Joyce was somewhere in his mid-twenties.

'What a *putain* that one would make,' Lepape said from the other side of the room.

Tahir turned to concentrate on the woman. The pimp was right. Sandra Bishop was beautiful. Even with a look of fear on her face, her curly black hair and dark good looks had not been done justice by the black and white photograph. There was some essence of this woman that a photographer would never be able to capture.

'You're much more beautiful than your picture,' Tahir said, smiling, then turned his grey eyes back to Michael. 'You're the fucker who killed Cavelli?'

'You mean the man you sent to Brussels?' Michael asked. 'Yes, I killed him.'

'How?'

'I garrotted him.'

'If Bruno Cavelli let you get behind him, then he was a bloody fool and deserved to die,' Tahir said. He looked at Sandra again. 'Move away from him.'

Sandra slid along the couch away from Michael.

'I guess it would be dumb to ask what all this is about,' Michael said.

Tahir smiled. Jeaune hadn't even informed them yet. They were going to die and they would never know the reason. He motioned Lepape forward. 'You've got yourself mixed up in something that you should have left alone.' He took the MAT from his companion. 'Search him!'

'Stand up,' Lepape said, in heavily accented English.

Michael complied immediately.

Lepape moved behind him. 'Now turn around and put both your hands on the back of the couch and spread your legs.'

Michael did as the fat man requested. As with Cavelli he had no doubt that the men intended to kill them. The only difference was that this time there were two of them and they were not as relaxed about him as the killer in Brussels had been. He felt the fat man's hands running over his body. If he was lucky he could get one of them, but the second one would certainly get him.

'He's clean,' Lepape said.

'Check his jacket,' Tahir said.

Lepape picked up the cotton jacket and felt it. 'Nothing,' he said, tossing it over the edge of the chair.

'Sit down,' Tahir ordered Michael. He passed the MAT back to Lepape.

'What do you want with us?' Sandra was getting over her initial shock. 'You can have your precious papers back. Just leave us alone.'

'Too late, darling,' Tahir said, hauling Jeaune to his feet. ' The Brussels flics want to talk to you about a certain dead body found in the basement of your apartment building. And while you're explaining the body, we don't want you bloody telling 'em about the papers.'

Michael noticed a small patch of vomit on the floor where the INSEAD professor had been lying.

'Tell Monsieur Blu that I don't want anything,' Jeaune whimpered. 'I am happy just to be of service to him.'

'Are those the papers?' Tahir asked, pointing his pistol in the direction of the papers sitting on the piano.

'Yes,' Jeaune said quickly. 'Please take them. I haven't told anybody about them.' A picture of the neat stack of copies nestling in his safe at Fontainebleau flashed through Jeaune's mind. He would make that bastard Blu regret the day he had sent his henchmen to beat him up.

Tahir moved to the piano and looked into the plastic bag containing the documents. The fat man stood at the other side of the room with the machine gun pointed in their direction. Michael doubted if possession of the papers was going to satisfy these men. He looked across at Sandra and caught her looking directly at him. She seemed to be willing him to do something about their predicament, but Michael couldn't conceive of a plan that wouldn't end in getting them all killed.

'What happens now?' Michael said, watching the grey-haired man examine the documents.

Tahir closed the bag and crossed the room to where Lepape was standing. 'Give me the 'works'.'

The fat man took the plastic box out of his pocket and handed it to 'Le Sergent'. 'Everything has been prepared. There's one vial of juice for each of them. It's a hundred percent pure. They'll have a high they'll never forget.'

Tahir slipped his pistol into his pocket and took the plastic box from Lepape. 'Keep them covered. If one of them so much as farts, shoot their fucking heads off.'

Michael watched as Tahir re-crossed to where he'd left Jeaune sitting on the couch.

'You first, Professor.' Tahir opened the plastic box on the coffee table and took out a syringe. He picked up one of the vials and carefully charged the syringe.

'What are you doing?' Jeaune said, cowering at the end of the sofa. He cursed himself for being so bloody greedy.

'The three of you are going to have a little orgy,' Tahir said, gripping Jeaune's arm and pulling him to his feet.

The puny professor went limp in the iron clutch of 'Le Sergent', like a rabbit blinded by the lights of an oncoming car.

'Unfortunately you got some bad dope.' Tahir pulled up Jeaune's shirt as Sandra gasped. 'You!' Tahir shouted at Michael, 'make one fucking move and one second later her brains will be decorating this room.' He grinned. 'If you don't have an orgy, could be that a dope buy went wrong, with you lot dying in a hail of bullets.' He laughed, and then turned back to Jeaune, who stood limply in his grasp. 'You're just about to die a fucking happy man, Professor.'

'No!' The shout from Jeaune surprised everybody in the room including Tahir. The professor threw his left hand at Tahir as 'Le Sergent' was about to plunge the needle into the vein on his right arm. As the two men grappled, Michael instinctively knew that this was the moment he was waiting for. Without thinking, he shoved his hand into the gap between the armrest and the cushion, tightened his fingers around the handle of the Smith and Wesson and pulled the gun clear. In one smooth movement Michael brought the pistol up and fired three shots in the direction of the fat man holding the machine gun.

Two of the shots caught Lepape directly in the chest. As he was thrown back against the wall his finger tightened on the trigger of the machine gun and he loosed twenty rounds in the direction of Michael and Sandra. He heard the click as the magazine in the MAT hit empty. The pain in his chest was excruciating and he looked down to see the front of his dirty white shirt already soaked in blood. The fat pimp tried to focus his eyes on the other side of the room and felt himself slide to the floor at the same time. Nothing was moving over there and he died happy, thinking that he had killed the bastard who had killed him.

Tahir had just landed a vicious punch to the side of Jeaune's head as the explosions from the 38 echoed in the room. The professor fell against him as bullets sprayed out from the MAT. Tahir felt two shots thud into the limp body on top of him just before he himself was flung back with a searing pain in his shoulder. He and Jeaune both crashed to the floor.

Michael waited until Lepape was motionless. He knew he should pump another round into the prone figure, but the bloody holes in the front of Lepape's shirt convinced him that the man was dead. Over by the piano, Jeaune and the grey-haired man lay tangled together. A pool of dark red blood had already formed on the parquet floor. Michael turned to Sandra, who had pressed herself into the corner of the couch, and then rushed to her and pulled her out from the cushions. 'Are you hit?'

'No.' Her reply was flat and toneless. 'Are they all dead?'

'The fat one is, and Jeaune. I'm not sure about the other guy. He's unconscious, but he may still be alive. Let's get out of here.' Adrenalin was pumping around his body as he pulled her to her feet. 'Those gunshots will have been heard, and the police will be here soon. I guess we should not be around when they arrive.'

Michael shoved the Smith and Wesson into his jacket pocket and scooped up the pile of documents from the piano. He half pulled, half carried Sandra up the short flight of stairs and out of the front door. The lift was still on the third floor. Michael pulled Sandra inside and pushed the button for the ground floor. The house was deserted and silent. Yet it was inconceivable that nobody had heard the shooting. He grabbed Sandra's hand and led her out of the building.

His heart was pumping as they walked out onto the rue Richpin. His first inclination was to run pell-mell down the street and away from Jeaune's apartment, but he had seen enough gangster movies to know that wasn't the right thing to do. 'Walk naturally,' he said, leading Sandra back the way they had come.

'They were going to kill us, weren't they?' Sandra said, finally finding her voice. 'Why? What's it got to do with us? What have we done?'

The rush of adrenalin was gradually subsiding in Michael, and although he felt like stopping to draw breath, he walked steadily on in the direction of La Mouette. 'We've stuck our stupid long noses into something that didn't concern us, that's what we've done. Finn was dumb enough to do the same, and he paid for his interference with his life. This whole business is much more serious than either of us ever realised. We should have understood that after they sent the man to Brussels to recover the documents.' Michael's intuition about the news value of the documents had been more than right. There was undoubtedly a story buried somewhere in the sheaf of paper, but it was problematic now whether he would ever live to tell that story. He looked across at Sandra and realised the enormity of the mistake he had made in forcing her to come along on what was proving to be an extremely dangerous odyssey.

The sound of a siren came from directly behind, but Michael never broke stride.

'Somebody wants very badly to suppress whatever is contained in these papers,' he said, as they reached La Mouette. Crowds were exiting from the gap between the high green fencing that led to the Bois de Bologne. Michael steered Sandra towards the crowd. 'They've already killed, and they've demonstrated that they're willing to continue killing in order to get the papers back.'

'Then give the bloody papers back to them,' Sandra said, as they slotted into the stream of people moving in the direction of the rue du Passy. 'If they want them so badly, then the only way we can save ourselves is to let them have the damn things.'

'It may be too late for that,' Michael said. 'That grey-haired man — what was his name? Tahir? — he knew who we were even before he entered the apartment. He knew my first name and my occupation.'

'Remember he said that you were more beautiful than your picture. I don't remember Jeaune taking any photographs of us. They know who we are, Sandra, and they're busting their ass not only to get those papers back but to get rid of anyone who could put the finger on them.' Michael glanced over his shoulder. There was no sign of the police following them.

'How did whoever wants the documents get to Jeaune?' Sandra asked.

'They didn't.' Michael had been thinking about that very point. 'Jeaune got to them, I guess. We already know that whatever is in these documents is dynamite. It's so explosive that five people as far as we know have already died because of them. Jeaune decided to cut himself a piece of the action. My guess is that he sold us down the river and tried to make some sort of a deal for himself.'

The sun had already set, but the air was still warm and humid. Sandra shivered as she looked around the scene of normalcy of which she was a part. The rue du Passy was exactly as they had left it less than an hour ago. The shops were the same and Parisians and visitors still sipped beers and coffees at the tables of streetside cafés. But something had changed for Sandra Bishop. She had witnessed the death of two more people — perhaps three — one of them killed by the man with whom she was now walking.

'You did it again, didn't you?' Sandra said, looking at him.

'It was either them or us.'

'I realise that.' Sandra slipped her hand through the crook of his arm. 'It's just that you're so cold about it. These past two days I've come to regard you as a warm human being. But in Jeaune's apartment you behaved like a machine.' He did not reply, and after a while she went on. 'Maybe we should go back to Brussels now.'

'I guess not.' Michael liked feeling her so close. 'The police would pick us up straight away, or perhaps whoever's behind this will have somebody waiting for us. We could end up being caught between the devil and the deep blue sea.'

'Then what on earth are we going to do?'

'I don't know,' Michael said.

They continued walking until they reached the Place de Trocadero and the semi-circular building of the Palais de Chaillot.

It was a hot summer's night in Paris, the streets were full of happy laughing people, yet deep inside Michael felt an overwhelming sadness. A part of his brain was telling him that he and Sandra were as good as dead. He hadn't known the men in Jeaune's apartment but he had recognised the type. In business parlance they were 'expediters'. They were the kind of people you called in to settle strikes, not through negotiation but by sending the strikers home with cracked skulls and broken bones. They were the kind of people you passed bad debts to at sixty cents on the dollar and never expected to see the debtor again. Michael and Sandra had become somebody's bad debt, and were now the object of the expediters attention. It wouldn't stop until they had been eliminated.

A photographer moved towards them, his jet black hair sleeked back by some greasy preparation. Sweat ran down his cheeks but he still wore his jacket. Michael's hand moved instinctively to the gun in the pocket of his jacket.

'Vous voulez une photo devant le Palais?' The photographer thrust his face in front of Michael and Sandra.

Michael's hand released the gun as he pushed the man violently aside.

'Con! Salope!' the photographer said, but moved away immediately to harass a group of tourists reclaiming their seats on a coach.

'Nearly a nasty accident,' Michael said, smiling at Sandra. This was the kind of dumb reaction he'd heard lectures on at the military academy. A fight in public was what they needed least at this very moment.

'I never know whether to admire you or to be frightened of your penchant for violence.' Sandra could see that her companion was completely on edge, and could feel a shiver in his arm as she held it. 'What does it feel like?' she asked.

'What does what feel like?'

'Killing somebody. I was watching you. You weren't really fazed. I was so scared that I couldn't even have told anyone my name, but you stayed completely cool. It looks almost as though you enjoyed it.'

He turned to her, his face angry. 'That's a dumb thing to say. I certainly didn't enjoy it. I didn't want to kill the guy in your *cave* or the one just now. I didn't have any alternative.'

'Sorry.' They walked on for a short while in silence. But Sandra could not stop herself from digging a little more deeply, and she then asked, 'Did you kill anyone in the desert?'

Michael had calmed down. 'I don't know. It wasn't that kind of war.' He saw in his mind's eye the carnage that the Legionnaires' fire had wreaked on the Iraqi armour. The desert had been littered with the remains of Arab vehicles, and within some of the torn shells of the tanks could be seen the charred bodies of the soldiers who had been incinerated in them. 'There's very little proximity in modern warfare. You can always tell yourself that the lap-top computers were the real killers. I left Kuwait convinced that I personally hadn't really hurt anyone.' He smiled wryly. 'I guess I always think of myself as a peaceful kind of guy. My "penchant for violence" you said. I guess the violence comes out when I'm threatened, and especially when I'm with someone else who is equally threatened.'

'That photographer just now wasn't threatening us.'

Michael did not respond at first, and Sandra, who had regretted her words as soon as they were spoken, was afraid that she had upset him again. To her relief, after a while he smiled.

'You're right,' he said. 'I guess I ought to go find him and apologise. But he wouldn't understand anyway.' He gave a humourless laugh. 'He just caught me at a bad moment.'

'I'm sorry. I shouldn't have criticised you.' Sandra squeezed his arm in apology.

'Honey', Michael said, 'you can criticise me as much as you like. I got you into this goddamn mess.'

'That's not true either. If anyone got me into it, Finn did.'

'Don't let's argue about it.' He flopped onto one of the benches facing the Avenue Kléber. 'The problem now is that we've got to find out what's in these documents, and we've got to do it somewhere where we can be more or less sure that the people who own them won't be able to find us.'

'That's a tall order.' Sandra sat beside him. Twice during the past few days she had been scared witless, and twice Michael had been there to save her life. She knew that she would have to stay close to him until the whole business was resolved, and she was beginning to realise that the thought did not displease her at all.

For a while they sat without speaking, watching the drivers practising kamikaze patterns on the wide space in front of the Palais.

Suddenly Michael said, 'I think I may have thought of somebody who could help us decipher the documents. One of my father's old friends is Professor of Law at Galway University. He wouldn't be quite as specialised as Jeaune, but he has the advantage that he won't sell us down the river.'

'My faith in academics has been somewhat shattered by Professor Jeaune. Are you sure we can trust him?'

'I'm sure,' Michael said definitely. 'Also we can hide out on the Aran Islands while he's looking at the documents.'

'What islands?'

'It's a group of islands off the coast of Galway. My father and mother were born there and we still keep a house on the big island. I used to spend my vacations there when I was a kid. Patrick Joyce didn't want his spoiled American brats to forget that their father came from nothing.'

'What are we waiting for? Why don't we go back to the car and collect our stuff? We could be at Charles de Gaulle by nine o'clock and we could possibly be on this island sanctuary of yours by tomorrow evening.'

'Hold your horses. The grey-haired guy back at the apartment said something about the Belgian police wanting to interview you. If we leave through Charles de Gaulle or any other international airport, passport control have the nasty habit of typing your particulars into their computers. The Belgian police might already have put out a request to report your whereabouts. So Charles de Gaulle is out of the question.'

'Then how exactly do we get there?'

'We'll head for Cherbourg and get the overnight ferry to Rosslare. If we're lucky we'll make tonight's sailing, and we should be in Ireland sometime tomorrow.'

Sandra stood up and pulled Michael to his feet. 'Let's get back to the car and off to Cherbourg. I want to get to this magical place where people aren't going to be trying to kill us.'

Patrick Tahir sat back in the taxi. His shoulder ached like hell. The bullet had passed through his flesh, leaving a clean wound, and he had stuffed a handkerchief into the puncture so that the flow of blood was now more or less stopped. The taxi driver ignored the rest of the traffic and ploughed straight across the Place de l'Etoile before continuing along the Avenue de Friedland and the boulevard Haussmann. Tahir looked at the elegant streets packed with the early evening crowds. He watched the laughing faces as they streamed along the shop-lined boulevards. Joyce and the woman were somewhere out there, but the question was where. A city the size of Paris could swallow two people completely, though Tahir doubted whether they would remain in the capital. He winced as the pain in his shoulder suddenly increased in intensity. 'Le Sergent' had come to only moments after Michael and Sandra had left the apartment. Pausing only to confirm that Lepape was indeed dead and checking to see whether the documents were still on the piano, he had left the apartment building and had just turned the corner when the sirens began to blare.

Despite his injured shoulder, he had managed to make his way without incident to the Avenue Victor Hugo. Now he was on his way back to the rue du Caire. Lepape's people would help him find a quack who would sew up his shoulder. He had been shot enough times to know that the wound was not dangerous but that if left to its own devices it could very well become so. He cursed under his breath as he replayed the events in the apartment on rue Richpin. That stupid bastard Jeaune had caused just enough of a diversion to give Joyce his chance. But where the hell had the gun come from? The bottom line was that it had been his mistake to underestimate Michael Joyce. He should have learned from Cavelli's death that they were dealing with someone who was either very lucky or very good. Tahir resolved not to make the same mistake again. Another dart of pain shot through his shoulder. Failure wasn't something that Patrick Tahir accepted easily. Somehow he would find a way to organise a rematch with Joyce. Somehow he would manage to recover the documents.

CHAPTER SIX

Jean Claude Blu sat despondently at his desk in the Tour Chemie. Tahir's phone call from Paris had shattered his hopes of remaining chairman of the cartel. He was more sure than ever that the whole chain of events, from Von Schick's discovery that enquires of a delicate nature were being made by one Finn Jorgensen of the European Commission to the latest fiasco in Jeaune's apartment, were being orchestrated by whoever was trying to bring the cartel down. Therefore the so-called journalist Joyce must in reality be an agent of that person. Tahir had found out the hard way that the American wasn't quite the amateur he appeared to be. Blu had been concentrating all his energy on Roger Morley as the traitor, but wondered whether he had allowed his hate to rule his head. He closed his eyes and tried to think which of his colleagues besides Morley could possibly be the traitor. All of their companies were dependent on controlling the market. Perhaps one of the *salopes* had a brain tumour and had gone crazy.

Blu turned on his desk lamp and pulled open the middle drawer of his desk. The light from the lamp shone directly on the box of sleeping pills. What sort of life would he have without the power and prestige of his position? He would be forced out of his office and into the concrete mausoleum his wife had created in the suburbs. There, amid people he scarcely knew, he would wither and die. He picked up the box and examined the twenty or so capsules containing tiny red crystals. He took out one of the capsules and held it up to the light. His eyes travelled to the panel that contained his drinks cabinet. A handful of capsules washed down with a half litre of whiskey would be enough to make the trip to the mausoleum unnecessary. Blu started to laugh. He tried to remember the last time he had wallowed in self-pity. Even in the darkest days of the Indo-China campaign, when it appeared that he would never see La Belle France again, he had not contemplated giving up.

He dropped the capsule he was holding into the box and snapped the cardboard container shut.

As he tossed the box back into the drawer, anger suddenly replaced his earlier self-pity. Somebody had tried to remove him as chairman of the cartel. However, he was still chairman of Chemie de France and would probably retain that position if he could bring about the downfall of the bastard who had intrigued against him. Even if it was his final act, he would nail the *salope*. Newton, Morley, Von Schick, Di Marco or Van Veen. Whichever one of them was responsible for his predicament was going to pay. There were two telephone calls to make. The first was one that Blu had never thought he was going to have to make and it was going to be very painful. The office of chairman of the cartel would have to be passed to Morley. Blu sucked in a deep breath as he thought of the humiliation he was about to suffer. Yet it was a bitter chalice that he could not refuse to accept.

The second call would be to Patrick Tahir. Joyce and his master, whoever that might be, had made a terrible mistake in leaving Tahir alive. One of the principal rules in dealing with wild animals was that if you shoot one you must make sure that you kill it. Joyce hadn't only wounded Tahir in the body. 'Le Sergent's' pride and professionalism had also been wounded. And while the shoulder wound would heal naturally, the wound in Tahir's soul would grow and fester. Such wounds can only be expunged when the person who inflicted the wound no longer exists. Blu had refused Tahir's request to pursue Joyce. However, the chairman of Chemie de France had refused without thinking. Tahir was like a mad dog who scented blood. Why should Blu deny him the opportunity to avenge himself? And if Tahir was around when Joyce's master was finally revealed, so much the better.

Michael and Sandra stood on the after-deck of the *St Killian* and watched the dark shape of the coast of France receding into the distance. The sea was like a black rippling cloak spread out before them. The breeze which had been warm close to the shore now had an ocean chill to it. Sandra felt a shiver running along her spine and moved closer to Michael. She turned to face him and saw that he was looking at her. He lifted his free hand and tilted her chin upwards. Sandra wanted to say no, but the word wouldn't form on her lips. Michael leaned forward and kissed her. The kiss was light, his lips brushing against hers before exerting a delicate pressure.

'Please don't,' she forced the words out as his lips moved away.

'I'm not happy about what has happened, but I can't say that I'm unhappy that we're still together,' Michael said, noticing that tears were forming at the corner of her dark eyes. He took his hand away from her face, but she followed his movement and pressed her cheek into his palm.

'I'm not unhappy that we're still together either.' Sandra kept her cheek pressed into his palm as she spoke. 'But I'm feeling scared and confused, and that's not helping me to sort out other feelings that I might be having.'

'I can understand that.' Her skin felt soft and smooth in his hand. Michael could still feel the taste of her on his lips and he wanted desperately to kiss her again.

Sandra pressed her cheek once more into Michael's palm and then put his hand away. 'It's too soon, Michael,' she said, looking over the stern of the ship at the white trail of water that the ship was leaving in its wake. 'After all that's happened I know I've got to make some changes. Right now you've got a central position in my life. After all, you've already saved my life twice. And, whatever you may say, I'm at least partly responsible for you being in this mess. That isn't a very good basis for trying to sort out my feelings about you. If we ever manage to get back on an even keel, then we'll be able to discuss our future.'

'I wish you weren't so damn logical,' Michael put his arm around her shoulder.

'Not only am I logical,' she said, removing his arm, 'I'm also very hungry.'

'I can take a hint,' Michael said.

The lights were burning brightly in Roger Morley's office at Commonwealth Chemicals. The telephone call from Blu had been one of the high points of Morley's career. It had been ten minutes of pure delight listening to the Frenchman explaining his abject failure. Morley's pleasure at finally acceding to the chairmanship of the cartel was heightened by the knowledge of the pain that the Frenchman must have been suffering on the other end of the line. Blu had been dealt a mortal blow.

'Is this all there is to go on?'

'Yes.' Morley looked across the table at the man he was going to depend on to recover the documents for him. George Patterson had come highly recommended as a man who could be depended on to find solutions to difficult problems. Morley watched as the Scotsman examined the papers that Blu had faxed to his office.

'Looks like you people have made a right royal cock-up of it so far,' Patterson said, throwing the batch of paper onto the table. 'Joyce and Bishop have somehow managed to evade two professionals. Unless they're absolute fools, they know they have documents of great value in their possession, and they're probably running. That means we have to find them again, and when we do, they'll be on their guard.'

'That was under the old management.' The chairman of Commonwealth had taken an instant dislike to his new employee. The man affected an air of superiority which was infuriating. Despite the humid evening, Patterson wore a three-piece suit which should have left him sweating, but didn't. The tall bony Scotsman looked more like an accountant or an academic than a trouble-shooter. A pair of wire-rimmed glasses completed the studious image and gave Patterson's bland angular face an owlish look. However, Morley couldn't fault the man's credentials.

Patterson didn't only look studious. Morley had learned that the trouble-shooter had earned a first class honours degree in Classics at Oxford before joining MI6. Unfortunately for Patterson he had been drawn into the maelstrom of Northern Ireland, and instead of following the official position of playing both ends against the middle, had decided to turn himself into the 'Lone Ranger'. He set up and ran his own little Protestant murder gang to rid the province of the scourge of the IRA. The Patterson gang operated successfully for two years and was responsible for murdering more than a score of IRA suspects.

Such activities sat uneasily with Patterson's superiors and his political masters. It was decided that the episode of the Patterson gang would have to be closed. The murderers were free to return to their home and hearth, where their mouths would have to remain firmly shut. Patterson had turned to servicing the needs of the business community by employing the skills and contacts of his previous profession. Wherever Morley had made inquiries among his peers for a man who could carry out a delicate task, Patterson's name was invariably mentioned.

'I expect you'll rectify the situation.'

'I expect I will,' Patterson said. 'I have a reputation for getting the job done. Do I limit myself to recovering your precious documents?' Patterson emphasised the word 'precious'. 'Or do I have to arrange for the removal of the protagonists as well?'

'I want the documents back and I want the whole affair buried.'

'And I will want fifty thousand pounds.'

'Fifty thousand pounds! You must be mad.'

Patterson started to rise from his chair. 'And you are wasting my time which, as you can see from the level of fee I charge, is very valuable.'

The Scot stood looking down at the chairman of one of Britain's largest companies. He didn't like pomposity, and both Morley and the surroundings of his office reeked of it. Patterson didn't need to be an art expert to see that the impressionist paintings that decorated the office were genuine. He wondered where the shipyard worker's son without so much as an A-Level to his name had developed his taste for art.

'Hold on a minute.' Morley motioned Patterson back into his chair. 'I can agree to your fee on two conditions.'

Patterson stood waiting.

'Firstly, it will be necessary for you to deal personally with this matter. And secondly, the fee will be contingent on success.'

Patterson smiled. 'You should have been told. I always deal personally with business and I always guarantee success.'

'Time is pressing.' Morley shifted his weight in his chair. 'When can you begin?'

'I already have.' Patterson scooped up the files on Bishop and Joyce from the top of the desk where he had placed them. 'You'll hear from me as soon as there's anything to report.'

'How will you find them again?'

'Chances are that they've already started to run. That means that they will use some form of transport. We'll start with the airlines and the credit card companies. If they flew somewhere they're on some airline's computer. If they've used a credit card to purchase a ticket, we'll have them. Providing they haven't changed vehicle, a few phone calls will have the security apparatus looking for them for us. Don't worry, locating them won't be such a problem. It hasn't proved difficult so far. Getting the documents from them and ensuring their silence appears to be the problem.'

Patrick Tahir had taken a room at the 'Méridien' at Port Maillot. Lepape's organisation had gone underground in anticipation of the squeeze that the police would put on his people to find out the details of what happened in the rue Richpin apartment. Gradually the story of the drug buy that went wrong would emerge, and the police hue and cry would die down. Lepape's organisation would gradually reappear under new management. Another link in the chain which Tahir had set up over the past thirty years had been broken with Lepape's death. Very few of the veterans now remained. Tahir could count them on the fingers of one hand, and fifty percent of them had become too infirm to be useful. Tahir winced at the pain that emanated from the tear in his left shoulder. The pain seared through him despite the morphine tablets the quack had provided. The wound had been cleaned and closed, but the nine-millimetre bullet had torn through the muscles and sinews. Tahir lay back and closed his eyes. Like the others in his network, 'Le Sergent' was beginning to feel his age. The lure of his retirement villa in Ceuta was becoming stronger. As soon as he had dealt with Joyce and the woman, he would tell Blu that he had decided to retire. Then he would find himself a young Berber like Farhana and live a life of ease in the sun. Locating Joyce and Bishop was his prime objective, and to accomplish that he would have to squeeze every contact that he and Blu had. The effort of pushing himself up from the bed brought beads of sweat to 'Le Sergent's' forehead. He rooted in his jacket pocket and removed the piece of paper on which he had written the name of Blu's contact in the Deuxième Bureau. By tomorrow morning the police forces of Europe would be on the lookout for Michael Joyce and Sandra Bishop.

Michael sat in the lounge of the *St Killian*, leafing through the pile of documents he had taken from Jeaune's apartment. They still appeared to be written in a language he was quite incapable of understanding. Jeaune's jottings on the margins were equally obscure. The other Joyce siblings with their degrees in law and accountancy would have had a much better chance of deciphering the tables which littered the pages. Calling on the talents of his family was something that had never crossed his mind. Anyway, he doubted if either he or Sandra would be allowed to put their foot on a plane for Boston. Seen in the light of a brilliant July morning when everything in the world seemed beautiful and bright, the huge ferry ploughing peacefully through a calm sea, while above their heads children played on the deck and Muzak poured over the public address system, the events in the basement in Brussels and the apartment in Paris had more than a touch of the unreal. Except that Michael had now killed two men and something told him it wasn't going to stop there. Like Sandra, he felt that some vital connection with his recent past had been broken for him. His co-operation with Richard Fryer and his life as a stringer in Brussels were definitively over. But what of the future? Some famous philosopher had said that one encounters one's fate by trying to avoid it. Maybe Michael had tried so hard to avoid his fate at Joyce Construction that he was actually moving in that direction. The thought didn't bring him much pleasure. Then there was Sandra. Earlier that morning, in the hours of wakefulness as the ship pitched to the movement of the Atlantic waves, he had watched her sleeping face. Whatever future he had, there would have to be a place for Sandra in it.

'You look like a man with very deep and dark thoughts.' Sandra's head appeared suddenly over his shoulder.

'Not so,' Michael lied. 'Trying to make sense of these documents tends to leave me with a feeling of inadequacy.'

'I have the same thing about neurosurgery but I don't let it bother me.'

'You've been keeping this talent for comedy pretty well hidden.'

'I haven't felt much like comedy lately, but who could fail to feel optimistic on such a beautiful day as this? We're still alive, and I suppose that's the largest bonus.' Sandra flopped down on the seat beside him and took the file from his hands. 'You wouldn't think that these pieces of processed wood could cause such havoc.'

'It's not the pieces of processed wood that are causing the problem — it's what's written on them.'

'Thanks for last night,' Sandra said, touching his shoulder.

'Something happened last night?' Michael said, smiling. 'I must be losing all sense of feeling.'

'Don't be silly. You know what I mean. Thanks for not coming on to me after I asked you not to.'

'The difficult I can do easily, but don't count on me to continue doing the impossible indefinitely.'

'You're a very sweet man, Michael Joyce.' Sandra leaned forward and kissed him on the cheek. 'And I'm very glad that we met — although I'd have preferred different circumstances.'

Michael could still feel the imprint of her lips against his cheek. There were many things he wanted to say, but saying them now might only complicate matters.

'What are our plans for today?' Sandra asked.

'My horoscope suggested a sea journey.' Michael put away the papers. He had already decided to abandon any further efforts at deciphering them. 'If we arrive in Rosslare as scheduled by five this evening, we should be in Galway by eight, and we'll connect with Fergus Maguire, my father's friend. Then we can travel to Kilronan tomorrow. In the meantime, I suggest that we benefit from this magnificent spell of good weather by taking a walk around the deck.'

Detective Danny O'Brien sat in the Vauxhall Cavalier perched on the hill above the port of Rosslare in the south-east corner of the Irish Republic. He looked down across the natural harbour with its twin berths lying beyond the series of corrugated sheds that constituted the customs area. There was no sign of movement. On a small knoll to the side of the customs area three semi-nude bodies lay cooking in the hot sunshine. There is an old Gaelic saying, 'Whatever is rare is wonderful'. And sunshine in Ireland was a rare commodity indeed. O'Brien let his eyes wander out to sea. Yachts with gaily coloured sails moved smoothly over the blue waters of the southern Irish Sea. Far out on the horizon he saw the looming shape of a huge ferry. The heat wave had turned the car into an oven, and sweat ran in tiny rivulets down the detective's ample cheeks.

'Why us?' Danny said, looking across to where his partner Liam Kelly lay with the passenger's seat tilted back.

'What?' Kelly said sleepily.

'I said why the fuck did they pick us for this job.' O'Brien's son was playing his first game for the Dublin minor football team and the detective had promised the boy that he would be at the match. That had only been last night. That had been before that bastard of a superintendent had called up and told O'Brien that he was going to be in the county of Wexford the following day and not at Parnell Park watching his son. And to add insult to injury, the bastard hadn't even bothered to apologise.

'Because we're the best,' Kelly said, and smiled.

'So now you're a fucking comedian as well as a copper.' O'Brien could feel the fire rising in his cheeks. Even with both doors open, there was hardly a breath of air in the car. He looked around at the remains of their lunch. The polystyrene box which had contained O'Brien's double cheeseburger sat on the dashboard in front of him. A ball of grease had solidified on the edge of the box and O'Brien thought of what he had consumed one hour earlier. He picked up the can of Coke from the dashboard and raised it to his lips. The liquid tasted warm and sickly sweet.

'The way the super was talking last night, the poor fool we're looking for must be a cross between Billy the Kid and Al Capone.' O'Brien looked over and saw that Kelly wasn't listening. The younger man had a habit of switching off when O'Brien launched into one of his diatribes. Just you wait,

O'Brien thought as his partner swatted a fly that buzzed around his mouth. Kelly had been on the Force and was still eager about catching criminals and gaining promotion. O'Brien wondered how long it would take the silly bastard to catch on. If you wanted to advance in the Force it wasn't just necessary to have your head shoved up your superior's arse, you had to be up there long enough to build a house. O'Brien turned on the radio and tuned in to the RTE sports programme.

'For Christ's sake, turn that thing off,' Kelly said, suddenly coming to life. 'I arrived home this morning after a night of sordid passion intendin' to sleep the day away. It's bad enough to be sittin' in this bleedin' oven without havin' that fuckin' thing blarin' in me ear.'

O'Brien turned the volume down until he could just about hear the voice on the radio.

'Thanks.' Kelly lay back and closed his eyes again.

O'Brien strained to hear the results. The announcer gave the match scores with the deep sonorous bass tone that was his trademark. Finally, he announced the result of the Dublin minor game.

'Yeh!' O'Brien exclaimed when he heard that his son's team had won. At least the boy wouldn't be too annoyed with him. The Special Branch detective looked at his watch. It was half past four. He pulled out the binoculars from the dicky-hole of the car and raised them to his eyes. The *St Killian* would be arriving right on time, and if their man wasn't on it, Kelly and himself could hot-foot it back to Dublin. The next ferry was the seven o'clock from Fishguard. Their relief was due on at six. Some other poor gobshites could continue the search for the Scarlet Pimpernel.

'Don't be on the fucking thing,' O'Brien said under his breath as he scanned the decks of the ship with the powerful glasses. The ferry was now close enough for the detective to pick out individual passengers on the deck.

The two Special Branch detectives sat in silence as the ferry manoeuvred itself into the port. As soon as the docking procedure had been completed and the bow of the ferry opened, O'Brien raised the glasses to concentrate on the cars that were already beginning to pour out of the belly of the huge vessel.

They snaked in a seemingly endless line towards the black corrugated sheds with their red and blue customs channels.

'Fucking hell,' O'Brien exclaimed, as he focused on the blue Peugeot which climbed up the ramp from the ferry to the quayside. He zoomed in on the small licence plate with the red lettering. 'We've got 'em.' He moved the glasses upwards and examined the young couple who occupied the Peugeot.

'Blast 'em anyway.' Kelly punched the leatherette dashboard in front of his seat. 'Why couldn't they have been on the next bloody boat?'

O'Brien watched the small blue car join the line of vehicles that were moving towards the customs sheds.

'Get down there and make bloody sure those idiots in uniform go through that car with a fine tooth comb.' O'Brien picked up the microphone which connected him to Special Branch Headquarters in Dublin, and slumped back in the driver's seat. The arrival of the Peugeot at Rosslare was going to put some anxious buggers out of their misery, but for him and Kelly it was going to be one hell of a long day.

'Welcome to Ireland,' Michael said, looking across at Sandra.

Every item in the car had been removed and was laid on the wooden bench that ran at an angle of forty-five degrees across the blue channel of the customs shed. The rear end of a hefty customs officer stuck out from the inside of the Peugeot, while the legs of another stuck out from underneath the car. Although Michael marked the two men as the kind of people who enjoyed the fact that their draconian powers permitted them to harass the public, he knew that he and Sandra were getting the treatment. This was the type of welcome to the auld sod afforded to known drugs and arms smugglers. Something in the state of Ireland was smelling very bad, but this wasn't the time to frighten Sandra. She was fully convinced that they had managed to evade their pursuers, whereas Michael was almost certain that the contrary was probably the case.

Michael first saw him as he glanced around the hanger-like building. He stood leaning nonchalantly against the office that was set into one of the corners of the customs shed. The man was dressed in a grey cotton tee-shirt and blue jeans and might have remained anonymous if he hadn't shifted his eyes away so rapidly when Michael looked in his direction. Perhaps I'm becoming paranoid, Michael thought, examining the young man. Was it possible that whoever was after them could have reasoned that they would flee to Ireland? Michael watched the young man as he walked away from the roughly constructed office. He thought of the man in the basement in Brussels and the two old men in Paris. The young man slipped around the corner of the shed and was gone from Michael's view.

The fat customs officer withdrew himself from the Peugeot and examined the meagre possessions laid out on the wooden bench. A car passed, and the drunken occupants roared with laughter as they passed the scene of customs officers giving some poor bastard a right going over. They gave Michael the thumbs up. We're all in this thing together. It's us against them. Sure, haven't we got a couple of extra bottles of booze ourselves? It's the luck of the draw, you poor bollocks. Except that much as Michael wanted to believe that it was the luck of the draw, something told him that both he and Sandra had been expected. Tentacles were reaching out from the centre of the web that was controlling the search for them. He might break one tentacle off, but the octopus would simply reach out another and another until it had snared its prey. You can run but you can't hide.

'We're all through here.' The customs man pointed at the clothes that had been spread on the table and started to walk away.

Michael recognised the dulcet tones of west Cork in the man's accent as he moved to gather up the few belongings that Sandra and he possessed.

'Are you quite sure you examined everything?' Sandra called after the customs officer's retreating back. 'You wouldn't like to take the car apart while you're at it?'

'Don't give the man ideas.' Michael took her arm and led her to the passenger seat of the car. 'The law gives these people legal powers way beyond their mental capacity to understand them. It's better not to antagonise them or we may be old and grey and the Peugeot will be a classic car before we leave this sweat-box.'

Michael eased the car forward around the barriers and towards the gaping hole at the far end of the shed. They emerged into the early evening sunlight and turned up the hill and away from the port. As the Peugeot climbed over the top of the hill and the panorama of green fields and blue sky opened before them, Michael felt the excitement grip his stomach just the same way as it had always done ever since the first time he set his eyes on his ancestral home. This familiar feeling always convinced him that there was something inside that complicated creature called man which stored information from the generations before. Somewhere within the body of Michael Joyce was an ancient memory of this land which almost moved him to tears every time he set foot in it. He knew that he had made the right decision in coming here. If he was right and they couldn't escape their fate, then Ireland was the place he would have chosen to die.

'I've got to make a call,' said Michael, pulling up beside the first telephone-box on the road into Wexford.

Sandra sat and watched him through the glass window of the phone-box. The fear of the events in Paris had dissipated and had become something unreal, just as the death of the intruder in Brussels had become unreal by the time they had arrived in Paris. Sometimes she wondered whether she was dreaming. Maybe she would soon wake up and find that whole escapade had been a fantasy, a personal mind-movie directed by a bored brain. She stared again at the man who had saved her life twice already. Was he the kind of man that she would invent for herself in a fantasy? She felt a shiver run down her spine when she realised that Michael Joyce probably was just such a man.

Michael left the phone-box and took his place behind the steering-wheel. 'I got him,' he said, switching on the engine. 'We've to meet him this evening in a small village called Clarinbridge just outside Galway.' The car moved off in the direction of the setting sun. 'You just sit back and enjoy the ride.'

'He either made you or he didn't.' The breeze flowing through the open car window cooled Danny O'Brien's hot face.

'Look.' Kelly's professional feathers had been ruffled by O'Brien's remark. 'I don't know whether the bugger made me or not. What I do know is that he gave me one hell of a long look back there in the shed.'

179

The two Special Branch detectives were a hundred and fifty metres behind the Peugeot as it made its way inland towards the town of Enniscorthy. O'Brien had received the order he didn't want but knew that he would inevitably get. They were to stay with the target. It was useless to point out that they had already been twelve hours on duty and that if the Peugeot was heading for Donegal or any part of Northern Ireland then they would be in for a seven to eight-hour drive. O'Brien cursed the unknown man and woman in the car ahead of them.

'You didn't happen to recognise either of them?' O'Brien asked.

'No.' Kelly sat back and relaxed. He cursed himself for telling O'Brien about being made. 'I haven't been through the IRA Hall of Fame for some time, but neither of them rang a bell. The bloke looked like a Paddy, but you can never bloody tell these days. Terrorists have given up looking like gurriers just so we can spot them a mile away.'

Ain't that the truth, O'Brien thought, staring at the two figures in the car in front of them. It was useless to speculate. It was his job to keep a tail on them and report back. They didn't pay him enough to think.

They passed through the market town of Enniscorthy with the Peugeot continuing to head north-west. O'Brien contemplated a trip to Donegal with trepidation.

The sky was a blaze of orange and red light as Michael steered the Peugeot out of Enniscorthy and on towards Carlow. He stared out at the bare fields and his nostrils twitched as the long-remembered smell of burning grass assailed him. It was strange that one of his earliest childhood memories was of travelling with his family from Galway city into Connemara, the hills ablaze with fires in the darkness of the night as the farmers burned the summer grass before the onset of winter. An occasional glance in the rear mirror of the Peugeot was enough to convince him that they were being followed. The grey car stayed just far enough behind them to keep contact, but near enough not to lose them. It was over. There was no possible chance of escape. For someone to have picked them up so quickly implied immense resources and influence far beyond anything that Michael or Sandra could conceive. They had been hooked, and it was now simply a matter of time before whoever wanted those damn papers reeled them in. Michael looked out on the brilliant summer's evening. Somewhere somebody was conspiring to take away this pleasure from him. Beside him in the passenger seat, Sandra sat staring out at the rolling countryside of County Carlow. The two plastic bags containing the copies of the documents lay in the boot of the Peugeot, the secret they contained remaining hidden. It was going to be a race against time. Michael knew that he had already been on the receiving end of two strokes of luck, and to expect more would be foolhardy. Even if Fergus Maguire managed to discover why those damn papers were so important, there was still no guarantee that their pursuers would immediately quit the chase. The kind of men that had been sent after them didn't just pack up and leave without seeing the job through. And there was Sandra. A beautiful woman with a dead lover in her recent past and an uncertain future that could lead to oblivion. Michael felt a need for her which was beginning to outweigh his scruples at taking advantage of her confusion.

George Patterson sipped a glass of malt whiskey and watched Humphrey Bogart hand Peter Lorre the package that every person living in the developed world knew did not contain the Maltese Falcon. The Scotsman loved the old black and white movies from the forties and fifties. He savoured the smooth taste of the golden Speyside liquid as he watched Bogart fox the baddies for the thousandth time. To either side of the 70cm television, the shelves were stuffed with videos of classic films. Patterson felt the glow of the whiskey spreading through his chest as he watched the closing minutes of the film he loved most of all. He could have said all of the lines himself, but he had too much reverence for the delivery of the masters to spoil even one second of the classic film. Sidney Greenstreet had just pulled a gun on Bogart when the phone started to ring. Patterson pushed the button on the remote control and the video made a whirring sound before coming to a stop. The picture of Greenstreet and Bogart was frozen on the television screen, a grainy grey image from the past.

Patterson lifted the phone and listened. He was a man of few words, so that when he did speak people listened. The voice on the other end of the phone had the tone that Patterson despised. Nobody spoke like that from birth. Patterson listened as the voice on the other end of the line droned on. He hadn't expected his ex-colleagues to produce the goods so quickly. The Service had been decimated since the end of the Cold War, but luckily for him that there were still a few hardy souls on the pay-roll who believed that what he had done in Northern Ireland had ultimately been in Britain's interest. Those hardy souls were the supplement to the meagre pension Her Majesty's Government deposited each month in the local branch of the Natwest Bank.

'Thank you.' Patterson emphasised his Scottish burr, hoping that the yuppie on the other end of the phone might be aggravated. 'I'll be travelling early tomorrow morning, so perhaps you could leave a message for me at Buswell's Hotel in Molesworth Street in Dublin concerning the final destination.'

On the screen in front of Patterson the images of Bogey and Greenstreet shimmered. Sitting in Paris, Joyce and the woman had virtually the whole of Europe to choose from. They could easily have run for Spain or Italy, and Switzerland, Holland and Germany were within easy reach. They could even have run to Bishop's home on the north coast of Wales. It was ironic that with such a wealth of choice, Joyce and the woman had chosen Ireland. After he had left the Service, the Scotsman had sworn that he would never be seen near that accursed island. But fate was deciding otherwise. He flicked a switch on the remote control and the image disappeared from the screen. Bogart and Greenstreet would have to wait for another night to complete their duel. Patterson moved back to his chair and picked up the crystal tumbler containing the remnants of his malt.

Tomorrow morning he would take the early shuttle to Belfast. His contacts in the UDA would be only too happy to provide him with a clean weapon. One good favour deserves another, and he had certainly done enough favours for the clandestine Protestant groups to warrant a lifetime of returns. As soon as he had picked up the gun he would head south by train. There was little or nothing in the way of customs checks at the Dublin train terminal at Connolly Station, and Patterson would be doing nothing to advertise his presence.

Patrick Tahir woke out of a sleep that had been constantly interrupted by the ache from his damaged shoulder. The phone by his bedside whirred discreetly rather than buzzing or ringing. 'Le Sergent' raised himself up on his right arm and pushed himself towards the telephone. As he picked up the instrument he saw his image in the mirror on the wall across from the bed. The white-faced old man who stared back at him from the polished glass convinced him that it was indeed time for him to make the move to the villa in Ceuta.

'Oui,' Tahir snapped angrily into the phone. His shoulder ached as he settled himself on the bed. He could almost feel the individual sinews and muscles seeking to repair the tears that the parabellum slug had caused.

'C'est moi,' the man on the other end of the line said, and Tahir instantly recognised the voice of Blu's contact within the Deuxième Bureau.

'Le Peugeot est arrivé en Irlande,' the man from the Deuxième Bureau said.

'Où en Irlande?' Tahir asked, picking up the two sheets that Gnechte had provided on Joyce's background.

'Pour le moment leur destination est inconnu. Ils voyagent.'

So Joyce and the woman were still on the move. It was just like roulette, Tahir thought, round and round the wheel it goes and where it stops nobody knows. Well, soon enough Mr Joyce and his charming companion would have to stop, and when they did, Patrick Tahir would catch up with them.

'Demain je serai à Dublin.' Blu's Lear was still sitting on the tarmac at Charles de Gaulle awaiting instructions. Tahir would order take-off for first light.

Blu's documents were no longer the motive for continuing the chase. Tahir was going to find and kill Joyce for himself, not for Blu. Joyce had avoided his fate in Jeaune's apartment, and in so doing had transgressed a basic law of nature. Nobody escaped Patrick Tahir, and Michael Joyce was going to be no exception. And he would kill the woman too.

A line of red light streaked the evening sky as Michael drove north-west through Portlaoise and on towards Athlone. The soft gold-red light illuminated the scorched fields and enhanced the normally drab market towns through which they passed. Michael had given up glancing in the rear mirror. The Vauxhall was still tagging along somewhere behind them. Outrunning their pursuers in the tiny Peugeot was out of the question, but at the same time it would be stupid to lead them directly to Fergus Maguire. The only possibility that Michael and Sandra had of staying alive was to be in a position to bargain, and for the present their ignorance of what the documents contained gave them little or no strength in that direction. It would take them a half an hour to reach Athlone and then a further hour to reach Maguire in Clarinbridge. Michael would have to come up with something, but his mind was devoid of ideas. He felt like a rat trapped in a maze. No matter where he moved their pursuer would manage to re-establish contact with them.

Sandra watched the flat lands of the centre of Ireland flash by. It could very easily have been her native Wales. Small slate-roofed farmhouses dotted the yellow-green landscape, giving the impression of a country almost devoid of people. Why shouldn't it be the same as Wales? Her home lay a short boat journey across the Irish Sea. She was as Celtic as her Irish cousins. Perhaps this common heritage was the reason for her growing affinity for the man at her side. They had known each other for four short days, but in that time they had spent almost every waking minute together. A plan was forming in her mind. Brussels and Finn Jorgensen were the past. She had come to realise that both her ex-lover and her job with the Commission had already been consigned to history in her mind. Neither had worked out the way she had wanted and so she had to be mature enough to walk away and start again. The future was uncertain and she didn't know yet whether it contained Michael. She only knew that the thought of not being with him caused her considerable sadness. Her feelings about the man who had entered her life with such force were beginning to crystalise.

'How much longer?' Sandra asked.

'Something over an hour.' A short enough time to develop a plan for losing their shadows, Michael thought. When the

Vauxhall had got close Michael had noticed that there were two occupants. Who exactly were they? The young olive-skinned man who had murdered Finn in Pamplona and had tried to murder Sandra and himself in Brussels had been a trained killer. So were the two old men in Jeaune's apartment. It was therefore safe, and prudent, to assume that the men in the car were the same kind of individuals.

'I might take a short detour into Galway city,' Michael said, noticing a sign which indicated that they were now thirty kilometres from Athlone and the River Shannon.

'I was the tour guide in Paris. Here I have to place myself in your capable hands. If you say that we detour to Galway, then that's what we do.'

Michael stared ahead at the sweep of the ring-road that would take them around Athlone, avoiding the narrow traffic-choked streets. His eyes swung in an involuntary movement to the mirror in time to see the Vauxhall enter the short motorway system behind him. Away to his left the soft evening light bathed the town of Athlone in an orange hue. The River Shannon rolled majestically through the centre of the small market town, making its timeless passage towards the Atlantic Ocean. It was a sight that would have done credit to the impressionist section at the Louvre. On such a beautiful evening and in such a place, it was bloody wonderful to be alive. The question that bothered Michael was how were they going to stay that way.

'I know it's a bit premature but I think that I could get to like this country,' Sandra said, as they exited from the eight kilometres of motorway system west of the Shannon.

'You're right. You are being premature. The Ireland that you're seeing right now is a rare sight. Normally you can't see the town of Athlone for the rain and gales. If you can love Ireland in the middle of winter when the rain and the cold and the wind forces you into the corner of some pub with a roaring fire, then you'll adore it on a day like today.'

'You know, it's amazing, but sometimes my mind tries to convince me that we're on a holiday. The events in Brussels and Paris seem like bad dreams that you wake up from to find yourself wandering around the Château de Versailles or in a Bateau Mouche on the Seine.'

'Or travelling through the heartland of Ireland,' Michael added.

'I've decided that I definitely don't want to pick up the pieces of my life in Brussels,' Sandra said, as they passed through a section of road where large evergreens shaded the tarmac surface.

'I thought the motto of the Commission staff was "once a *fonctionnaire*, always a *fonctionnaire*".'

'Oh, I have no doubt that there will be hundreds of applicants for my post as soon as I vacate it, and quite honestly I hope whoever gets it finds great happiness. I honestly do. But it's finished for me.'

'You know what they say "act in haste, repent at leisure". Maybe you should give yourself a few months to let the trauma subside and then decide what to do.' Michael castigated himself for talking such shit. They didn't have the prospect of months ahead of them. Statistically speaking, their luck had run out long ago. It was they who should have died in the basement in Square Marguérite and in the duplex in Paris. Somehow they had avoided their fate, but a person was only entitled to so much luck in one lifetime. The men in the car a hundred metres behind them represented their future.

'Leaving Brussels has nothing to do with Finn or with what's happening now. Maybe this whole business has helped me to crystalise thoughts that I was trying to suppress. It's easy to roll along in a comfortable existence. Nice car, nice flat, nice boyfriend. You can ignore the plastic people that surround you and convince yourself that you're living in the real world, but it's as false as the "Donna Reed Show" or Bill Cosby and his happy family. Perhaps my recent contact with the real world has been sufficient to convince me that there's more to life than the office/home routine.'

'Give yourself a break. Most people would have wilted under the kind of pressure that you've been exposed to. An ordinary person could easily have been unhinged by the trauma of Finn's death. The attempted murders were the kind of icing on that particular cake that would have had even the mentally strong reaching for either the whiskey or the Valium bottle.'

'Maybe,' Sandra said simply, and continued to look out the side window at the receding countryside.

Light was failing as they passed through the east Galway towns of Ballinasloe and Loughrea. There was a subtle change in the scenery as the hedges that separated the green fields gave way to the stone walls that typified the landscape of the western coast of Europe. Just visible in the growing gloom, great chunks of granite dotted the middle of fields, cold grey stones deposited by the retreating icepack like unwanted children.

By the time they had reached the T-junction in the village of Oranmore, Michael still had not come up with a definite plan for shaking his pursuers. The left-hand road led to Clarinbridge and Fergus Maguire. Leading the occupants of the Vauxhall there was out of the question. Michael turned right towards Galway city and away from his rendezvous with Maguire.

Detective Danny O'Brien was bushed. He had been on the job for sixteen hours already. Galway was fifteen kilometres down the road, and if they continued their progression westwards there was only the Atlantic Ocean as the ultimate destination.

For Jesus, sake, stop, O'Brien thought, feeling the cramp biting at his right leg. Why couldn't some other team have taken over the pursuit? The answer was simple — money. Getting some other poor buggers out on the road would probably cost fifty quid more. O'Brien brought the Vauxhall a little closer as they began to enter the outskirts of Galway. Sticking to the Peugeot had been child's play on the wide open road, but the narrow streets of Galway would present a totally different situation. O'Brien was twenty metres behind when the Peugeot swung left on the outskirts of the city.

Michael travelled along the narrow road that led to the dock area of the city. Somehow he had to get a lead of a few minutes on the car behind him. It was nearing ten o'clock and Maguire wasn't going to wait forever. The Peugeot skirted the docks and turned onto the road that ran parallel to the wide expanse of the River Corrib on its path through the centre of Galway. Michael eased the car into a parking lot which bordered the banks of the quietly flowing water.

'Why are we stopping?' Sandra asked, as the Peugeot came to a halt facing the river's waters, which looked dark and threatening in the evening gloom.

'There's something I have to do before we get to Clarinbridge. Wait here.' Michael climbed out of the car before Sandra could respond.

The Vauxhall pulled into the parking lot and stopped twenty metres away from the Peugeot. Danny O'Brien watched as the driver got out of the car and began walking along the bank of the river, heading away from the city.

'Liam,' O'Brien said, killing the engine, 'our friend is going walkabout. Why don't you see what he's up to?'

'He's probably lookin' for somewhere to have a crap.' Kelly felt an unwelcome movement in his own bowels. 'The bastard must have a bladder made out of one of them Yak skins.' The young policeman opened the passenger-side door and pushed himself reluctantly into the evening air, which was still balmy from the heat of the day.

Michael sucked in breaths of the salt air as he made his way downriver towards the sea. This barren stretch of land was where his ancestors had landed their sailing boats and traded with the Spanish and French merchants who had plied the wine and brandy trade along the west coast of Ireland. To the left stood the symbol of the city, the Spanish Arch, a moulding pile of masonry which only recently had been the object of a belated restoration effort by the city fathers. Michael stopped, bent to pick up a stone and skipped it across the smoothly running water as he had done when he had been a child. The young man he had noticed in the customs shed in Rosslare had stopped thirty metres along the bank and stood staring into the river. OK, Michael thought, let's get this over. He moved quickly away from the river, heading for the Spanish Arch. As a child he had wandered those narrow streets while his father had sat in a dockside pub regaling his companions with tall tales and true of the fabulous land to the west. It was a scene of cobbled streets and dilapidated deserted warehouses that could have been transposed from any northern European port.

Michael turned into Quay Street. Run-down brick buildings lined the narrow cobbled artery. The half light of the evening disappeared almost completely between the three-storey buildings, leaving dark shadows where the tight alleys cut between the ancient brick warehouses. Michael slipped quietly into the nearest alley and stepped into the shadows. He waited for the tell-tale noise of feet on cobbled stones. The words of the Legionnaires unarmed combat instructor began to run through his brain, as his ears registered the first sound of pursuing feet. The small Vietnamese corporal was a proponent of the substance rather than the form of the martial arts. The object of the exercise was to immobilise the enemy. The position of the feet and the hands were vital to the main purpose of unleashing a blow. Feet began to scurry, indicating that the pursuer knew his quarry was no longer in sight. As the young man in jeans raced past Michael's position, the American stepped out and launched a chop at the rear of the man's neck. The position of Michael's hand was not absolutely correct and he hadn't had time to worry about the orientation of his feet, but the young jean-clad man fell pole-axed to the ground. Michael silently thanked the little Vietnamese instructor. Quickly he bent over the prone body and ran his hands along the outside of the pockets. His pursuer didn't appear to have a weapon, but Michael could feel a small hard rectangular object in the right-hand pocket of his jeans. He pulled out a small leather wallet and flipped it open. The sight of Detective Constable Liam Kelly's warrant card staring at him from the middle of the wallet shook Michael. Toughs could be hired by the hundred kilos in every town and city on earth, but it took a certain kind of juice to swing the forces of law and order behind you. The desperation Michael had been feeling about their situation returned, magnified by a factor of a hundred. They were dead. If whoever was behind the pursuit could mobilise local police forces in the search for them, then it was only a matter of time before the net closed on them. Michael replaced the wallet in the young police detective's pocket and began moving back towards the car.

Danny O'Brien watched the young man approaching along the bank of the river and looked beyond him for the familiar figure of Liam Kelly. There was no sign of the young bugger. O'Brien watched as the dark-haired man made his way to the Peugeot. Perhaps Kelly had stopped to relieve himself. If so, O'Brien would have the bastard's skin. He heard the Peugeot's engine burst into life and instinctively turned the ignition key in the Vauxhall. 'Come on, you silly bugger,' he said under his breath, as he watched the Peugeot move along the river bank and past his position. The detective slipped the car into gear and was preparing to follow the Peugeot when Kelly appeared from behind the Spanish Arch. 'Hurry up,' O'Brien said, and glanced quickly over his shoulder in time to see the Peugeot disappearing around the first corner.

Michael accelerated the Peugeot into the narrow streets that surrounded the dock area. He turned sharply left and then almost immediately right.

'That break has certainly put some pep in your step,' Sandra said, bracing herself against the right-hand door. 'Either that or you're in training for next year's Monte Carlo Rally.'

'I just decided to see what this little baby is capable of,' Michael lied, and glanced into the rear mirror. There was no sign of the Vauxhall.

'You do have insurance, don't you?' Sandra asked.

'I was hoping that you weren't going to ask me that question.' Michael wheeled the Peugeot into a sharp left-hand turn, and accelerated away in the direction of the road on which they had entered Galway. He was on his way back towards Dublin, but he would branch off at Oranmore to make his rendezvous with Fergus Maguire.

'At least you can drive,' Sandra said, as she righted herself in the passenger seat.

Danny O'Brien's Vauxhall turned the first corner on two wheels.

'You stupid young bastard,' O'Brien said, as he surveyed the empty street before them. There were two narrow streets on the left-hand side and two more on the right. The area into which the Peugeot had turned was like a rabbit warren. O'Brien accelerated ahead and turned down the first street on the right.

'The fucker hit me with some kind of martial arts blow.' Kelly rubbed at the tender spot behind his ear where a bump had already risen. 'I went out like a bloody light.'

'Do tell,' O'Brien said, surveying another empty street. The superintendent in Dublin would flay them alive for this. 'You'd better get on the horn and report that we lost them in Galway city. My guess is that they'll probably continue west, but for Christ's sake don't say that on the radio. The way our luck is running they'll probably be heading in the opposite direction.'

'These are not exactly in my line of business.' Fergus Maguire put the papers he had been examining into the plastic bag and laid them on the bench beside him. 'But then again, I'm in no condition at the moment to decide what is and what is not my line of business.' He picked up a pint glass of Guinness and drank a quarter of the contents in one mouthful.

'But you can decipher what they relate to?' Michael asked hopefully.

'As soon as the fuzz in my brain clears I suppose I'll be able to give you at least an educated guess.' Fergus Maguire wouldn't have believed a word of the story that he had heard from anyone but Michael Joyce. While Patrick Joyce had been known to stretch the truth somewhat, speaking normally with what the Indians used to call a forked tongue, that particular trait was totally absent from the youngest Joyce. If Michael Joyce said that he was being pursued by a gang of murderers intent on putting him and his beautiful companion six feet under, then Fergus Maguire had no doubt whatsoever that, however improbable the story, it was absolutely true.

They were sitting in the back snug at Willie Moran's pub outside the village of Clarinbridge.

'We don't have much time.' Michael thought of the warrant card in the pocket of the man he had pole-axed in Galway. With the police on their side it wouldn't be long before whoever was after them would pick up their trail.

'For Christ's sake, Michael, you've only just given me the papers. Give me at least one day to have a good look at them. I'll start on the blasted things first thing tomorrow morning.'

'Jeaune made some notes which I couldn't make head or tail of but which might speed up the work a little.' Michael was oscillating between bouts of desperation, in which he felt that no matter what they did there was no way that they would be allowed to survive, interspersed with limited optimism that if, by some marvellous fluke, they discovered what dark secret lay hidden in the pages in the plastic bag, then they might just possibly escape with their skins. Sandra looked radiant in the half light of the snug. Here, surrounded with the trappings of civilisation, good food, good drink and good company, it was easy to forget that they were running for their lives.

'You know I'll do my best, Michael.' The old professor slurred his words as he put his arm around Michael's shoulder. 'I'd do anything I could for you, and not just because of my friendship with your father. Behind it all you're really the best of them. Your grandfather was no mean judge of character and he often said that you'd make a fine man. I think he was probably very right in that assessment.'

'I'm sorry, Fergus.' Michael laid his hand on the arm of his father's friend. 'This bloody business has me on edge. I know you'll do your best.'

'Count on it, Michael.' Fergus nodded at Michael's travelling companion who was demolishing the remains of what had once been a plate of smoked salmon and crab. 'Your friend is what we call in this region a "good grubber".'

The minute Fergus Maguire had met Sandra he had taken an instant liking to the girl. She was attractive and bright and as far as he could tell she had that very rare quality of genuineness. Over a lifetime in academia, Maguire had developed what he liked to call an 'inbuilt bull-shit detector'. 'I think the "big fella" is going to like her,' Fergus said, winking at Michael and taking a noisy slug from his Guinness.

'And who might I ask is the "big fella"?' Sandra was thinking that if Michael's friend was an example of the kind of person they would meet in Ireland, she would have to revise her plan to head 'down-under'. Fergus Maguire had that quality which is normally called impish. He was almost entirely bald except for a few strands of grey hair which hung over the back of his neck like the flap of a kepi. The lack of hair on his head was compensated by the two tufts of curly light brown hair that adorned his cheeks. On some people the tufts of hair would have appeared as an affectation, but on Fergus Maguire they seemed as naturally present as his two eyes or his nose. Sandra wondered whether the hair had been present at Fergus's birth. The Galway University professor was small, perhaps 170 centimetres, and rotund. Sandra wouldn't have been at all surprised to find him dressed in green and sitting at the foot of a rainbow guarding a crock of gold.

'You've already heard me speak of one Patrick Joyce,' Michael said, smiling. 'Well, he's quite a large man physically, so the people on the islands naturally call him the "big fella".'

'Thank you, Fergus, for what I must assume to be a compliment,' Sandra said.

'It is indeed, my darlin'. Michael's father has always had a fine eye for the ladies and I'm sure it's a trait that can be found in all the Joyce men.'

The door opened and the barman stuck his head into the room. 'Are ye goin' home at all tonight, folks?' the young man said, smiling. 'The boss wants to close up.'

Maguire gathered up the empty glasses from the table and handed them to the barman. 'You can tell the boss to send us in three more pints of stout and then we'll be on our way.'

'You'll have his licence taken away,' the young man said, taking the glasses.

'I sincerely doubt that,' Maguire said. 'The guards know well enough to stay away from this place. Be a good man now and bring the drinks.'

The barman disappeared, shaking his head.

'I'd say that you've certainly kissed the Blarney Stone,' Sandra said, laughing.

'That's only for foreigners anyway,' Fergus said. 'Now what sort of arrangement have you made for tonight?'

'I was thinking that maybe we could get a couple of rooms in Galway,' Michael said. 'Then tomorrow morning we could catch an early ferry to Aran.'

'I'm quite sure that you could get a room somewhere in Galway,' Fergus said, as the door opened and the barman deposited three creamy pints of Guinness on the wooden table. 'You're a sound man, Peter.' Fergus distributed the pint glasses as Michael handed the barman a ten pound note. 'Keep the change,' Fergus said to the barman's retreating back.

'You're very *flathúlach* with my money.' Michael picked up his glass and took a swallow.

'What's *flathúlach*?' Sandra asked, following Michael's lead.

'Generous, darlin'.' Maguire toasted Michael and Sandra. '*Sláinte mhaith.*' He took a long swallow from his glass, the creamy head of the black liquid hanging on his upper lip like an old man's moustache.

'Back to your problem,' Fergus said, setting the glass down reverentially on the table. 'Why the hell should you go looking for a room in Galway when I've got a perfectly good empty cottage in Baile na hAbhainn? The two of you can spend the night there and it's only a stone's throw into Rossaveal tomorrow to pick up the ferry.' Maguire removed a key from his jacket pocket and handed it to Michael.

'That sounds wonderful,' Sandra said, before Michael could raise an objection.

'The girl is far too good for you,' Fergus said, smiling at Sandra.

'It's not that way at all,' Michael started to say.

'Enough said.' Fergus handed Michael his glass. 'A wink is as good as a nod to a blind man. Finish up your drinks and get on the road.'

The stars adorned the black Connemara sky as the Peugeot sped westwards past the city of Galway and continued along the coast road through the village of Spiddle. Sandra sat quietly looking into the dark countryside. It was an unfamiliar sight which should have felt threatening. But it didn't. Being with Michael made her feel safe. There was something real about her companion which had been missing in all the Euro-phonies among whom she had lived in Brussels. Michael was earnest and up-front in comparison to some of the Eurocrats who felt they were vital blocks in the edifice of the new Europe. She looked across in the darkness at his face. The sculpted features were similar to those that stared out from sixteenth-century engravings of Pizarro's Conquistadores. Oh Christ, Sandra thought, as she stared across the dark interior of the car, I'm falling for this sod. Just two weeks ago her future had seemed mapped out for her, and now there was only uncertainty and the possibility of a potentially disastrous relationship. What had she and Michael in common? She had no idea what music he liked or whether, like her, he preferred the movies to watching television. What sports did he play? It was like looking at a complicated painting from a distance. She could see the big picture — the involuntary involvement in the Gulf War, the family back in Boston and the aspiration to be a Pulitzer Prize winner. But the detail had been glossed over. She would have to find out a lot more about this sweet but deadly man before she entrusted herself totally to him.

Michael looked into the driving mirror but saw no signs of the telltale lights which would indicate the presence of a car behind them. He was in no doubt that they had shaken off their pursuers, but he was also certain that the men seeking them would soon pick up the trail. At least the documents were now in Fergus's hands, and nobody knew that except Sandra and himself. The tarmac road stretched ahead hugging the rugged coastline. Michael had travelled this road thousands of times, but each time he saw the jutting majesty of the coastline of County Clare across the bay, he felt he was home. Out there in the darkness, beyond the stone walls and the barren fields, three mounds of rocky land rose out of the sea, shaped like the humped backs of whales.

Fergus's cottage lay at the tip of a small inlet sheltered from the Atlantic by the headland which formed Rossaveal Bay. Michael parked the Peugeot on the gravel patch directly in front of the cottage. An almost full moon cast a silver light on the whitewashed walls and the neatly thatched roof.

'Home, for tonight at least,' Michael said, as he cut the engines.

Sandra looked at the tiny building bathed in the soft moonlight. 'It's like something out of a picture postcard.'

'A damn expensive picture postcard.'

'Some things never change,' he said, as he opened the door of the cottage. He wouldn't attempt to count the number of times he had accompanied Fergus and his father to late-night drinking sessions here. Within the cottage's white walls he had learned that the man with the ham-sized hands who had built Joyce Construction could also tease a delicate melody from the tiny buttons of a concertina. In America Patrick Joyce was a businessman, an imitation WASP vying with the descendants of the Pilgrim Fathers for his share of the cake. In Ireland Michael had learned that his father was a dreamer, a poet and a musician. Two very separate lives and one person.

Michael flicked on the light and stepped back to allow Sandra to enter.

They stood together in the doorway. Michael put his hands on her shoulders and she turned to face him. He bent and kissed her. Their kiss held all the pent-up passion of the few days they had spent together. Michael took her hand and began to lead her towards a door in the corner of the room.

'No, please, Michael.' Sandra pulled away from him.

'For God's sake, Sandra,' Michael said, his frustration evident in his expression. 'I love you and I want to make love to you.'

'And I want you to make love to me,' Sandra said, holding on to his hand. 'But not yet.' She moved towards him and hugged him. 'Oh God, I'm being such a bitch. Please be patient with me. I'm so damned confused that I don't know which side is up.'

'It's OK.' Michael brushed a black curl off her cheek and kissed her where it had been. 'That door leads to one bedroom, and that door,' Michael nodded at the far side of the livingroom, 'leads to the other.'

Sandra smiled. 'You know, the Scots put a bolster between betrothed couples. It's a pity the Irish don't have the same tradition.'

'That can be arranged. Even if I have to scour the cottage for a bolster.'

'I don't think that a bolster would be sufficient to stop you. The tradition says a lot for the self-restraint of the Scots.'

Michael crossed the room to a large wooden chest that stood in one corner. He opened the heavy lid and produced two duvets and a pair of sheets.

'No bolsters, but Fergus said this stuff is both clean and dry.' He tossed a sheet and a duvet to Sandra. 'See you in the morning.'

Sandra caught the bed linen and moved towards Michael. 'Thank you for understanding.' She kissed him quickly on the lips. 'Sleep well.'

'That won't be easy,' Michael said, as he watched her slip the latch on the bedroom door.

CHAPTER SEVEN

'We can't take the car?' Sandra said, as Michael stuffed the few clothes he possessed into a canvas bag he had purloined from the cottage.

'God damn it, I told you that the *Prince of Aran* was a ferry. If it had been a car ferry I would have said so.' Michael knew that his anger was unwarranted, and realised that he was being very childish. The disappointment of the previous night still hurt. He ached to possess this woman, but every time he felt she was within reach she pulled back, leaving him feeling empty and frustrated.

So that's the way it was, Sandra thought. Michael Joyce was the same as every other man she'd known. He wanted his way and when he didn't get it he behaved like a petulant child. She had been right to hold fire with him. All that kindness and consideration had probably just been his particular wrinkle to get into her pants.

Although it was scarcely ten o'clock, a bright orange sun was already peering over the eastern horizon from a cloudless blue sky. Even the Atlantic Ocean was playing its part in the summer scene, the small swell being the only disturbance on the otherwise flat surface of the dark blue waters. Michael looked westward at the three black humps that appeared to float on the still sea. The Aran Islands seemed close enough to touch. It was part of local tradition that when the islands appeared near, the weather was going to be fine.

The small harbour was beginning to bustle. Three cars, two with French licence plates and one from Germany, had pulled in directly behind Sandra's Peugeot, and a battered red coach bearing the legend 'Prince of Aran' on the side was disgorging twenty or so young rucksacked passengers. At the end of the quay the 'Prince', a red-painted rusting hull, sat bobbing gently.

Michael looked carefully at the group of young people as they descended from the bus. Just because they had given the cops the slip in Galway didn't mean that whoever was after them had forgotten them. The men in Jeaune's apartment had looked like a pair of refugees from a pensioner's day outing. Perhaps the next lot of assassins would look like college students and carry rucksacks on their back. Who could tell? Michael watched the earnest young faces, searching for the tell-tale sign that would announce a potential killer.

'See somebody you recognise?' Sandra asked.

'What?'

'You're staring so hard at those kids that I thought you might have recognised one of them.' Sandra was sad that the rapport of the past few days seemed to have been broken.

'No,' Michael said simply. Sandra's question made him realise what a bloody fool he was being. The guy he'd killed in Brussels and the old men in Paris had been professional murderers. Such people didn't go around advertising their calling like encyclopaedia salesmen. There could very well be a killer in the group now gathered beside the barred gangway of the *Prince of Aran*, but there was no way in heaven or earth that he was going to be able to divine the mind from the sunburned faces.

A Ford Capri with panels of various colours roared along the quay and stopped directly across from the small ferry. Two men dressed in tee-shirts and jeans and wearing gumboots climbed out of the back seat and made their way to the gangway. The driver's head emerged slowly from the car and looked with disdain at the thirty or so passengers gathered at the foot of the gangway. The body that followed the head of tousled black-grey hair was thin and lanky. Tom Fitzgerald, the captain and owner of the *Prince of Aran*, stretched his arms out in front of him and surveyed the rest of the quay. His eyes fell on Michael and Sandra.

'Michael, you old reprobate.' The glint in Fitzgerald's eye affirmed his pleasure at seeing the young American.

Michael just had time to say to Sandra, 'Meet Tom Fitzgerald, the captain of the "Prince" ', before being grabbed in a bear hug.

'And who is this wonderful-looking woman?' Fitzgerald leered over Michael's shoulder.

Sandra found herself looking directly into the darkest eyes she had ever seen. The eyes were set into a chiselled face the colour of seasoned mahogany. If there was a Mrs Fitzgerald, then the poor woman's heart had definitely been broken several times.

'This is Sandra Bishop,' Michael said, extracting himself from Fitzgerald's grip.

'You're a wonder to behold, Miss Bishop.' Fitzgerald lifted up Sandra's hand and kissed it. 'I hope your stay with us is going to be long and pleasant.'

Sandra smiled. The words were uttered as a simple greeting, but somehow Fitzgerald managed to convey a sexual overtone.

'Nice to meet you, Mr Fitzgerald,' she said casually.

'I presume I'll be having the pleasure of your company on this morning's cruise.' Fitzgerald looked only at Sandra while he spoke.

'You will,' Michael smiled. Watching Fitzgerald in his role as Ireland's Rudolph Valentino was one of life's small pleasures. 'Shouldn't you be helping your jolly Jack Tars to ready the vessel for the perilous crossing to the islands?'

'Perhaps I should.' Fitzgerald grinned. 'Will you be staying long, Michael?'

'A few days at least.'

'Why don't you visit me on the bridge as soon as we sail?' Fitzgerald said over his shoulder. 'And bring your Duty Free with you.'

'Quite a character,' Sandra said. 'But I pity the poor woman who's married to him.'

'Like most Irishmen, Tom fancies himself as a bit of a Lothario. As far as character is concerned, you haven't even scratched the surface.' Michael picked up the two canvas bags containing their clothes and made his way to the rear of the crowd who were waiting for the chain across the gangplank to be lifted. He glanced around the faces. No obvious candidates for 'murderer of the month'.

Sandra stood beside him in the queue. 'What's the matter, Michael? You're edgy, and you're looking at everyone in sight as though you're afraid of who they might be. I thought we were going to be safe here while Fergus looks at the papers.'

'I guess that business in Paris has wound me up pretty tight?' Michael said. 'I'm beginning to jump at my own shadow.'

'I know the feeling,' Sandra said, as one of the sailors released the chain and the crowd began to pour onto the small ferry. Her earlier suspicions of him were fading, and she realised that the tension generated by the fear of death which had enveloped them in Brussels and Paris was being augmented by the growing sexual awareness between them.

As soon as Michael and Sandra had scampered aboard the ferry, the sailor withdrew the gangplank. They could feel the throbbing of the engines beneath their feet, and before they had found a place on the rough wooden benches on the forward deck, the *Prince of Aran* began to move away from the quayside. Neither Michael nor Sandra noticed one of the fishermen at the end of the quay reeling in his line. He closed and packed his rod into a fishing bag with the air of a man who hadn't had a bite and didn't expect to get one. The man walked slowly back along the quay to where a Volvo station-wagon sat parked. He tossed his bag into the rear of the car before slipping into the front seat. The fisherman lifted up a car-phone from the arm-rest and dialled a number in Dublin.

The Lear jet bearing the logo of Chemie de France landed at Dublin Airport at about the same time as the *Prince of Aran* pulled away from the quay at Rossaveal. Five minutes before landing, the pilot had announced that the high pressure area that lay almost stationary over western Europe would provide another stunningly hot day. Temperatures were expected to rise to thirty centigrade. The captain completed the weather forecast with the hope that Monsieur Tahir would enjoy his sojourn in Ireland.

Tahir left the jet and was escorted by the commercial attaché of the French Embassy towards the Customs area. The sun was already beating down and beads of sweat had gathered on the brow of the Chemie de France chief of security. Tahir's left arm hung in a white cloth sling. 'Le Sergent' was a quick healer, and the stiffness caused by the wound he had received in Jeaune's apartment was already beginning to ease. As he strode across the tarmac ahead of the small balding figure of the attaché, Tahir reaffirmed his resolution not to underestimate Joyce again. There was something in Joyce's background that had been overlooked, and that something was the vital element that had allowed the American to escape twice with his life while better men had perished. He felt the comforting weight of the PA15 MAB in the canvas bag he carried in his right hand. One of the prerogatives of travelling by executive jet was that whatever you wanted, whether it was drugs or women or weapons, could come along without the full scrutiny of airport security.

The attaché rushed ahead and opened the glass door leading to the passport control area. 'Le Sergent' breezed through and presented his blue-covered passport to the official on duty. After a cursory look the official returned the passport, and Tahir entered the sovereign area of the Republic of Ireland.

'Où sont-ils?' Tahir asked, as the attaché led him out of the main concourse building towards the car-park.

'We have received no news since last night,' the attaché said.

'Don't fuck me about,' Tahir said harshly, without breaking stride. 'Unless you want me to turn your tidy fucking world upside down.'

The attaché was quite convinced that the man walking slightly in front of him was capable of anything. 'The Irish Special Branch lost the Peugeot in Galway last night, but they've blanketed the area. They should have been picked up by now.' The attaché had been liaising with the Special Branch, but he had no idea why the couple were being tailed. Neither did he care. The first rule of making a career in the diplomatic service was to know the absolute minimum. That way, when the shit hit the fan one could disclaim all knowledge quite legitimately. 'As soon as we reach the embassy I'll put a call through to my contact.'

The attaché pointed to a silver Renault 25 with CD plates. Tahir tossed his canvas bag into the back seat and climbed wordlessly into the passenger seat. He was beginning to feel his age. As soon as Joyce and the woman were out of the way he would allow the warm North African sun to heal his old bones.

Tom Fitzgerald took a slug out of the bottle of Smirnoff Blue Label Vodka that Michael had brought to the wheelhouse. The *Prince of Aran* ploughed sedately across the short stretch of the Atlantic Ocean which separates the Aran Islands from the coast of Galway.

'I'm sure there are some maritime regulations prohibiting the captain from drinking on duty,' Sandra said with a laugh, watching the skipper lower another healthy swig from the rapidly emptying bottle. 'I distinctly remember the captain of the *Exxon Valdez* being sent to prison for being drunk on duty.'

'God save us from clever women,' Fitzgerald said, and took another gulp from the bottle before reluctantly passing it back to Michael.

Michael grinned. 'For a start,' he said, taking a small drink from the bottle, 'this isn't a supertanker and Tom has already done away with his fair share of ferries. The law of averages says that only one skipper in ten thousand ever gets to lose his ship, but somehow Tom managed to get rid of two of them. And there was a strong rumour circulating at the time that the question of insurance was uppermost in the skipper's mind at the moment the boats were lost.'

'That's bloody unkind,' Fitzgerald said, and started laughing.

Sandra looked through the stained window of the wheelhouse and saw that they had covered almost half the distance between the mainland and the three small islands rising out of the dark blue waters of the Atlantic Ocean. Their lives were still in danger and she was sure that Michael was holding something back from her. The fear of death should have been uppermost in her mind, but she found herself concentrating instead on life. Sandra had always wondered how people in war zones could proceed with their daily lives with the knowledge that death could strike at any moment. Now she knew. The desire to survive overcame any inertia that the fear of death could engender. She was enjoying herself, and she could laugh again — and so could Michael. She looked across the wheelhouse at him. His black curls dangled over his forehead, and she was gripped with a desire to kiss him. Instead she smiled. Through the window she saw the looming shapes of the islands bathed in a Mediterranean-style sun, and wondered whether they would provide the sanctuary that Michael promised.

George Patterson had arrived at Aldergrove Airport in Belfast on the first shuttle from London. He was met by one of his old comrades in arms, a senior member of the Ulster Defence Association and one of the commanders of the clandestine Ulster Freedom Fighters. The two men had often collaborated in removing Catholic terrorists. His contact drove him through the town of Portadown, and to a well-kept whitewashed farmhouse. Patterson never ceased to be amazed at the range and quantity of firepower that the Ulster Freedom Fighters had amassed. The array of weapons that was secreted in the farm's barn would have kept a small war going for a couple of months. The Scotsman was modest in his requirements. He refused the offer of a Kalashnikov and instead selected a Browning Hi-Power 9mm, with the British Army serial number still visible on the handgrip. He slipped two magazines of 9mm Parabellum shells into his jacket pocket, and then had his contact drive him to the border town of Newry, where he caught the Belfast to Dublin express.

He arrived in Dublin at eleven-fifteen in the morning, hired a car at a small agency across the road from Connolly Station, and drove immediately to Buswells Hotel in Molesworth Street. The message at reception was short. Joyce and the woman had embarked for the Aran Islands on the morning ferry. Patterson cancelled the room he had reserved and returned to the car. With a bit of luck he could be in Galway by mid-afternoon and by this evening he would be on the Aran Islands. The business with Joyce would be completed by the next day and he would be back in London, fifty thousand pounds richer, by the end of the week.

Patrick Tahir had often visited Ireland in the company of his mentor at Chemie de France. His one abiding memory of the fishing trips to the west of Ireland was the omnipresent rain. He was therefore surprised to find himself bathed in warm sunshine as the attaché drove him to the French Embassy in Aylesbury Road.

As soon as they arrived at the period mansion which housed the embassy, the attaché led Tahir directly to his office. 'Le Sergent' waved away the offer of coffee. The sooner he found Joyce's whereabouts and dealt with the situation, the sooner he would be in his villa in Cueta recuperating.

'*Ils ont pris le bateau pour les îles d'Aran ce matin,*' the attaché said, as he put the phone down. The diplomat thanked God silently. He glanced across at his visitor. The man looked decidedly ill. With the reason for Tahir's visit nestling in the west of Ireland, there would be no need for this potential liability to hang around Dublin. The attaché had done his duty in providing a service to the monkeys on the Quai d'Orsay. If a diplomatic incident ensued, let it be on their heads.

'*Je les connais,*' Tahir said. He had visited the bleak western islands on one of the Chemie de France fishing trips. 'Le Sergent' sat back and thought. As far as he remembered, the islands could be reached by air from Galway or by taking a ferry from either Galway or Rossaveal in Connemara. The Chemie de France jet was still standing at Dublin Airport. Galway would be less than one hour away on the Lear.

'*Apportez-moi à l'aéroport,*' Tahir said, rising swiftly.

The attaché sighed audibly. Who the hell did this sack of shit think he was ordering around? The diplomat remained seated.

Tahir was not impressed by the attaché's show of reluctance. He leaned across and pulled the man out of his chair.

'*Je n'ai pas le temps pour jouer.*' The menace was clear in 'Le Sergent's' voice. He released his grip on the man's shirt and lifted up his canvas bag from the floor. '*Maintenant,* do it now, asshole!' Tahir's accent would have been completely at home on the streets of Chicago. He would take the jet as far as Galway and then hire a car. Joyce was within striking distance again.

The attaché brushed down his ruffled shirt and picked up the keys of the Renault from his desk. As he held the door of his office open for Tahir, he was thinking of the indignities one had to suffer in the service of one's country.

'Up to a few years ago there was no jetty.'

It could have been her imagination, but Sandra thought she detected a slur in Michael's voice. Her companion and the erstwhile skipper of the *Prince of Aran* had managed to do away with a half litre of vodka during the hour and a half journey Although in fairness she had to admit that Fitzgerald had demolished most of it.

'The ferry used to anchor in the centre of the bay,' Michael continued, 'and small boats used to come out and row people ashore. I guess the returning Yanks used to think it was "cute". But it was goddamn inconvenient.'

Sandra wondered whether her new friend suffered from an identity problem. After all, if there was a sub-group of humanity that could rightly be labelled 'returning Yanks', he would certainly have been included in it. She smiled to herself.

Fitzgerald was using any concentration he still maintained to manoeuvre the 'Prince' into a position alongside the quay at Kilronan, the big island's main village. His two Jack Tars threw lines to the quay from the bow and stern of the ferry and two men reluctantly left a group of hackney car drivers and tied up the 'Prince' to the quayside.

'All ashore what's goin' ashore,' Fitzgerald said, slapping Michael on the back.

The skipper of the 'Prince' stowed the remains of the Smirnoff in a locker below the chart table and left Sandra wondering whether he would add a third boat to his tally of disasters before the day was out.

The rucksacked tourists disgorged themselves onto the quayside as Michael and Sandra made their way down to the deck from the wheelhouse. More than half a dozen horse-drawn carriages were lined up on the quay, and the small knot of men who had been awaiting the arrival of the 'Prince' began to ply their wares to the arriving tourists.

'See you on the return trip, darlin'.' Fitzgerald launched a slap at Sandra's bottom and was disappointed when she adroitly avoided the contact.

'That man's a pest,' Sandra said, as she stepped onto the concrete jetty at Kilronan.

'He's only trying to be friendly,' Michael said.

'That's a matter for debate, with the deciding vote being cast by that section of the community that normally wears skirts.'

She smiled. 'Still, I suppose you're bound to defend him. You men always stick together.'

Michael glanced quickly at her. He had been aware that she had reacted badly to his churlish behaviour earlier — he had been a fool not to apologise for it immediately — and he was relieved now to see that her eyes were laughing at him. 'We stick together because it's our only defence against you lot,' he said, lightly.

He felt happy. The sun was shining, a few shots of vodka had produced a nice buzz, and he was in the company of a beautiful and intelligent girl. All would have been well with the world if it hadn't been for the presence of the Special Branch on their tail. Michael thought back to the meeting with Maguire in Clarinbridge and wondered whether he had impressed on the inebriated professor sufficiently clearly the need for a quick solution. He reckoned that at most they would only have a couple of days before they were located.

'What now?' Sandra asked, intruding on Michael's deep and dark thoughts.

Michael was about to answer when he was grabbed rudely from behind. He dropped the canvas bags to the ground and stamped down hard on the foot of the man holding him. The arms that held him were instantly released and Michael whirled to face his assailant.

'Holy Mother of Jesus!' The man was jumping on one foot along the jetty. 'You ignorant young pup!'

'God, Tim, I'm sorry,' Michael said. He grasped the old man around the shoulders and hugged him.

'You have a fine way of saying hello to your friends,' Tim said. He had stopped hopping about and was screwing up his weather-beaten face in pain. 'I think you've been spending too much time dealing with them muggers in the States.' The old man returned Michael's hug.

'Sandra, let me introduce you to Tim O'Flaherty,' Michael said, standing back from the embrace.

'Nice to meet you, Tim.' Sandra stepped forward and shook Tim's hand. O'Flaherty had a ruddy face which could have been the product of either the weather or an over-indulgence in alcohol. A soiled tweed cap perched on top of his large head, with tufts of grey hair protruding. If she hadn't just been introduced to him, she would have wanted to embrace him herself. There was a quality about Tim O'Flaherty that made him look like everybody's favourite uncle.

'This man,' Michael said, putting his arm around Tim's broad shoulder, 'was given the delicate task of instructing all the Joyce children in the noble arts of fishing and sailing, and nobody could have done the job better.'

'You might have given us some notice of your arrival,' Tim said, smiling at Michael. 'There isn't an ounce of food in the cottage, bar some tea and coffee, and the place hasn't been aired for months.'

'Stop behaving like a mother hen,' Michael said. 'Since you haven't landed yourself an unsuspecting tourist, you can take Sandra and me to the cottage. We'll stop off at a shop and stock up with whatever we need.'

'There's nothing like the returned Yanks for ordering the locals around,' Tim said, and picked up the two canvas bags from the quay. 'I suppose you still recognise my cart.'

Werner Von Schick, the man known as 'Schuman' at the European Commission in Brussels, paced up and down his office. It had all been planned so meticulously, and yet it could so easily come apart at the seams. He had spoken with Blu and Morley and had learned the fate of the documents he had so carefully planted on Jorgensen. The journalist Joyce and Jorgensen's lover had proved to be such a useful addition to the scenario that he felt sorry he had not planned for the kind of diversion they had created. They were a bonus that he could not possibly have counted on. But now that they were in the game, he fully expected them to go on playing their part until their time to exit arrived. The only blot on an otherwise faultless plan was the fact that the pompous British ass sitting in the Commission offices in Brussels was at least a week behind schedule in examining the complete set of papers on the operations of the cartel which Von Schick had so graciously supplied. He could understand the need for caution, but did those idiots in Brussels need him to draw a map for them? Elliot was the type of British civil servant who wanted to be presented with a career-enhancing coup but who didn't really want the risks entailed in snatching it.

The German looked out at the brilliant sunshine. Northern Europe was basking in one of its rare heat waves. Soon he would bask in the admiration of his colleagues. The results of his little plan had already been spectacular. Who could have imagined a few short weeks ago that an institution like Jean Claude Blu could have been replaced as the chairman of the cartel? Von Schick could imagine the intense personal pain that Blu was experiencing. The ex-chairman had an ego the size of the Eiffel Tower, and by now he would be skulking in his office tower in Lyons thinking of ways to explain his disgrace to his colleagues on the Chemie board. Von Schick had also anticipated Jorgensen's murder. It had all been part of the plan. The greater good sometimes required sacrifices to be made, and the chief of Mannheim Chemicals had been instrumental in subtly pushing the cartel into the decision to kill the Dane. For his plan to succeed, it had been necessary to create an environment of panic and fear. Within two short weeks the Treuhandanstalt, the German government body responsible for the privatisation of the industry of the former East Germany, would announce that Mannheim Chemicals had bought out the whole of the East Germany chemical industry, creating a giant that would in its turn dominate the European industry. Werner Von Schick would need a breathing space to create this monolith, and that breathing space would be provided by the chaos that a case against the other members of the cartel would entail. What would emerge from Von Schick's plan would be a new European chemical industry dominated by Germany. It would be a return to the glory days of the nineteen thirties when IG Farben ruled the industry. There would be no need for a cartel. The prices would be set by Werner Von Schick and by him alone.

After they had bought ample provisions in Kilronan, Tim O'Flaherty drove Michael and Sandra in his cart to the cottage. Rounding the corner of a small hill, they could see before them the bay of Kilmurvey, which lay beneath a perfect blue sky, the bright sunshine reflected in brilliant light from the white strand.

'It looks like a South Sea Island,' Sandra said.

'Today, yes,' Tim said, urging on his old horse, 'but you stand here on a wet and windy winter's day when a heat wave like this is a million miles away. The South Seas wouldn't be the first thing you'd think of. It would more likely be Siberia.'

'Stop spoiling the woman's pleasure.' Michael gave Tim a playful punch in the shoulder. 'That's our house.' He was pointing towards the edge of Kilmurvey Bay.

Sandra followed the line of his finger to a house perched on the very edge of the ocean on the northern sweep of the bay. Its white walls glistened in the sunshine, the building being set into relief against a backdrop of black limestone rocks.

'It's beautiful,' Sandra said, feeling that this was about the only phrase she had used since she'd arrived on Aran. The scene that lay before her was a picture from a travel brochure. And yet she knew it was real. In a few moments she would descend from Tim Flaherty's jaunting car and would be able to prove that it was all true.

The sight of his grandparent's house, now totally renovated by his father, always caused a stirring in Michael's heart. It was in that small house that Michael had sat at the feet of an old man with a head of steel-grey hair like bristles on a brush and a face that looked as if it had been carved directly from the island's limestone. While the wind whipped the mighty ocean against the rocks at the edge of the bay, Michael had listened to the ancient stories that had been handed down in the oral tradition of the first Celts.

'What's that?' Sandra was staring back over her shoulder at a long low-lying rock formation which stretched along the hill overlooking the bay. Even in the sunshine it looked dark and foreboding.

'Dún Aengus, the fort of Aengus,' Tim said, gazing up at the ancient ruin. 'As to what it is, even the experts in the universities are divided on that one. Some say it was named after a leader of the Fir Bolg, the Neolithic tribe that inhabited Ireland before the arrival of the Celts. In fact it was one of my own ancestors who was responsible for carrying that little gem of oral tradition. There are others on the island who simply call it Dún Mór — the big fort.'

'Can we go there this afternoon?' Sandra said, looking at Michael. Something about the place seemed to call to her.

'I guess so,' Michael said. 'Your wish is my command.'

They had reached the house and Tim brought the jaunting car to a halt on the gravel path directly across from the front door.

'It looks bigger from close up,' said Sandra, surveying the cottage.

'Only the best for Patrick Joyce,' Michael said, walking past her to a group of rocks beside the house. He bent and slipped his hand into a crevice in the rocks, wondering exactly how long his ancestors had used this hiding place. When he removed his hand it held a decaying leather bag. Michael tipped the bag and a key fell into his hand.

'I see you people are heavily into security,' Sandra smiled.

'With Tim and my cousins about, who needs video cameras and the like? There isn't a trick that they miss.' Michael had already toyed with the idea of telling Tim about their predicament but had decided against it. There was no way that he could contemplate dragging Tim or any of his relations into the dangers that he and Sandra faced.

'Do you intend to stand there all day or are you going to open the door?' Tim O'Flaherty held two plastic shopping bags in his huge hands.

Michael opened the door and stood back to allow Sandra to enter. She had never seen anything so perfect. The inside of the cottage had been restored with a care that attested to a great love. The central room, which was similar to Maguire's cottage in Rossaveal, rose to a beamed ceiling, and was dominated by a magnificent stone fireplace, in front of which were a couch and easy chairs. Sandra could imagine sitting before the fire on a winter's evening, listening to the howling of the wind and the crashing of the Atlantic breakers. On both sides of the main room, tight-pitched wooden spiral staircases wound towards dark-stained wooden doors on the floor above.

Tim passed her and opened a door in the rear wall of the central room.

'The kitchen's through there,' Michael said, dropping the two canvas bags on the floor. 'It contains every labour-saving device known to man.'

'It's absolutely beautiful,' Sandra said, letting her eyes run over all the subtle touches that Patrick Joyce had incorporated into his parents' house.

'Everything is packed away,' Tim said, when he eventually came out of the kitchen.

'Can we meet you later for a drink?' Michael asked. They would need to go to Kilronan later to make a call to the mainland. If Fergus Maguire was as good as his word, there would be some news by evening.

'I've never been known to refuse,' Tim said, through smiling lips. 'I'll be back about four o'clock.' He doffed his cap to Sandra, and ambled through the front door.

'I don't know about you, but I can't resist that beach for one moment longer,' Sandra said.

'You're beginning to echo my thoughts.'

'That could be dangerous,' Sandra smiled, and leading Michael by the hand she moved into the sunlight. 'This is every yuppie's dream come true,' she said, as they walked towards the deserted beach. 'You know, my colleagues in Brussels spend thousands of pounds for a couple of weeks at some Club Med hideaway where a totally artificial "get-away-from-it-all" scene has been created.'

'I don't think the people here would appreciate a Club Med stuck in the middle of Kilmurvey Bay. And I don't think that Club Med would waste its money on a location where the number of days of sunshine a year is less than the number of fingers and toes of the normal individual.'

They had reached the edge of the sand and Sandra bent to remove her sandals before stepping onto the beach.

'That's wonderful.' She could feel the warmth of the sand rising through her feet. The warm sun beat on her shoulders and the blue ocean ahead of her looked cool and inviting. She looked along the empty white sands. 'I suppose a swim wouldn't be out of the question.'

'What about swim-suits?' Michael asked.

'There doesn't seem to be too many spectators and I'm not squeamish about being seen in my underwear.' The Joyce cottage was the only building within two hundred metres of the beach.

Sandra ran to the edge of the sea and slipped out of her dress. Michael could see the dark triangle of her pubic mound through her thin white cotton panties.

'I hope I'm not going in alone.' Sandra whipped off her blouse and immediately ran into the cool water.

Michael slipped out of his jeans and tee-shirt and ran after her. The water was wonderfully refreshing compared to the searing heat of the sand. When he came out of his flat dive into the waves, he saw Sandra swimming strongly parallel to the beach. He took off quickly in her direction.

'This is heaven.' Sandra stood on the bottom and her bare white breasts emerged from the sea. The dark brown nipples were fully erected. Michael moved close, his desire for her overwhelming. He took her in his arms, and when she held up her face to him, kissed her on the lips, crushing her to him as he did so. Her nipples were like small stones against his chest. The blue waters of the Atlantic swirled around them as their bodies moved together. His tongue flickered in her mouth again, and his hand slid into her cotton briefs and up between her legs. Sandra could feel his erect penis against her thigh, and she reached down to take it in her hand. For a few moments they explored each other's body before she guided him into her. They were standing in the middle of Kilmurvey Bay, but they felt so alone that they might have been on the moon. As Michael entered her, Sandra gasped, and then allowed her feet to come off the sandy bottom, and floating on her back, her hair like a fan on the water, she wrapped her legs around his waist. He held her buttocks as he thrust into her. Slowly she felt her orgasm begin, deep within her being, and she raised herself up and clung to his shoulders as the blood began to pound in her veins. She cried out with pleasure as the orgasm built up, and Michael felt her teeth biting into his shoulder as his thrusts accelerated and his own orgasm approached. Holding each other tight, they both came in an explosion of shuddering

214

sensation, and then, unwilling to break apart, covered each other with salty kisses until their hearts had ceased to pound and they had returned from their private world of ecstasy, and were standing once more in the waters of Kilmurvey Bay. 'I think we might just have scandalised the parish of Kilmurvey,' Michael said, planting a soft kiss on her lips. The salt taste of her filled his mouth and the feel of her was still on his penis. Michael Joyce was in love, and it felt so sweet that he could have exploded with joy.

'I doubt if we're going to scandalise anyone,' Sandra said, looking round the empty beach. 'There's no one about to scandalise. But I wouldn't care if there was.' Their lovemaking had been wonderful for her. She knew for certain now that she was in love with Michael. Brussels and Finn seemed a million years ago. This was where she was destined to be — here, with the small eddies of the Atlantic playing around her feet, and the Joyce cottage standing on the shore and calling to her as her own home.

'I'd like to do that again,' she said, only this time maybe we should try it in a bed. Until today I'd never made love in the sea and I've never made love in a thatched cottage. Two firsts in one day wouldn't be at all bad.'

Dominique Leriche crossed her legs for the fiftieth time and permitted her skirt to ride higher. It had been a frustrating morning for someone who had been trying to get the undivided attention of Jean Claude Blu. The chairman of Chemie de France was usually more than receptive to a view of exposed thigh, but on that sunny morning in Lyons Blu's mind seemed to be on other things. Blu's assistant had been disconcerted from the moment she had entered the office. Overnight her chief had been transformed from a dynamic executive into a tired old man. She would still sleep with him to advance her career, but the prospect of screwing the ancient wreck who sat behind the chairman's desk didn't have quite the same appeal as it had some days before. She recrossed her legs, making sure that her skirt rode high enough to expose a flash of white cotton pants. It was time to abandon the waiting game. The sooner she got this geriatric into bed the better. It would be a shame if the game she had played with the old bastard over the past months came to nothing.

'*Assez*,' Blu said, abandoning all efforts to get some work done. He really had had enough. The feeling that had been growing in his stomach over the past few days had now taken over his entire body like some raging cancer. The same inner voice that he had listened to so assiduously over the years was now shouting that he was fucked. And that same voice was telling him that it was not simply a question of losing his job at the cartel or even the chairmanship of Chemie de France. The threat was total. He was not going to be permitted to fade away and tend his roses. Blu looked across at his delectable assistant and felt absolutely nothing. The realisation that his sexual drive had disappeared only made him shrink further into himself.

'It's finished for today,' Blu said, pushing the papers on the desk away from him.

'Are you feeling okay?' Leriche leaned across the desk towards her boss exposing the deep cleavage between her firm young breasts.

'Yes,' Blu answered with a little of his old sharpness. 'Now get out.'

Dominique Leriche turned on her heel and began to march towards the office door. It would be a cold day in hell before Jean Claude Blu would get another opportunity to lay her like the one that he been given that morning.

Blu watched her petulant exit from the office and decided that she needed a new appointment. He dictated a note to the personnel manager instructing him to find the most Godawful executive post in Chemie de France and to put Dominique Leriche into it. His hand shook as he held the small tape recorder that he used for dictation. It was all coming apart at the seams, and so was he. One part of him wanted to fight, but a logical review of his situation came down heavily in favour of despair. Blu stood up from his desk and lovingly ran his hand along its edge. He looked around his office but gained no solace from the fine paintings or the antique furniture. He hadn't been home in several days and it was perhaps time to see whether the old woman living in Fontaine could bring any light into this new dark existence. Blu doubted it.

George Patterson traversed Ireland from east to west and was five cars behind Tahir's Ford Sierra as they moved west along the coast road from Galway and into Connemara. He was considering extending his trip by a couple of days and making a holiday of it. By tomorrow he would have disposed of Joyce and the woman, his already healthy bank balance would be looking even healthier, and there was really no good reason he could think of for not spending a few days wandering through the Emerald Isle, perhaps looking up some of his old comrades. The view across Galway Bay was extraordinary, with the Aran Islands appearing close enough to touch. A few days up North when the Joyce business was concluded would be just the ticket.

Nicholas Elliot took a white handkerchief from his pocket and wiped a film of sweat from his brow. He reflected that the founders of Europe must have suffered a collective brain-storm when they had decided on the capital of Belgium as the seat of the major European institutions. In July and August, the Gods drop a heavy blanket of humidity over the city. The humidity extracts water and energy from every pore until work becomes an impossibility. Elliot had already been at his desk for eight hours, and his head was beginning to ache. He popped two Panadol into his mouth and washed them down with a glass of Evian. They were almost ready to launch the 'dawn raids' on the offices of the chemical companies. Those taking part in the raids would be kept in the dark until the last minute. Elliot had been through this process many times before, but there was something about this particular case that was different. The whole affair was not quite pukka.

Elliot stared at the door as Georges Lafonde rushed into the room. Lafonde's bushy eyebrows were more furrowed than usual and the dark hooded eyes looked as if they were about to release a deluge of tears.

'We've got a problem.' Lafonde dropped into the chair in front of Elliot's desk. Elliot hadn't seen his assistant this agitated in years, and beads of sweat broke out on his forehead.

'Calm down and tell me what's happened.' Elliot hardly recognised the cool voice as his own.

'Vincent Ryan, one of the lawyers in our chemical cartel team, received a call from his old professor early this afternoon. This may be a coincidence, but his professor asked him a series of questions that relate exactly to the ongoing investigation. It was all hypothetical, of course, but according to Ryan, there can be no doubt that this man was presenting our case against the chemical cartel for an opinion.'

'I suppose Ryan didn't have the wit to pursue the matter,' Elliot said, fighting for control as he felt the chances of the 'K' and possibly his job disappear.

'Ryan is one of our better people,' Lafonde continued. 'His professor, Fergus Maguire, was very evasive on the source of the enquiry, but Ryan was sure that he had substantial information on the case we've been building.'

'Did the professor try to draw Ryan on the matter,' Elliot asked, as he tried to shake off the fatigue caused by the humidity and to consider all the possibilities created by the professor's enquiry. Three months of hard work and a forty-year career hung in the balance this evening.

'No. He was simply tapping an old student on a point of competition law,' Lafonde replied.

'Then we might possibly salvage something from this potential disaster. Get Ryan up here straight away and get me the Irish commissioner on the line. I want to know where Maguire got his information from, and I want to make bloody sure that the lid is kept on this business for at least one more day.'

Tahir and Patterson were passengers on the same ferry, which ploughed across the calm waters of the Atlantic towards the Aran Islands. 'Le Sergent' watched the approaching coastline and thought of Joyce and the woman. This time there would be no mistake. Cavelli and Lepape would not have died in vain. He looked at the small islands. He hadn't remembered them as being so small. Finding Joyce would not be a difficult matter. The rabbit had run for its warren, thinking it would be safe once it was inside. But this warren would prove to be a trap.

Patterson sat on a wooden bench near the bow of the ferry. He was just another tourist reading a book on the Aran Islands that he had purchased in Galway. Knowing the terrain was an important consideration in the success of his mission. MI6 had taught George Patterson many skills, and the most vital of those was not the art of killing itself, but the planning of the kill. Any fool in possession of a weapon could use it to end the life of another human being, but the skill came in killing and slipping quietly away. Patterson looked up as the bow of the ferry dipped, and saw the shape of the islands up ahead.

A cool breeze blew across the land from the Atlantic, mitigating the fierce heat of the sun, when Michael and Sandra finally left the cottage in the late afternoon. Their love-making had been slow and gentle, the complete opposite of their coupling in the water, and afterwards they had eaten a light lunch washed down with a chilled bottle of white wine.

'OK,' Sandra said, slipping her hand into Michael's. 'It's your turn to play the guide.' She had never felt as happy as she did at this moment. Finn had never brought her even a modicum of the pleasure Michael had given her in one single afternoon.

He led her along a rough path towards the forbidding rock fortress on the top of the hill. 'The fort backs onto a cliff, so that it can only be approached from this direction. Whoever built the place wanted to use the natural terrain as much as possible for defence.'

To their left was a large green field which climbed in the direction they were walking, culminating finally in a small hillock. 'That small hill,' Michael pointed it out with his finger, 'is called Caoineadh na Mná, which means the weeping of the women. The field below the hill was the scene of faction fights on the island even up to quite recently. The local women would stand on the hill and watch as their men laid into one another. The two main causes of death on the island were the ocean and that field.'

They walked on past the field with the grisly history, and began the climb towards the rock fort on the summit of the hill. Within minutes they were walking through a forest of upright limestone slabs, which extended in a wide semi-circle around the fort.

'These slabs don't look very natural,' Sandra said, moving carefully between them.

'They're not,' Michael said. 'They're called *chevaux de frise*. A sort of front line of defence for the fort. The ice-age deposited a lot of limestone slabs in this area and the Celtic or pre-Celtic tribe that built the fort set the slabs in the ground in such a way that an attacking army would be forced to move forward slowly and expose themselves to whatever the defenders had to throw at them. A secondary consideration was that anyone who succeeded in ripping off the defender's cattle would have a hell of a job driving them through a veritable forest of limestone slabs. Not an easy task if someone is trying to shove a spear up your ass while you're driving the cattle.'

They moved slowly through the ancient slabs. Sandra slid her hand over the rough rock which was sharp around the edges. 'They look like soldiers standing there. Did you ever wonder what kind of people put these rocks here? They lived and loved on the very spot that we're walking on and the only thing that's left of them is the rocks they set into the ground to protect themselves.'

'I think you'll find that they left something more behind than the rocks. There are plenty of people on the island whose family tree extends all the way back to the people who built this fort. My grandfather had stories of Irish mythology which could very well have been based at a camp-fire somewhere on this hill.'

They went past the *chevaux de frise* to a roughly semi-circular open area that lay directly in front of the four and a half metre high outer walls of the fort. Small openings, large enough to accommodate one person at a time, were cut at intervals in the wall at ground level. Sandra and Michael went through the first opening which was over three metres thick, and found themselves in a grassy area between the outer wall and an inner wall.

'This is the outer keep,' Michael said, walking across the grassy enclosure. 'The experts say that this was a grazing area for the cattle of the people gathered in the fort, although they must have been pretty small cattle to have got through those openings.'

The inner wall was similar to the outer in both size and construction. They squeezed through the opening in the inner wall, which was fully four metres thick, before emerging into a large semi-circular space littered with rocks.

'This is the central keep,' Michael said.

In the centre of this space was a huge rectangular slab of dark grey limestone, some six metres long, which was raised about a metre above the ground. Beyond it the ground ended in a sheer cliff which descended to the ocean below.

'I see what you mean about only being approachable from the land side,' Sandra said, looking down over the edge of the cliff at the swirling white waters. 'It looks as if the fort was originally circular and that half of it fell into the ocean. Anybody living here certainly wouldn't want to suffer from vertigo.'

They walked hand in hand around the inner fort.

'What's the significance of the slab?' Sandra asked, as she shivered involuntarily despite the warm weather.

'That I don't know.' Michael felt the shiver and pulled her to him. 'Have you caught a chill?'

'No.' Sandra moved closer to him. 'That rock gives me the creeps. Look at how symmetrical the thing is. The sides are almost perfectly perpendicular and the top is virtually flat. Don't you get the impression that there was some reason for building the fort around it.'

'There is a school of thought,' said Michael, 'which says that Dún Aengus is not a fort but an ancient place of worship for the old pagan gods. Some people see that slab as some kind of altar on which sacrifices were made.'

'I'm sure they're right,' Sandra said, forcing a smile she didn't feel. 'I think I've seen enough of the fort. Do you mind if we leave now?' Without waiting for his agreement, she hurried away, almost running until she was beyond the outer wall.

'Are you all right?' Michael asked when he caught up with her. He wrapped his arms around her.

'I didn't like it there very much. It made me shiver.' She gave a little laugh. 'But don't worry — I'm fine now. Really.' She kissed him lightly and then broke away.

'The way you were running, I thought you were thinking of going back to the cottage and that soft and comfortable bed,' Michael said. 'At least, I hoped that was what you were thinking.'

Sandra laughed again. 'You've had your quota for this afternoon.'

'But I guess there's still a quota for this evening. How about tapping this evening's reserve in advance?'

'Michael Joyce, you're incorrigible,' she said. 'We've got a phone call to make — remember? I want to know what Fergus has to say and whether we're going to get out of this business with our skins intact.'

The telephone kiosk outside the pub in Kilronan was out of the dawn of the telecommunications age. The air inside the small box was stagnant, and the clicking sounds from the handpiece were at least evidence of relays mating somewhere, hopefully in order to connect Michael to Galway, some sixty-five kilometres away. As Michael stood anxiously listening to the whirring and clicking, he began to lament the passing of the age of the carrier pigeon.

'Yes?' Fergus Maguire's voice appeared to come from the other end of the galaxy, and could barely be distinguished over the background atmospherics.

'Fergus, it's Michael.'

'Michael, thank God you called now. If you'd waited ten minutes you wouldn't have got me. Listen carefully, Michael. I had a stroke of luck on deciphering those papers you left with me. One of my ex-students who works for the European Commission was able to help me out.'

'I asked you not to go outside with this,' Michael said angrily. The experience with Jeaune was too fresh in his mind.

'Don't worry, Michael, I didn't mention anything about either you or Sandra. The papers you gave me relate to the operations of a petrochemical cartel. It appears that a number of companies have been screwing their customers blind for a very long time. By setting up certain cosy arrangements, they've managed to cream off hundreds of millions of pounds. The amounts of money involved makes it easier to believe your

222

story. But there's another strange twist to this tale. The European Commission are about to close the net on these people and there's a certain amount of apprehension in Brussels about how the papers you've been carrying got into circulation.'

'What's the bottom line, Fergus?'

'The bottom line as you call it, my young friend, is that within a day or so the people behind this scam will be history. When the Commission dumps on them, you and Sandra will be the furthest thing from their minds.'

Michael felt a huge weight lifting from his shoulders.

'The Commission are sending their jet to take me to Brussels.' Maguire's voice was excited. 'They want to examine the papers, but no matter what they find in them, the axe will certainly fall on the cartel .'

'Thanks, Fergus.' Michael didn't try to hide the relief in his voice.

'Don't thank me. The boys in Brussels had this one well and truly sussed. They've been working on the case for months, and it's lucky for you that events appear to be coming to a head just in time. Listen, I've got to be off to the airport. I'll contact you when I get back. You and Sandra can enjoy the sunshine in peace now.'

The line went dead, and Michael replaced the handset slowly. He let out a huge whoop that drew amused looks from the sunbathers lining the wall beside the phone-box.

'It's over.' Michael pulled Sandra from her chair outside the pub and hugged her. He felt a great wave of happiness and relief welling over him. It really was over. Their lives were no longer in danger, and the bastards who had been trying to kill them were about to get the kind of kick up the ass they deserved. As soon as the Commission broke the cartel, he and Sandra could go back to Brussels and explain the body in the basement, and the shoot-out in Paris. They were going to survive, and he and Sandra did have a future together. To add icing to the cake, he would soon be in a position to write a series of articles on his contribution to the downfall of the petrochemical cartel. He looked into her smiling face and reflected that he had never loved the way he loved this girl.

'You seem to be into public displays of affection today,' Sandra said. 'I take it that the news from Fergus was good.'

'Not just good, fantastic.' He explained what Fergus had said.

'If the Commission was already working on breaking the cartel,' Sandra said, 'how on earth did Finn get his hands on the documents and why was he working in parallel with his colleagues?'

'I have no idea,' Michael replied. 'I suppose the people at the Commission will be looking for the answer to that question themselves. Right now I'm just happy that the whole mess is about to be cleared up and we can get on with our lives.'

Sandra felt the same relief as Michael, but it was tempered by a feeling of apprehension. 'Getting on with life' didn't have the same meaning as it had had one week ago, and she wondered whether it would have a different meaning one week from then. She and Michael had been thrown together by circumstances, and somehow or other they had contrived to become lovers. Now that the circumstances that brought them together no longer existed, would they still harbour the same feelings about one another. She reached out and took the hand of the man who had given her more pleasure than she had ever thought possible, and then kissed him lightly on the cheek. 'Would getting on with our lives include you going inside this establishment and returning with an ice-cold glass of lager?'

George Patterson sat sipping an ice-cold pint of Guinness not five metres away from the table occupied by Michael and Sandra. The evening sun was still hot and he had pulled his chair into the shade of an awning. Although running for home was the natural reaction, Joyce must have been out of his mind to seek refuge in this tiny island. Trying to find a single individual in London, Rome or Madrid would have been a gargantuan task, but finding a man on a sparsely inhabited island was a piece of cake. It had been even easier than Patterson had thought. Stepping off the ferry, he had made his way to the terrace of the pub overlooking the harbour, and Joyce and the woman had simply wandered into view. It was one of those strokes of luck that people dream about, but which rarely happens. He was able to observe them both without any fear of arousing suspicion. Sandra Bishop was indeed beautiful. Nevertheless, Patterson looked at her without any prurient interest — he could not remember having had a sexual feeling for any living creature. It was an advantage in his business. He saw her simply as a pawn in a game she would never understand. Michael Joyce was an altogether different proposition. Patterson fancied himself a solid judge of character, and his first estimate of Joyce was that he was someone to be wary of. There was something in the determined set of the face that indicated a fierce individualism, but it was the dark eyes that most drew Patterson's attention. The Scotsman had seen enough similar sets of eyes in Northern Ireland to recognise the hardness in Joyce's stare.

Watching him and the girl, he had no doubt that they were lovers. That was also to his advantage. People in love tended to be so wrapped up in themselves that they became careless.

'If I was one of the travelling people, I'd say that there was a look of love between ye.' Tim O'Flaherty flopped into the chair beside Michael, well aware that he was interrupting an intimate tête-à-tête. 'I'm dyin' for a pint.'

'Easier done than said.' Michael stood and entered the pub.

'You're goin' to make a lovely couple,' Tim said.

Sandra looked into Tim's smiling eyes, and immediately felt like hugging the big islander. 'Don't you think you're jumping the gun a little?' she said.

'I don't think so at all,' Tim said, taking the pint glass of Guinness from Michael's hand. 'I've been around long enough to recognise the real thing when I see it. *Sláinte.*'

'*Sláinte,*' Michael said, taking his seat and responding to Tim's toast. 'I took Sandra to Dún Aengus this afternoon. She believes that those who say it was a place of worship once, not a fort, are right.'

'There's something odd about it,' Sandra said. 'It made me shiver.'

'You're not alone in that.' Tim placed his half-empty glass on the table in front of him. 'Many's the time I've had a chill come over me when I've been standing in the centre of the place.'

'I thing there's a feeling of death there,' Sandra said.

'You have the second sight?' Tim asked.

'No, I don't think so. But I just felt sure that people had died there — as sacrifices, perhaps.'

'You could be right,' Tim said. 'Nobody knows. We don't know who the people were who built Dún Aengus, or what they used it for, and men will still be postulatin' theories on the origin of them damn rocks when we're all dead and gone.'

'And they'll probably do their best postulating with pints of Guinness in their hands,' Michael said, smiling.

Tim took another draught of his Guinness. 'Did your friend catch up with you?' he asked.

'What friend?' The relief that Michael had felt after the phone call to Maguire evaporated like sand running out of an hourglass.

'One of the boys picked up a fella off the afternoon ferry. He said he was a friend of yours and asked to be driven to your cottage.'

'What did he look like?' Michael glanced at Sandra and saw that she shared his apprehension. He would have preferred her not to have heard what Tim said, but it was too late now.

'According to Gearóid he speaks like a Frog — somewhere in the sixties with short grey hair.'

Michael didn't need any further description. It had to be the old man called Tahir who had nearly killed them in Paris. He must have been alive after all — wounded and unconscious, but certainly not dead as Michael had hoped — when he and Sandra had fled from the apartment. And Maguire had got it wrong. Whoever was at the centre of the cartel wasn't aware that everything was over, and had therefore neglected to call off the hounds. As far as Michael was concerned, Tahir could have the goddamn papers. But of course it wouldn't end there. Even if Tahir's master did know that the affair was finished and had called him off, the old man would still be after them, seeking revenge for what had happened in Jeaune's apartment.

'It's him, isn't it, Michael?' Sandra said quietly. 'The old man who tried to kill us in Paris. He wasn't dead, was he? When we left Jeaune's apartment, I mean.'

'There's no way we can tell for certain whether it's him without seeing him, but yes, I guess you're right.'

'Would somebody please tell me what the hell is going on?' Tim asked. 'One minute it's all laughter, and suddenly the atmosphere is thick enough to cut. I take it that this friend of yours isn't exactly a friend.'

'It's a long and complicated story, Tim,' Michael said. 'But you've got the kernel of it. The guy that Gearóid picked up certainly isn't a friend.'

'No problem. We'll round up a few of the boys and the Frog will be on the next ferry back to the mainland, never to return.'

'Somehow or other I don't think it would be that easy, and anyway I've no intention of involving you in my affairs.' Michael took Sandra's hand in his. 'What I would like you to do for me is to take care of Sandra this evening and tonight.'

'No problem.' Tim emptied his glass. 'I pulled the lobster pots today and lo and behold if I didn't come up with three beauties. Both of you are invited for dinner at my place. Ready for a refill?'

Michael nodded.

'No way, Michael,' Sandra said, as soon as Tim's broad back disappeared through the front door of the pub. 'I'm sticking with you.'

'Not this time,' Michael said, squeezing her hand. 'I'll be much happier knowing that you're safe with Tim. Maybe I can negotiate with this guy. As soon as he hears that the axe has fallen on the people he works for, he'll probably back off.' He didn't believe that for a moment, but he hoped that Sandra would. 'You're staying with Tim and there's no discussion on that point.'

Patrick Tahir lay in the tall grass six hundred metres from the Joyce cottage on the small hill called Caoineadh na Mná, which Michael had shown to Sandra earlier that afternoon. The heat of the day had finally subsided, and after sweating for much of the afternoon Tahir appreciated the cool of the evening. He removed a chocolate bar from his pocket and bit into the runny brown stodge. He hadn't eaten since lunch but he felt no hunger. He ate now only to pass the time and because he knew that ultimately his body would need the calories the chocolate provided. 'Le Sergent' glanced at his watch. It was eight o'clock, and there was still no sign of Joyce or the woman. Patience wasn't just a virtue in Tahir's business, it was a necessity. The cottage lay empty below him. He had always favoured killing by stealth. Joyce and the woman would return to the cottage and they would sleep, no doubt, the sleep of the sexually sated. Then Tahir would sneak into the cottage and kill them. He took the MAT out of the canvas bag and loaded a full magazine. This time there would be no mistake.

The deep blue sky was streaked with red fingers of cloud, and the normally turbulent waters of the North Sea lay still, as Roger Morley looked from his office across the landscape of South Shields.

'What a wonderful bloody day,' he said, as he sipped a glass of chilled Dom Perignon.

'It is a new beginning for Commonwealth,' James Brown, his executive assistant said. 'Now that you're chairman of the cartel you can regain the market share we lost to the continentals.'

Morley sipped the bubbling liquid. 'I wonder what my old friend Jean Claude Blu is doing this evening. Drowning his sorrows, I'll bet.' He looked at the portraits that adorned the walls of the boardroom. A series of grim-faced north-eastern stakanovites looked out from his office window. These were the dour Geordies who had built Commonwealth into one of the world's premier chemical companies. Morley wondered where his portrait would rank among the greats.

'To the new chairman of the cartel,' Brown said, and raised his glass.

'Thank you,' Morley said. For him the toast was hollow. The papers that Blu had been trying to retrieve were still missing. Morley would prove himself the true chairman when he had accomplished that which his predecessor had failed to do. Patterson was his expensive trump card.

Brown took his boss's glass and refilled it from the bottle standing in the ice-bucket on the bar of Morley's office. The new chairman took the glass and watched the bubbles rushing to the surface. As he gazed at his reflection in the glass panel of the cabinet, he wondered whether a greater national future awaited him. He lifted his glass to his reflection in a silent toast.

Although it was nearing ten o'clock in Brussels, the European Commission building at 150 Avenue de Cortenberg was as alive with officials as it had been at ten o'clock that morning. Most of the activity was centred on the eighth floor, and in particular the office of Nicholas Elliot. This was the director general's forte. Years of Sandhurst training had produced an individual who was completely in his element as the battle approached. While his aides flagged from exhaustion, Elliot was positively glowing with energy as he made the last-minute arrangements for the teams that were being dispatched to Lyons, Milan, Rotterdam, South Shields and Frankfurt. A special team from the US Security and Exchange Commission would be raiding Newton's office in White Plains in New York. By noon of the following day they would be in possession of enough evidence against the cartel to put them out of business permanently, and to put at least some of the people responsible behind bars. Elliot signed the final batch of papers and dismissed his staff for the night. There would be precious little sleep for anyone, but there was nothing more to be done until the dawn raids were launched. The director general removed a bottle of Glenlivet from his desk drawer and poured himself a stiff measure. He sipped the golden liquid, feeling the heat descend from his mouth into his stomach, and reflected on the somewhat bizarre conversation he had conducted earlier in the evening with Professor Maguire. It was too early to conclude that Jorgensen had been murdered by the cartel, but if one scrap of evidence emerged that the Irishman's strange story was true, then nothing on earth would save the members of the cartel from the full weight of the law. Elliot had already vowed that the murderers of his man would not be allowed to while their days away in some luxury open prison alongside the inside traders and the corrupt fund managers. Only one task remained. Elliot picked up the telephone and laid it on his desk while he sipped the whiskey. He really should inform Commissioner Combes about the dawn raids on the chemical companies. Elliot finished his whiskey and contemplated with anticipatory pleasure the visit to Buckingham Palace for the investiture of his knighthood. He replaced the telephone on its cradle. There was no point in disturbing the commissioner at this hour.

The light had almost totally faded from the Connemara sky as George Patterson watched Michael Joyce take his leave of the woman and the old man outside the cottage on the southern side of Kilmurvey Bay. So that's the way it is, he thought. Joyce was casting himself as the sacrificial goat. The poor bastard was trying to save the woman, but in fact he was signing the death warrant of the old man as well. Patterson waited until Joyce was a hundred metres down the road before moving off silently behind him. As soon as he had disposed of Joyce and located the documents, he would return for the woman and the old man.

The warm air enfolded Michael as he made his way along the tarmacadam road that led towards his father's cottage. It was perhaps three kilometres from Tim's place to his own, and the young American had set off at a brisk pace. As he marched towards the strand at Kilmurvey Bay, Michael glanced up the hill towards the fortress of Dún Aengus. The dark rocks stood out against the backdrop of the fading light, forming a sinister black shape across the horizon. Michael had viewed this scene a thousand times without any feeling of apprehension, but tonight it was different. He couldn't shake off the feeling that someone was watching him. His eyes scanned the hills, looking for some telltale sign of the old man from Jeaune's apartment. He hurried quickly along the road, anxious to reach the security of the cottage and his father's rifle.

Tahir saw the figure approaching from the distance. He swivelled himself into the correct position and slid the short muzzled MAT forward. He felt that he could take Joyce here in the middle of the road with ease. That would have sufficed to avenge Lepape, but the question of the documents would still have to be dealt with. His original plan should be adhered to. Joyce and the woman would die in their sleep, and he would have ample time to locate the missing papers. All would end exactly as he had planned it several days ago in the office at the top of the Tour Chemie. Tahir watched as Michael strode along the road towards his cottage. He was concentrating so much on the American that he almost missed seeing the dark figure that moved along the hedgerows directly behind Joyce. Tahir was puzzled for a moment, but then he remembered that Blu had been forced to relinquish control of the cartel to the Englishman. They too must have located Joyce, and the figure tailing the journalist was probably someone like himself. Well he'd be out of luck — no one but 'Le Sergent' would have the pleasure of killing the bastard Joyce and his whore.

Michael opened the door of the cottage and stepped cautiously inside. Moving from room to room he quickly established that he was alone. He went to the cupboard in the main bedroom and removed the lightweight Marlin Model 70 from the wall holder. He pulled out the small magazine from the underside of the rifle. It was empty. A box of shells was lying on the floor. The slightly battered cardboard box was disconcertingly light. When he opened the box, Michael found himself staring in disbelief at four small .22 rounds. The Marlin might be useful for hunting snipe, but it would be of little use if the Frenchman was armed as he had been in Paris. Michael was well aware that a bullet from a .22 would have little impact on a human target unless it hit one of the main organs. He slipped the four shells into the rifle, switched off the lights, and went to the window facing the road.

Tahir watched Michael enter the house and then switched his attention to the figure moving smoothly through the shadows. The man following Joyce was sometimes hard to pick out against the bushes and dark limestone rocks, but Tahir was able to follow his progress towards the cottage. 'Le Sergent' had been in the business long enough to recognise a fellow professional. The man following Joyce was very good. Tahir lay still and slipped the safety catch on the MAT.

Patterson moved quietly along the narrow road that led to the Joyce cottage. He hugged the hedges and the stone walls, trying as best he could to conceal his approach from a watchful eye in the cottage. He slipped the Browning out of his pocket and removed the safety catch. It was prudent to assume that Joyce had some kind of weapon at the cottage, and Patterson had no desire to join those who had already fallen foul of Michael Joyce. The light from the cottage cast a yellow beam across the stone pathway that led to the front door. Patterson was sitting at the end of the lane that led to the cottage, contemplating his next move, when the beam of light was suddenly extinguished.

Tahir watched the dark figure crouching at the end of the path. He would probably be able to pick the man off with a burst from the MAT, but that would only serve to warn Joyce. There was no downside in playing a waiting game. Whichever way the affair beneath him resolved itself, Patrick Tahir would be on hand when the winner emerged.

Michael looked into the darkness and saw no movement. Nevertheless he could not shake off the feeling that he had been watched as he walked along the road from Tim's cottage to his own. His heart pounded in his chest and the blood raced in his veins. He felt that his luck was tottering on the edge. The only positive aspect was that Sandra was safe with Tim. His fingers shook as he slipped the catch on the window as noiselessly as possible. A cool Atlantic breeze blew into Michael's face. A quarter moon cast a faint silvery light towards the strand at Kilmurvey, while Caoineadh na Mná and the hill leading to Dún Aengus were set as dark shadows against a star-studded backdrop. Michael scanned the darkness again. There was still no discernible movement.

Patterson felt rather than saw Joyce's face at the window. He slipped quietly around the side of a large limestone boulder that stood in front of the cottage. A low stone wall separated the cottage from the field adjoining it, and would provide perfect cover for someone who wanted to make their way unseen to the rear of the house. Dropping to the ground, he began to make his way along the wall and towards the rear of the Joyce dwelling. Michael Joyce was about to get a surprise he would never forget.

Michael glanced at his watch. It was approaching eleven thirty. His head shot up as a sound came from the field beside the cottage. He pulled back the hammer on the Marlin, eased the rifle through the partially opened window and pointed it in the direction from which he thought the sound had come. The field was dark and silent. Michael cursed his nervousness. He released the trigger and eased the Marlin back into the livingroom. The noise had probably been caused by a rat or a field mouse. A blast from the Marlin would have been several degrees of overkill.

Patterson recommenced his progress towards the rear of the cottage. The noise of the Browning scraping against a limestone rock had almost given him away, but he had lain absolutely still when he heard the noise of the rifle's hammer being cocked. He reached the end of the wall separating the field from the garden of the cottage, and moving smoothly over the grey stones, made his way to the back door of the house. With the Browning at the ready, he turned the handle and pushed softly against the wooden door. It resisted the subtle pressure. A Yale lock had been fitted to the door at eye level, but that was only a minor irritant to a trained operative. Patterson rooted in the side pocket of his bush jacket and removed a lock pick. He slipped the pick into the lock and smiled to himself when it opened almost instantly and soundlessly.

'If you make one movement I'll blow the living shit out of you.' Michael put the maximum amount of menace into his voice. He could see the dark shape of the automatic pistol in Patterson's hand and he was prepared to pull the trigger of the Marlin if that hand moved. 'I'm pointing a fully loaded rifle directly at you, and something tells me that you already know what kind of damage it could do.' Michael stood at the end of the short corridor that connected the livingroom to the back door.

'You're the boss.' Patterson affected a southern Irish accent and stood absolutely still. This wasn't part of the plan. However, all was not lost. A certain amount of improvisation would be required.

Michael held the rifle rock steady as he examined the man who stood outlined in the doorway. One thing was certain, even in the silver half-light cast by the moon. This was not the old man from Jeaune's apartment in Paris. The intruder was considerably younger than the man called Tahir. Michael stared into the darkness trying to make out the features on the thin face. The wire-rimmed glasses made the man look more like his father's accountant than a trained killer.

'Who the hell are you?' Michael asked.

'Special Branch,' Patterson said. 'I've been sent over from Dublin to keep an eye on you.' The accent was flawless, and the content of the message would only confuse Joyce.

'Why didn't you keep an eye from outside?' This guy was altogether too smooth, Michael thought. 'Why sneak into the house with a gun in your hand?'

Patterson turned quickly and fired the Browning twice at the shape holding the rifle, before diving backwards through the open door and into the darkness of the back garden.

Michael fired the Marlin as soon as he saw the man move. Almost instantly he felt a sharp pain as the first slug from the Browning ripped through his left side, chopping through a rib before exiting from his back. The second shot had flown wide of the mark. Michael ignored the pain and fired a second time at the dark figure moving through the back door.

'Shit!' Patterson cursed, as he scurried to roll behind the stone wall outside the cottage. What an almighty cock-up, he thought, slamming his fist into the hard earth. He felt a slight throbbing in the fleshy part of his thigh and realised that he had been hit. Rolling over onto his back he pushed himself up against the wall. Blood had already begun to seep through his trousers. The entry hole was tiny. Patterson quickly removed his belt and tied it around his upper thigh in a tourniquet. The wound wasn't significant. To be killed by a .22, one would have to be very unlucky indeed. As soon as he had finished off Joyce, he would have to get back up North and find a friendly doctor.

Michael felt the blood trickle down the inside of his shirt. The wound stung more than pained, and he moved quickly towards the front door of the cottage. He wondered who the hell the new player was. What really counted was that the man had the same thing in mind as the old men in Paris. He wondered whether either of the shots he had fired had struck home. With ammunition in short supply, this was not the time to be trapped inside. Michael slipped the catch on the front door and crawled outside across the gravel in front of the house. He didn't stop until he reached the cover of a large limestone boulder directly in front of the cottage.

Sandra was sitting silently in Tim's spare bedroom when she heard the shot. The initial crack was followed by two louder explosions. She ran into the livingroom. Tim was standing in front of the empty fireplace.

'Michael's in trouble. I know that shot came from the cottage.' Sandra ran her fingers through her dark curls. 'I'm going up there.'

Tim moved to face her. 'The lad told me to keep you here no matter what happened,' he said, putting both hands firmly on her shoulders. 'He'll sort it out himself.'

'No, he bloody well won't,' Sandra brushed Tim's hands away. 'Those men in Paris wanted the two of us dead. If Michael or you think that they're going to be satisfied with just one of us, then you're badly mistaken. As soon as they manage to kill Michael, they'll turn their attention to me, and maybe even you. Do you have a weapon in the house?'

Tim shook his head. 'Only if you consider fishing tackle to be a weapon.' He nodded at the pile of fishing gear in the corner of the room.

'You don't have anything?' There was a tone of desperation in Sandra's voice. There had been no more shooting, and that could mean that Michael was already dead. She felt a huge wave of despair washing over her. She ran to the fishing gear and began to pull the wicker baskets from the bottom of the pile. The first basket contained row after row of delicately made flies. She tossed it aside and picked out the second basket. The serrated-edged knife caught her eye as soon as she raised the lid. She picked it out of the basket and held it in her hand.

'Don't try to stop me,' she said as she turned to face Tim. 'Michael's in trouble up there and I'll be damned if I'm going to look the other way.'

The big islander looked at her and then stood aside. Faced with the Celtic fire blazing in her eyes, and the determined set of her chin, he knew that resistance was useless, though what young Michael would say when he learned that she had escaped from his care, he dreaded to think. And what dangers would the girl face, and how would she survive them? Holy Mother protect her, he thought, and meant it as fervently as he had ever prayed in his life. The best thing that he could do now would be to try to get help. 'I'll head into Kilronan and get the guards,' he said.

Michael was beginning to realise that his options were limited. There was no question of a fair fight. The Marlin with its two remaining bullets was no match for the pistol he had seen in the intruder's hand if it came to a shooting match. Somehow he would have to contrive a situation in which he could get the drop on his adversary. His only chance lay on the hill directly above him. If he could reach the rocks at the top of the hill, he might stand a chance of setting up an ambush. However, it was at least a mile to Dún Aengus and there was precious little cover on the way to the top. For the first hundred metres or so he would have a measure of protection from the hedgerows in the narrow lane directly across the road from him. After leaving the lane he would have to cross at least three hundred metres of open ground before he hit the *chevaux de frise*. Once within the forest of limestone slabs, he would be relatively safe. It would take one hell of a marksman to hit him in the middle of all that stone. Beyond the slabs there would be another hundred metres of open ground before he reached the outer wall of the fort. The pain in his side was burning, and he was aware that he was loosing blood steadily. He looked up the hill directly across from him and saw the dark shape of Dún Aengus looming across the skyline. This wasn't going to be easy. He began to move carefully away from the cover of the boulder and towards the lane that led up the hill towards the ancient fort. His side ached as he pulled himself through the grass towards the road.

As soon as he reached the edge of the road he summoned all his strength and launched himself across the exposed stretch of tarmacadam.

Patterson could feel the tourniquet feeding the throbbing in his thigh. A dull ache emanated from his left leg as he lay behind the stone wall. What a bloody idiot! Not only had he managed to get himself injured, he had also displayed himself to his target. Such an example of gross incompetence would not have impressed his former superiors at Century House. The sodding journalist had a charmed life. He heard a sound from the front of the house and carefully raised his head in time to see Joyce propelling himself across the road and into the darkness of a bushy lane. Patterson quickly raised his Browning and fired three shots in the direction of the lane. Although he knew there was little or no chance of hitting Joyce, there was always the possibility that Lady Luck might just have changed sides. What the hell was the bastard up to, Patterson wondered, raising his head and peering into the blackness of the lane.

As soon as Michael reached the temporary sanctuary of the narrow lane, he began to climb upwards. The brambles and thorns pulled at his clothes and ripped at his exposed flesh. Although his eyes had become used to the night light, the darkness of the lane was total, and he stumbled forward as quickly as he could, wanting to put as much distance as possible between himself and the man with the pistol before he reached the exposed ground. The lane was only a hundred metres long, but it climbed steeply upwards. Michael's breath came in great gasps as he forced himself forward.

Patterson came to a stop just across the road from the entrance to the lane, and crouched behind a boulder in case Joyce was waiting for him in the blackness. Every one of his faculties was operating at full power. He heard the sound of bushes rustling and what sounded like the tearing of cloth up the hill, and wondered if Joyce was trying to draw him into an ambush. He waited several seconds before launching himself across to the lane, which appeared as a black hole of tangled bushes and briars. He fired two shots into the darkness in case Joyce was hiding there. The entrance to the lane was empty. The scotsman began to move forward cautiously.

Sandra ran quickly along the road towards the cottage, gripping the fishing knife firmly in her right hand. She heard a volley of shots from the darkness ahead of her. Please, Michael, be alive.

Michael left the cover of the hedgerows, and saw the task that was ahead of him. A shaft of moonlight illuminated a wide stretch of boggy grass interspersed with small boulders. The pain in his side was intense, and he wished that he could stop. He forced himself to run forward, stumbling across the soft terrain. The apparent weight of the Marlin had been increasing as he had climbed higher, and he pulled in great gulps of air as his feet pounded onwards. The *chevaux de frise* was only two hundred metres ahead, but to Michael the distance was of marathon proportions. He pushed himself forward in the sure knowledge that very shortly he would be a perfect target.

Patrick Tahir watched as Michael came out from the lane and began his mad dash across the open ground that separated him from the limestone slabs surrounding the rocky edifice on the brow of the hill. The Frenchman had heard the shots at the cottage and had rightly deduced that Joyce was making a fight of it. He had been unable to see what had happened, and was contemplating leaving his position on the hill in order to investigate, when he saw Joyce sprint across the road and into the straggle of bushes that led up the hill. Tahir watched him run on towards the limestone slabs, almost one hundred metres in front of him. Soon it would be time to move.

Patterson detached a briar from his jacket as he reached the top end of the narrow lane. He dropped to the ground and crawled forward cautiously. There was no sign of Joyce. He left the lane and looked upwards across a wide expanse of short grass. Joyce was two hundred and fifty metres ahead of him, making pell-mell for what looked like a mass of standing rocks. Patterson quickly raised the Browning and took aim.

Michael heard the bullet singing off a rock directly behind him, and immediately went into a zigzag running pattern. His lungs were at bursting point and his legs felt like lumps of lead. The pain in his side had abated slightly. He heard the boggy ground at his feet make a sucking noise as the earth absorbed the impact of the 9mm slug. Up ahead he could clearly see the dark vertical rocks standing like erect soldiers guarding the forbidding fort on the summit of the hill. He pitched himself to the left as another bullet cut the air where he had been a split second before. Only twenty more metres and he would be safe.

The cottage was still and empty as Sandra pushed open the front door. She moved quickly through the house, confirming that Michael was no longer there. Where could he possibly have gone? She went back to the front door and looked up at the dark fort which dominated the area. It was then that she caught the first sight of the figure running for the *chevaux de frise*. From the door of the house she couldn't see plainly who it was, but she knew that it had to be Michael. The figure stumbled and then went on as before. A shiver ran down Sandra's spine. Without thinking further she ran forward, following the path that Michael and Patterson had taken some minutes before. The knife was still gripped tightly in her right hand and her mind was in turmoil. Why couldn't the bastards have left them alone? Hadn't Finn's death and the deaths since then been enough for the greedy ghouls? She reached the entrance to the lane and began the climb towards the summit of the hill.

'Shit!' Patterson shouted, as the figure disappeared into the field of standing stones three hundred metres ahead of him. He jerked the empty magazine from the Browning and tossed it into the darkness. It hadn't been an easy shot under night conditions, but his luck had been completely out. Joyce had not helped by varying his zigzag patterns. There was either more to Joyce than met the eye, or the man had a highly developed sense of survival. Patterson removed a fresh magazine from his jacket pocket and jammed it into the Browning. Now he had to negotiate the several hundred metres of open ground that Joyce had succeeded in crossing.

Tahir slipped out of his lair and padded across the side of the hill. His watch station was at about the same level as the start of the *chevaux de frise*, but some five hundred metres to the side of it. He saw Joyce reach the safety of the standing stones, and his pursuer making his way cautiously behind him. Tahir crawled along the ground, with the MAT lying across his arms. His shoulder ached as he pushed his body across the rocky terrain. He didn't want to arrive at the point where Michael had entered the field of limestone slabs before the man who was chasing him. Tahir was going to bring up the rear, unknown to both.

As soon as Michael had penetrated into the mass of upright slabs, he stopped and lay back against one of them. His shirt was soaked with a mixture of sweat and blood and his legs felt weak. He drew in great gulps of air, but there never seemed to be enough to satisfy his aching lungs. He looked around, contemplating a possible ambush in the middle of the stones, but rejected the idea. The slabs were so closely packed that the rifle would be of only limited use. Suddenly a spasm gripped his stomach and he whirled round and sent a stream of vomit onto the earth beside his feet. He tried to keep his retching silent as he forced the last of the puke from his lips. He leaned back against the slab again. His body cried out for rest, but Michael knew that he would have to go ahead through the limestone slabs as quickly as he dared.

Patterson reached the *chevaux de frise* at the same time as Michael had reached the end of the barrier. The Scotsman didn't like the situation. It was the perfect place for an ambush. Anger wasn't an emotion that Patterson succumbed to easily, but he was bloody damn angry with himself right now. He was performing like a rank amateur. Somehow he had already committed the cardinal sin of losing contact with his target. Joyce could be anywhere. He could have pushed on ahead or he could be lying in wait in the middle of this mass of stone. The Scotsman was beginning to regret his decision not to take a UDA hard-man along with him. A second gun would certainly have tilted the balance in his favour. But it was no good crying over spilt milk. The outcome would still be the same. He would get Joyce. It would just be that little bit more difficult than he had anticipated. Patterson began to move carefully through the maze of standing stones.

Sandra was about to leave the lane when she saw the figure moving towards the *chevaux de frise* from the left-hand side. A shaft of moonlight revealed the head of close-cropped grey hair, and Sandra knew that she was looking at the old man from Jeaune's apartment. She crouched under a bush at the edge of the exit from the lane and watched the old man's progress as he cautiously approached the limestone slabs. Further ahead there was no sign of Michael, but only the looming presence of the fort. Sandra suppressed a shiver as she thought of the ancient fort on the hill. It was eerie, and frightening, and even at a distance it spoke to her of death.

Michael ran in a zigzag pattern across the grassy area that separated the standing rocks from the outer perimeter of the fort. He was virtually all in, stumbling to the ground when he was nearly half way to the semi-circular outer wall, and was beginning to wonder whether the man below him had already given him a mortal wound. He might not be dead yet, but he was certainly headed in that direction. He staggered the last few yards to the outer wall. The entrances to the fort were at ground level, and Michael eased himself down below the rocks, pulling the Marlin behind him. Operating on some kind of internal autopilot, he found his way into the fort and stumbled the thirty metres to the inner wall. His eyes fogged as he located an entrance to the inner keep, and he shook his head to clear them. Unless he could keep some kind of grip on himself, the killer would have no difficulty in finishing him off. Michael slid beneath the wall and emerged into the central keep. This was where he must set his ambush. Beyond the ground of the keep he could hear the Atlantic breakers smashing against the sheer edge of the cliff. The central keep was in almost total darkness, a realm of dark rock and shadows. Michael moved away from the entrance and slipped into a crevice in the ancient wall where stones had been removed from the original structure. He slumped to the ground, standing the Marlin against the wall beside him. An overpowering tiredness welled over him. His body keep shouting at him to close his eyes and to give it rest, but his brain responded that if he closed his eyes he would probably never open them again. He prayed to God that he could resist the temptation to sleep.

Patrick Tahir reached the lower edge of the *chevaux de frise* and began to make his way cautiously through the field of slabs. This was the critical period. Any premature contact with either Joyce or the man following him could prove disastrous. He would prefer to have one of them out of the way before he revealed himself. However, this was not something that he could plan for. Planning hadn't been much use at Jeaune's apartment, and Tahir was quite happy to improvise. It had always been his forte.

Sandra watched the old man enter the *chevaux de frise*, then she left her position at the edge of the lane and began to make her way up the hill. She was halfway across the open area below the limestone slabs when she was gripped by fear. What on earth was she doing on this lonely hillside on a tiny island off the west coast of Europe? Up ahead of her was a ruthless killer, probably armed to the teeth, while she had only a fishing knife to protect herself. The dark shadow cast by the fort hung over the slabs directly in front of her. A terrible feeling of dread came over her and her legs suddenly went to jelly. Up in the fort were death and destruction — and the man she loved. If there was any true feeling between her and Michael, then she would have to go on. She steeled herself against the fear and ran upwards towards the fort.

Patterson moved cautiously across the final few metres of clear ground in front of the outer wall of the fort. Joyce had to be behind the stone wall somewhere, and he would be waiting. The

Scotsman made his way to the nearest entrance and squatted down to view what was on the other side of the wall. The area beyond the wall was grassy and clear, an ideal killing ground. Skirting the entrance, he made his way along the wall until he found a point where so many stones had been removed that it was easily scaleable. He shinned up the rough stones and flattened himself on the top of the wall. The grassy area was about thirty metres across. His eyes scanned the darkness of the outer keep and could find no sign of Joyce. This was trickier that he would have wished. Joyce was on home ground, and there were enough loose stones around to hide ten Joyces. With the Browning held at the ready, he dropped silently onto the ground of the outer keep. Somehow he would have to cross the open ground. He squinted, trying to penetrate the dark patches on the inner wall. There was nothing.

From the upper edge of the standing slabs, Tahir watched Joyce's pursuer drop from the top of the wall into the outer keep. Tahir had visited the prehistoric fort on his only previous trip to the island and he was aware of the general layout. Things were proceeding very much as he had anticipated. He moved forward confidently.

Michael felt himself drifting, and had to pull himself back from a brink where sleep seemed like the most wondrous of God's creations. He sank further into the shadow, and a feeling of apprehension gripped his stomach. What if it ended here, he thought. His body could easily be dumped over the cliff and smashed on the rocks below. No one would ever find him. And for what? Because he had seen a man being murdered during the running of the bulls and had been nosy enough to follow the affair to the bitter end. He looked at the black slab in the centre of the central keep and remembered Sandra's dread of the stone. The thought of Sandra forced his mind back to the present, and sharpened his senses enough to hear the slight sound that came from the top of the wall to his left.

Patterson lay on top of the inner wall and continued to survey the dark central keep. It contained even more rocks than the outer keep and the central area was dominated by a large dark stone rising out of the ground. Beyond the stone he could hear the persistent crashing of waves. Patterson dropped silently from the inner wall, and immediately crouched close to it. He gazed around the dark keep. If Joyce was there, he was very well hidden. The Scotsman was suddenly gripped with the fear that Joyce had somehow evaded him after leaving the limestone slabs. He banished the nagging thought from his mind, and began to move slowly along the wall.

Michael could just about follow the progress of the dark figure that approached in a crouch along the side of the wall. Beads of sweat dropped regularly into his eyes, blurring his vision. The man from the cottage was now only fifteen metres away. The American stopped breathing.

'I can see you perfectly, and this time if you so much as twitch I'm going to blow your fucking head off.' Michael's voice had such strength that he thought for a second that somebody else must have spoken. 'Drop the gun, then stand up and move into the centre of the fort.'

Patterson looked into the recess from which the sound had come. Joyce had found some very effective cover, and if the rifle was truly pointing at him and Joyce was even a reasonable shot, then the game was up. Patterson let the gun drop to the ground and moved away from the wall.

'All the way into the centre of the keep, or so help me I'll put a slug into you just to speed you along.' Michael watched the thin-faced man as he moved towards the rectangular stone in the centre of the fort. 'Climb up on it,' Michael said, when Patterson stood beside the stone.

Patterson could hear the quaver in Joyce's voice. He knew he had hit him back at the cottage. If the wound was bad, then Joyce would be on his last legs. It was time to humour the bastard until he could find out just how bad the damage was. He pulled himself up on the large flat stone, and stood looking into the shadow from which Michael's voice came.

'Who sent you?' Michael asked.

'Guess.'

'What do you want?'

'You've been a naughty boy.' Patterson had dropped his Irish accent and his voice was tinged with a slight Scottish burr. 'It appears that you've stolen some papers and the owners are anxious to retrieve them.'

'It's over.' Michael coughed, and spat blood onto the ground at his feet. 'We know what's in the papers and so does the European Commission. By tomorrow your boss's little scam will have been blown sky high, so there's no point in trying to get the papers back or in silencing Sandra and me. Soon the whole world will know their filthy little secret.'

'What's that you Americans say "it isn't over until the fat lady sings"?' Patterson looked around him theatrically. 'I'm afraid there isn't a fat lady around to help you out. I've been hired to retrieve the papers and to ensure your silence.' Patterson began to walk across the top of the stone towards Michael's position. 'And that's exactly what I'm going to do.'

The burst of gunfire caught both men unawares. A line of 9mm Parabellum slugs from Tahir's gun ripped into the earth beside Michael and continued across the keep before tearing into Patterson's stomach, sending chunks of flesh and streams of blood flying into the dark night air. Patterson's body was flung backwards by the force of the burst, and the Scotsman was dead long before his body smashed into the black stone on which he had been standing. Michael ducked instinctively as the firing continued. Bullets swept back in his direction, sending chips flying from the stones beside him. He swivelled automatically and fired both the rounds remaining in the Marlin magazine at the origin of the machine gun fire.

One bullet struck Tahir's side. It felt more like a sting from a bee than being hit by a piece of flying lead. 'Le Sergent' ignored the pain and pushed a second magazine into the MAT. Rolling to the side, he sprayed the area from which the rifle blast had come.

Sandra stood by the outer wall of Dún Aengus. The burst of courage that had brought her up the last part of the hill had gone and she was paralysed by her fear of entering the darkened fort alone. She imagined that she heard moaning from beyond the walls. Oh my God, she said softly to herself. A terrible fear gripped her. She wanted to drop her knife and run — anything to get away from this horrible place where ghosts whistled around the primitive walls. The burst of gunfire from behind the wall made her jump, and then the realisation that Michael was in mortal danger helped propel her through the entrance to the outer keep.

Michael dropped the Marlin and crawled away from the wall towards the huge stone on which Patterson's lifeless body lay. The Browning was out there somewhere on the grassy floor of the keep. He heard the noise of the new magazine being slipped into the machine gun and was well away from his previous position by the time bullets began to chop up the ground around the fallen Marlin. He was almost spent and he knew it. His body ached to be allowed to lie down, and his eyes longed to be allowed to close and accept the nothingness of sleep. The last drops of adrenalin coursed through his body, forcing him to stay conscious long enough to counter the threat.

Patrick Tahir's body ached as it had never ached before, the only thing that kept his concentration on his task was the blood lust he felt for Joyce. He hadn't heard a sound since he fired the last burst, so perhaps he had already killed the American. All he had to do was to get to the stupid *salope* and make sure he was dead or finish him off if he was still alive. 'Le Sergent' fought the pain in his body and began to crawl towards Joyce's position, hugging the cover of the wall as he went.

Michael felt around for the Browning, but could not locate it. Time was running out. He slipped onto the rectangular stone and crawled slowly towards Patterson's body, keeping to the seaward side of the dead man so that he would not be visible from the inner wall of the keep. Sweat streamed into his eyes as he searched the dark pools cast by the wall of stones. The movement was slight, but he located the moving form of the old man. Although he couldn't be sure, Michael believed that he had scored a hit. The old man was crawling slowly and carefully towards the position Michael had fired from. Within seconds he would be level with Michael's position on the stone. Michael sucked in large breaths, filling his lungs for the exertion he knew was about to come. The pain in his side had subsided to a dull ache, and he tried to banish all thoughts of his injury from his mind. As the old man drew level, Michael rose quickly and sprinted off the rock, throwing himself directly at the crawling figure.

Tahir heard the noise to his left. He pulled the MAT around into a firing position just as Joyce landed on top of him. The force of the collision knocked the MAT out of his hand and it skidded across the rocky floor of the keep before settling unseen in the shadows. Tahir swung his right hand up and caught Michael a glancing blow on the side of the head. Michael clung to the old man, and the two of them rolled away from the inner wall of the keep and past the stone to the edge of the cliff. Michael could hear the roaring of the ocean below as he struggled to get a grip on Tahir's throat. Air came in huge gulps into the American's mouth. His arms felt like lead weights as he wrestled with the Frenchman above the sixty-metre drop. Everything was happening in slow motion. He wanted to tear at the old man's throat but his hands were no longer fully under his control. There was no force left in his fingers.

Tahir's left arm was almost useless, and even under normal circumstances he could not have hoped to resist the strength of the younger man, but his right hand ran along Michael's side and he felt the wet sticky patch, and the discovery of Michael's injury gave the Frenchman an added incentive. Michael could feel his strength ebbing as he was pushed nearer to the edge. He thrust his knee into Tahir's groin and at the same time used his remaining strength to roll away from the edge of the cliff. The two men crashed into the black rectangular stone in the centre of the fort. Tahir pulled Michael to his feet, and punched at Michael's side with his right fist. Michael gasped in pain as the fist made contact with his shattered rib. Clouds began to float across his eyes and he prayed for the darkness to descend on him. His eyes closed and he knew that he was finished.

A deep animal roar of exultation came from Tahir's throat as grabbed Michael's throat with his right hand and began to squeeze.

Sandra saw the two men struggling at the edge of the raised stone. She moved quickly across the keep and, summoning all her strength, plunged the serrated knife deep into the side of the old Frenchman's neck. The knife forced its way in, severing muscles and tendons before shearing the windpipe. She pushed the knife until it would go no further. Tahir released his grip on Joyce and turned sharply, jerking the hilt of the knife out of Sandra's hand. A stream of dark sticky liquid already covered her fingers and palm. She stumbled back as the stricken man turned to face her. He opened his mouth to speak but no sound came and dark red blood bubbled out from between his open lips. He took a step towards her and she retreated before him. His face was twisted in a horrible grimace as his legs continued to propel him forward. He put his hand to the hilt of the knife and began to pull it from his throat. Blood streamed from the wound, soaking his neck and running down his throat.

Sandra screamed in horror and fear. She was so intent on Tahir that she hadn't noticed that she was on the edge of the cliff.

Tahir tugged at the hilt of the knife, but all his strength had gone. He looked beyond the woman and saw the sea and his white villa perched on the hill overlooking Cueta. The blue sky extended to the north past Gibraltar and on into Spain and he could smell the warm desert air that blew up from the Sahara. He released his grip on the hilt and walked jerkily forward over the edge of the cliff and into the crashing waters below.

Jean Claude Blu sat at the breakfast table in his elegant mansion in the Fontaine district of Lyons. During the night he had made the fateful decision that he would fight to hold his position as chairman of Chemie de France and do everything in his power to undermine Morley in his role as chairman of the cartel. Blu was dotting the 'i's and crossing the t's' on his new strategy when the telephone rang.

'*Votre assistante.*' His wife handed him the phone without further comment.

'*Est-ce vous, Monsieur le Président?*' Dominique Leriche's voice came over the phone almost before Blu had put it to his ear.

The chairman of Chemie de France had heard the sound of panic often enough to recognise it in his assistant's voice. *'Oui, c'est moi,'* he replied, his apprehension rising rapidly.

'You must come to the office immediately, Monsieur.' Leriche was shouting to make herself heard above the clamour in the office. 'The executive offices have been taken over by officials of the European Commission and the police. They are emptying the filing cabinets and loading everything into cardboard boxes. Monsieur Di Marco has already called from Milan and Monsieur Van Veen from Rotterdam. The same thing is happening in their offices.'

Blu replaced the phone on its cradle without speaking. He stood up wearily and left the kitchen without speaking to his wife. He crossed the hall of his nineteenth-century merchant's manor and entered his study, closing and locking the door behind him. His feet dragged as he crossed the room and stood before a glasscase set on the wall. His eyes passed lovingly over his colonel's dress uniform. His ornamental sword hung beside the uniform, pinned to the back of the case was the medal of the Légion d'honneur, and at the side of the case was a regulation army issue MAS 9 mm automatic set in a stiff leather holster. He opened the case and removed the pistol. The gun had served him well in Indo-China and Algeria and was, like every other item in the case, kept in pristine condition by his *femme de ménage*, the wife of an old soldier, who knew the true worth of such mementos. Blu removed the magazine from the handgrip of the gun. There were three cartridges in the magazine, which he carefully replaced. He walked to the desk of the study and sat down. Slowly he slipped the safety catch from the MAS.

Roger Morley's Jaguar sped through the gate of Commonwealth Chemicals and drove directly to the building housing the chairman's office. Morley had received the news of the dawn raid at his home in Newcastle, and had left immediately. Calls from his car phone had confirmed that raids had taken place on the offices of all the members of the cartel, without exception. Blu and Von Schick were untraceable, while Di Marco and Van Veen were both hysterical. A call to the States had elicited the information that Dan Newton had been taken into custody by Federal Marshals at exactly the same time as the offices of the European members of the cartel were being raided. The whole operation had been carried out with military precision. The most ominous sign for the future was that Morley's tame Member of Parliament was unavailable and would probably remain so for the rest of the week.

Morley's office was like a scene from a madhouse. The room was packed with people. Morley focused on two men, wearing jackets with 'European Commission' stencilled on the back, who were emptying files from his filing cabinets into the cardboard boxes that littered the floor. The broken locks of the filing cabinets lay on Morley's desk.

'What the hell do you people think you're doing?' Morley grabbed one of the officials by the shoulder.

'Excuse me, sir.' A young man wearing a suit stepped forward, producing a police warrant card from his pocket. 'These men are carrying out their duty. I would be grateful, sir, if you left until they've completed their work here.'

'Do you know who I am?' Morley was almost apoplectic with rage.

'I don't care who you are, sir?' the policeman replied courteously. 'As soon as we've finished, you can have your office back again. If you have any queries you should address them to the European Commission.'

Roger Morley's face turned an ashen grey colour. They were finished. All of them. The fines from the Commission might be only the tip of the iceberg. The board would undoubtedly call for his resignation. But it might not stop there. The British government had already put some very rich and powerful men behind bars for manipulating the shares of Guinness Plc. A picture of George Patterson flitted across Morley's mind, and he suddenly felt like throwing up.

Walter Von Schick sat in the office of his executive assistant. His own office had been commandeered by some thugs from the European Commission.

'Mr Elliot will be with you presently,' the voice on the telephone said calmly.

Von Schick wanted to scream. The duelling scar that ran from the corner of his eye to his thin lips was a vivid white against the redness of his face.

'Good morning, Schuman.' Elliot's uppercrust accent came on the line.

'Let's drop this Schuman shit,' Von Schick said angrily. 'You promised me that there would be no raid on our premises. "For services rendered" you said.'

'That was when you were a simple whistle-blower and before I learned that one of my officials had been gratuitously and callously murdered by you and your friends.'

Von Schick didn't like the coldness in Elliot's voice. 'What the hell are you talking about?' The German's tone was still indignant, but his skin had gone instantly cold.

'I'm talking about the death of Finn Jorgensen, which I intend to have fully investigated, and if I find that you have played any part in the death of that poor man, then I will see that you are pursued with the maximum vigour. Do I make myself clear?'

Schick opened his mouth to protest his innocence, but realised that whatever he said, the truth would come out in the end.

'I presume your silence indicates that this conversation is terminated. I wish you good day.' Elliot's tone was icy cold.

The phone went dead in Von Schick's hand and he slumped back in his assistant's chair, still clutching the humming instrument.

The outline of the ceiling came slowly into focus. A strip-light cast an eerie white beam which seemed to stretch from the ceiling right into Michael's brain. He wanted to raise his hand to shade his eyes from the searing light but found that he couldn't move. As the strip of light came more into focus, so did the dull pain that pervaded every part of his body.

'He's awake.'

Sandra's smiling face came into view directly above his head and he tried to speak. The effort of moving his lips seemed quite beyond him.

'Thanks be to God.'

Michael recognised the sound of his mother's voice. With an enormous effort he turned his head and saw his mother and father sitting at the bedside.

'Don't try to talk,' Sandra said, stroking his brow. 'First off, you're going to live, so don't have any worries on that account. Secondly, it really is over this time. The cartel's been broken and the officials in Brussels are putting a damning case together. While you've been lying there resting yourself, I've been interviewed around the clock by the Belgian police, the French police and the Irish police. Some of them even came in to take a look at your inanimate form. You would think they'd never seen a Rambo character before.'

Michael forced a smile.

'I've also had an opportunity,' Sandra continued, 'to get to know these wonderful people. In fact they've been kind enough to invite me to spend the rest of the summer in Cape Cod helping their son to convalesce. And you know what? If you're agreeable I'd really like to take up that invitation.'

Michael smiled and drifted off to sleep, thinking that if what had just transpired was a dream, it was the best dream he'd ever had.